A CANDY
COATED LIE

A CANDY COATED LIE

A Maggie and Odessa Mystery

Jill Brock

The characters and events in this book are fictitious. Any similarity or real persons, living or dead, is coincidental and not intended by the author.

For my family and friends who always believed.

JILL BROCK

CHAPTER 1

Small, raised bumps in the shape of Texas decorated the inside of my left wrist. A minute ago, I could have sworn it wasn't there. I sat at a corner table in the rear of the Blue Moon, our family restaurant in Queens, New York, and sighed. The last remnants of the Tuesday afternoon lunch crowd lingered in the dining area.

On my right side sat my fiancée, Lee. Silent, stoic, and pretending to be interested in the proceedings. His furtive glances kept me on edge. On my left sat my best friend Maggie. She pretended not to care about the proceedings as she worked her way up to the tenth level of Candy Crush on her phone.

How does an impromptu wedding planning meeting morph into a struggle of wills? Mid-June was the height of wedding season. As the owner of the O So Sweet bakery, I should have been filling orders.

"Shrimp or crab?" My sister, Candace, glared at me with the practiced impatience I came to recognize over the years. Being older by several years entitled her to some respect and obsequiousness, at least in her mind. Her voice made the irritated spot itch. Parts of the state of Louisiana appeared.

"Are you listening, Odessa?"

"Yes, Candace, I always listen to you," I proclaimed.

Maggie's blue eyes widen in disbelief. A passing waitress stopped, steadied her tray before moving on. Even she didn't believe me.

"Shrimp or crab?" Candace repeated with a face that reminded me of our mother. Honey brown skin, beautiful smoky topaz almond-shaped eyes always made me pause. The resemblance made it difficult to tell her to take a flying leap off something short and steep.

"Is it important?" I complained. Because which crustacean I eat at my wedding didn't rank as my top five priorities. One irritated fiancée and best friend, three unfinished cakes, and my sanity sat at the top of that list.

"You have an unfinished menu and a fiancé too busy saving the world." Candace raised her nose up at Lee and sniffed. The same way wolves did just before they eat you.

Every time Candace made disparaging remarks toward him, he squeezed my thigh. Whether it was about being a lawyer, catholic, divorced, or white, out of sight of my sister, he kneaded into my leg. I'd become a human stress toy. When Candace shot down any of Maggie's wedding suggestions, she kicked me in the ankle. Between the bruising and my rash, my wedding's color theme might have to change.

"You pick," I said out of exasperation.

"McKenzie!" Candace barked, never once lifting her head from her tablet to acknowledge Lee.

The cracking sound was Lee's spine stiffening. His superhuman restraint not to strangle my sister when so many men had failed, made me love him.

"Yes." The tightness in Lee's voice matched the intensity of the grip on my leg.

The squeak I made caught everyone's attention. Lee eased the pressure as it turned into something else as he rubbed the spot. His hand worked its way up my thigh. Thankful the table hid us, I blocked his advance with a well-placed hand and a warning expression.

To get everyone back on point, I placed Lee's hand in his lap and snatched away Maggie's phone. The Candy Crush World Championships would have to wait.

Lee sighed with a mixture of exhaustion and frustration.

"The Blue Moon is doing the catering. You'll opt for shrimp to save money. The extra will allow you to invite more of your relatives. So why ask us?"

"This is your wedding," Candace said with some exasperation of her own.

Lee said nothing, leaving me to explain to my sister how pointless this was. Feeling like a hostage negotiator, I leaned in across the table as my sister and I locked eyes.

"Candace, why don't we give out tee shirts that say, Wilkes Family reunion and oh, P.S. Odessa's wedding. Stop adding third cousins to the guest list. Do the damn menu yourself, pick the flowers, and do the seating, because you will anyway." I sat back and scratched. Lee's hand covered mine to stop me.

"Shrimp it is," Candace said, indifferent to my tirade. Then she stood up, gave us each a triumphant smile before she turned and left. Maggie, Lee, and I shot her murderous looks.

Lee dropped his head in his hand and sighed. His hand went back to my thigh. As a source of comfort, I didn't have the heart to stop him.

"If I were your wedding planner, this wouldn't happen." Maggie stood up and snatched her phone from my hand. Her five-foot stature did nothing for her indignation. Yet those angry blue eyes, flaming red hair, and pixie face made her resemble a crazed fairy.

"You'd turn my wedding into a psychotic princess party. I do not do Disney," I explained for the umpteenth time.

"That's not true." Maggie pouted, which only proved my point.

"If Candace calls me again for this, I'll snatch the first judge and we'll elope, Odessa," Lee warned.

I crossed my heart.

"I promised you a no fuss wedding while you're on this crazy case. Forget Candace and worry about your clients. I will Kung Fu block everything else."

"Kung Fu," he mused and smiled. Past his wire-rimmed glasses, I saw the lines around his tired, hazel eyes deepen. With the ease of tension, I leaned in for a kiss, a reward for his patience with my sister and me.

"Odessa." Maggie's warning tone stopped me. I followed her gaze to the front of the restaurant. Two suited men and Candace stood in deep conversation. My sister's usual imperious demeanor appeared shaken.

"Cops," Maggie announced.

As an office manager for a private investigator, she could spot a civil servant from a hundred yards. Her fan girl crush included a framed picture of Jack Webb during his Dragnet days hung in the office.

The men appeared to be plain-clothes city detectives. Their loose-fitting, dark suits and comfortable shoes all but announced them. To confirm this, the taller of the two men flashed his badge. My sister pointed in our direction.

I turned to Lee.

"Do you think something happened at the LaGuardia Apartments?" I whispered.

Lee said nothing. Dark hazel eyes locked on the two men approaching.

A problematic case involving tenants and a landlord consumed Lee's every waking moment. The landlord harassment of the tenants had turned ugly, often with Lee intervening. My concern rose each time he left the house to deal with the problems at the LaGuardia Apartments.

Lee sat stiff, eyes fixed on the coming storm and another sleepless night. Maggie remained frozen for a moment before retaking her seat. Between the two, I sat and scratched over the state of Alabama.

"Ms. Wilkes, I'm Detective Brody and this is Detective Starzynski," the shorter of the two men said, with a square face, prominent brow, and snub nose, like a boxer with too many fights under his belt. A faint scar framed the corner of his left eye. His thin lips set in a permanent bloodless scowl. It made him look constipated.

"Excuse me?" I shifted away as their attention fell on me and not Lee.

"What's this about?" Lee shot me a sideways glance filled with questions.

"The detectives need to talk to Odessa." Candace took up a position next to me. This made it clear to anyone who cared that she was still my big sister. According to Candace, Lee would have to put a ring on it before he usurped her authority in my life.

I scratched.

"Why do you need to talk to Odessa?" Maggie demanded. The short detective named Brody brows shifted up, a familiar expression when meeting her for the first time. Most expected her to throw fairy dust at them.

"Can we talk alone?" His tone had a weary edge.

I had a list. First, I needed to finish my cake orders. Second, I refused to marry anyone in a courthouse hallway. Last but not the least, I didn't want to talk alone with any New York City detectives.

"We can talk here," I insisted.

"You're sure?" Starzynski said and took a side glance at Lee.

I nodded.

Brody exhaled noisily as if he missed an opportunity to water-board someone. Out came a well-worn notebook, which he flipped through before he made eye contact again.

"Did you receive a phone call at 11:06 last night from the Airport Terminal Hotel?"

"Excuse me?" I said.

"Someone made a phone call to your bakery shop." Brody nodded toward my shop. "We talked to the girl in the shop next door, and she said any voicemail would go directly to your phone when the store is closed."

The detectives were right. My phone did receive voicemail if no one picked up at the shop. But, who would call me that late?

"Did you?" the taller one prompted.

"What?" I struggled to get a clear thought in their presence.

"Receive a call?" Brody reiterated with some impatience.

Candace's last-minute meeting sidetracked me from going through the day's messages.

"No, I haven't checked."

Brody sighed again. "Could you?"

Without thinking, I reached into my back pocket to retrieve my phone. Lee held out a hand to stop me.

"Again, what's this about?" Lee asked.

The men locked eyes the way men do when someone needed to get a ruler.

"You the fiancée?" the tall one, called Starzynski, said in a smug tone. What had Candace told them?

"Yeah, he's the lawyer." Candace's words came out like there was a nasty taste in her mouth.

The two men stiffen.

"You're not in any trouble, Ms. Wilkes," Starzynski reassured in a softer tone. Maggie, who once explained about the bad cop, good cop scenario seemed impressed.

Yet, Lee's question went unanswered. Their evasiveness was par for their profession, but they weren't the secret police.

"It's clear, you're in the middle of an investigation and time is paramount. So why don't you tell her what you can, and she will cooperate to the best of her ability," Lee asserted.

This eased me to know someone supervised this crazy train.

"Last night there was a murder at a hotel near Kennedy airport. The victim, a woman, called your shop just before she died. We're curious as to why?"

"I know New York is the city that never sleeps, but really!" I said non-plus. From the set of Lee's jaw, I knew I'd missed a point.

"Why would a murder victim call a cake shop that late? So, can you play the message?" Starzynski said.

I glanced at Lee, who seemed curious as well. Maggie stared at the phone as if she might snatch the phone and play it herself. What did I have to lose? I didn't want to hinder a murder investigation. I searched my phone for the message menu and pressed play for yesterday's messages. As expected, there were various calls from customers, except the last one. Recorded at six minutes after eleven, from an unknown number. A dead woman called me.

"I know this is strange, even crazy, but I'm trying to connect to Leland McKenzie. My name is Heather McLaughlin. He knows me..."

The pressure and white noise in my head overtook the words that followed as I turned to see Lee. His face contorted in anguish like an unexpected punch to the gut. I didn't know what to do. I had no Kung Fu for this.

CHAPTER 2

At the precinct, Lee disappeared into a room with Detective Brody. I preferred Starzynski. Not that either one of them was better. Starzynski seemed the more sensible of the two. Brody's anger issues wouldn't resolve with a month's vacation and Prozac.

"He's over compensating," Maggie explained about Brody.

"For what? The lack of hair, height, and personality?" I glared at the door Lee disappeared behind.

If Brody thought Maggie was a nuisance, I was public enemy number one. Not handing over my phone without question put me on his no friends list.

"He doubts Lee's alibi," I said.

The night of Heather McLaughlin's death, Lee received a phone call. Not from Heather, but from a tenant living at the LaGuardia Apartments. An altercation there involving the police made him leave the house that night.

"They can't ignore it," Maggie insisted.

Queens was the largest borough in the city; it stretched over seventy miles. The LaGuardia Apartment building sat in a neighborhood that faced Manhattan. At the opposite end of the borough sat the Terminal Hotel. Its proximity to Kennedy Airport was its only appealing attribute. Between them was New York traffic that could make driving five miles a day-long event.

"Does Brody think Lee had a flying car?" I sighed, with arms crossed, and sat back in the rigid plastic chair.

Regulated to a waiting area, Maggie and I sat in the Detective Squad. For over two hours we observed the human circus flow in and out of the room. While Maggie found this fascinating, I preferred doing my taxes. Watching only confirmed my belief about most criminals. They were stupid. A prime example was a young man of about twenty being interviewed by a detective. He appeared affable, even articulate. The only hint he was on the wrong side of the law were the handcuffs he wore.

Maggie and I sat in rapt astonishment. Who would think to rob a donut shop a few blocks away from a precinct? How many brain cells does it take to know you might find a few police officers taking a coffee break and having a donut or two? It seemed this donut thief was a few brain cells short of a happy meal.

"That place is always busy," the man clarified in an animated tone.

The detective's exasperation said it all. With each detail of his master plan, the detective twitched and typed the report.

"Everyone loves donuts," the man concluded. "Anyway, who guards donuts?"

"Why is he confessing?" Maggie stared in disbelief.

"In a donut shop filled with police officers, he cut the line, demanded money and two glazed donuts. What would his defense be?" I replied.

The detective taking the report seemed to agree and held up his hand for the confession to stop.

"Take Butch Cassidy to lock up," the inpatient detective said. "I can't take anymore, for Christ's sake."

"Could have psychological issues?" Maggie suggested as a uniform officer took the hapless man away.

"Stupid is not a mental diagnosis. It's a religion some people worship." I pointed at the thief as he left the room. "There goes the high priest."

Maggie faced me with pursed lips of disapproval. She had more faith in humanity than I did. Considering the profession, she wanted to aspire to, I didn't hold out hope she'd have that long. Yet, my cynicism always surprised her.

"Stop being so negative, Odessa."

Really!

For two hours, I sat. Waited for the return of my confiscated phone. Listened to a donut thief give his dissertations on the justice system. Sympathized as an intoxicated couple gave their cringe worthy confession of love. Wondered if Lee would go home with me tonight, or if I would have to arrange bail.

"I'll let you stay positive." I gave her a reassuring pat on the leg.

Maggie hugged me for reassurance. Normally, I would deflect her public displays of affection, but I didn't. I wanted to believe in Maggie's Tinkerbell magic. But Peter Pan only dealt with a one-handed, overdressed pirate. Putting my hands together and saying I believed in fairies wouldn't get Lee out that room with Brody.

Then Lee came out of the room with Brody.

No handcuffs. No screams of righteous indignation or bail money needed. Nothing. They shook hands like grownups.

"Odessa!" Lee caught sight of me and smiled. The smile had no muscle behind it and did little to push away my concern. Heather's death had derailed him. He walked toward me with the gait of a man who needed to sit down but wouldn't. His effort to be strong for me just felt infuriating.

"They're done with it." Lee held out my phone.

"Okay," I mumbled and took it.

"Are you all right?" His concerned voice helped to unfreeze my brain.

"Yeah," I said with a little too much enthusiasm.

Though his face no longer held the tightness of shock, he remained unfocused. It made me wonder. How close were he and Heather? If what Lee said was true, he worked with Heather during his marriage to his first wife, Julia. A time when Lee and Julia's marriage failed. Did Lee seek solace in the arms of another woman?

"Can we go?" I begged as wave after wave of the human homage to bad choices passed us. Some of these people would not go home.

"Sure," Lee said.

A sense of relief hit me as we headed for the door. That feeling died when Lee caught sight of Starzynski coming out of an office. We stopped. He wanted to ask the detective something before we left. I groaned and almost pulled him back when he walked away.

"Are you all right?" Maggie said, reading my taciturn mood.

"I need out of this place." I scratched the state of Florida that formed on my arm.

"Stop that." Maggie pushed my hand away.

The scratching stopped as I watched the two men. Lee stood, head bowed and listening. Starzynski talked. The conversation ended with no arrest and a handshake.

"See, we can go." Maggie gestured as Lee headed our way.

The weak smile I plastered on hurt, but I didn't want Lee to worry. A reassuring arm went around my waist as he guided me out the detective's room. Thank god he did, because I wanted to bolt out of there, like a thief with a pocket full of donuts.

Twenty minutes later, Maggie was in her car at the Blue Moon parking lot and driving off for home. A part of me wanted to go inside to prove to Candace that Lee wasn't in lockup. I overrode my need to gloat.

When we arrived at our house in the small Queen's neighborhood of St. Albans, my relief was almost palpable. Inside, I double checked the front door when Lee locked it. I stopped when I found him staring at me.

"You alright?" His voice held doubt.

"Perfect!" I said between clench teeth.

Lee kept staring.

"What?" I threw up my hands in frustration. "I wish people would stop asking me that."

Lee reached out, took me by my outstretched arms, and pulled me into a hug. My head collapsed on his shoulder. Between the wedding planning, the cake shop, the news of death, I wanted to crawl into bed and not come out. Absent of that, Lee's shoulder would do.

"The police seemed satisfied with my alibi. They confirmed I was at the 106th precinct and how long I was there. So please stop worrying," he whispered.

"Really?" I pulled back to gaze into his eyes. There was a degree of belief I wanted to give him. Yet, I sensed there was something he wasn't telling me. How close was he with Heather?

Lee nodded.

"It's a transient hotel and someone broke into her room. They think Heather tried to stop them and some kind of struggle happened. She died from blows to the head from a weapon, maybe a pipe. They have no other motive than that. A housekeeper at the hotel saw someone, but her account was so conflicting they can't trust it. Anyway, her descriptions of the person she saw didn't match me. I'm about a foot taller, with darker hair, and I wear glasses. So please, baby, take a breath," he implored.

I took a breath and wrapped my arms around him. My imagination got the better of me. Maggie had been right, I thought the worst. A friend of Lee's died a terrible death, and I'd made it about me. I had a devastated fiancé and all I could do was scratch my itch.

"I'm so sorry, Lee."

We stood in the tiny foyer wrapped in each other's arms. The silence felt like a comfort, a break from the chaos of the day. It always made me pause and remember how far our relationship had come. The first time we met, Maggie almost knocked him out with her oversized pocketbook. He completed the introduction by hitting me with a Key Lime pie. We consummated our relationship the same night my ex boyfriend stalked me. Any normal person would run in the opposite direction. Our attraction overrode our common sense.

Nestled in the crook of his neck, I whispered, "Are you all right?"

He took a moment to answer. He sighed and spoke, "Why was she in New York? Why she couldn't reach me and called you instead? Why that hotel? I don't understand."

Lee pulled away and the darkness that enveloped him at the initial news of Heather returned. I cursed myself for stirring everything back up. Yet, he hadn't answered my question. He wasn't all right.

"God, I'm tired," he announced, pushing up his glasses and rubbing his eyes.

"And hungry, so I'll whip up something quick." I dropped the rest of my stuff on the small foyer table and headed for the kitchen. "Take a shower and it will be ready when you're done." At first, he protested. He wanted nothing but to go retreat in his small home office. There, he would brood over Heather, her death and knowing Lee, how he'd failed her.

"Shower, dinner, and bed," I instructed firmly. A hint of a smile threatened to emerge from his lips but faded. He came to me for a kiss. A quick touching of lips, a kiss meant to appease if nothing else.

"There's some ham left and Esperanza's bread. How about that?" I offered.

The Blue Moon's chef's Sunday Virginia ham was a favorite of Lee's. Every time George Fontaine made it, I always brought some home. Along with the rustic round French bread made by my assistant, Lee couldn't resist.

I shooed him upstairs and waited for the sound of the shower going. The moment I heard running water, I reached for my phone. Convinced I was doing the right thing, I punched in the familiar number.

"He will kill me," I said to myself.

Heather was a friend from Lee's past. A past he rarely discussed. Admittedly, I had no desire for Lee to indulge in reminiscing about a time that included his ex-wife, Julia. Yet, no matter how I twisted it, I knew Lee. Heather's death and how she died would torture him. It would be his unanswered question. If I wanted my old Lee back and standing up at our wedding, I wanted to get him his answer. So, I had to talk to a pint-size redhead. A woman who found joy in chasing the rabbit.

CHAPTER 3

"If this color exists in nature, it's not on this planet," I said. The dozen sculpted bright yellow sugar paste flowers sat in neat rows on my worktable. A jaundice yellowish tinge covered my fingers. They ached from pressing the sugar paste into delicate hydrangeas.

"Ms. Bentley used the word electric sunshine," Esperanza, my baker's assistant, said. The sheen on her caramel colored skin hinted at the effort she'd put into making dozens of the flowers.

"There is another word I'd use, but let's wait until the check clears." I needed a break and pushed myself away from the steel workbench in my cake shop. The stain on my hands made me wonder why I'd given up my job in advertising and traded it in for temperamental brides. Then I remembered. I didn't give it up. They fired me.

Four years ago, I worked for a top-rated advertising agency in New York City. As a project manager, I thought my future seemed set. Along with the job came the perfect boyfriend. As an investment banker, Davis Frazier was the Ken to my Barbie and the Kim to my Kanye. When I lost my job, Davis didn't think too much of my downward spiraling employment choices. He soon became the vinegar to my baking soda like a bad student experiment. He thought we needed a break. I took the time to think about my life and place in the universe. Davis took the time to marry someone else. Those memories made me not mind my yellow fingertips.

"Why don't you try gloves?" Esperanza said. A recent culinary school graduate, she'd become invaluable at the shop.

"Can't work with gloves to do sugar work." I stood at the large sink trying to scrub my hands back to the right shade of brown.

"Ms. Bentley called again." Esperanza's coal-black eyes had turned sheepish. Her youthful naivety made her an easy target for pushy brides. Naomi Bentley was pushy. A twenty something, obsessed with television bridal shows and the perfect wedding.

My hand washing stopped, and I glared at Esperanza.

"They got a bigger venue," she said apologetically. Despite her dark skin, she couldn't hide her blush.

"I don't care if they have Madison Square Garden. No." I pointed a soapy finger at her.

"Sorry, but I kinda said okay. I'll do the extra flowers," Esperanza suggested. Anxious eyes stared back at me, contrite and earnest.

"Yes, you will." I sighed. Beneath my breath, I cursed Ms. Naomi Bentley. For extra measure, I sent nasty thoughts to the company who invented the food color. When the front door chimed and interrupted my growing list of things to curse, I checked my watch. Maggie promised to come by and I had lost track of time. Naomi's cake would have to wait—again.

"Granny can get it," Esperanza said.

Esperanza's Guatemalan grandmother used to go to the neighborhood activity center. A recent Mommy and Me swimming classes cut her daily senior swimming group down to once a week. She arrived at the shop one day to announce that toddlers had overrun the center like locust. Armed with yarn and her knitting needles, she found a space in the corner and knitted.

"I need a break." I raised my hands in resignation and took off my work apron. Deep in concentration, Esperanza continued her work on the flowers as I left.

At the front of the shop, the shabby chic style gave the place a cozy feel. Maggie stood in front of a beverage bar made from reclaimed wood. Mrs. Gonzales sat behind it, next to a beautiful vintage Italian coffee maker.

"Hey!" Maggie said when she saw me. She took the cup of coffee Mrs. Gonzales held out to her.

"I'll have one of those," I said as I joined the women.

The polished copper coffee maker spewed steam. Mrs. Gonzales wrinkled but deft hands made me an espresso with expertise. Purchased on a whim when I first opened the shop, I couldn't get the damn coffee machine to work. It forced me to place it off in a corner, turning it into a piece of expensive decor. A few days after leaving the center, Mrs. Gonzales gave the machine a cursory glance, then put aside her knitting and went to work. Some moments later she placed a perfect cup of espresso before me. I didn't care how she got the thing to work, her coffee was delicious. Before long, the shop had a 70-year-old Guatemalan barista. The senior swim team would have to wait.

"How was the morning rush?" I asked my senior barista. With the antique coffee machine working, Mrs. Gonzales garnished a growing fan base from the early morning commuters.

"Wonderful," she said with a wide, infectious smile. She spoke Spanish with little concern if I understood or not, but I got the gist.

Her smile made me forget about my aching fingers and Naomi Bentley.

"Where's your lovely boy?" Mrs. Gonzales said to Maggie with genuine disappointment on her face. Maggie's 9-year-old son, Rocket, had hit it off with the older woman. Fascinated with Mrs. Gonzales' ability to knit at the speed of light.

"With his grandmother." Maggie's tone sounded like a complaint.

"What is it this time?" I grinned.

"The Nassau County Chamber Music Festival," Maggie replied.

I clutched at the space over my heart and feigned pain.

"Not funny." Maggie huffed. "I had to bribe him with a movie and Chucky Cheese for him and two friends."

"Christ, Maggie, he's nine."

"I tried, but the woman ignores me." Maggie crossed her arms in frustration. Maggie's mother-in-law, Lenora Swift, had the mindset of a pit bull and the social boundaries of one.

"I could talk to her." My disingenuous smile made Maggie's eyes widened with fear.

"No. The last time you had a little talk with her, she threatened to call the police."

"She misunderstood my intent." I shrugged and gestured to one of the shop's cafe tables.

"She threatened a restraining order." Maggie took a seat at one of the wrought iron tables.

"Maybe Rocket can get one for his grandma," I offered.

Maggie sighed in resignation.

I laughed and sipped my coffee. The strong aroma filled my nostril and gave me a jolt. The weariness of working on the flowers faded. Even the idea of my godson trapped by his overbearing grandmother didn't bother me. Rocket was a smart kid, he'd find a way to unglue himself from that woman.

"We need dessert!" I declared and took two fruit cream pastries from the glass dessert display. I placed one of the puff pastries in front of Maggie and took a seat. Maggie's eyes crinkled in delight at the dessert. Thoughts of Lenora Swift vanished.

"God, that's delicious!" Maggie closed her eyes and smiled.

I gave her a moment to gather herself and remembered the reason why she'd come by. With a sip of her coffee, she sat back and narrowed her gaze on me.

"You're sure you want to do this?" Her warning tone made me stop in mid bite. Maggie felt uncertain about what I wanted her to do, something about a lack of trust.

"This coming from a woman who removes the fuses from the weed whacker."

"That's different." Maggie stuck out her tiny chin.

"How?"

Her lips tightened into a thin line.

This woman had the neighborhood handyman on speed dial. The doctors at the emergency room knew her husband, Roger, by his first name. She encouraged Roger's belief she only did secretarial work at McAvoy Investigation. Conceding I wouldn't let this go, she relented and told me what she found.

"Most of the stuff I found was the usual. Where Heather went to school, place of birth..." Maggie stopped and cocked her head to the side with an expression of doubt. I knew that look. It was the unusual stuff that hooked her.

"What?" I prompted.

"At first glance, Heather was just a girl from Staten Island. Grew up, went to school, and got a job."

"And..." Her hesitation began to annoy me.

"And then, she fell off the face of the earth." Maggie's brows rose for emphasis. "For years, I couldn't find anything, and then suddenly she shows up at that hotel near the airport, out of nowhere."

"Homesick?" I questioned.

"Her mother is still here at one of those assisted living facilities. A fancy one. But, there's no record of Heather ever visiting her mother recently." Maggie pulled the large leather satchel she always carried onto the table. Inside could include anything from her son's overdue library book, to a book on the steps on procedural investigation. She pulled out a steno pad and began to flip through several pages until she settled on the one she wanted.

"Heather's mother lived on Staten Island all her life. Married, had Heather, and never worked. Her husband left her a decent pension when he died of a heart attack when Heather turned sixteen. Four years ago, Heather sold the family house, placed her mother in a nursing home on Staten Island, then moved her to Magnolia Adult Care and Housing. I did a quick inquiry of Magnolia. Their specialty is dealing with Alzheimer."

"Why did she move?"

"Magnolia is a step up and can better deal with her illness." Maggie flipped through more pages.

"Of course, I couldn't get any personal medical detail or visit her. But, I saw the visitor's log. Only two people visited in the last six months, none of them were Heather. From what I could get from the staff, there was a woman named Lucy Le Sueur. Some kind of case worker, but she didn't visit often. The other was a man who visited often." Maggie stared up at me with a knowing expression.

"What aren't you telling me?" The pastry in my stomach shifted.

"The guard remembers the man because he's always nice to her and gave her some advice." Maggie sounded purposefully cryptic.

"What kind of advice?" My stomach rolled again. A prelude before jumping down the rabbit hole.

"The legal kind." The words came out like a tease.

Maggie wanted me to connect the dots. Her obvious discomfort digging in Lee's past would make getting information difficult. If she was Pandora's friend, she would have told the girl not to open the damn box and to have a spa day.

"Lee?" I blurted out.

She gave a reluctant nod. "Dark hair, tall, professional, and wore wire-framed glasses."

The coffee cup had been on my lips, but I didn't take a sip. I sat there frozen and took in the implications. Lee had gone to visit Heather's mother, not once, but several times. Why, if Heather had left the city? That begged the question how close were they? Four years ago, Lee's marriage to Julia had imploded. Had Heather's arms offered comfort? I hated feeling jealous of a dead woman, but my head and my heart weren't speaking at the moment.

"He told the police he hadn't talked to her for years," I said without much confidence.

"He said he hadn't seen her." Maggie cocked a brow at me.

"He hadn't seen her," I repeated with annoyance. Just like Lee to twist words, damn lawyer.

"The guard said Lee often talked to the administrator about Mrs. McLaughlin. Probably to check on the care she was receiving. Very businesslike, but nice and polite," Maggie added.

"He was taking care of her mother." I set the coffee cup down to push it away. The half-eaten pastry sat on the table. I scratched the irritated patch of skin on my arm as thoughts whirled in my head. Lee had said nothing, except that Heather had been his friend. Then he told the police a half-truth.

"How far do you want to go with this, Odessa?" Maggie asked, interrupting my dark thoughts.

In truth, I didn't know. In the back of my mind, I wanted to believe Lee would tell me everything and all would be right. However, I used to believe in Santa Claus and the Tooth Fairy. Now I believed Santa would show up at my house with the Tooth Fairy as his date before Lee told me anything.

CHAPTER 4

In the days that followed, only one of the top New York City newspapers carried the full story on Heather's death. In a city of millions, her murder didn't merit front page status, but it gained some attention. The articles said little about the reason for her being at the Terminal Hotel. It noted the small hotel's recent problems with vagrancy and assaults. The hotel's nearness to the airport seemed its only shinning point.

Our small house in Queens became littered with news stories of Heather's death. The stories became a constant reminder that Heather was gone, but not forgotten. I had to maneuver around them like emotional landmines. When Lee came home one day to announce he made funeral arrangements for Heather, I didn't know what to think. Our words had dwindled down to nothing most days. Heather's death somehow robbed us of our words. If it weren't for the cat, we'd barely speak at all.

"It's a cat," Lee announced one day as he came through the front door. As if I couldn't recognize the animal glaring back at me.

On the day of Heather's funeral, Lee arrived with a large pet carrier in one hand and a Pet Smarts bag under the other.

The cat was the size of a small dog or at least looked like it ate one. The heavy, coated brown tabby pattern covered a wide body and a pair of tufted huge paws and ears. Imperious, oblique, wide set green-gold eyes stared back at me. The glare had such a level of indignation; it reminded me of my sister. Unsure of whether to help or get out of the way, I said nothing at first and watched. He clumsily struggled to enter through the narrow foyer to make it to the living room.

"Yeah, that's a cat," I agreed with trepidation. "Why do you have a cat, Lee?"

After unburdening himself, Lee fell onto the couch and loosened his tie.

"One of my clients, Mr. Jimenez, took ill this morning and I couldn't find anyone to take his cat. The super threatened to toss him into the garbage chute."

"No one?" Certain there was a zoo missing one of its animals, I stared at him in disbelief.

As one of Lee's clients, Mr. Jimenez lived in a building that had a civil case against a slumlord. A horrible man named Cezar Comaneci. Lee wanted to bury him beneath the LaGuardia Apartments he neglected.

Lee shook his head.

"The doctors think a few days. Long enough to get his pressure under control," Lee said apologetically. He pushed himself off the couch and took a step toward me. The slight smile he wore didn't hide the tiredness in his eyes. This thawed my resistance a little.

"Honey, I tried to find a place that would take him, but they most only took dogs."

I laughed. "Trust me, if you get this thing to bark, he'd pass for one."

Without warning, a deep trilling sound came from the cat, followed by clicks and a halfhearted meow. The cat pushed its large paw through the small bars of the cage. After doing this several times, its paw connected with the latch. The door popped open. I stepped back as it squeezed its large frame through the small opening. Curled up in the confined carrier case, I misjudged its size. The damn thing was massive. It sniffed the air a few times before it brushed its huge body against my legs. After depositing enough cat hair on me to knit socks, it walked away and hopped onto the couch. It pawed at the cushion with long curled nails, walked in a circle a few times before settling down.

"What the..." I stopped when I heard a deep purring that bordered on snoring.

We stared at it in amazement, too afraid to move in case it might do something worse.

"Let me set up his things before we go to the service." Lee broke his gaze and retreated to the kitchen.

"A few days, right?" I followed because the large food bag was hard to miss. He said nothing as he set up the litter box, food, and water bowls by the back door.

"Promise." Lee gave me a thankful kiss after he finished. "Let me change and we can go."

There was no time to respond as Lee bounded up the stairs to the bedroom. In two hours, we had to be at Heather's funeral on Staten Island. Rendered speechless, I made my way back to the living room to watch our new guest stretched out on the couch. Half of me wanted to strangle Lee. The other half loved the man who'd take on a client's cat.

When Lee reemerged, dressed in a neat, dark suit and a solemn expression, I held my tongue. Moments later, we're in the car headed for Staten Island. Despite answering a few questions about the cat and Mr. Jimenez, Lee fell into a familiar silence. Something propelled me to speak.

"What was she like?" I pulled my gaze away from the slow-moving traffic on the Belt Parkway.

Lee's mouth hitched into a half smile. "You would have liked her. Heather would have admired your shoe collection."

My brow cocked up in appreciation of a fellow shoe aficionado. My cake shop required less of a fashion statement than my previous job. So, my patent leather black Jimmy Choo pumps sat collecting dust in my closet. Sometimes, I missed that part of my life and Lee knew it.

"Working at Mercier, Koenig and Layng could be a grind. Heather's presence made it less of one. How she cared about people made her everyone's friend." His grip on the steering wheel tightened. Even now, Heather affected him.

"Things at the firm changed. She found it difficult to stay," Lee said, his tone sad and regretful.

Had Lee's fond memories made him ensure someone noted Heather's passing? He found no information about friends who might want to attend her funeral. A death announcement in the paper might attract a few curiosity-seekers and nothing more. By the time we crossed the Verrazano Bridge into Staten Island, even I wondered who would come.

Upon our arrived at Saint Anne, Lee took time to talk to the young priest about Heather. There, only for emotional support, I kept my distance. I sat in the first pew as they talked before the service.

The huge brick church was cavernous. An assortment of stone saints stared down at me from perches on the wall. A large photograph of Heather stood by her plain oak casket. She was a stunning beauty, with raven hair, blue-green eyes, and translucent skin. Pleasing to any red-blooded man, maybe even a man like Lee.

So, transfixed by the image and thoughts of Heather, I only noticed Lee's presence when he took my hand. I looked up to find the priest at the pulpit ready to begin the service. My gaze fell on the few mourners who'd arrived. Some, I suspected didn't even know Heather. Yet, a few rows over sat a pair of women. Their familial features hinted at being related, perhaps mother and daughter. The older woman, in her late seventies dabbed at her eyes. Her companion sat stone still and indifferent.

"We gather here today to celebrate the life of Heather Mary McLaughlin..." the priest began.

"Do you know those people?" I whispered to Lee, who turned to spy the women a few feet away. He shook his head and admitted he knew no one in the church. Yet his eyes caught on someone leaning against the back wall by the large front door. His brow furrowed for a moment before turning away. The focus of his attention was a rail thin man in his thirties. Dark brown hair, sharp cheekbones, and like me, his unkind gaze locked on the portrait of Heather. Dressed in a mud colored brown, ill-fitted suit, he stood by the front entrance as if he was about to bolt.

The service passed by in a dull haze. Distinct moments pulled me from the fog in my head—Lee's release of my hand, the sound of a woman weeping, the ending of the service when the priest offered the prayer for the dead, my sudden strong dislike of Heather, and the guilt that followed.

"You okay?" I turned to Lee who also appeared caught in his own emotional traps. He offered a smile that didn't quite reach his hazel eyes.

"Let's go," he said flatly.

"What about the burial?" I had given up the entire day with the understanding I would attend Heather's burial as well.

"She wanted cremation and her ashes given to her mother," he replied.

That surprised me. Not because of the instruction for cremation, but on when and how he got them. Considering Heather's mother's condition, who had given them to him?

"Then we go home." I knew this wasn't the time or place for twenty questions.

When Lee gave me a genuine smile of relief in response, it felt like a sign of the lifting of his mood. Was it possible the storm that Heather McLaughlin brought had passed? If this meant Lee would move on, I could live with that.

"Let me talk to the priest for a moment before we go."

When he walked away, again, I was alone with my thoughts—the sadness of the service, the thin attendance, and the sorrowful remnants of a life lost. Her photograph stared back at me as a reminder that Lee had a life before me. When my dislike of Heather returned, I forced myself to turn away to the people leaving the church. The mother and daughter had gone, along with the man in the ugly brown suit. Even they couldn't linger in this place.

"Ready?" Lee said and pulled me from my thoughts.

"Yes," I said with resolve. Once again, he took my hand and pulled me from my seat.

Outside, the afternoon had turned unseasonably cool. Dull gray clouds hung low in the distance as the air held a threat of rain. A sudden chill overtook me as I tighten my hold of Lee's hand. Distracted, I hadn't realized Lee had stopped in mid-stride at the top of the stairs. He stiffened and pulled back without warning. The action caused me to take a misstep on a step and pitch me forward.

"Dessa," Lee yelled.

I gasped in surprise at losing my footing as Lee's arms grabbed my upper arm. Out of nowhere, a man appeared at my other side with a hand about my waist. I stared in shock as if to make sense of his sudden presence. Shorter than Lee, with dark blond hair, he gave me a concerned smile.

The source of Lee's distraction had been an older man standing at the base of the steps. With his eyes locked on Lee, he stood frozen in the moment.

"I have her," Lee said in a brusque tone as he pushed away the man's arm and drew me close. The stranger stepped away without protest.

"Thank you," I said in earnest, to counteract Lee's unfriendliness.

Lee took his time as we walked down the steps. When we reached the last step, the older man approached.

"Leland." The voice, rich and compassionate, seemed to stir Lee from his resentment momentarily. The men stared at each other for what seemed like forever before Lee spoke.

"Maxfield," Lee said.

"It seems I am always breaking my promises to you," Maxfield said with a sigh.

Those questions I put aside came charging back like a brick to the head. This wouldn't end with a prayer for the dead. Heather had brought Lee and the man called Maxfield here as surely as she'd sent invitations. In the distances, gray clouds gathered.

CHAPTER 5

Maxfield Layng began with small talk as he leaned on an ornate walking cane. Made of some dark polished wood, the head was an impressive arching silver wolf's head. His measured, yet melodious voice lulled me into mild adoration. Yet, the cautious air of a lawyer remained as he stood stiff in Lee's presence. Pale blue eyes stared back, uncertain. Lee gave nothing away. My own uncertainty was as thick as the air before a summer storm.

The man who tried to help stood off to the side, silent and watchful. The older man introduced him as Kip Waller one of the firm's associates. From Waller's eager attentiveness, their relationship appeared more personal than professional.

"I hear congratulations are in order." Maxfield gave me an infectious smile and pointed to my engagement ring.

"Yes, thank you," I said with forced cheeriness. From the coolness of Lee's mood, we weren't inviting Maxfield to the wedding.

"Aaron said it's in a few weeks," Maxfield said.

Aaron Boyer was a divorce lawyer and a senior partner in Lee's firm. He encouraged Lee in our relationships and delighted at the news of our engagement. Aaron was a devotee of my Key Lime pie and regular at the Blue Moon; however, Maxfield's name never came up— ever.

"You and Aaron still talk?" Lee struggled to hide his surprise and annoyance. Boyer had a lot to explain to the both of us.

"Rarely, but enough," Maxfield replied, with what sounded like honest regret. "You will always remain our favorite subject of conversation."

"Why are you here, Max?" Lee's tone went chilly.

Maxfield frowned. "I cared for her, too."

"You knew Heather well?" I interjected to defuse the growing tension.

"Yes, even longer than Lee. Beautiful, clever, and I regret, unappreciated." Maxfield's face softened as his eyes clouded in remembrance. I'd seen that expression on Lee.

"Did you read the notice in the paper?" Lee asked.

Maxfield nodded.

"Also, the cause of her death." Maxfield's lips tighten in a grimace. "To die like that in a dingy room with the view and smell of garbage."

Something in Lee's face reacted to the pain in Maxfield's voice. If these men shared nothing else, they shared that.

"If anyone in the firm had to attend, I guess it would be you." Lee conceded with reluctance.

Lee's curtness annoyed me. Short of drowning puppies, what had Maxfield done, short of paying respect for a woman they both cared about?

"Lee, I miss her, too." Maxfield brightened as he fed off the exchange.

Maxfield acted like a man looking for forgiveness. Lee looked like a man willing to give it if the circumstances were right. My presence was an impediment to this, and I wanted to give them privacy.

"Why don't I go wait in the car," I offered and stepped back. Maxfield shook his head.

"Please, no, this is not the place to talk, to bring up old wounds. Not here." Pale blue eyes turned toward the church and our gazes followed. A silence appeared and threatened the hard-fought civility between the men. Maxfield's lips broke out in a wide smile that crinkled the corners of his eyes as if he'd just remembered something.

"I had a thought, nothing too casual. No place too quiet that we'd force ourselves to speak," Maxfield teased with a hint of playfulness. "A formal place where the rules of decorum need the best behavior. Where there would be no time for old memories to haunt us."

Lee's eyes narrowed in suspicion.

"A place where your lovely fiancé and you can come as my guest for an evening, enjoy yourself, and avoid me if you wish."

"Are we going to England?" I joked.

Maxfield laughed. Lee didn't.

"Occasionally, the Carmen Smyth Gala can be pretentious."

"Why does that name sound familiar?" I wracked my brain to remember. Then it hit me, and my mouth got stuck in the open position of shock and awe.

As a rich New York socialite, Carmen Smyth remained civic minded until her death in the nineties. She threw over-the-top charity balls to fund several causes and got her rich friends to donate. Over the last twenty years, the event became the highlight of the city's social calendar. With media coverage, it was the place to be. When I worked in advertising, the agency handled several companies for the gala. Corporations liked charities for publicity. The Carmen Smyth charity ball was the perfect storm of media and money.

"Be serious, Maxfield," Lee chided.

"Why not!" Maxfield said, cocking a judgmental brow at him.

Lee remained mute, possibly unable to think of a logical reason.

"I want to go." I raised my hand. The food and wine at some of these events were envy worthy. Some of the city's finest dessert chef vied for a spot on the caterer's menu.

"No, you don't," Lee snapped. From the annoyed expression I knew I had, Lee registered my displeasure with a sigh.

"The people who go to these things are pompous asses and you wouldn't like them," Lee explained, his manner apologetic.

"Honey, I don't want to make friends. I want to get out of my apron, put on my Jimmy Choo's, and dress like a grown up. As much as you think it is, cake batter is not my perfume of choice," I replied.

"Why don't I sweeten the pot," Maxfield said and gave me a conspiratorial wink.

I smiled, as Lee gave me a warning glance.

"Aaron told me about this case you were handling pro bono. I can set up a fund and make it one of the small charities at the ball. As commendable as pro bono work is, Aaron has a small firm and its resources are finite," Maxfield insisted.

For a moment, there was a promising glint in Lee's eyes. Though he wouldn't admit it, I knew what little money and resources Aaron gave him for such work. Often, our joint checking account dipped for unknown reasons.

"Forget it, Max." Lee turned to leave.

After a few steps, he stopped when he realized I wasn't by his side. Next to Maxfield, I stood with arms crossed and glowered at him. Though getting dressed up and going out with Lee thrilled me, his refusal to help because of pride infuriated me more.

"Odessa?" he said, his tone filled with confusion.

"Let me not be the cause—" Maxfield stopped when I put up a hand. From his surprised expression, I guessed not many people demanded his silence this way.

"This man isn't offering you charity," I said while trying to control my temper. Lee returned and faced me. "He offered to help the families who need charity and a little help."

"Odessa, you don't understand—" Lee began before I put up a hand to stop him. There was no surprise there, he'd seen the hand before.

"Yesterday you said they might condemn that building to get those families out. Where are those people supposed to go? They can't move in with us, because we barely have room for Mr. Jimenez' cat."

"Odessa!" Lee pleaded.

"Someone is offering you help, and you refuse? They don't care about what happened between the two of you."

"Odessa, it's not about the money," he said.

"Then what is it about?" I asked, waiting for an answer I knew wouldn't come. If I haven't gotten answers from him before about a dead girl, two detectives, and a funeral, why would I now?

"Do you want to marry me?" My incredulous tone held a dash of threat.

"What!" Lee's eyes widened in alarm. "This has nothing to do with us getting married."

Lee hated when I took side trips in arguments. The lawyer in him liked unobstructed roads, no alternative routes or detours. Foolish man believed arguments with me had road maps.

"It does." I stepped close and lowered my voice. "Because the man I planned to marry wouldn't put his pride before the welfare of people who put their trust in him. You're not that person. So, Lee, put on your big boy pants and tell Maxfield you're taking the offer."

A multitude of emotions played in his eyes before he gave a tight-lipped smile. "Fine," he said. "But you'll regret it."

I laughed. "That's what my sister said about marrying you."

Maxfield seemed bemused if not confused at our exchange. "Wonderful, I'll have Kip make the arrangements."

Out of view of Lee and Maxfield, Kip Waller stood with a bemused smile. His discreet nod of approval said a lot about a man who appreciated my not so subtle manipulation.

"Thank you, Maxfield, and Lee's families from the LaGuardia Apartments thank you." I felt proud.

Lee remained stoic. You would have thought I asked him to give up his Yankee season tickets.

"Lee, I know seeing me wasn't what you expected or going to the gala. But I hope it's an opportunity for us to talk at least," Maxfield said with some contrition.

"I'll go, but I won't promise more, Max," Lee said.

Maxfield nodded before facing me.

"Ms. Wilkes, it was a true pleasure meeting you." He gave me a quick bow before turning his gaze on Lee. In an instant, Waller appeared in a black sedan. He opened the car door as Maxfield hobbled unevenly from the gravel beneath him. His unsteady gait gave him an air of fragility that put me further on his side.

I watched Lee as he watched the two men drive away. His displeasure would play out in hours of silence. Discussion on Maxfield and Heather wouldn't happen unless I started them. Our drive home was proof of that, with only two or three words spoken between us. The traffic on the Belt Parkway toward Queens didn't help. It only dragged out the silence. Questions on what happened at the church only would ignite an argument and more silence. I wasn't stupid. In the mood Lee was in, he might pull over to the parkway shoulder, open the car door, and ask me to walk home. So, I kept my mouth shut.

When Lee turned onto our block, it relieved me to see our little Tudor inspired house. I held my breath as he pulled the car into the driveway. The walk to the front door took decades. Before Lee put the key in the door, I stopped him. Now I was home and not left on the roadside, I had to say something. I'd sided with Maxfield and encouraged Lee to do something he didn't want. He had to believe I was still on his side.

"We'll go to the party and get a lot of money. Then we'll run out like bandits," I reassured and pulled him into a hug. He was stiff to the embrace. "I promise."

Lee relaxed once he put his arms around me. His head dipped to nuzzle my neck. When he pulled back, a slight smile played across his lips.

"In your Jimmy Choo's," he said with his familiar sarcasm. Of course, he was right, running was out of the question.

"No, we'll walk away slowly, with a great deal of dignity," I mused.

His smile widened.

"You want to take this inside?" I gave him a lecherous grin.

The first sight I saw upon entering was the comatose body of the cat. It obliterated any amorous intentions in an instant. Spread eagle on the living room floor, with his head resting on a half-eaten bag of kibble, made me think it was dead. Then I heard the snoring.

"Oh my god," Lee said.

I shook my head and glared at him. "God has nothing to do with this."

CHAPTER 6

The Henderson-Bentley wedding imploded. I rated it up there with a ten-car pileup on the Long Island Expressway. How could a group of well-dressed people act like they were auditioning for the next reality television show? Easy, throw in free-flowing champagne and family drama. Well-dressed people screaming, and yelling was very photogenic. The crux of the problem lay with Uncle Hal.

"This won't go well," I said.

The Alderson Gallery, a converted factory in Long Island City, hosted many of the city's finest weddings. Its view of the Manhattan skyline, spacious accommodation, and catering made it the perfect place for Naomi's two hundred plus guests. What Naomi's wedding planner didn't expect was an arrival of a former family friend, Uncle Hal. She hadn't missed the resemblance the bride had to Hal, nor did anyone else. Why Hal took this moment for a confessional was anyone's guess.

"Should we do something?" Bebe Dunn asked with caution in his voice. The Blue Moon's sous chef came in handy when the cake weighed more than I did.

"If anyone throws punches, remember to protect the cake." I put the last of the neon yellow sugar paste flowers near the top. Situated off to the side by the cocktail table and bar, we had a full view of the goings on. The cake, a six-tier extravaganza of color and flowers, took center stage. However, the cake came in a distant second after Uncle Hal's appearance.

"I'm more worried about you." Bebe gave me his usual scathing glare. A look that often questioned my sanity and judgment. His unblemished chocolate color skin and acerbic world-weary observation endeared me the first time we met. At 15-year-old, he started as a dishwasher at the Blue Moon. Three years later, he'd worked his way up to assistant chef. His once gangly adolescent frame now replaced with something that could play for the New York Giants offensive line.

"Why me?"

"Why is it, every time I work with you something happens?" Bebe questioned.

"You make it sound like it's my fault." I pouted.

"Last time, someone tried to kill you." He cocked up a brow.

"Again, not my fault," I protested. Not that Bebe was wrong, but it wasn't my fault crazy followed me.

"The guy in the funny suit should worry about getting punched." Bebe pointed to Uncle Hal.

Dressed in a sky-blue tuxedo that looked two sizes too small for him, Hal pleaded his case to the bride's father. The issue being, who should walk the bride down the aisle? The poor bride stood huddled behind her future husband crying her eyes out and ruining her makeup.

I'd hoped the Henderson-Bentley wedding would be a distraction for me. A sullen fiancé, my out-of-control wedding, and a bathroom rug masquerading as a cat took up too much space in my head. The encounter at Heather's funeral and Lee's reaction to Maxfield Layng still had my stomach in knots. After the funeral and cleaning up the mess the cat made, I'd called Maggie for some much-needed clarity.

"Didn't you say this Layng guy seemed nice?" Maggie said after I told her what'd happened at the funeral service.

"The man could give Santa Claus competition. Lee wasn't buying it, though, and that bothered me. Lee loves Santa Claus."

"He does love Christmas, but Santa Claus doesn't have a history with him," Maggie reminded me.

"Who is this guy Layng?"

"Are you asking me to find out?" Maggie didn't hide her tentativeness. Would opening a can of worms before my wedding be smart?

How smart was I if I ignored the obvious? There was something about Heather McLaughlin's death. There was something wrong with Lee and his refusal to talk. Maggie once remarked that people hid the truth to protect the ones they love or themselves. I didn't think Lee was self-serving. The only other option was that he was protecting me. From what, was the question.

"Yes, Sherlock."

"Don't call me that," Maggie complained.

"I know Frank McAvoy's name is on the front door, but I know who the real investigator is. Frank couldn't find a clue unless it was wrapped up with bacon and shoved into a donut," I quipped.

"Frank is a good detective." Now she sounded defensive. Maggie protected Frank, even from me. As a retired New York City detective, Frank was on his third divorce. He had the fashion sense of a third-rate car salesman and the emotional IQ of one. Without Maggie, Frank's investigation agency would die a slow death

"Frank's good at chasing adulterous husbands, wayward wives, and missing UPS packages," I retorted.

"Why can't you two get along?" Her voice had that Mommy tone.

"You want the long story or the short?"

At first, Maggie's need for working with Frank had more to do with him as her mentor. To become a licensed investigator, in New York State, a licensed investigator had to mentor you. As time passed, Frank begrudgingly appreciated Maggie's value to his business. Besides being an office manager, bookkeeper and all-round work wife, Maggie had skills. Even though she looked like one of the Lords of the Ring elves, she had a way of finding the truth. People trusted and confided in her in ways they never would with the socially inept Frank.

"Neither," an exasperated Maggie huffed. "Listen, O, I'll look into this Layng guy, but I can tell you now, Lee won't like it."

"I know." Would I put myself on a path of truth or self-destruction? Either way, Lee wouldn't be happy. "What would you do?"

Maggie said nothing at first. "Yes, I'd want to know. Lee is a little overprotective at times," she said.

"He hates it when I break the law," I teased, trying to find levity in the conversation.

"It's good he's a lawyer, but Lee loves you," Maggie reassured.

"Yeah, that too."

After the phone call I went to bed as I was exhausted from the day's events and drama. Lee sequestered himself in the home office downstairs for most of the night. When I woke the next morning, the weight of his arm over me felt reassuring. I lingered, not slipping out of bed like the usual start to my day. I wanted, if not needed, the contact. A day planned for the Henderson-Bentley wedding and the chaos that loomed ahead. I didn't want the peaceful moment to end.

The memory of the morning and my sense of comfort vanished as the volume in the room increased. I longed for the comfort of my bed. There, I didn't think about Heather, Maxfield, or whether my wedding was really a family reunion. I ached for that moment.

"The groom's pretty pissed," Bebe said, breaking me from my reverie.

"Pissed would be an understatement." I watched as several groomsmen tried to stop the groom from punching Hal.

"I give it five minutes before someone calls the cops." Bebe's sardonic tone belied his young age. Despite being nineteen, he understood human foibles, sometimes more so than I did.

It took ten minutes before the police arrived. Uncle Hal noticed them too and bolted. Fortified with a few cocktails, I had to give him credit. Hal was nimble. Like a world-class soccer player, he dodged two groomsmen and the maid of honor. Naomi's father stood in front of his daughter in a protective stand as Hal shouted out endearments to her. The guests hugged the walls and watched. When Hal turned in our direction, I jumped in front of the cake table. In my hand was a replica of the bride and groom done in modeling chocolate. As Hal lumbered toward me, I held it out like a talisman.

"Stop!" I said with more ferocity than even I expected. Amazingly, he stopped in front of me and wobbled. I sneered at him. I've seen Candace use this trick on small dogs, drunks, and prepubescent boys.

"You're a tall drink of cocoa." His slurred words were mixed with an unmanly giggle. Hal took a step toward me as if he'd like a sample.

"Bebe," I barked.

Bebe stepped around me and grabbed Uncle Hal in a bear hug. A noticeable sigh of relief came from the crowd. Hal squirmed, cursed, and reeked of alcohol. I held up the figurine's inches from his face.

"Shame on you," I said. "Greatest day of her life and all she'll remember is a drunk in a bad suit."

"I have a right... I have a right." Hal twisted to no avail.

"You ruined this wedding and ruined this moment for her. Shame on you," I said.

Bebe released him when the cops placed handcuffs on him. Behind them the future Mrs. Henderson, eyes red with tears, looked like she wanted to disappear.

"Why does everybody think this event is about them? It's about her," I yelled as the police took Uncle Hall away.

"Crazy." Bebe looked in my direction.

Off in a corner, bridesmaids enveloped Naomi in taffeta and flowers to usher her away. Naomi's father followed the cops and Uncle Hall out, screaming profanities. Naomi's mother sat in one of the pews shell-shocked. The groom, an earnest-looking man of around thirty, stared at me as if I had answers. I had none and shook my head. The rest of the guests headed for the cocktail table like a herd of wildebeest. The disaster of a wedding became an afterthought to everyone catching up with each other's news.

"It's turned into a family reunion." I scanned the well-dressed crowd in disbelief at the insensitivity. The need to get as far away from the Henderson-Bentley wedding couldn't happen fast enough. News of the wedding's cancellation came from the dumbstruck wedding planner. So, Bebe and I packed up our tools. We were out of the venue within fifteen minutes and heading for the parking lot.

We had parked a few streets down on a residential street. I led the way with Bebe close behind. When I reached my shop's pink van, stenciled with the shop's logo on its side, I paused. The words I KNOW YOU written in what looked to be deep brown paint glared back at me. The writing was crude as if written by a child. Disgusted at the sight of my vandalized van, I cursed. Then I cursed again as I surveyed the surrounding area. Certain the culprits were long gone, I took a closer inspection of the van.

"Miss O." Bebe grabbed me by my arm and pulled me back. He stepped before me to take a closer inspection of the vehicle.

"We should remove it." The thought of driving around with that on my van was not an option for me. Without thinking, I reached out to touch a section of the paint when Bebe pushed my hand away.

"Don't touch that," he exclaimed.

"Why?"

Bebe leaned in and sniffed one letter. Then he did it again.

"What are you doing?" I asked, confused.

"Miss O, that ain't paint." He took a step back.

"What do you mean, that ain't paint?" I stared at the writing. The paint color was a reddish brown and thinned out in many places. "What is it?"

"Blood."

CHAPTER 7

"Are you going to tell him?" Maggie asked as she held up her cellphone to snap a picture.

The sight of my reflection in the full-length mirror stopped me from answering. I resembled an angry wedding cake topper. In Gateau's Bridal Shop, Maggie found the ugliest bridal dress in creation. It was a corseted concoction that cinched my waist and jabbed at my ribs. My outright disgust completed the ensemble. How I let Maggie talk me into one of her fantasies said more about her powers of persuasion and my inability to say no. What I planned as a last-minute fitting for my wedding dress devolved into Maggie treating me like a doll.

"No," I answered finally, as I tried to find what protruded into my side.

"Can't have it both ways," Maggie said as she snapped a picture with her phone. "You can't complain that he won't tell you things and then hide this from him."

"This is different."

Maggie lifted an imperious auburn brow up at me, but I tried to ignore it. This was my friend's passive aggressive way of saying I was so wrong, I bordered on stupid.

"Graffiti, that's all it was. Anyway, I had Bebe with me."

"Bebe can't always be with you. Odessa, you can't ignore this." Maggie crossed her arms and jutted out her tiny, pointed chin. If you could imagine a pissed off pixie, you'd guess this image didn't fill me with concern. She was right, though, and I couldn't ignore the message. The thing was, I didn't understand what the message meant.

"Right now, the van is the least of my problems," I said, refocusing on my priorities and the thing sticking in my side. Was it possible a dress could kill you?

"Can I get out of this now?"

A deflated Maggie sighed and reached out to help me off the pedestal. The stiff and voluminous fabric made a crunching noise every time I moved. Maggie needed help from one of the sales girls to get me out of the damn thing.

"I wish you'd enjoy this," Maggie lamented. The sour look I gave her summed up my feelings.

"I had a simple wedding plan," I said and tried not to scratch. "My sister and best friend decided that's not good enough."

"We want the best day of your life," Maggie replied.

"Candace has invited more people than I know. The minute I let my guard down, you pull out your fairy wand and dress me in one of those medieval torture dresses."

"You're being unreasonable," Maggie said.

"The reason brides act like Godzilla is because they can't breathe. No breath, no oxygen to the brain. No brain, rational thought goes out the window. So, if I seem like I want to murder you and stuff you in the truck of my car, that's why."

"Sometimes, O, I can't understand why you're not having fun." Maggie pouted with disappointment.

Failing to convert me into a Disney princess, she refocused her concern back to my other problem. Someone went out of their way to find me.

"Don't think I pissed off anyone lately," I reassured her. The eyebrow shot up again. I huffed in protest. "I never count family or friends."

"What about indirectly?" Maggie stood at a rack of gowns and sighed wistfully. Each one uglier than the next. She pulled out a mermaid style dress with too much lace. My response was to put my finger in my mouth and gag. Maggie huffed.

"Indirectly?" Now it was my turn to raise a questioning brow. I knew how to piss off someone, but never indirectly.

"Lee." Maggie held up another dress in triumph. This one had too much tulle. I shook my head. Maggie shoved the dress back onto the rack and huffed. It was hard to play dress up when your doll refused to play.

"Lee," I repeated. Unless there was a gang of angry bakers after me, I couldn't think of anyone who might vandalize my van. At the moment, Lee had a list of people who didn't particularly like him. Current and former legal opponents topped the list. I would throw in Candace, but I didn't think she'd trash my van. All she had to do was get the entire First Baptist congregation to pray for Lee to break a leg before the wedding. There was a pissed off slum lord from the LaGuardia Apartments Lee had a civil suit against.

"Didn't you say the landlord is playing hardball with the tenants? Wasn't an apartment vandalized? If the landlord is using those tactics, why would he stop there? What's next? What about the lawyer's girlfriend?" Maggie asked.

That question made me pause. Lee could be as tenuous as a pit bull. If the landlord had tried to intimidate him, he'd never tell me. He would think it was part of the job. What would he do if he knew the landlord came after me?

"The landlord, Comaneci, has these goons masquerading as maintenance men. They do whatever they want. They don't do repairs and the building is falling apart. A few families have left already."

"Their only hope is if Lee wins the civil suit. This would hold him accountable for the tenants' pain and suffering. Lee has to win," Maggie said.

"He'll win, but it takes time," I said. Which means, I can't tell Lee about the vandalism, especially if it's linked to the LaGuardia Apartments.

From Maggie's sour expression, she didn't like the idea.

"If the worst they could do is vandalize my van, I can live with it."

"What if it doesn't stop with the van?"

It was a question I didn't want to answer. The only thing I was sure of was I didn't want to be the reason Lee pulled out of the LaGuardia Apartments' civil suit.

"Between LaGuardia Apartments and Maxfield Layng, Lee can't sleep or eat. Do you know he's still in contact with those detectives? That makes everything worse. Every time he talks to them, he gets quiet and defensive."

"He seems pretty torn up about it." Maggie held up a simple but elegant veil for me. "This would go nicely with your dress."

I had to agree. Maggie's selection of the veil was my concession to her. I'd never be her Disney princess, despite her efforts. I headed back into the dressing room to change back into my own clothes. All the while, Lee came to the forefront of my thoughts. When I return to the main salon, I found Maggie waiting by the door. She frowned at the sight of me.

"What's wrong?" she asked when I reached her.

"Lee thinks if he doesn't talk about it, I won't think it bothers him. Four years ago, he walked away from a great job, divorced his wife, and gave up law. Whatever happened, Heather McLaughlin was there. While he's cut off ties with Maxfield, he kept them with Heather, no matter how tentative. Why?"

"That's a good question." Maggie nodded as she followed me out of the shop. "I've looked into Maxfield Layng a little. It seems he's well respected amongst his peers. He's won a ton of cases, big flashy ones. A few years ago, they gave him an award and the people who came included the governor. The newspaper articles on him talked about his influence, how he became a career maker, just by association. Though he's not as active as he once was, his involvement in certain cases still carries weight."

"Then why is Lee the only man who doesn't want to be around him?" I turned to her. The late afternoon sun held no warmth for me. The busy sound of traffic in front of the shop felt muted and my head crammed with thoughts. As my wedding day approached, Lee acted less and less like the man I wanted to marry. A side of him appeared that I didn't recognize—sullen, silent, and conflicted.

"There might be an answer for you at the gala," Maggie said as we walked to her car.

"Lee tried to talk me out of going again last night. He wanted to go alone and deal with Maxfield himself. He went on and on about how I wouldn't enjoy myself." I sighed. It was almost as if he didn't want me to be around Maxfield.

"What did you do?" Maggie asked.

"I showed him the dress I bought. I told him if I didn't get to wear it to the party, he would, on pain of death." I smiled.

Maggie laughed. "Can't imagine Lee in a cocktail dress."

"Well, neither could he and he stopped asking. Even though I made it sound like I wanted to go to the gala for a night out in the city, I couldn't tell him the truth," I confessed.

Maggie nodded her head in understanding.

"That you want to find out what his past looked like. Talk to Maxfield Layng and get an idea about their relationship and why they had a fallen out."

I nodded. We stood by Maggie's car, but didn't enter.

"It's a time Lee doesn't talk about. He left the firm, divorced Julia, and didn't practice law. Now someone they both cared about has died and it's thrown them back together. I'm confused by Lee's resistance and Maxfield's eagerness to reconnect."

"At the funeral, I took his side with the gala. He might be grateful enough to talk. If not, I'll beat him into submission."

Maggie laughed. "That's more your style. Either way, Lee won't like you digging into his past. Especially a past he wants to keep buried."

"If Lee knew half the things I did without telling him, he'd never let me out of the house." I snorted at the accusation.

"If he finds out you want to go to the gala to spy on him, he'll do more than lock you in the house."

"This coming from the woman who edits everything she says to her husband when it comes to her job," I replied.

How many times had she asked me to go with her to investigate or tail some wayward spouse in the middle of the night? Asking her husband was out of the question. Her narcoleptic boss, Frank, was of little use. After midnight, he'd turn into a snoring corpse.

"Why are you looking at me like that?" Maggie feigned innocence.

A promise of a girls' night out often morphed into one of her surveillance jobs. Once at a restaurant, Maggie insistence on a selfie that had more to do with the cheating husband in the next booth.

"Try to be discreet."

This time I had to laugh. Maggie and I had switched roles. At the gala, I was to play the spy. Use my charms on Maxfield Layng in the hopes he give me a clue about Lee's past. More importantly, Lee's true relationship with Heather McLaughlin. What hold did she still have over him? All the while, I had to convince Lee I wanted to use the gala as a date night. I would put on my brand-new dress, slip on my Louboutins and lie to Lee on the true nature of the night. Give him a half-truth wrapped up in something sweet. A candy-coated lie that would make it go down easier if he found my real reason. At least I hoped so.

CHAPTER 8

Lee and I arrived in Manhattan on the West Side around seven. The city being the city, we parked at the closest parking lot a few blocks away from the event. Hand in hand, we walked down Columbus Avenue in a comfortable silence. A rare moment of amity, free of wedding plans, Candace, tenants, and a furry houseguest. Lee was handsome in a tailored suit with his hair freshly cut and the day-old stubble gone. Yet, he walked as if each step was his last. His grip on my hand was tight. At any moment, I expected him to pull me back and demand to return home.

"You look nice," I said.

An appreciative smile emerged, and he leaned in close.

"Let's get a hotel room someplace. Order room service and turn off our phones," he whispered.

A part of me melted. Most of those parts lived below my waist, the other parts wanted to ignore his poor attempt at distraction. Tempted as I was to disappear into some Manhattan hotel, Lee didn't fool me. Second thoughts about Maxfield plagued him. It made me second guess my decision. Against his better judgement, he'd come because of me. We stood a block away from the museum, each rooted in our own indecisiveness.

"What about the LaGuardia Apartments?" I questioned. Would his absence affect the outcomes of Maxfield's efforts? Would Lee care? He was a good man, he would care.

A Candy Coated Lie

Something in Lee's face changed. A resolve, a slight hardening around the eyes and a firm set to his mouth. He walked again in the direction of the museum, taking me with him. Lee didn't speak again until we were on the gala's receiving line and handed a host our invitations. My guilt knocked on the door of my conscious and wanted entrance. I ignored the knocking.

As we entered, the Victor A. Friis Museum seemed like a perfect place to hold a charity ball. It was a former mansion of one of the city's infamous 1800s industrialists. He made millions exploiting coal miners or something like that. His recompense was to donate his mansion and its content upon his death to the city. The museum's profits were going to a variety of New York City charities.

Once a family home, the museum had a large outdoor garden, a rarity in Manhattan. It hinted at a time when the city had more space and fewer people. Large tents covered much of the outdoor space. In the background, a jazz band played. Illuminated bars edged along the tents. Lee cut through the growing crowd and headed for one. I followed.

As if by magic, Kip Waller popped up in front of us. Wallers' knack for appearing out of nowhere was almost magical, if not disconcerting.

"You must have come in at the west entrance," he said, somewhat out of breath.

"Yes." Lee brushed past him. This left me with a somewhat perturbed Waller, who shook it off with a shrug.

"He needs a drink," I said, my tone apologetic.

"Still not keen on being here?" Waller surmised. His lips quirked up in understanding and gestured us to follow Lee.

"Where's Maxfield?" I scanned the growing crowd for a white-haired man.

"Working Dina Holbourne. Normally, her charities are animal related. You know, zoos, shelters, and such. Maxfield will guilt her into contributing to the human species for the first time in years." Waller sounded boastful.

I search the crowd hoping to see the telltale shock of white hair amongst the crowd. With most of the men dressed in the typical uniforms of dark suit and entitled looks, it was hard to find him. Also, the venue's lighting made it difficult. Whoever organized the gala tried to mimic soft, almost candle like lighting. Under it, hair like Maxfield's looked blond.

"It's nice for him to do this," I said as we walked toward the bar where Lee stood talking to the bartender.

"I haven't seen him this animated in months. McKenzie's fund is in good hands," a boastful Waller said as we reached Lee at the bar.

When Lee turned around with two drinks to face me, he didn't have his happy face. One glass held what looked like scotch or whiskey, the other, a martini. Lee stepped past Waller to hand me the martini. The moment reminded me of one of Lee's old movies he loved to watch. The one with Bette Davis when she declared the night would get bumpy. I sipped my drink for fortification.

Finally, Lee acknowledged Waller's presence with a weary sigh.

"Were you their compromise?" Lee asked.

Waller's brows furrowed in what looked like confusion. It didn't last long.

"They actually interviewed me for it," Waller quipped. "I beat out twelve associates and two law clerks."

I stared at them confused.

"Maxfield hasn't been in a courtroom in years. Aaron said he had a mild stroke," Lee explained.

I couldn't decipher the look Lee gave Waller. I didn't know whether he pitied or envied his current position.

"What are you talking about?" I said, frustrated with the secret boy code going on between them.

"Maxfield is one of the founding partners at Mercier, Koenig and Layng. If he wanted, he could come to work naked and no one would say a thing," Lee said.

"When clients come in, they want to see him. It's his name they trust," Waller said. The men seemed to exchange something about Maxfield Layng I'd yet to understand.

"So, your job is to..." I couldn't find a subtle way to ask Waller if he were an overpaid babysitter.

"Make sure he's happy." Waller gave a self-effacing smile. "It's easy. He doesn't ask for much. I ensure the world around him is what he likes."

"What do you get out of this?" I asked.

"That you can say you worked under Maxfield Layng. In some circles, that's enough," Lee said.

Waller shrugged. "A few doors might open."

"Be careful which door you walk through," Lee warned in an uncharacteristic chilly tone.

Waller's pleasant demeanor shifted, but once again recovered. Then he pointed at a large group of people. In the center stood Maxfield. His almost instinctual awareness of Maxfield's presence impressed me.

"Do you have a tracking device on him?" I quipped.

Waller laughed.

"Max draws a crowd. They want to be seen with him because he is famous and infamous," Waller said.

"Infamous?" I asked.

Lee sighed.

"Maxfield in the courtroom was to eviscerate his opponents without them even knowing it. Max made it into theater," Lee said in a way as if the memory was uncomfortable.

"Like a surgeon, he was efficient. An actor in the courtroom, changing his demeanor and mannerism to suit the jury. Judges applauded his knowledge of the law. Other lawyers feared sitting across from him," Waller chimed in.

It was hard to reconcile the man Lee and Waller spoke of with the one I met at the funeral. Or had that been an act? Had Maxfield played me like one of his jurors? Was the decision to come to the gala mine or his? I like to think I wasn't that easy to manipulate. As I watched Maxfield approach, I wondered.

Even from a distance, I saw how he commanded the room. Absent of his ornate cane, he made his way through the crowd like a king amongst his subjects. He hid his unsteady gait by keeping his pace slow. Occasionally a nearby chair's back or a friendly shoulder steadied him. When he caught sight of us, the partygoers parted like the Red Sea as he made his way to us.

"Kip found you, good." Maxfield reached out and took Lee's hand to shake. "It's been a profitable night, my boy."

"Thank you, Max," Lee said. I caught the resistance in his voice if no one else did.

Out of nowhere, Waller handed Maxfield a drink. Lee spied it and frowned. Remembering Maxfield's condition, I stared, too. Yet he didn't drink. A prop used to let those around him know all was well.

"So glad you made it," Maxfield said with a smile. I was under no delusion those words were for me. Lee's presence pleased him. Yet, Lee stood silent, letting the past stand between them.

"Barring any complications, you can access the fund in a week," Waller reassured.

"Kip will expedite this quickly," Maxfield promised, giving his assistant an appreciative smile.

Lee offered a weak smile as the tension eased from his face. As if handed cue to engage, Maxfield fell into a conversation about the venue, the guests, and the magnificent art on view.

"When you get a chance, you and Odessa should view the open galleries," Maxfield suggested. When the men began a long discussion about the logistics of the fund, I got lost in the legalese. Happy that Lee seemed interested in talking, I took a step back.

"Ladies room," I announced and handed Lee my half-finished drink. His stern, if not pleading look told me not to leave. With a shrug and a wave, I cut into the well-dressed crowd and left him. Lee and Maxfield didn't need a mediator or referee. If they did, they had Waller.

A Candy Coated Lie

Five minutes later, with freshly applied lipstick, I emerged from the bathroom. I wasn't ready to return to the men, so I acted on Maxfield's suggestion and viewed the galleries. It would give me a chance to clear my head of the martini and placate my guilt about dragging Lee to the gala.

In several rooms, I strolled passed the Dutch Masters and French sculptures. I took my time. Before long, I'd gotten so turned around and found myself in a grouping of smaller rooms deep within the gallery. With each room, the sounds from the garden lessened. When I tried to find my way out, the sound of Lee's voice stopped me. I was surprised at his presence inside and I didn't enter at first because there were other voices. Ones I didn't recognize.

"I think it providence," an unfamiliar voice said.

"That's ridiculous," an annoyed Maxfield barked.

"That may be, but it gives us an opportunity to settle this," another unfamiliar voice said.

"I don't need to settle anything," Lee said coolly.

"It's just like you to pull this, Eric," Maxfield scolded.

"We only want to know what McKenzie thinks," a male voice said.

"You blindside him with this crap and expect him to go along for old time's sake. He's not one of your associates!" Maxfield said. The full force of his persona clear.

"Maxfield, I don't need you to defend me," Lee interrupted.

"Why don't we all calm down," a calmer voice said.

"I don't want Lee to think I brought him here for this!" Maxfield barked.

"I'm going to find Odessa and leave this to you, Max." Lee's voice had a measure of control, barely.

Panicked that he might catch me eavesdropping, I turned to leave. Something tall and hard stopped me, or more like someone.

"Sorry," I said, looking into the handsome face of a dark blond-haired man.

"No, I'm the one who's supposed to say I'm sorry," he said with a lopsided grin. "I shouldn't have been so close."

He had been close, too close, and I took a step back in panic. Then I bumped into something equally hard. I turned to see Lee. His lips pressed hard in a tight line as his gaze locked on the man before me. The last time I saw that face was when Lee had cornered a man he thought had run me off the road. It took Maggie and me to stop him from popping his head like a Pez dispenser.

The man cocked his head to the side and his smile widened.

"You don't look happy to see me, Leland."

CHAPTER 9

The person that stood next to me was unrecognizable. Lee stared at a man he clearly hated and did nothing. Would my presence, or the watchful eyes of his former law firm associates, stop him from punching the stranger? By the tight set of his jaw and penetrating gaze, I knew he wanted to. When one man, a distinguished looking black gentleman, suggested privacy, Lee gave him a withering stare. At one-point Maxfield held up a hand between them as if things might come to blows.

They wouldn't. Lee's facial expression resembled the control he often gave my sister. A way to counteract Candace's constant baiting. He hadn't punched her yet.

"I'm sorry." A contrite Maxfield placed his hand on Lee's chest. If Lee didn't believe the honesty in the old man's eyes, I did. Unless Maxfield's behavior was an Academy Award-winning performance, his anger felt real.

"Mercier thought coming to the gala might be the best place to meet." The blond man nodded at the black man.

"When I told you about the gala, it wasn't an invitation." Maxfield snarled at the man called Mercier.

Mercier raised both hands in mock surrender. "I saw an opportunity."

Lee turned a steely gaze on him. "For what?"

Mercier replied, "Resolution!"

Maxfield huffed in annoyance and pointed a finger at the man. "Of all times, you pick now!"

"We doubted Lee would come to the office if he asked him, no matter the enticement. You won't return our phone calls." One of the suited men directed at Lee.

Like Mercier, he exuded a sense of authority. With a receding hairline, fleshy jowls, and a face that held resentful eyes, he reminded me of an angry accountant. To tell you the truth, they all looked like they belong to a funeral directors' union.

"What conversation could I have with anyone at Mercier, Koenig and Layng?" Lee's biting tone had a negligible effect.

"It doesn't have to be this way, Leland," the man replied. From the commanding presence of this man, I wondered if he might be the third partner from Mercier, Koenig and Layng.

"Don't blame them. My father pushed for this." The blond man held up a hand in his defense.

"Daddy says come home and make amends," Lee said in contempt. The first sign of his control failing.

The blond man shook his head. "More like, I'll make amends if you let me come home."

"I doubt I am your ticket back to New York," Lee said.

"No, but you could be the reason I stay. You've met my father, everything has a condition." The stranger wore a bemused smile.

From the stilted expression on Lee's face, his remark had no effect.

"As I recalled, my last conversation with your father involved having me arrested," Lee said.

So focused on the man before him, Lee didn't notice my surprise reaction. The man did. His smile widened. Was he goading Lee?

"Well, you broke my nose, cracked two ribs, and threatened to eviscerate me." The stranger's face twinkled with mischief.

Lee stiffened.

"Stop this. This isn't the time or place, Ellison." Maxfield's commanding voice froze the men in their place.

"I understand that now," the man called Ellison said, his tone apologetic yet his satisfied smirk said more.

"A good time?" Lee snapped. Hell freezing over might happen first, I thought.

"You're right." Ellison held up his hand in mock surrender. He was about to turn to leave but stopped. His eyes fell on me. "I'm told congratulations are in order."

Waller stood just beyond the small group and gave an audible moan. Maxfield glared at Ellison. The other men shifted uncomfortably. Lee's jaw clenched, along with his fist. Ellison's attempt at civility hit a nerve. I felt like an outsider, clueless of their inside jokes.

This had to stop.

I held out my hand in greeting.

"Hi, I'm Odessa," I said, with a forced smile. Five minutes into meeting Ellison, I didn't care for him. I didn't much care for Mercier, Koenig and Layng either. They resembled a pack of wolves as they surrounded Lee. I understood wolves. They couldn't compare to a pack of bridesmaids at a bride's bouquet toss.

Ellison gave Lee a cautious glance before he took my hand to shake.

"I'm sorry, I didn't catch your name." My memory was fine, but at a loss to find a safe topic to discuss. The price of milk, the weather, the level of discomfort I felt.

"Ellison..." His handsome face took on a well-practiced boyish quality.

"Ellison Yves Schaeffer, of Schaeffer Pharmaceuticals," Lee informed. "One of Mercier, Koenig and Layng's biggest clients. Last I remember they made up thirty percent of the firm's income."

"We're one of many clients the firm handles," Ellison said with a false sense of modesty.

"Humility doesn't suit you." Lee's tone went frosty again. "Neither does civility, common sense, and restraint."

"A lot has changed since we last met." Ellison sounded defensive for the first time.

"Daddy banished you, right? Mongolia?" Lee quipped.

"South Korea." Ellison's smile faltered.

"Still doing anything to please your father and using the firm to help." Lee gave the men surrounding him a condemning glance. "Am I the first on your redemption tour?"

Ellison shook his head. "Not the first, but the hardest."

Lee chortled. "Modesty and contrition. What's next, abstinence? No, you had to achieve that to come home."

The expression on Ellison's face darkened. These men knew how to push each other's button.

The rash on my arm flared in protest as I watched. These men had a history, a bad history. Lee's tentative control of his temper prevented the encounter from going nuclear. How long would that last?

With the press at the gala, an altercation would be front page news. Maxfield's efforts would amount to nothing. He'd convinced people to give to the fund because of Lee and his cause. They don't want to have second thoughts regarding their contribution.

"Well, that's interesting," I interrupted brightly. Lee glared at me like I'd put on a clown suit.

"Really?" A surprised Ellison raised a dubious eyebrow.

Whether in advertising or running a cake shop, clients were problematic. Being the expert, you knew what was best, at least most of the time. Ellison wanted to make amends and Lee balked at the idea. How to put the two on common ground was the task.

"Besides saying hello to old acquaintances, you must be here for the charities as well?" I ignored the perplexed gaze of the surrounding men.

"What?" Ellison responded, dumbfounded by my question.

"Odessa!" Lee cautioned. This man lived with me. Where I wanted to go didn't have a map. He hated when I didn't have a map. Maxfield's gaze danced between Lee and me. I pitied the dumbfounded expression on his face. Yet another man who needed a map.

"Schaeffer Pharmaceuticals got these fine gentlemen out on a night like this to support a worthy cause is high praise. Why would you imagine this was all about you?" I teased Lee, who didn't find me amusing.

The gentlemen in question continued to stare at me as if I were an umbrella giving tax advice.

"What are you saying, Odessa?" a tentative Maxfield asked.

The corner of Waller's lip quirked up into a smile. Perceptive as always, he understood, I would push his bosses into a corner.

"I know what she's saying." Lee faced me.

Not wishing to see his ire, I gave Ellison my full attention.

"Schaeffer Pharmaceuticals can't be seen showing up just for the food," I said with no humor.

"What?" Ellison's brow furrowed.

"Excuse me, Miss..." Mercier interjected.

"You missed the point. What impression would Schaeffer Pharmaceutical make coming to a famous charity ball and donated nothing?" I said.

Maxfield laughed with delight.

As educated as these men were, my point took a moment to register. The comical expressions of surprise and embarrassment came in waves. Just beyond the group, Waller gave me an appreciative nod of approval.

"How would they find out?" Koenig complained.

"Odessa used to work at a top-rated advertising firm in New York. She's promoted several companies at this event. Free publicity for those seen to be giving and for those who just show up for the food." Lee added with a bemused look of his own.

"I recognize a reporter or two or three," I lied. "They would love to report on Schaeffer Pharmaceuticals excellent charity work."

"We didn't come here for this!" Koenig complained.

Lee's contemptuous gaze fell to Koenig. "I did."

Ellison chuckled in surprised. "I don't think Lee would take a dime from me."

I bat my lashes at him. "Heavens, why not?"

A long silence came upon the small group. Had I missed something?

"Because he slept with Julia and broke up my marriage," Lee explained coolly.

My appraising glare at Ellison deepened his furrowed brow. Julia ruined her marriage for this man? This smug, entitled, privileged little dilettante had been her choice. Once again, my opinion of Lee's ex-wife dropped. If my opinion dropped any lower, I'd need a shovel to find it.

"Lee!" Mercier exclaimed. Several guests' heads turned in our direction of the man's raised voice.

Ellison gave me a told you so expression I didn't much appreciate.

"Oh, well, that changes everything." I said, breaking the awkward silence. Sometimes, you had to go through a storm to survive it.

"Odessa!" Lee cautioned again.

Something as incidental as Julia's poor choice, a rich boy, and a group of stodgy old men wouldn't stop me, and he understood that about me. His expression of benign acceptance of what I was about to do allowed me to continue.

"Hypothetically, what would you donate to a fund that helped abused tenants?" I asked.

"Ohm... I guess five thousand," Ellison considered with an uneasy laugh.

"Kind of light, don't you think?" I feigned distress. "Is Schaeffer Pharmaceuticals a second-rate pill mill?"

"No!" Mercier protested.

"Didn't think so. All they can offer is a measly five thousand. A Girl Scout on a rainy Saturday afternoon could get that much." I cocked my head to heighten my disappointment.

A non-plus, Ellison nodded in agreement. "What do you suggest?"

"It's not for me to say what you should give. It wouldn't make up for you sleeping with Julia or Lee cracking a few ribs and a busted nose. Short of making amends, any generous offer would say something, wouldn't it?" I said coyly.

The corner of Maxfield's lips lifted in a smile.

"A positive inclination your father might appreciate," Maxfield offered.

Ellison thought about it for a while before his gaze fell to Lee. "Would you take it?"

A resigned Lee sighed. "Since Odessa asked so nicely, yes I would."

"Okay, how about ten?" Ellison suggested.

"Let's make it twenty and we can call it a night." I walked back to Lee's side and entwined my arm with his. He took my hand and gave it a firm squeeze. A few of my knuckles cracked.

"The law firm will match it," Maxfield proclaimed over the sudden protest of the others.

Waller's smile widened. Had I acquired a fan with my ability to put the partners of Mercier, Koenig and Layng in a corner.

"Fine," Ellison conceded with a laugh. "Lee, I know this doesn't—"

"It doesn't, but it helps the families I'm trying to help. That makes it easy," Lee said before turning to Maxfield. "Thank you, Max, for what you did tonight. And, I don't blame you for this circus. I'm going to take Odessa home. The atmosphere is a little stuffy for me."

"No, you go, my boy. It was my pleasure." Maxfield nodded in my direction.

After Lee shook Maxfield's hand, Maxfield leaned over and kissed me on the cheek. I thanked him for Lee and the families of the LaGuardia Apartments. Despite his firm blindsiding him, Maxfield had done a good thing.

"Goodnight everyone," I gave them a girly finger wave as Lee and I turn to leave. Though Lee wanted to rush away, I took my time.

"Remember, slow and with a great deal of dignity," I reminded him as we walked away from the small group.

He chuckled.

"The view from behind is spectacular," he said as he slowed down to let me walk ahead.

"Thank you, sweetie," I said, as I put a little more sway in my step.

CHAPTER 10

Over a plate of scrambled eggs and buttered toast, Lee told me about Ellison Schaeffer. This story explained the year Lee gave up the law and people. Lee brushed aside his absence as his time of reflection. When he returned to practice law, he landed at Aaron Boyer's small law firm in the borough of Queens. As far away from Mercier, Koenig and Layng as he could get. Lee went from a law firm of over two hundred to a small firm with five lawyers, two law clerks, and a receptionist on maternity leave.

With the gala being a distant memory, the peaceful quiet of our little kitchen became a sanctuary. Lee sat at the table, barefoot, dressed in sweatpants and a tee shirt, his hair still wet from the shower. He stared down at a plate of half eaten eggs. I stood by the kitchen sink, a big mug of chamomile tea in my hands. Still in the cocktail dress, my only concession to comfort was the removal of my shoes.

"Ellison's family pharmaceutical company is Mercier, Koenig and Layng's premier client." Lee pushed the plate away and leaned back in his chair.

"How did Ellison meet Julia?"

"This story isn't about Julia." His hazel eyes cautioned me.

"This is about her," I protested.

"You're getting angry." He slipped off his glasses, rubbed his face, and sighed.

"No, I'm not," I lied. I rated Julia's adultery with war crimes, wearing socks with sandals, and disco.

Lee's response to my half-truth was a dubious raise of an eyebrow.

"This is my story, Dessa. I know who the villain is in this piece. Trust me, Julia isn't the villain," he mused, I suspect trying to make light of my ire toward his ex-wife.

I hadn't expected his impish smile as he reached out to me, an invitation for connection I thought we both missed. I feigned reluctance for half a heartbeat before I stepped over to him.

"I want to explain what happened tonight. The why and the how." He placed his hands on my hips to pull me close.

"At the end of this, will my opinion about Julia change?" I teased.

"I won't pin my hopes on that." He laughed.

Though Lee was on good terms with his ex-wife, Julia and I wouldn't be sharing recipes. Lee's willingness to take full responsibility for his failed marriage was irksome. In deference to him, I kept my hostility toward Julia in check, to a point. He pulled me onto his lap.

"Because of Schaeffer Pharmaceutical and the firm, Ellison and I became friends. Julia and I would go on double dates with whatever girl Ellison dated. We became close. Maxfield encouraged the friendship, considering Ellison's wild crowd."

It was hard to contain my surprise at the news of Lee's friendship with Ellison. I shook my head in disbelief. Lee nodded confirmation.

"The only one who had influence over him was his father and Maxfield. His father bullied him. Max cajoled him."

"He's a charmer," I joked, but Lee's eyes held no humor.

"At Mercier, Koenig and Layng it was a heady time for me. As a first-year associate, under Max, I worked on important cases and embraced the responsibility. This got me closer to Max and further away from Julia. When you're sitting at the foot of Zeus, you don't notice if the world is burning."

"Didn't Julia complain?" I asked.

Lee shook his head. "She thought I wanted this. My time at the firm meant she had to give up her dream to work with an environmental group in Washington when I got out of law school."

I cocked a brow at this.

"This is the same Julia who now works as a lobbyist for the oil industry." My lips curled in disgust.

"Biofuel!" Lee retorted.

"Whatever." I rolled my eyes.

"Again, this is not about Julia," he warned and gave me a playful pat on my rear.

"Around this time, Ellison became more reckless than usual, drinking and drugging. Even Maxfield had trouble keeping him under control. I was knee deep in litigations and never even noticed."

"What made him turn on you?" I asked.

Lee pulled me onto his lap. My head rested on his shoulder as he drew me closer. I sensed Lee needed a moment before he expelled his demons. To give voice to the anger that had displayed itself earlier that evening.

"I got too close to Maxfield."

"Jealousy?"

"A few years earlier, Max lost his son in a car crash. The death almost destroyed him and caused his marriage to fail. So, he poured everything into his work. In a way, Ellison and I became the son he lost. Max and I had the law in common and it brought us close. Because of his close relationship with the Schaeffer family, it gave him Ellison. After a while, Ellison's antic wore on Maxfield. A period of benign neglect described their relationship. This drew me closer to Max."

"Sounds like Ellison didn't react well to that," I said.

Lee nodded.

"Julia grew distant. The work load got heavy. This one case with Schaeffer Pharmaceutical turned bad."

"Schaeffer Pharmaceutical?"

"A major suit brought all the partners on board to defend Schaeffer. Koenig was lead counsel, but Maxfield steered the boat. Because of Max, I was there, ready to follow him. Look at Waller. Sent by the partners to keep an eye on Max after his stroke. I'm sure Maxfield won him over with an encouraging pat on the shoulder. He drank the Kool-Aid. Like Waller, I felt the need to please him."

"What changed?"

"The pharmaceutical case. By the time it ended, Max and I were at odds with each other, emotionally and morally." Lee caressed my arm, his focus no longer on me, but a distant spot in the past.

Before he continued, his other hand fell to my thigh and slipped beneath the hem of my dress. He found that place on my inner thigh and stroked it more out of his comfort than anything. My reaction made me put my hand atop his to stop it. I needed him to finish and if he kept on, I wouldn't care why he wanted to punch Ellison.

"Ellison used his position with the family and the firm like a concealed weapon." His brow furrowed with the memory.

"I don't understand?"

"Ellison worked for the company as head of marketing. How the company marketed its drugs was part of the suit. That kept him around Mercier, Koenig and Layng, so he knew of the problem Max and I were having over it. I was too blind to see what he was doing. Because of his jealousy, he drove a wedge between Maxfield and me. My friend had become my enemy."

"He went after Julia?"

Lee didn't respond, and I knew why. He had brought Ellison into their lives. Inside that chivalrous half-baked brain of his, he felt responsible. He could forgive Julia as if she didn't have a choice. Trust me, she had a choice.

"He sounds wacky." This wasn't a professional diagnosis of Ellison's narcissistic behavior, but it was close enough.

"He had her convinced that he loved her. Two lost souls commiserating over the loss of a husband and a father figure to the firm. It was bullshit." Even now, it still hurt him.

"A one-night stand, I can understand. A moment of weakness or stupidity, you pick. But, Julia had an affair. The dumbest choice in the history of humankind." My annoyance grew with each word.

"Odessa, this is not about Julia," Lee warned.

"She chose a spoiled brat over a man who loved her. It's about her." My irritation with Julia was like a boulder rolling downhill. It wouldn't stop until it got to the end and rolled over her.

Lee held me tighter to cull my growing ire.

"I neglected our marriage because of the firm," Lee said, as if that was answer enough.

"This isn't taking the blue pill or the red pill. This isn't the lady or the tiger. That's the bullshit. Ellison used Julia's weakness against her. He used Julia against you."

"You weren't there." A flash of his anger had returned.

"If I had been, would I have done what Julia did?" I said with anger of my own.

Lee stared back as if the question was absurd.

"Would I have done the same?" I repeated.

"You're not Julia." He sighed and turned away.

"Damn straight, Skippy. I'm not sure I'd make a better choice, but it wouldn't be with my husband's friend." I grabbed Lee's face with both of my hands and forced him to face me.

"Because if I did that, slept with my husband's best friend, that meant I hurt you, not only by betraying you, but by taking away someone who could have supported you over the betrayal. Julia and Ellison got the results they wanted. Ellison by destroying your marriage because of his stupid jealousy and Julia destroyed it because of your neglect. I know rocks less passive aggressive than those two. I won't weep for either of them, especially Julia." My face grew hot with anger.

Lee's body tensed, and nostril flared with his breathing. His embrace on me eased. My hands fell away from his face as I wrapped my arms around him.

"I would have demanded you choose me over Maxfield, that damn law firm, and everything. I'd tie you up in the basement until you came to your senses. Candace and her prayer group would give you an intervention and bring Aunt Renne for good measure. I would have stepped over Ellison's bloody corpse to get through to you," I proclaimed.

Lee's embrace tightened again.

"You'd use your 80-year-old aunt against me?" Lee asked.

"Without a doubt, Skippy."

The tension in his face melted away and replaced with a bemused smile.

"You're not Julia." Lee stroked my cheek and ran a finger across my lips. When he kissed me, Julia and Ellison became the furthest thing from both our minds. Afterward, we sat in companionable silence, digesting our thoughts and newfound revelations the evening had brought. My head back on his shoulder, his embrace tight around me again, I took a deep breath.

"Ellison told me about the affair in Maxfield's office. Ellison interrupted an argument Max and I were having. I'd gone there to confront Max about the problems I had with a lawsuit involving Schaeffer. Ellison burst in and confesses about the affair."

"What an asshole."

"Ellison let me know Maxfield knew about the affair. Maxfield told him to end it before I found out."

"Why wouldn't Max tell you?" I said, surprised at this revelation.

Lee raised an eyebrow. "I was waist deep in the Schaeffer litigation. Finding out the truth about Julia and Ellison..." Lee closed his eyes. "His exact words were, it would distract me."

"Distract!"

"He believed Ellison didn't take his affair with Julia serious and my marriage could survive it. Before he involved himself with Julia, he was already in a tumultuous relationship. Max even went to Julia and convinced her to end the affair."

"How very French of him," I said snidely. "Why did Ellison tell you at the office?"

"He thought Maxfield's presence might temper me," Lee said.

"Did it?" I questioned.

"I broke his nose and cracked a rib or two." Lee's eyes had a gleeful glint. "It took two associates to pull me off him. Later, Maxfield convinced Ellison's father not to press assault charges."

"Maxfield was trying to help," I said, not quite believing it.

"They all expected me to get over it. Like the worst thing I'd lose was Ellison as a friend. I quit." Lee laughed. "Maxfield had been right in one aspect. When the dust cleared, Ellison hadn't been serious about Julia. While he was with her, he was also seeing someone else."

"Who in the right might would hook up with Ellison?"

"Heather."

CHAPTER 11

Maggie sat on one of the tall workshop stools. Her feet dangled above the floor. Dressed in jeans and a little league coach's tee shirt, she looked like a petulant child. With her head cocked to the side, she gave me a suspicious look as I prepared to make a Key Lime Pie for Lee's boss, Aaron Boyer.

"So, this is a bribe?"

A thick file folder intended for Aaron lay on the edge of the counter near her. With the law firm only a few blocks away, Maggie's visit to the bakeshop was a pleasant surprise. The visit inspired me to go with her to give Aaron a surprise visit of my own.

"I wouldn't call it a bribe." I tossed a dozen key lime rinds in the trash. "More like persuasion."

An auburn brow arched in disbelief. Not sure whether she questioned my motives or my methods. Her doubts concerned me less than the measuring cup filled with lime juice she slid out of my reach. I guess she didn't like my response.

"You think giving Aaron a pie will get him to tell you about Maxfield Layng and this Ellison guy?" She slid the cup further away.

Annoyed with her, I turned my attention to cans of sweetened condensed milk.

"Don't you think you should drop this?" she asked in a tone the bordered on maternal.

I did not respond. Instead, I opened the cans of evaporated milk and dumped them in a bowl. Next, I put graham crackers in the food processor for my crust. Each time she tried to give her opinion, I pushed the processor's button to drown her out. When she'd had enough of this, she threatened to dump the lime juice down the sink. I stopped the machine. Key Limes are small; it took forever to juice enough for the pie.

Still not willing to answer, I poured the contents of the blender into a bowl, added melted butter, and mixed. I dumped this into a pie pan and pressed the mixture down along the side and bottom before placing it into the oven.

"I don't know who's worse, you or Rocket." Maggie's comparison of me with her 9-year-old son told me what she thought of me now.

Aaron was not only Lee's boss, he was a close friend and mentor. My questions might put undue stress on Lee and Aaron's relationship. She thought my visit to Aaron was a mistake.

"This won't help," she insisted. McAvoy investigation did a lot of work for Aaron. Over time, Maggie and Aaron had become friends.

"Listen, I would let it go, but after the gala, I can't," I explained. "A few days ago, Kip Waller called Lee and let him know that the legal funds were available. When Lee called to thank Maxfield, he kinda brushed him off. Not once, but several times. Maxfield made himself unavailable."

"I thought Lee wanted nothing to do with his former law firm."

"At first he did. After Heather's funeral and seeing Maxfield, I thought both men wanted reconciliation. After Ellison showed up, everything went to crap."

"Something's changed." Maggie's blue eyes stared back at me.

"Yeah, Lee wanted to punch Ellison and went all dark and moody. Maxfield plays referee but is now showing Lee the cold shoulder. What's that about?"

Lee acted like Maxfield's sudden change didn't bother him, but it did. That wistful expression of hope on Lee's face at the gala vanished the moment Ellison showed up. Now with Maxfield missing in action, the look cemented itself.

"Can I have the lime juice please, or do you have more questions?" I scowled at her.

Maggie slid the measuring cup back in my direction. "So, Ellison came to the gala for what?"

"He said to make amends with Lee about Julia." I shrugged. Part of me didn't quite believe him, the rest didn't trust him.

"What did Lee call it?"

"His redemption tour or something like that. Ellison's father insisted on it from what I understand. His old firm buddies showed up for backup. Lee was not happy."

Maggie shook her head. "Then the thing with Heather?"

I nodded.

"Lee wouldn't go into details. When I pushed, he shut down."

"God, this doesn't sound like him." Maggie's frown mirrored my concerns about Lee.

"Despite Maxfield being missing in action, because of the fund, they're still connected. I have this uneasy feeling we haven't heard the last of Maxfield or Ellison. Either way, Aaron will know. Maxfield may not be talking to Lee, but I bet he's still talking to Aaron," I insisted.

Maggie pointed to the mixing bowl.

"You think a pie will loosen his tongue? He never told Lee he was in contact with Maxfield. Why would he talk to you?"

My lips twisted up into my best evil grin, but I was sure it resembled a smirk. For half a moment, I wanted to throw in a diabolical cackle for emphasis but didn't. Instead, I removed the pie crust from the oven to cool.

"Even Superman has his Kryptonite. This is Aaron's." I smiled at the thought. Aaron Boyer once threatened to divorce his wife to marry me because of his love of my Key Lime pie.

"Aaron might tell me if Maxfield plans to pop back into Lee's life again. The only thing I want Lee to worry about is Candace becoming his sister-in-law."

Maggie's eyes widened in horror, then soften.

"She might mellow out once you're married." Her hopeful expression didn't last long. "Forget I said that."

"Exactly. Last time they talked, Candace hinted at Lee converting to a Baptist before the wedding. Suggested I keep my last name and then told Lee to cut down his guest list to the wedding. He will strangle my sister and I won't stop him."

"Sounds like something Candace would say." Maggie nodded in understanding.

"When is your appointment with Aaron?" I asked.

Maggie checked her watch with the Minnie Mouse face. An anniversary gift from her husband, Roger, on their last trip to Disney. It would be like Roger to buy her such a gift. Maggie loved it.

"We've got time. I promised the report on the Poulsen's divorce today, but he said not to rush, he had nothing scheduled."

Aaron loved using Maggie in his divorce cases. Unlike her boss, whose approach was like a bull at a vegan picnic, Maggie was subtle. She once convinced a cheating wife to tell her everything in a Starbuck's line waiting to buy coffee. Her deceptive waif-like appearance and non-intrusive style got people to trust her.

"Odessa, you remember that saying about letting sleeping dogs lie?" Maggie said.

"Even sleeping dog have teeth, sweetie." I bared my teeth for proof.

Maggie's shoulders slumped in resignation. She slid over the file folder and tapped it with her fingers. "The Poulsens, married fifteen years. One day, they stopped trusting each other. It got so bad, Mrs. Poulsens called the cops on her husband. He'd taken her hostage in their own house."

"I trust Lee." I sounded a little indignant but didn't care. "It's Maxfield and Ellison."

"I thought you liked Maxfield?" Maggie's frowned.

"Do I really know him? I forced Lee to go to the gala, and see what happened," I said.

"You don't think Maxfield changed his mind about reconnecting?"

I shrugged.

"Lee's stress level is high enough with the LaGuardia clients and my sister breathing down his neck with changes to the wedding. Maxfield popping in and out does not help."

Maggie said nothing. What was there to say? Lee wasn't acting like himself. Though she wanted to stay positive, even Maggie couldn't throw happy dust on this.

Thirty minutes later, the oven timer chimed. I took out the pie. Once cooled, I would edge with toasted coconuts and top with a swirl of whipped cream. It would be perfect. If Aaron didn't tell me what I wanted to know about Maxfield, then I'd lost my touch, or he was on a diet again.

With the pie, we left the shop in Esperanza's hands. The walk to the nearby small, brick office building that housed Lee's firm took only ten minutes. Along the way, she tried to convince me to toss the pie and go back to the cake shop. I ignored her.

We arrived at the neat, little, brick building, which sat on a corner lot. Built in the thirties, it kept its style. Stainless steel detailing blocks of glass windows and curved canopies adorned the building. We rode the old, shaky elevator to the top floor. The law firm took the entire space. It opened onto a décor that changed little since Aaron's father opened the firm in the late forties. Polished wood paneling and glass partitions gave the place a trendy retro vibe.

The minute we stepped off the elevator, Walter, the law clerk, blocked our path. He eyed the pie box. He'd recognized it from the dozen or more I've brought to the firm since I began my relationship with Lee.

"This is for Aaron," I warned

"Aaron doesn't share," Walter said coolly.

The rotund lawyer hoarded my desserts like a prisoner of war. With his office in full view of everyone, he felt no shame in eating in front of them. I couldn't argue with Walter's assertion.

"Sorry, Walter. Next time I'll bring extra," I offered in the hope he wouldn't make a scene or tackle me. His lips twisted into a wolfish grin. Half the office had the same look. I began to feel like zombie bait.

"Busy as Aaron is, I'm sure the office wouldn't mind a break," he said to several watchful eyes staring at Maggie and me. "I bet those cookies Esperanza makes would go good with her grandmother's coffee."

A frequent visitor at the bakery, Walter could recite the menu like the pledge of allegation.

"That sounds like a bribe," Maggie admonished.

Walter didn't care. Instead, he stared down at the pie box. Walter was no fool. Because of Lee, my presence wouldn't garnish any mistrust. Even Maggie was a regular visitor because of her work with Aaron. The both of us and dessert equal major manipulations. Lee and Aaron were our usual targets. The food meant Aaron. Me in something short and tight meant Lee.

"Fine, I'll send something over when I leave," I conceded.

Walter's smiled. "No worries, I'll go pick them up."

"You've got to be serious," I said in exasperation.

Walter's smile widened. "I guess you know Mr. Mackenzie is at a deposition at the courthouse. It's a shame he missed you."

Of course, I knew this. If Lee were around, I wouldn't get near Aaron with the dessert.

"The fact you can undermine a great legal mind with dessert should bother me." Lee once told me. I groaned, handed Maggie the pie box, and called Esperanza to place an order for the office. Satisfied, a smiling Walter took a large step to the side and added a bow for good measure. A few of the office workers applauded. I huffed in disapproval.

Once passed Walter, our only other obstacle was the office's receptionist. A temp covering for the one on maternity leave, Amber Kim was easy compared to Walter. Only slightly taller than Maggie, the twenty something receptionist had a self-contained maturity one didn't often find at that age. Quick with a smile that always crinkled her wide-set coal black eyes. She believed you couldn't live without well shaped black pump. Once a former shoe addict, I bonded with

Amber the first time we met. We compared fashion styles in the same manner old soldiers talk about the war.

"Nice pumps," I said, eyeing a pair of what looked like a tan calfskin Dolce & Gabbana knock offs.

I held out the pie. "Can I have five minutes with Aaron?"

"I'll need a little more time, but I'll be less fattening." Maggie waved the file at her.

Amber's usual cheerful demeanor faulted as her almond-shaped eyes squinted in concern. She nodded toward Aaron's office.

"He's in with someone," she said apologetically.

"That's okay, I can..." I stopped.

The sight of Maxfield sitting in Aaron's office made my stomach clench in surprise. The rash on my arm flared in protest. As if sensing my presence, both men turned and saw me. Frozen in confusion at Maxfield's presence, I didn't stop the pie box as it slid from my hand. When it hit the floor, pieces of pie splattered across my leg and feet. I didn't care.

CHAPTER 12

When I worked in advertising, I became good at reading clients' faces. Most clients had little physical traits which let me know how well my pitch was going. The executive for an auto parts company loved pulling on his tie when I used too many big words. The sales rep who could never look me in the eyes when the campaign became too sexualized. There was always something.

Maxfield and I held each other's gaze as Boyer ranted about the pie that now decorated my feet. We ignored Maggie and Amber as they tried to clean up the mess. His congenial smile and expression of concern confused me more than clarified. I wouldn't invite this man to play poker at my house.

"Are you okay, Odessa?" Maxfield said in a melodic tone that soothed jurors and judges.

Unsure of his intent, I said nothing.

"You made the one with coconuts," Boyer lamented. "Did you trip?"

"You ruined your shoes," a wistful Amber said.

"Lee isn't here," I said as the thoughts floating in my head came out.

Maxfield smile broadened, and he nodded. "Aaron told me. We've been having some miscommunication."

Miscommunication!

I rolled the word around my head a few times and it didn't fit. Few things rattled Lee, except me. Candace on full wedding meltdown didn't get that much of a rise out of him. Yet, the lack of response from Maxfield to his messages or phone calls did. I'm sure he's doubting his decision to involve himself with Maxfield again. That pissed me off.

"How did this happen?" My calm tone surprised me. Inside, I didn't feel calm at all.

"What's going on here?" Boyer asked, his attention no longer on his destroyed dessert. Like at a tennis match, his gaze danced between the two of us. Maggie's quick reaction saved a small piece of the pie, which she held out to Boyer. This pulled his attention away from Maxfield and me. Good one, Maggie.

"Maxfield wants to explain about the miscommunication." My tone was skeptical, and I didn't care. The edges of Maxfield's smile faltered, but not enough anyone would notice much. Had I found Maxfield's tell?

"The only explanation I have is a new secretary." Maxfield's expressive face found its grin again. He patted the spot over his heart and bowed in acquiescence. If he expected me to believe Lee's calls got misdirected by a bad secretary, he must think me an idiot. Or even worse, Maxfield thought his Santa Claus charm worked on me.

"Secretary? What new secretary?" Boyer chimed in as he held what remained of the bribe, I baked him. The pie now looked more like Key Lime pudding than anything else. With a disregard to his company, Boyer stuck his thick finger into the mess and licked the dessert off. A deep sound of pleasure emitted deep from within him.

"She's a scatterbrain." Maxfield chuckled.

"Are you hiring your relatives again, Max?" Boyer dug into the dessert again.

Maxfield nodded. "A daughter of a colleague."

The conversation faltered when Boyer jabbed the last bit of dessert into his mouth. A handkerchief appeared out of nowhere as he wiped the remnants off his face. When he morphed back into sweet divorce lawyer I knew and loved, I relaxed.

"Your desserts must be extraordinary, Odessa," Maxfield said with bemusement.

"You should taste her Rhubarb and Blackberry mousse cake. Melts in your mouth," Boyer said as he shut his eyes and moaned. No doubt remembering the two pieces from lunch the other day at the Blue Moon.

I was pleased that at least Boyer appeared content; however, my uncertainty grew. Lee once said Maxfield could be a charmer and as manipulative as hell when he wanted something. My indecisiveness came because I didn't know what Maxfield wanted. At first, I thought he wanted to get back into Lee's good graces and bond over a lost friend. After the gala, there were doubts. Maxfield raised money for Lee's cause. Yet in the next breath, disavowed him. Now he sat in Boyer's office talking as if nothing happened. Sixteen-year-old girls weren't this fickle.

"I felt neglectful not responding and wanted to come in person to give my apology. Aaron told me Lee was in court. Thought this might be a good time to catch up with Aaron while we waited," Maxfield said. His affable expression reminded me of the man from the gala, pleasing and willing to please.

I responded with a smile. Still unsure of which Maxfield stood before me. The legal god or the tottering old scholar lost in his past regrets. Either way, I set the ball in motion by forcing Lee into his line of sight.

"I'm sure Lee will understand," Boyer encouraged.

"He will?" Maggie blurted out. She recovered with a giggle she reserved for idiots, salesmen, and her boss. "I'm sure he will."

"Why don't I take you to the Blue Moon for some braised ribs," Boyer said with delight. "Finish the meal off with Odessa's mousse."

Then began a long conversation about their favorite food haunts when at law school. Maggie and I waited as Boyer and Maxfield exchanged friendly banter. The men joked and teased one another like one of those old-fashion comedy skits.

"Geno's off 8th street. The best pizza," Boyer exclaimed.

A doubtful Maxfield shook his head. "No, they had the best co-eds."

"No, that was the Greek restaurant in old town, outside of New Haven," Boyer insisted.

When the conversation devolved into Maxfield's favorite Manhattan restaurants, Boyer countered with the list of the Blue Moon's best dishes and dessert. Somehow the discussion morphed into a show from the Food Channel. I waited. If Maxfield had an excuse, I wanted to hear it. His defense of a dizzy secretary didn't play for me. I wanted to redirect the conversation. Then the last person I expected to see appeared from nowhere and stopped me.

A confounded Lee stood in front of the closing elevator doors.

From his expression, you would have thought he caught me in bed with an elephant, a circus clown, and a meter maid. His presence didn't get my attention, it was his appearance. Lee looked like he'd been rolling around on the ground with my clown and meter maid and stomped on by the elephant. I forgot Maxfield, the pie, and those unanswered questions.

"What the hell happened to you?" I ran to him. An efficient Amber took his briefcase and the jumble of files he carried. She reappeared moments later with a cool, damp towel for me. Lee winced as I dabbed at the growing bruise on the left side of his face. His torn pants revealed a bloody knee. The scrapes on his hand looked nasty. With his glasses missing, his eyes narrowed on the small group before him. They stopped at Maxfield.

"What..." he winced again when I touched the dried blood off the corner of his mouth and flinched away.

Like Houdini's assistant, Amber appeared with a small first aid kit. She pulled out disinfecting pads for me. When I touched the pad to the cut, Lee jerked away. He gave me a threatening scowl when I tried to apply the pad again.

"What happen?" Maggie came up behind me, along with Boyer and Maxfield.

"I'm fine," Lee reassured, but from the looks on everyone's faces, no one believed him. "Let me go into my office and sit down, okay? It's been a morning from hell."

This seemed like a reasonable compromised as we all followed him to his office. He hobbled as he made his way to his office. Lee fell into his only concession to luxury—a leather-bound chair I got him for his birthday. The rest of his office looked like the one at home, an organized mess.

"Oh, god, sitting down feels good." He pulled at his tie to loosen before taking a deep breath and stretched out his injured leg.

"What happened?" Boyer demanded.

"Is anything broken?" I touched him everywhere. When I reached to touch by his torn pant, Lee's hand grabbed me. He shook his head in warning. I inflicted enough pain for the moment and stopped.

"I fell," Lee said.

"Where? Off a cliff?" I didn't hide my annoyance with his limited explanation. In all the years I've known Lee and his passion for rock climbing, he never came home like this. It was like he took on a mountain and the mountain won.

"At the courthouse. I went to talk to Judge Sorensen." The hair Lee had been too busy to cut flopped down, covering much of his eyes. When he fingered combed his hair away from his face, I saw another bloody scrape.

"Did you have a fight with Judge Sorensen?" I said.

I knelt beside him. My fingers traced the edges of the bruise. Lee acquiesced to my ministrations for a while.

"What's going on, Lee?" Maxfield stood over him with arms crossed and a look of concern.

Moment's like that made me doubt my concern over Maxfield's intention. Despite their past, these men cared about the other. Each wanting something from the other. What Lee wanted, I kind of understood. Maxfield once played a large part in his life. Like going to the circus, enjoying the acts, eating popcorn, and laughing at the clowns. Then one of the clowns punches the lion tamer, and the acrobats are trying to kill each other. When the circus returns, you're a little wary. Lee stared at Maxfield, like an invitation to the circus. What Maxfield wanted, I wasn't sure.

"Who did this?" Aaron asked.

"Lorena Ramos is missing." Lee sighed. "I scheduled a deposition for her. When I couldn't find her, I wanted the judge to give me more time," Lee said. "She's the strongest witness I have against the building's owner and I can't find her. Although sympathetic, the judge can only do so much."

"I don't understand. What has that to do with you falling?" I asked.

Lee gave me a sheepish glance. "Didn't watch where I was going. I ran into one of Comaneci's so-called maintenance men. Don't know why they were there, but we slammed into each other."

At over six feet two inches, there was more muscle behind that suit then anyone would expect. When work didn't overwhelm him, he loved to rock climb for recreation. I often told him, hanging from a rock wall wasn't a sport, it was survival. With nothing to climb, he'd find a pickup basketball game on Saturday at the local YMCA. So, Lee was no easy push over.

"It happened on the courthouse steps. I didn't see him, and I bounced off him like a rag doll." Lee's shoulders slumped.

"Did anybody see?" Maggie questioned.

Lee shook his head. "Everything happened so fast." He bent down and inspected the tear on his trousers. "That's going to hurt."

"You think!" I stood, glaring down at him. Lee wanted to play the attack off as some accident in front of the others. Comaneci has been notorious with his dealings with his tenants. Why would he stop with lawyers? Now, one of Lee's key witnesses had gone missing. This made me think of my van.

"Are you all right?" Maxfield's asked me.

The state I was in, I couldn't judge Maxfield's sincerity. Lee's case just got physical. Things could get a lot worse than Maxfield's mind games.

"I'll find your tenant."

Everyone turned to Maggie the moment the words came out of her mouth. From the determined set in her azure eyes, I knew things just got worse.

CHAPTER 13

When meeting Maggie Swift for the first time, you assume her to be a well-balanced person. Her pixie appearance lulled you into a false sense of safety. I understood otherwise. Her pocketbook would contain her son's retainer along with a can of pepper spray. For laughs and giggles, she followed strangers to practice her surveillance skills.

When she wanted to become a private investigator, she found Frank McAvoy in the yellow pages. The ex-New York City Detective turned private investigator never knew what hit him. Before he realized what happened, she took over. In time, she doubled his client list and increased his fiber intake.

I stared down at a battered Lee. His eyes stayed on Maxfield. His former mentor loomed large in the small office as he remained a quiet observer. I sensed Lee wanted to ask questions. So did I. They would have to wait.

While working for the tenants of the LaGuardia Apartments, one of Comaneci's men waylaid Lee. The likelihood of that happening again appeared high. Those odds increased if he went looking for his missing witness. Now Maggie wanted to throw in her two cents, giving Comaneci a new target.

Maggie sat at the edge of Lee's desk and plastered on a magnetic smile. To his credit, Lee appeared cautious if not wary.

"Let me find her." Maggie's eager face said everything.

"You mean Frank," Lee corrected. Without a license, Maggie needed to work under Frank's supervision.

"Of course, I mean Frank. I'm talking about the corporate we." Maggie made a circling gesture with her fingers.

"Frank McAvoy corporate?" I laughed in disbelief.

Maggie cut me a nasty look, which I ignored.

"Whether Lorenia Ramos left on her own or coerced by Comaneci, either way she stalls your case. The judge can't give you a continuance forever," Boyer said.

"Do you think he would stop at Ms. Ramos?" Maggie continued. Was this a reference to my vandalized van?

Lee took a deep sigh which made him touch a tender spot on his side. Did he realize he couldn't run all over New York City? Lee appeared to waiver.

"Whoa!" I held up both hands. "What makes you think I want you to find her even when I don't want Lee too?"

The indignation on both Lee and Maggie's face said they didn't appreciate my tone.

"I'm sure Lee went to Lorena's home and asked the neighbors about her. He searched in obvious places, in full view of everyone, including Comaneci's people." Maggie wagged her finger at Lee.

When Maggie showed no concern about Comaneci, I worried. Delusional people can live with any nutty decisions they make. The people who surround them, not so much.

"Didn't think anyone would notice me looking for her. When I went to her job, they told me she took some time off. People like Lorena don't have the luxury of taking time like that. I wanted to search further, but I needed to tell the judge I had a problem." Lee rubbed his eyes.

"I'm sure you went straight to the court." Maggie shook her head in disappointment.

"Yeah, where some Comaneci's so-called maintenance men happened to be," I stated.

In the hopes that he might be on my side, I turned to Boyer to put an end to both Lee and Maggie's search. Boyer appeared caught up in his own contemplation.

"Let McAvoy handle the search." Boyer nodded at Maggie. "Try to find another tenant to testify, if you can."

Maggie beamed.

"No!" I pointed my finger at her. Frank wouldn't see this case. Maggie would raid the office slush fund, give Frank some money, and point him toward Atlantic City. He'd go humming and skipping all the way.

Maggie lips pressed tight in a scowl. Azure eyes that belonged to a wood nymph darken as her ire grew.

"Can I speak to you for a sec?" Maggie's eyes widened.

"No." I shook my head. At least in the office with the men I felt safe. In a fair fight, my height and weight would do nothing in a battle of wills. I wimped out. A determined Maggie's unflinching glare propelled me out of the office.

When we stepped outside, the sight of Kip Waller surprised me. He stood by Amber's desk talking. I hadn't seen him when we arrived, but his sudden presence didn't surprise me. He was the human Finding Waldo, lost in the background. If Maxfield was around, how far could Waller be?

A relaxed looking Waller chatted admirably with the shy receptionist. Whatever he said pleased her, because she laughed coyly. When she pulled out her phone, Waller did the same to possibly exchange numbers. Such was the way of modern dating.

Unwilling to have Maggie scold me again, I opted to talk with Waller. Maybe he'd give the answers I wanted. So, I headed in his direction.

"Odessa," Maggie complained as she followed me.

"Hi, Kip," I called out, ignoring her.

Amber appeared startled by our sudden appearance and made busy work of files on her desk. The act fooled no one. Waller smiled at us, like someone caught with their hand in the cookie jar. He took an appropriate step back and put his phone away.

"Interrupting something?" I teased.

"No!" Amber insisted. No one bought that either. Amber was a pretty girl, no one would blame Waller for wanting her number.

Before Maggie had a chance to remember why she pulled me out of the office, I made a quick introduction. Waller did what most men did upon meeting her. At any moment, they expected gossamer wing to pop out and one of their wishes granted. Maggie's firm handshake and no nonsense greeting belied that fantasy in an instant.

"We didn't see you when we arrived," I said.

"Had to return to the car, forgot something." He waved an envelope at me. "Need some signatures for the tenants' fund."

"If Lee hasn't thanked you, I will." I gave him an appreciative smile. Though Maxfield suggested the legal fund, I knew the dirty work went to Waller.

Waller shrugged and looked passed me to Lee's office. No doubt curious about the conversation going on without him. I preferred the one about the forgetful secretary I wanted to have with him.

"Lee and Maxfield keep missing each other." I kept my tone conversational.

"What?" Waller surprised expression morphed into a mild annoyance. "Oh yeah, the secretary from hell."

"Secretary from hell?" Maggie interjected.

Waller let out a frustrated sigh.

"She's somebody's daughter or niece or whatever. The girl lost an internship at Marie Claire, and we are her consolation prize."

"Really!" My opinion about Maxfield shifted again. I couldn't keep up with how I felt about the man.

"God damn Schaeffer," Waller muttered. The mention of Ellison Schaeffer confused and intrigued me.

"Ellison!" I prompted.

Waller's eyes scanned the office. Then he asked if he could speak alone with me. I agreed and ignored Maggie's pout. I suggested a small conference room that kept us out of view of Lee's office. Waller followed and to my surprise, he closed the door after we entered.

"I'm only saying this because I didn't want you to think badly of Maxfield," Waller began.

A few moments ago, I thought Maxfield a duplicitous old man with control issues. Waller's revelation changed my mind once again.

"Why would I assume that?" I lied.

"Because of Ellison," Waller said. "I'm only telling you this because of Maxfield." He lowered his voice still further. "Maxfield's hoping to reconnect with your fiancé. He's getting older and has regrets. You understand?"

"Lee is one of his regrets?" I asked.

Waller acknowledged this with a brief nod. "I don't know the details, but Maxfield felt responsible for how things ended. He was elated when Lee took his offer to fund the lawsuit and come to the gala."

"Ellison shows up and ruins the moment," I added.

"Yeah." Waller's lips pursed with scorn. "To please Ellison's father, the other partners took it upon themselves to have Ellison at the gala. They read McKenzie wrong, thinking time had softened him."

"That's an understatement. Was Ellison always like this?"

Waller nodded. "Rehab, scandal, and women. Not exactly in that order. His return hasn't been easy."

"Why blame Ellison for Maxfield's secretary?" I wanted Waller to get to a point before I got too old.

"Ellison's father put him in charge of Schaeffer marketing again. He's been at Mercier, Koenig and Layng and spending more time with Maxfield. Mr. Schaeffer likes that because Maxfield keeps Ellison in check."

"So." I shrugged. The inner workings of Mercier, Koenig and Layng didn't concern me.

"It's clear Ellison and your fiancé don't like each other. His reemergence in Maxfield's life hasn't set well with Ellison."

"Lee is competition?" I huffed in disbelief.

"Somewhat. Because of familial ties and friendship, Maxfield inherited Ellison. Unlike Ellison, Maxfield chose Lee to befriend.

Mackenzie has all the qualities Maxfield wished he saw in Ellison and he knows it," Waller said with a smirk.

Ellison wouldn't receive any birthday cards from Waller.

"Tell me how you really feel," I joked.

Waller laughed.

"Maxfield's a great man. Ellison's presence undermines that. When I found out the secretary hadn't given Maxfield your fiancé's messages, I talked to her. Ellison promise to introduce her to an editor of a fashion magazine if she did a little favor for him," Waller said.

"Why would he do that?" I stared at him in disbelief.

"You mention Mackenzie's name and Ellison sees red," Waller said. "Once Maxfield knew about the mix-up, he wanted to come to explain what happened."

I didn't know whether to be glad Maxfield saw through Ellison's deception or not. With Maxfield, you inevitable get Ellison. Ellison's Machiavellian tendencies could prove troublesome.

"If we're lucky, they'll ship him back to Korea," Waller said with satisfaction.

"Could it be the Korea in the North?" I shook my head amazed.

Waller smiled.

"What happened to making amends with Lee?" I asked.

"From the family dynamics, Ellison's father doesn't believe in free rides. He made Ellison work his way back home. Outwardly, he does as his father asks. Subconsciously, he can't help himself from doing what he does."

I couldn't help but ask my next question. "What do you get out of it? If Ellison is messing up your dream job, why stay?"

Waller didn't answer right away. When he did, the wicked smile he wore said a lot about him.

"My other option at Mercier, Koenig and Layng would be a sixty-hour work week. Partners who don't respect you unless you're billing twenty-four seven and no weekends. Beside which, I like Maxfield. That's lightweight compared to other associates. I'll never have that relationship he had with Lee and I don't want it. Ellison doesn't see me as a threat. What I want is to make my boss happy and for him not have another heart attack."

This seemed believable, but I thought there must be more. Encouraging Maxfield and Lee's reconciliation would only irritate Ellison.

If Waller was disingenuous, I couldn't tell. I sensed he cared for Maxfield, beyond what the man could do for him. Unsure of what to say or do, I didn't push it any further and took Waller at his word.

"How much trouble could Ellison be?" This was a stupid question. Lee's relationship with Julia and Maxfield were notches on his belt.

With a raised brow, Waller contemplated the question for a time before answering. "Let's say, his own family needed him a continent away."

CHAPTER 14

A few days after seeing Maxfield at Lee's law firm, life went back to normal, at least I thought so. In Maxfield's apology about the miscommunication, Ellison's name never came up once. Also, the apology came with a dinner date I didn't want to accept, but Lee did.

When I met Maggie at the Blue Moon for lunch, I talked to her about Maxfield's apology. Astute as always, Maggie questioned Maxfield's sudden reappearance in Lee's life.

"Why now?" she said as she ate her chicken salad.

"Heather," I said, staring at my plate. George made my favorite—poached eggs, smoked salmon over spinach, and Challah bread.

"Could Maxfield want something more?" She scooped up a candied walnut to eat.

"Tell you the truth, I don't know. He says he wants to reconnect with Lee but it's a relationship that brings its own drama," I said.

Maggie nodded. We discussed the wedding for a while, her son, Rocket, and a bridal shower. A shower I didn't want. Maggie insisted I did. The topic ended when I wouldn't respond to her pleas of throwing me a shower. We enjoyed our meal for a while until Candace deemed a limitation to our peace and quiet and came to our table. Before she even spoke, she stared down at my plate.

George's affectionate gesture of making my favorite dish annoyed my sister. The dish wasn't a regular menu item and the Blue Moon chef made it just for me. Candace took this act as a personal affront to her authority. Despite being in charge, George did whatever the hell he wanted and ignored her. People loved his food and Candace wouldn't dare fire him. More to the point, I was his favorite Wilkes sister.

"Yes, Candace." I stopped eating, put down my fork, and looked up at her. She took a deep inhalation, crossed her arms, and sighed.

"What happen to McKenzie's face?" She sounded as if this was a problem for her. As if Lee's bruised face would ruin the wedding's color scheme.

"Marble steps," I said.

"Marble steps?" Candace pinched her lips into a tight frown. I tried to decipher what annoyed her more, Lee's bruises or my inability to keep him locked in a closet until the wedding. My eggs congealed as I waited for Candace to tell me.

"What if I told you we had rough sex, would you go away?"

The other brow shifted up and was joined by a frown. Candace stepped back, turned, and walked away. Maggie's shoulders did her silent laugh thing. Pleased with myself, I returned to my meal. My peace lasted only a mouthful.

A familiar voice pulled my attention. There Ellison Schaeffer stood chatting up my sister. I nearly dropped my fork. Once again at her station at the front, Candace pointed in my direction. My fork went down along with my appetite. I needed to tell my sister to stop telling everyone my whereabouts. First the police and now Lee's sworn enemy.

"You've got to be serious," I said in disgust. This got Maggie's attention as a well styled Ellison approached our table. His handsome face gave off such a sense of perfection that it made a cynic like me look for cracks. Though the Blue Moon's food rivaled any Manhattan restaurant, I didn't believe Ellison would cross a bridge to Queens for a taste. His smile heightened my suspicion as he stood before our table.

"Let me guess, you were in the neighborhood," I said with no humor. Ellison's smile widened in a meaningless grin.

"I went to your lovely bakery, but your... barista told me you were having lunch," he said, before turning his gaze on Maggie. "Sorry to interrupt..."

He stared at Maggie for a moment and frowned as though puzzled.

I sighed recognizing the look. With Maggie, some men didn't know which one of their fantasies they wanted to put her.

"Why are you here?" The sight of him, put me off my lunch. My cool tone didn't appear to faze him as he took an uninvited seat between Maggie and me.

"I'm sure you find this awkward," he said. "So, I'll make this quick. You might have guessed I've been trying to connect with old friends and acquaintances."

I muffled a laugh without success. "Where does Lee fall?"

"After the gala, you have your doubts?"

This time I laughed with no hesitation. Ellison, funny, who would have thought?

"Doubts? Me?" I crossed my arms across my chest. The universal signal, he would have to elaborate.

Ellison's expression of contrition broadened my smile. A recognizable expression often found on Maggie's 9-year-old son, Rocket. He used the expression when he burnt off his friend's eyebrows with his science kit. My godson's face held the innocence and the charm of a Machiavellian prince. Ellison could take lessons.

"How did you find her?" Maggie interjected.

"Excuse me?" Ellison turned to my friend.

"This is my bestie Maggie. How did you find me?" I pushed aside my plate and gave Ellison my full attention. Maggie did the same. Ellison appeared flustered for a moment by the two sets of eyes boring into him but recovered.

"When I heard Leland and Mackenzie was roaming through the gala with a woman introduced as his fiancée, my curiosity got the better of me," he admitted. "The Smyth gala is all about being seen and gossip. No one escapes. Within fifteen minutes, I had your name."

I feigned a thoughtful expression and nodded. "That explains that, but to my next question. Why are you here?"

Ellison laced his hands together on the table. Head bent down, I thought he might pray. Instead, he returned with a heartfelt expression. I wanted to applaud. Again, Rocket did the face better.

"At the gala, I explained for my returning home, let's say, I'm required to do penance for my sins." A devilish grin played across his face. "My return is contingent on my mending a few fences with people."

I tempered my reaction. Why did Ellison come to see me? If his family required him to ask Lee for forgiveness, did his contribution to the fund not appeased his father?

"One being Lee?" I interjected.

Ellison nodded.

If what Waller said was true, how could Ellison renew his relationship with Maxfield? The cause of his ruination remained. Ellison disliked Lee, and Maxfield wanted to renew their relationship.

"So, what do you want from me?" I sat back in my chair. I suspect Ellison knew a frontal approach to Lee wouldn't work. Lee would shut him down in a heartbeat and punch him. Did he expect me to soften his way?

"I want to be in a room with Leland and not be in fear of my facial features," he mused.

Neither Maggie nor I thought that was funny.

"Why would Lee be in a room with you?" Maggie asked.

Ellison hesitated until I gave him an impatient look. I needed the answer to her question. He cut his eyes to Maggie, apparently still not ready to continue. She straightened in her chair to convey a clear message. She would stay and not be silent. Ellison continued.

"If Maxfield is talking to Leland, trust me, he wants him back. If Max thinks it's good, my father does, too. This would seal the deal for the firm and they'll try their best for it to happen," Ellison said with certainty.

I hadn't expected that to come out of Ellison's mouth. My mind raced back to every contact I had with Maxfield. I took him for a man wanting to rekindle an important relationship in his life. Did I mistake his kindness with hidden ambition? Like Ellison, did Maxfield think me the key to Lee?

"Maxfield doesn't often mentors associates. When he does, he takes it personal. He's made three State Attorneys, a federal judge, and a senator," Ellison said.

"What does your issues have to do with Lee?" Maggie asked.

"My little issue with Lee's wife kinda derailed Maxfield's plans for Lee." Ellison tried to appear contrite but failed.

"Little issue?" I mocked. Lee's desire to punch him seemed reasonable now. I wanted to punch him. "You believe Lee would go back to work for Maxfield, so he can complete a grand plan for him?"

"Why else would he go out of his way to reconnect? Why else would those partners be at the gala? Maxfield wants Lee and they live to keep Max happy. Also, Maxfield hates fundraising, but did because of Leland. He'll befriend him again and pull him back into the firm. And if that happens, Leland and I must mend our differences. I'm willing to kiss the devil."

I took a moment to decide how to take him. Was he desperate enough to track me down to help him with Lee? Whether he would kiss the devil wasn't the question, considering they were blood relations. His words about Maxfield's recruitment of Lee stuck in my head. Should I believe this, or ignore Ellison's paranoia?

"Do you know him?" Maggie pointed to the front of the restaurant.

I followed her gaze to the large windows at the front. Outside on the sidewalk, a tall, gaunt man stood like a statue. His laser focus appeared to be on our table. With his back to him, Ellison hadn't seen the man until he turned around in his chair. Ellison's affable expression vanished in an instant. He couldn't hide his recognition of the man. Not certain, but the stranger did look familiar to me.

Dressed in worn khakis, a wrinkled green Oxford shirt, he didn't quite seem homeless. His presence made the patrons at the tables closest to the windows uncomfortable. Yet staring was all he did. But, if he continued to put the customers off their meals, Candace would do something soon if he didn't go away. And it wouldn't be nice.

"A friend of yours?" Maggie questioned. Ellison's smile pressed into a tight, thin line.

My brain tried to force the memory of where I'd seen him before. The harder I tried the more elusive the memory became. Between Ellison's discomfort and the man's look of loathing, my curiosity won out. I bounded off my chair to stop Candace from doing anything before I could talk to him. Did Ellison need to make amends with someone else? Before I had a chance, Ellison dashed passed me. Maggie followed. I ignored Candace's questions as I slipped passed and exited the restaurant. Within seconds, Ellison was on the man.

"Did you follow me here?" Ellison shouted, his fist twisted in the man's shirt collar.

The man tried to pull away. Only then did I see the plastic shopping bag laden with something heavy in his hand. His face red with anger and fury almost overshadowed his actions as he pulled away from Ellison. Ellison's flinching away distracted me before I realized the man brought up the bag to toss. Before I turned away and close my eyes, I saw several Blue Moon customers gasp in horror.

Oh crap!

CHAPTER 15

I suspected Benjamin Moore Million Dollar Red wasn't quite the blood color Billy Pace expected. His aim wouldn't win any prizes either. Ellison's quick side steps allowed him to escape most of the carnage. Thank god I had my mouth closed when Pace threw the paint. Fifteen minutes of scrubbing with dishwashing liquid didn't improve my mood or appearance. My sensitive skin was raw with the effort of trying not to resemble a traffic accident victim. The small Blue Moon tee shirt and a spare pair of George's oversized chef pants garnished me a few looks as I made my way to the desk of Detective Oscar DeSmidt at the nearby police station.

"Thank God the paint was water base," Maggie said to DeSmidt taking the report.

Young, attentive, he paid way too much attention to Maggie. DeSmidt's mouth quirked into a smile as he began to type. I glowered at Maggie. Once again, I found myself on the wrong end of the confrontation that had nothing to do with me. How Maggie seemed to escape these little skirmishes untouched eluded me.

"How did you not get anything on you?" I glowered at her. Maggie's quizzical expression said she didn't have a clue and shrugged. If she didn't question her magical fairy shield, why should I? Yet I did. Maggie's quest to become the next Sherlock Holmes often left me in a painful situation.

"Nothing ever happens to you," I complained.

Maggie took offense to this. "What about my kidnapping, home invasion, or that mobster that threatened me?" She ticked off on her fingers.

"Where was I?" I said in a huff. "Next to you. My medical insurance premiums have gone up."

"You make it sound like it's my fault?" Maggie sounded hurt.

"I thought I attracted crazy, but it's you." I narrowed my gaze on her. DeSmidt did the same. Was he changing his opinion about Mrs. Swift?

"I'll admit we've come across a hornet's nest or two, but I don't poke the nest," she shot back.

"What's that supposed to mean?" I crossed my arms across my chest

"Odessa, sometimes you should say nothing. You feel the need to open your mouth and grab men by their man parts and twist." A flicker of annoyance flashed in her azure eyes. Detective DeSmidt shifted in his seat away from me as Maggie and I scowled at each other.

"Do you know why this happened, Detective?" Maggie asked, not before giving me an accusatory side eye.

"Ms. Wilkes, you got in the middle of a long-standing feud with William Pace and the Schaeffer family," DeSmidt explained.

"I'll assume you're not talking about Family Feud?" I mused.

Maggie sighed as if in annoyance with me.

"What she means, Detective, is should she worry about Mr. Pace?" Maggie's face had gone soft and feminine. Her attentive gaze and congenial smile disarmed the hapless detective. Clearly clueless to Maggie's subtle questioning, DeSmidt divulged a great deal. Whether charmed by her easy smile, motherly qualities, or fairy dust, I didn't care.

Four years ago, Ellison got a restraining order against Pace. The order lapsed after Ellison left the country. Four years ago, Lee left his wife and the legal world. Four years ago, seemed the touchstone for everything. To think Pace related to that somehow intrigued me. The revelation made Maggie's ears twitch at the thought of a connection between the men. Ellison was no help. After making his statement to the police, he left without a word. Would he even tell me?

"Is it possible you'll let me talk to Pace?" I asked. DeSmidt's eyes widened in surprise considering my first reaction after the attack was to strangle Pace. To dissuade his concerns, I put on my best congenial face.

"Why?" His doubtful eyes gaze back at me.

"Well, he didn't want to attack me, he wanted Ellison Schaeffer. If he apologizes, I won't press charges," I said. Thank God Candace stayed at the Blue Moon. Her presence would put Pace's life expectancy in question.

"That's a wonderful idea." Maggie beamed in delight. With Pace jailed, asking questions wouldn't be possible. DeSmidt threw up his arms, apparently frustrated by our change of heart. Upon arriving at the precinct, I threatened to disembowel Pace with a dessert spoon. Maggie treated him like a player on her son's soccer team with poor sportsmanship issues. Now, we wanted to drop the charges and ask a serial stalker some questions.

"Less paperwork." Maggie said the magical words that got the detective moving.

Twenty minutes later, we were in a small interviewing room with a remorseful looking Pace. As a precaution, he remained cuffed on the metal loop on the table across from Maggie and me. DeSmidt stood in the corner, keeping a watchful eye on us all.

I couldn't rid myself of the sense Pace and I had met. He didn't seem to recognize me, so I pushed the thought aside.

"Mr. Pace, we know you didn't mean to hit Odessa." Maggie placed her hands over his. In full mommy mode, she comforted him with kind words and reassurance. Pace seemed desperate enough to appreciate the gesture.

"She doesn't want to make this situation worse," Maggie continued.

Pace's eyes widened in surprise as his haggard features said everything. On closer inspection, he appeared frailer than expected and in need of a barber and sleep. I guessed his age at forty, but DeSmidt said Pace was only twenty-nine. His rumpled clothes, drawn features, and world-weary stare, a defeated Pace seemed hopeful.

"Thank you." An unsteady smile appeared on his face.

"She wants an apology and we can all go home," an impatient DeSmidt interjected. "For whatever reason, Mr. Schaeffer didn't seem interested in pressing charges. So, if the lady is nice enough not to press charges, then get on with it."

Maggie gave the detective an admonishing glare that silenced him.

"Give him a chance, Detective. Mr. Pace wants to do the right thing, don't you?" Years as her son's soccer coach, Maggie knew a thing or two about boys behaving badly.

To be honest, worse things have happened from being friends with Maggie while she pursued her dream. I've been stalked, concussed, and driven off the road. Still, I wouldn't mind an apology. What Pace had done was nothing in comparison. It came in a heartfelt one, with Pace almost in tears. By the time he finished, even DeSmidt looked like he felt bad at his earlier tone.

Pace insisted he would make any reparations necessary. Considering his current state, I didn't see how that was possible.

"I should have stayed away from Schaeffer." His pale gray eyes threaten to tear. "I read in the paper about him attending a party."

"The Carmen Smyth gala?" I said.

Pace nodded.

Maggie faced me. The curious expression she wore told me we were Alice again. Pace had become our white rabbit. She waited for me to acknowledge this. I took my time. Now, people from Lee's past life had dropped in my life like landmines. Pace was another one. Would he be more informative than Maxfield or Ellison or disruptive? Unsure of my next step, I took a deep breath.

"I appreciate your apology and won't press charges," I began. "You look like you could use a friend and meal, Mr. Pace. Let me offer you that?" This appeared to shock everyone, even Maggie, who smiled at the turn of events. DeSmidt stood with his mouth open, looking confused.

"Ms. Wilkes, are you sure you want to do that?" DeSmidt said. The detective gave me a look that now questioned my sanity. Did I have my doubts, yes, but I wanted answers. Maybe Billy Pace had them.

To convince the detective, I channeled my 80-year-old great Aunt Renne. She would forgive the devil if he promised to attend church every Sunday. She forgave me when I didn't.

"Bear with each other and forgive one another, if any one of you has a grievance against someone. Forgive as the Lord forgave you." I used the same pious bible quote my Aunt Renee used when Candace and I had a big fight and refused to talk. Scientists should study my aunt's ability to silence two combatant black women.

"Ms. Wilkes!" A dumbfounded DeSmidt shook his head, uncuffed Pace, and took him out for processing.

This gave me time to talk to Maggie alone. The minute the door was close, I couldn't get a word in edgewise.

"Didn't you say the case that made Lee leave had to do with Schaeffer Pharmaceuticals? Do you think Pace knows anything? Four years ago, is about the same time everything else happened. Or was this one of the many sins Ellison is doing penance on?" She took in a breath. "If Ellison is looking for forgiveness, why isn't Pace on his list? Why didn't he press charges? Here he was making all nice-nice with you and he tried to choke Pace. Do you believe Maxfield's intent? I don't trust Ellison."

She paused enough for me to respond.

"We'll take him to the Blue Moon, feed him, and then ask him a thousand questions. Okay? The first of which, does he know Lee?"

Maggie agreed.

To his credit, DeSmidt processing Pace in record time gained him points in my book. I thanked him. Maggie gave him an encouraging pat he appreciated more. He warned us again about Pace. I plastered on a smile that might have the detective wondering about Pace's safety or my sanity. Pace slipped into the back of Maggie's car before he could respond.

As we drove off, Pace continued to apologize all the way to the Blue Moon. Once there, he seemed reluctant to return to the scene of his crime. Maggie had to coax him out of the car. The signs of his misdeed removed, no doubt by my sister.

"You've got to be kidding me," Candace said as she barred our way into the dining area.

"I'm over the whole thing," I said nonchalantly and tried to walk past her.

She blocked my way.

"This nut job attacked you." Candace turned her heated gaze on Pace, who shrunk back. Candace in full rage was a scary sight.

"When I lost my job, and everything fell apart, I had a little emotional problem. If you treated me this way, I would still be in bed with the covers on my head. So be a good Christian or I'll call Aunt Renne," I warned.

When I reminded Candace of my bouts of anxiety after my firing, that made her pause. She had pulled me back from the brink kicking and screaming. I loved her for her intervention. Despite her complaints, Candace was my biggest defender. She stepped aside. Calling my Aunt Renne might have motivated her as well.

"He'd better behave." She pointed and finger at Pace.

"I've done a lot worse." I pushed her finger down and walked past her.

At a back table, away from watchful eyes, I treated Pace to a steak dinner. Between bites, he apologized again and again. While he ate, Maggie and I had coffee. I would have preferred a cocktail or two, but I needed to keep my wits. Pace finished the meal with a large helping of my Dutch apple pie and coffee. As he ate his dessert, it was then I remembered where I'd seen him before. At Heather's funeral standing by the church entrance. He'd been the man Lee had looked at. This only heightened my curiosity.

"Why did you attack Ellison Schaeffer?"

A slight pall came over him, but he recovered. Whatever had happened still affected him after three years. The way Heather still affected Lee.

"My sister." Pace looked away.

"What did Ellison do to your sister?" I felt intrusive, but I had to know. He faced me, eyes bright and determined.

"He killed her."

CHAPTER 16

Despite the chaos of the past few days, I sat at my workbench sketching. The new Bentley-Henderson cake was due. Uncle Hal and the New York City Police high-jacked the first wedding. Naomi Bentley's father promised his daughter a Hal free wedding. This included a secret new venue, wedding dress, and cake. In typical New York fashion, he gave me a week to come up with another over the top cake design. Considering the last few days, I was ready to give Naomi a fifty percent discount for an ice cream cake from Carvel.

"I like that one," Esperanza said over my shoulder. A rough sketch of a five-tier cake of white roses and delicate draping stood out amongst the designs. I liked it too because it didn't need a thousand Day-Glo flowers.

"Let's keep the same favors she selected before." Pleased, I held up the drawing for a better look. "If she wants it in a week, white roses are fine."

"Don't you think she'll want the cake she had before?"

I shook my head. "Would you want to be reminded of a nightmare?"

"Uncle Hal?"

I nodded. Regrettably, Uncle Hal's whereabouts were unknown after someone bailed him out.

"How could someone be so insensitive?" Esperanza's youthful face stared back at me. Barely into her twenties, her personal disappointments were few. Jerks with agendas hadn't yet entered her life. This made me think of Ellison and Maxfield.

"Sometimes people want what they want," I mused and handed the drawing to her. "Could you email this to Naomi for confirmation?"

Esperanza took the sketch and headed to my office to scan and email the drawing. I stared down at the various drawings on the workbench. There were other brides in need of cakes, I thought as I flipped through the sketches. As ideas popped in and out of my head, my thoughts kept going back to Ellison and Maxfield. My inspiration vanished at the sudden lack of focus. Frustrated, I called someone with an unwavering one. I pulled out my cell phone from my apron pocket.

"Hey Sherlock," I teased.

"Don't call me that," Maggie complained.

"Where are you?"

"At the office with Frank trying to explain why people pay us."

"I know why we get paid," a gruff, male voice came from the other side of the line. From the sound of his voice, I could tell she had me on the phone's speaker. "I don't want to go to the Bronx."

"Frank's got a thing about the Bronx?" Frank McAvoy seemed to have a thing about everything, I mused.

"Yeah, the Yankees, He hates them." Maggie's exasperation with her boss and mentor amused me.

A few years ago, Maggie Swift was an ordinary housewife with an insurance salesman husband, a kid, and a dog. She lived in a post WWII house in Hicksville and coached her son's soccer team. Her decision to become a private investigator came as a shock to her family and friends. The only one who didn't appear shocked was her son, Rocket.

"So, if he was tailing someone, and they drove to the Bronx, he wouldn't follow?" I clarified.

"Seems that way." Maggie sounded irritated.

New York State required mentorship with a licensed investigator before Maggie could be one. As an ex-cop, Frank McAvoy fitted that bill. If he'd known Maggie would increase his caseload, check his carb intake, and force him to work for a living, I'm sure he would have said no.

"Put on your big boy pants, Frank, and go," I demanded. Our contentious relationship drove Maggie crazy. Frank took advantage of Maggie's good nature. He thought women should be silent. This explained his three ex-wives.

"Stay out of it, Odessa," Frank commanded.

This was an invitation to give my opinion.

"If you want, Frank, I'll go with you and hold your hand." Certain that my placating tone rankled him, I smiled.

"Odessa," Maggie warned.

"Why don't I give you an Ouija board and a crystal ball to find Lee's tenant," I mocked.

"I should talk to that fiancé of yours and warn him," Frank shot back.

"Frank!" Maggie shouted.

"No one warned your ex-wives, Frank," I retorted.

"Odessa!" Maggie yelled again.

"Witch," Frank cursed.

"Coward," I said with glee.

"Enough!" Maggie demanded and disengaged the speaker phone.

"Hey, Maggie," I said, my voice cheery and upbeat.

"Why do you do that?" Maggie's annoyance with me was heard in her voice.

"Because if I did it to Candace, I would need to move to another country. With Frank, I'd only have to go to the Bronx."

She sighed audibly.

"Is there a reason you called besides wanting to set Frank off?" She sighed.

Normally doing Frank would be enough, but I had a thought. I want to talk to Billy Pace again.

"Really?" She seemed surprised but pleased. "So, do I."

Pace's relationship with Ellison intrigued us both.

"From what you said, Billy didn't recognize Lee at the funeral. Which meant Lee left before the Pace's lawsuit of Schaeffer Pharmaceuticals. I did a search and the case never went to trial. They settled."

"Doesn't seem like Billy did," I added.

"Billy's parents sued, not him. They settled and took the money. Billy didn't care. He blames Ellison directly, not only the company."

"Considering Ellison's personality, I don't blame him."

"The suit claimed the company encouraged a hostile work environment. The stress caused Billy's sister to kill herself. Considering they settled, it might be true," Maggie said.

"Not necessarily. The publicity of a lawsuit is more damaging even if they weren't in the wrong. They might consider settling cost effective," I explained. No matter how good your product was, a bad reputation made it worthless.

"Is that why you want to talk to Billy?" she questioned.

"Schaeffer Pharmaceuticals had other legal issues before that. Lee left because of it. It just had me wondering if it was all connected. Lee's case and the Paces."

"I can look into it. Do you think Billy has any answers?"

The last time we spoke, Billy wanted someone to hear his story and that of his sister. Would a cake shop owner and inspiring private investigator do? I got the sense that Billy would talk to a parking meter and a stray dog if they'd listen.

"Give me a couple hours to see what I can find out about Schaeffer Pharmaceuticals and the law suit. Call Billy and see if he'll meet us," Maggie said.

Already on the scent of something, I called Pace. He picked up on the second ring.

Once again, he apologized about the incident in front of the Blue Moon. Then he thanked me for the meal and leftovers. When he finally took a breath, I asked him if Maggie and I could speak to him about Ellison. I stated I had concerns about Ellison and wanted to know more about him. You would have thought someone asked him to attend the next royal wedding. He went on a tirade about Schaeffer Pharmaceuticals and corporate America. After five minutes, I stopped him. We agreed to meet. Unfortunately, it would have to be at his job, a laundromat in Astoria, Queens.

After hanging up with Billy, I waited for Maggie to pick me up later that afternoon. Esperanza ensured she could handle the shop on her own. Mrs. Gonzales showed me her stash of confectioner sugar stashed behind the counter. Maggie admonished me for encouraging her.

"Worst come to worse, I'll tell him it's a Guatemalan blessing." I offered my best grin as I ignored Maggie's look of disappointment.

Before we drove off, she handed me a newspaper article printout on Schaeffer Pharmaceuticals. I noted the date of the report on the newsworthy litigation with the company. Lee still worked there at the firm.

"Read the next section I highlighted," Maggie said.

I did. Just like the Pace civil suit case, the company admitted to no wrongdoing and settled. In one of the financial reports, the settlement was in the millions.

"The suit claimed the company mislead doctors about a drug series they manufactured. They promoted the drugs as an alternative to other most addictive drugs on the market."

"Was it?" I asked.

Maggie shrugged. "The thing is, they didn't settle for that. They settled for something called off-label marketing."

"What's that?" I asked.

"Off-label marketing happens when a drug company markets a drug for more than what it was designed. Like a drug that might be good for diabetes, but also helps you lower your high blood pressure and lose weight. Also, Schaeffer exaggerated how less addictive it was, compared to similar drugs."

"How much?"

"Hundreds of doctors switched their patients, only to find the drug was equally addictive if not more."

"So, Schaeffer Pharmaceuticals toted this new wonder drug, and they lied?"

Maggie nodded as she navigated the streets of Queens. Avoiding the congested parkway, we took many of the side streets through the varied ethnic neighborhoods that made the borough so famous.

"The off-labeling was a secondary charge. The doctors claimed the drug had severe side effects not found in the clinical trials. You know when you see those drug commercials and they list those horrible side effects? Well, the doctors claimed the drugs caused several deaths."

"That's a big side effect," I said.

"The opposition couldn't prove it. They even had testimonial that said the opposite. The judge wanted to get them on something, so he slapped them with the off-labeling," Maggie said.

"So, Schaeffer dodged a big bullet." I flipped through the pages and continued to read. We rode in silence for a while until we stopped at a light near Northern Blvd.

"After the paint thing, I checked into Billy," Maggie said with a hint of guilt. At first, I didn't respond. For Maggie, this was typical behavior. She didn't like unknowns and Billy Pace was a big one. Her ability to find out things no longer surprised me. Not only was she deft at research, she had a way of making interesting friends with access to information. This included a computer whiz kid with legal problems, a former court reporter who shared Maggie's love of eighties music, and a thirty something police detective with mommy issues.

"He lives in a place called Harbor House in Long Island City. It's supportive housing for people with mental disabilities. From his phone bill, he's been living there for a while. His last resume included a work program that probably got him his job at the laundromat." Maggie avoided eye contact with me. Cheating spouses were one thing. But invading someone's personal medical information was a line Maggie rarely crossed.

"He's had a few arrests on drug charges, disturbing the peace, rehab, and now Harbor House. After his sister's death, he relapsed but seemed to have bounced back."

Maggie's brows lifted.

"You don't have to tell me Billy is left of center. The red paint to the face proved that point," I reminded her.

"Yeah, but remember, whatever he tells us might not be true," she said.

Maggie was right. Yet, considering Ellison's reaction, I tended toward believing Pace. What I didn't want to do was to exacerbate any psychological issues Pace may be dealing with. Ellison's return rekindled a burning desire to demand justice for his sister. I didn't want to add fuel to that fire.

"Technically, he stalked Ellison," she informed me.

"You say it like it's a bad thing."

"Odessa, it is. This time red paint, what's next?"

It was like Maggie to make me concerned about Ellison's wellbeing.

"If we're lucky, he'll go back to Europe."

"I'm serious," she insisted.

"I know," I conceded.

Billy was living his life when Ellison graced New York with his presence again. Ellison had a way of opening old wounds. Did he deserve something more than a can of red paint thrown at him? I think he did. I suspected Pace would agree. We only differed on the method. Pace wanted to draw and quarter Ellison. I, on the other hand, thought he just needed to leave New York City and find Jesus.

CHAPTER 17

The Woodside Laundromat sat on a corner lot. Small compared to the mega Wash and Go we'd passed four blocks back. The place had none of the modern conveniences as the Wash and Go. No Wi-Fi, drop-off services, or convenient parking were available at the small laundromat. Its only customers were two women. One, a stooped shouldered geriatric and the other, a twenty something with her nose in a paperback. They had Billy Pace. Maggie and I found him touching up the storefront signage on a shaky wooden ladder with a can of paint. We approached him with care, in the fear he might fall off.

"Hey, you came." Pace's mouth opened in surprise at the sight of us.

"Are you busy?" Maggie placed a hand on the ladder to brace it. My concern focused on the can of paint in his hand and my proximity.

"Go inside. I'll be finished with this in a minute." Pace acted like a man eager to talk.

Maggie seemed unwilling to let go of the ladder. While Pace held a can of paint, I didn't have a problem putting some distance between us. A reluctant Maggie followed me into the small and outdated laundromat. We took a seat on a row of hard-plastic benches. A stooped old woman took notice of us and abandoned her vigil on a washer machine. She shuffled her way over dressed in a faded flowered housedress with white hair tinted with blue highlights. She gave us a wizened smile.

"You one of William's social workers?" the old woman whispered conspiratorially. Before we could respond, she leaned in closer. A generous amount of Chanel No. 5 and baby powder hit my senses, and I almost gagged. "Billy is doing a really excellent job here."

Maggie and I nodded in agreement and leaned back to get some fresh air. When the woman reached inside the dress's pocket, she pulled out a worn black-and-white photograph of a woman and a man in a tight but playful embrace.

"My husband, Leo. Handsome, isn't he? Have you seen him?" She gazed down at the picture wistfully. Maggie took the photograph. I leaned close to see. Youthful faces stared back at us from the aged photograph.

"It's Coney Island!" Somehow Maggie deduced the photograph's place of origin.

"Yes, oh yes, 1962 near the Nathan's hot dog stand." The old lady sighed in a warm response.

"Mrs. Stankowski!" Pace said as he entered the laundromat. "I didn't forget your cup of tea, I promised."

Mrs. Stankowski's eyes brightened and abandoned us to follow Pace toward the back of the laundromat. Maggie held the picture, studying the faces of the young couple.

"It's not her." Maggie showed me the photograph.

"What?" I turned to see her gaze locked on the old woman as she disappeared with Pace into a back room. Maggie's statement got the attention of the woman with the book.

"How did you guess?" The woman stared in amazement as she placed her book into her lap.

Maggie held up the picture and sighed.

"The woman in the picture is a foot taller, different facial structure, and not Mrs. Stankowski. This may be Mr. Stankowski, but the woman with him is not his wife he's hugging."

"You know her?" I nodded toward the old lady.

"Everyone knows Mrs. Stankowski. She always shows everyone that picture. If you wait long enough, she'll tell you how she lost her husband and best friend in the crowd at Coney Island."

Maggie's blue eyes darken as her gaze fell on the photograph again. She'd have a few choice words for Mr. Stankowski and his friend.

"Since Billy came, he treats her sweet. Makes her tea, listens to stories about that dog of a husband." The woman gave a disapproving shake of her head and returned to her book.

A moment later, Mrs. Stankowski and Pace appeared with her cup of tea. He guided her to a seat by the washing machine she abandoned when we arrived. Once he had the old lady seated with her tea, he came over to us. He noticed the photograph in Maggie's hand and asked for it.

"I'll give this to her later. A few minutes without Mr. Stankowski would be good." He took the photograph from Maggie.

"Can you talk?" I asked.

"Wait, I forgot something." He turned and dashed away. Pace returned with a large accordion style file in his arms. Worn from time, the content inside threatened to slip out. Maggie almost snatched the thing from him. Nothing got that woman hotter than finding answers to questions.

"Is that entire thing about Ellison?" This made me wonder how much Pace knew about Schaeffer.

"Mostly on my sister and her time at Schaeffer Pharmaceutical." Pace's expression turned dark. "My parents sued Schaeffer Pharmaceuticals over what they did to her."

"Why?" Since hearing about Pace's sister, I could only guess as to why the family sued the company.

"Deena worked for that company for over fifteen years. Then something changed about four years ago. She stopped calling home, lost weight, dropped her friends. Then things got worse. Six months later, Deena committed suicide."

"Where does Ellison come in?" I felt the first hint of doubt about Pace. Was this about the company or Ellison?

"Ellison pushed her out and made his attacks on her personal. Even when she left the company, he still harassed her." Pace's voice tightened with his anger.

The woman with the book looked up. I suspected our conversation was more interesting than the book she held. I gave her a pleasant, but focused gaze to encourage her to get back to her reading.

"Can we take these with us?" Maggie's eyes brightened at the idea.

Pace nodded. "They're copies."

I kept my eagerness in check. Yet, one unanswered questioned nagged at me. His appearance at Heather's funeral, and did he recognize Maxfield? Did he have a can of red paint ready for him?

"A few weeks ago, you attended the funeral of Heather McLaughlin." I spoke tentatively.

"You sat with the guy with the glasses?"

I nodded. "They worked at the same law firm for a time."

Pace's face darkened with concern. The expression of doubt on his face made me worry. Would Pace think me guilty because of Lee's association with the firm?

"Lee left the firm and doesn't much care for Ellison either," Maggie injected, reading Pace's sudden shift in mood.

"In fact, he hates him," I reassured. "That's why Ellison came to visit me at the restaurant. He's going through some kind of redemption tour. But nobody is buying his bull, especially my fiancé. They bring out the worst in each other, so I need to keep Ellison as far away from him as possible."

Pace said nothing for a while before nodding. A signal to say we were not the enemy. At least I hoped not.

"Why did you come to Heather's funeral?" Maggie questioned.

"I read about her death in the paper and thought Ellison might show," he said finally.

"They dated." I remembered what Lee told me. Ellison zeroed in on the hapless pretty law clerk.

"When Ellison harassed Deena, I confronted him. Several times, he was with her, that Heather woman. That woman would be at his apartment or at dinner together and such. Then he got a restraining order against me, so I followed her. Since I couldn't be around his place, I still could be around her. He'd show up now and then, so I knew where to find him if I had too."

"Had to what?" Maggie shifted uneasily in her seat.

Pace shook his head as if a foul thought became lodged there.

"Nothing happened. But I let his girlfriend know, I could get to him."

"You talked to Heather?" I asked. Pace's tenacity surprised me.

"Yeah. In fact, she warned me instead. She kinda thought me stalking Ellison was a joke." Pace's lips curled up in disgust.

"A joke?" From Maggie's expression, she didn't find stalking someone humorous.

"Heather said Ellison took what Deena did as a personal betrayal. She also thought Ellison was a borderline sociopath and I should be careful." Pace's face flushed with anger.

"Yeah, that kind of describes him," I nodded.

"Heather didn't fear him?" Maggie asked.

Pace shook his head. "When I saw them together, Ellison turned into this submissive dude. I've seen her yell at him and he took it. He'd follow her around like a puppy dog."

"Really!" This made me wonder. No longer the sweet girl that Lee painted her to be, my impression of Heather shifted—again.

"Did you ever see Heather again in any capacity?" Maggie asked.

Pace nodded.

"Yeah, when my parents started a wrongful death suit after Deena's suicide. They called me in to do a deposition at that fancy law firm. In the reception area, I saw her talking with two men, one with white hair, the other fat and balding. Heather was making a scene. When the white-haired guy reached for her, she slapped him, hard. The bald guy grabbed her, because I thought she would hit the other guy again. He rushed her into another office."

The description sounded like Maxfield and Koenig. When Pace went to the law firm to do his deposition, Lee had already quit the firm by then. I didn't have to worry about Lee meeting Pace because they had never met before.

"Did you hear what they argued about?" I hoped Pace had overheard the conversation.

Pace shook his head.

"What happened then?" Maggie prompted.

"The next day, the company offered a big settlement and my parents took it. I told them not to, but they needed the money. I wanted the truth to come out. They didn't listen," Pace said.

"Heather shows up and suddenly they settled the lawsuit," I pondered to no one in particular. Why had Heather returned? She'd quit the law firm by then.

"Well, she was there at the time Ellison harassed Deena," Maggie interjected. "She could testify to Ellison's treatment of your sister."

"Maybe she blackmailed him," the woman with the book shouted out.

We all stared at her. Sheepishly, she returned to her book.

"I hate to say this, but she has a point. Heather could prove the harassment case against Ellison if she wanted. But why sacrifice her golden goose?" I admitted.

"When did Ellison start to harass your sister?" Maggie asked.

"Before Deena's demotion. She got secretive about her work. She became preoccupied with a lawsuit the company was involved in. After the case ended, they demoted her and later they fired her. A few months later, she died. I found this at her apartment." Pace pointed to the folder.

"If Ellison harassed your sister during the Schaeffer's class action suit, he and Heather had to be together then. Before his affair with Julia," Maggie said.

"Or at the same time," I replied.

"Maybe she wanted revenge," the book woman proclaimed.

Again, we glared at her, but I sighed in resignation. Once again, the woman had a point.

My impression of Heather shifted again. I wondered how she felt about Ellison's affair with Julia. Heather started up with him again when the affair ended if she left at all. Though the thought of Ellison two-timing both women wouldn't surprise me. Julia became a means to an end. Ellison wanted to upset Lee and disrupt his relationship with Maxfield. How did that sit with Heather? Was she a go-with-the-flow kind of girl? Not the impression I got from Pace's contact with her. She had things on Ellison, a lot of things. Did she use it against him?

"That explains something," Maggie said.

"What?" I turned to Maggie.

"How Heather could afford an expensive nursing home for her mother?"

This answered one of my questions. Heather wasn't a go-with-the-flow kind of girl at all.

CHAPTER 18

After our visit with Pace, Maggie asked me if I wouldn't mind going to the Bronx. Since my afternoon was pretty much free, I agreed. Also, the borough was a no-fly zone for her boss, I didn't mind keeping her company. Possible information about Lee's missing tenant might be available. Maggie refused to miss the opportunity because Frank McAvoy had deemed an entire borough as his personal hell.

"So, it isn't the Yankees?" I said as we drove over the RFK bridge that connected three of the five boroughs of the city.

"No, more like the money he lost on the team." Maggie sighed. "He bet on them, he lost, and cursed the entire team, stadium, and the borough."

"Every time he comes here something bad happens?" I asked.

"First, they put a parking boot on his car. He broke his big toe while following a client's husband. Then a lawyer at the Bronx courthouse punched him."

"Sounds pretty bad," I admitted. It took a lot for me to feel sorry for Frank. A hefty parking fine, a broken toe, and a black eye would do it. Yet the expression on Maggie's face said otherwise.

"That happens when you ignore parking tickets and don't pay them. You break your toe when you confront an irate husband in the middle of his bowling tournament. Those balls are heavy. He could have avoided the black eye if he hadn't slept with the lawyer's wife," Maggie said.

I laughed. My laughter stopped at the sight of one Cezar Comaneci's apartment building. Situated on the Bronx Grand Concourse, the building could have been in a third world war zone. Comaneci's masterpiece of neglect stood out like a middle finger in the neighborhood. Until I saw that building, I never quite comprehended the depth of Lee's frustration with the landlord.

"I checked a city advocate watch list. This building has nine hundred and thirty citations. There is a list of the top one hundred worst landlords in New York City and Comaneci is working his way to the top ten. Someone should make him live here," Maggie said as she opened the driver's side door. Before she stepped out, I grabbed her by the arm.

"Why are we getting out of this car?" I said with trepidation. In this neighborhood, her suburban self-righteousness stood out like a beacon of trouble. I didn't want one of Comaneci's goons to tell her she didn't belong.

"We can't talk to Lorena Ramos' aunt sitting in the car," she said as if her reasons were obvious.

I pointed to Comaneci's building and hoped the panic on my face said enough. I didn't want to go there. Maggie was unfazed and gave me a pat on my hand as if this would calm my fears. It didn't.

"Easy, O." Maggie pointed to the building next door. "She lives in this one."

The building next door was a beautiful Art déco revival. Compared to the hell hole next to it, the building seemed safe enough. I let Maggie go. Still reluctant to leave the car, I hesitated. Maggie had a way of getting me into situations that required running and Kung Fu.

"Come on," she insisted as she headed for the building's entrance. I got out of the car.

Inside, we got buzzed in by Alma Deleon, Lorena Ramos' aunt. At any moment, I expected to see one of Comaneci's goons jumping out. They threatened Lee, his tenants, and though there was no proof who vandalized my van, they threaten me. Unable to relax, I began to scratch my rash.

"Odessa!" Maggie stopped abruptly.

"What?" I jumped in alarm. Before I had a chance to bolt, she held me by my arm.

"Look." She held up my arm to show me I'd scratched myself raw. I cursed myself for my nerves getting the better of me.

Maggie acted with the immediacy of a mother with a 9-year-old boy. She dug into her large saddlebag pocketbook. Out came a tube of anti-itch cream. When had she brought it? She seemed quite pleased when she finished. I, on the other hand, felt like an idiot because I couldn't stop myself.

"Relax," she pleaded. Her unconcerned face stared up at me. "This building isn't owned by Comaneci. Mrs. Deleon reassured me we'd be safe."

"Safe would be getting back into the car and driving back to Queens," I retorted.

Not feeling any safer, I still followed the little redhead to Mrs. Deleon's apartment at the end of the hall. It took all my effort not to scratch, not think of Lee's bruised face, my van and the lack of escape routes. My rumination about our demise ended when Mrs. Deleon opened her apartment door.

Once inside, the delicious aroma of something cooking in the kitchen assaulted us. An inviting, yet reserved Mrs. Deleon gestured for us to take a seat on an overstuffed sofa. My eyes gravitated to family photographs which decorated much of the room. What also got my attention was the young boy in a Catholic school uniform sitting at the table hunched over a notebook. He looked up only to acknowledge our presence.

"Say hello, Eduardo," Mrs. Deleon said in an authoritative tone. The boy said a quick hello before returning to his books. We returned the greeting.

"Thank you for seeing me, Mrs. Deleon," Maggie said as we took a seat on the sofa.

"No problem. What's this about?" She sat in a lounge chair across from us. Despite her invitation, she held a wary gaze.

Maggie turned towards the boy and then to Mrs. Deleon. Her furrowed brow told me she didn't like the idea of talking in his presence. Mrs. Deleon turned to the boy as well. The sternness in her face softened.

"Eddie, take your homework into the bedroom. I need to talk to these ladies," she said. Without a word the boy complied, gathering up his belongs before heading to the back of the apartment.

"And don't turn on the TV," she added. We heard an audible groan coming from the back.

"If only I could get my son, Rocket, to behave like that," Maggie said wistfully.

Mrs. Deleon frowned in confusion. "You named your son Rocket?"

"It's more a description of him than a name," I offered. Her tight expression returned as if to remind her we were only welcome to a point.

"You are?" Mrs. Deleon asked as a well arch brow rose.

"Rocket's godmother and the fiancé of the lawyer looking for your niece," I said. I didn't want to beat around the bush.

"Technically, I'm here to talk to you about your niece, Lorena, really," Maggie said, giving me a warning look of her own.

"How did you find me? We don't have the same last name."

Maggie gave Mrs. Deleon a sheepish smile. "You signed one of Lorena's petitions. At the beginning of the suit, she was quite active. Lee McKenzie got the tenants to sign a petition to send to their local representatives. She helped collect them. I checked the names, and most were family and friends who either lived in the building or nearby. You were also on her contact sheet she gave to Lee's law firm. Then there is her son, Eduardo."

Mrs. Deleon's frown deepened. "What about her son?"

"He goes to the Sacred Hearts Academy on scholarship." Maggie raised a hand when Mrs. Deleon was about to question how she knew.

"Facebook."

"Goddamn social media," she cursed. "I told her, don't put her business out there."

"Sound advice, Mrs. Deleon. She's being a proud mom. I understand that. Considering how involved she was in the lawsuit, I'm sure she wanted to make a better life for her son. A good mother wouldn't pull her son out of school if she didn't have to. She gives him to someone who'd protect him, make sure he does his school work, and loves him," Maggie said softly.

Mrs. Deleon sat back in her chair and crossed her arms, still defensive.

"Lee said she was active at the beginning of the lawsuit. Then the trouble started. The building repairs stopped. Men telling tenants to leave. They showed up at her job. Then they vandalized her apartment," Maggie said.

"Disgusting men," Mrs. Deleon cursed.

"She had her son to think of when Comaneci threatened her. Lee understands, and he wouldn't force her to testify," Maggie said.

"He can't force her if he can't find her." Mrs. Deleon jutted out her chin.

"Yeah, but they can find him," I injected. I was surprised at my sudden annoyance. I sympathize that Lorena Ramos needed to protect her child, but at the cost of what? The better life she wanted would never happen. Men like Comaneci wouldn't allow her to have a better life.

"That's not her problem anymore," Mrs. Deleon said.

"But the problem is mine. Because he won't stop. The more they push, he'll push back," I said.

"Isn't it his job?" Mrs. Deleon retorted.

My face flushed with heat. "Getting hurt is not his job."

Mrs. Deleon stared at me stone faced.

"Odessa," Maggie said to calm me, but I wasn't having it.

"I want him to stop, but he won't. I won't stand in his way either. I wouldn't know how. Because the thing I admire most about him, the thing I love, is that he could stand up against people like Comaneci. He is a man who could defend people unable to defend themselves. From what Maggie said, your niece is the same way. She found the strength to stand up against the son of a bitch."

"What Odessa is trying to say—" Maggie attempted to say, but Mrs. Deleon waved her off.

"I know what she thinks she's trying to say. But Comaneci is dangerous."

I gave a derisive laugh.

"Yeah, Comaneci is dangerous, and he's afraid of Lorena," I said.

Mrs. Deleon shook her head. "He's not afraid of her."

"He is, Mrs. Deleon," Maggie confirmed. "Comaneci's men crossed the line when they went into your niece's apartment and vandalized it. Everything went from simple building violations to assault. Also, Lorena expertly documented everything that was going on in the building," Maggie added.

"I helped her," a small voice said from the hallway which led to the bedrooms. We all turned to see Eduardo.

"Eduardo go to the room," Mrs. Deleon demanded. The child stood still. He looked small in the oversized burgundy school jacket. The school's emblem was an embroidered gold heart pierced by a flaming sword. His deep brown eyes were equally intense as they stared back at us.

"I helped her take pictures and talk to the people. I wrote a report about it for school. I got an A, and the teacher wrote Momma a letter about how good it was. She framed it. When those men came in, they broke it, stepped on it." His eyes shifted away as if caught in that horrible memory. "I recorded them with my phone when they came. They didn't know."

"What!" we all said in unison.

"I thought they might hurt Momma. They wanted her to stop getting signatures. Taking pictures of the broken things in the building. Momma wouldn't stop. She said it wouldn't get better if she stopped. Teacher said I should be proud of her. I am," he said defiantly.

"You have a video of them in the apartment?" Maggie asked for clarification. The boy nodded. "Why didn't you say something?"

The boy looked at his aunt. No doubt, after the attack, Mrs. Deleon demanded that her niece stop. Mrs. Deleon was a woman you didn't say no to, especially Eduardo. As he held out the phone to us, the sight of the brave little boy made me smile. Yet the tears that ran down his aunt's proud, but terror filled face made me pause. She understood the implications.

It took only a moment for Eduardo to pull up the video he saved. The sight of two men terrorizing his mother heightened my anger. They had been relentless, cursing and threatening and laughed as they did it. Somehow, Eduardo had recorded it all.

The fear that made me hesitate before became a distance memory. Unlike Maggie, I didn't want to give Comaneci and his men a stern talking to or explain the error of their ways. Even going directly to the police wasn't enough for me. I wanted the satisfaction of burying them beneath one of their buildings.

Then I had a really bad idea.

"Sometimes social media is your friend," I said as I took the phone from Maggie. She complained, but once she realized what I was about to do, she stopped. It didn't take long to upload the video to YouTube.

Mrs. Deleon began to protest when she realized what was happening.

"It makes one Lorena Ramos into thousands," Maggie reassured her. "Comaneci can't intimidate the world."

The first comment came within fifteen minutes.

"I hope someone went to jail for this," it said.

"They will," I replied. "They will."

CHAPTER 19

After the revelation about Heather's relationship with Ellison and dealing with Lee's witness, I came home around nine o'clock exhausted. The only thing I wanted was a hot shower and bed. I managed shower, but never made it to bed. My way blocked by a six-foot-two-inches male wearing wire-rimmed glasses and a pissed off attitude. Lee stood arms crossed, steam coming out of his ears. Still wet from the shower, my only defense was a towel.

"Have you lost your mind?" Lee bellowed.

"You're home late." I tried to step passed him and ignore the slight shade of red his face was turning. Lee moved to block me.

"You uploaded that video?" His hazel eyes narrowed.

"Maggie was there too, you know. How do you know it was me?" I said in my defense.

He laughed scathingly.

"She was the one who told me." He pointed a finger in my face.

I pushed it away, annoyed with both my fiancé and my backstabbing friend.

"I thought it was a good idea at the time." I huffed and tried to take another sidestep, which he blocked.

His eyes widened in both shock and indignation. He did that laugh again and grabbed me by my shoulders and gave me a little shake. I lost the towel. We both stared down at it. Lips set in a tight grimace, he tried to keep his eyes on the towel. We stood there, him in his business suit, me in my birthday one. I felt a power shift coming on and smiled.

"I'm cold," I complained playfully.

He picked up the towel, handed it to me.

"This should keep you warm," he said and walked out the bedroom door.

"Crap," I said and sighed. I'd have to make things right somehow or my new best friend was a towel.

Before heading downstairs, I slipped on one of his favorite tee shirts. In the hope that he wouldn't want to get blood on it, it might stop him from wanting to kill me. I found Lee stretched out on the couch, his arm covering his eyes. The furry monster masquerading as a cat stood guard on the back of the couch. As I approached, it made a horrible mewing sound. The damn thing was like a personal alarm. Lee removed his arm to see me.

"I don't want to play," he warned.

"Can I say I'm sorry?" I offered.

The arm went over the eyes again. Lee's rebuff usually didn't last long. The cat jumped on his stomach and started kneading him with his claws out. Lee yelped and sat up to get the cat off. The cat took his time before jumping down. It brushed up against my legs, meowed in satisfaction before it disappeared into the kitchen. The sound of crunching followed. If I didn't know better, I could have sworn that cat forced Lee to stop ignoring me. From the disgusted expression Lee gave the cat, he'd come to the same conclusion.

"I'm sorry," I repeated.

Lee pulled at his tie to loosen it, almost choking himself. When I stepped forward to help, he leaned away. Free of his tie, he loosened his shirt and lay back against the sofa exhausted.

"Lenora Ramos called me. She wasn't happy her son did that video." Lee rested his head back and closed his eyes. I took this opportunity to pounce and straddled him to sit on his lap. Equally annoying as the cat, I was harder to brush off.

"I am sorry. I should have told you about the video. I will never do it again," I said.

Lee placed his hands on my hips. For half a minute, I thought he might shove me off, but he didn't. Instead, he took a deep inhalation and then another.

"The video does make Ramos more willing to testify," he conceded.

"Over ten thousand hits." I pumped a fist in the air. Lee didn't cheer along.

"Comaneci can't afford any more violence. The courts are watching, so that's good," he said. "But you should have told me first."

"Promise."

If I kept hanging around Maggie, I didn't know how long that promise might last. To be fair, we'd found a way for Lee's missing witness to come back. Maggie would have preferred a subtle approach then me doing something out of anger. Yet the video got everyone's attention. The situation at Comaneci's buildings wouldn't go ignored for long. In a city of millions of opinionated New Yorkers, they wouldn't remain quiet. They would turn on him in a New York minute. I wanted to be there when they lit the bonfires.

"I sent a copy to the judge, along with a statement from Lorena and her son. We'll see what happens," Lee said. "Is that my Yankee shirt?"

The soft cotton gray tee shirt with Derek Jeter's number on it was too big for me, though it draped in the right places to intrigue Lee enough not to complain. Not a possessive man, Lee looked like he wanted his tee shirt back. Before we got distracted by my wardrobe issue, I needed a question answered.

"Can I ask you something about Heather?" I said as I struggled to keep Lee from pulling off the tee shirt. This stopped him cold. Nothing kills foreplay like a dead woman.

"Now?" His exasperation palpable, made me question my timing.

"One question, I promise." I crossed my heart again. "I'll even give you back your shirt right now." I began to pull up the shirt, but Lee stopped me.

"I don't think I can talk about Heather with you naked," he reassured me.

Ever since Maggie and I left Billy Pace, the revelation about Heather and Ellison nagged at me. Had he ended his affair with Julia to start up with Heather again? From what Pace said, Ellison's harassment of his sister started way before Lee had left the firm. During a time when Ellison supposedly had an affair with Lee's ex-wife. Was Ellison just a womanizer and a jerk?

"This may have to do with Julia," I warned.

This got Lee's full attention. That laser like focus he used with judges, prosecutors, and hostile witnesses fell on me.

"What?" Lee said.

I felt his body tense.

"Ellison and William Pace." I felt tentative.

"What about them?" From his pensive stare, this wasn't a topic he wanted to delve into with me.

"His sister worked at Schaeffer for several years in research and development. Billy claims that Ellison harassed her and forced her out of the company. She later committed suicide. Ellison and Pace have a contentious relationship."

"You seemed to know a lot about this." He pulled me off his lap to sit next to him. Whatever mood I tried to achieve with the tee shirt was now officially dead.

"A little redhead. She got curious about Pace and Ellison. You know her," I said.

Lee's brows furrowed.

"Yeah, I know her and her trusty sidekick. Why are you digging up stuff about Ellison?" A hardness crept into his voice.

"Well, you won't tell me anything and I don't like people showing up at my bake shop or throwing paint on me." This seemed to be my only defense.

"There is nothing to know. Ellison is an asshole. If he harassed that girl, I wouldn't put it past him. He's good at it. Heather found out the hard way," Lee said.

This time it was my turn to look at him bewildered. If it had gone bad for Heather, it had gone bad in the end, according to Pace. Unlike

Pace's sister, Deena, Heather had taken her diamond encrusted marbles and gone home.

"I guess relationships can go bad," I offered.

Lee flushed hot and his hands clenched into fists. "Relationship!" he cursed. "That self-absorbed bastard stalked her."

Stalked!

"What? No," I protested.

"Ellison terrified Heather." Lee seemed adamant in this belief.

Had Pace been wrong? He recounted numerous times Heather and Ellison were together. Never once did he give Maggie or me the impression that Heather was in fear of her life.

"How do you know?" I asked.

"She came to me. Told me what he was doing," Lee explained.

"When did you know they were even together?"

"Heather was the law clerk who worked on the litigation for Schaeffer Pharmaceuticals. Ellison's job was to represent the company. She was a beautiful girl. Ellison liked beautiful girls."

"Was this the same time Ellison had an affair with Julia?"

Lee's lips tightened, and I thought he would storm off, but he stayed. Though I knew he no longer love his ex-wife, he still cared for her. He also knew how I felt about Julia. She'd betrayed him and broke his heart. She would never get a pass from me.

"Yes, I guess. After Heather left the firm she was still in contact with me and told me what Ellison was up to," Lee confessed.

"So, you're saying she left the firm because of Ellison's affair with Julia. When Ellison dropped Julia, he tried to get back with her. Heather wanted nothing to do with him, but Ellison thought otherwise. So, you are telling me that's why she left New York. Are you sure?"

Lee shot me an incredulous look. "Of course I'm sure. I helped her leave."

"Excuse me!" I said.

"Ellison stalked her. He got mean and damn near threatening. So, I helped her leave New York," Lee said.

"Why didn't you go to the cops?"

"Heather didn't want to involve the cops. It would look bad for the firm. She just wanted to leave it all behind. I told her it was a mistake, but she wouldn't listen." He seemed to lose some of his anger.

"Is that why you take care of her mother?" I asked.

Lee nodded.

"Heather was a great girl." Lee turned away, caught up in some memory of Heather.

Yes, her death was tragic, but was Heather the girl he believed her to be?

"Ellison had lots of money and resources. Heather didn't want to be found, so she disappeared," Lee said.

"Did he stalk Julia?" I asked tentatively. Whatever dark place Lee began to turn to, my question pulled him out.

"No," he said as if that were the dumbest question I'd ever asked.

"He just stalked and harassed sweet little Heather," I said.

"Julia wasn't like Heather." He shifted uncomfortable next to me.

"She would have gone to the police."

Lee needed.

"Ellison was already having problems with his reputation. Exposing the affair would have made it worst. Even Ellison didn't want that. Afterward, she realized that Ellison went after her because of me. In his sick way, he was jealous of my relationship with Max. Once she figured that out, she hated him."

"Did she expose him?"

"No." Lee shook his head. "She thought I'd been hurt enough."

"Did you ever see Ellison harass Heather?" I asked.

"I saw the flowers, notes, and gifts he gave her. He was relentless," Lee said. "Heather was young, and impressionable. Ellison poured on the charm. At first, she was flattered, but he pushed and pushed for more. She didn't know how to say no to him."

"How could a good girl from Staten Island stand up against a man like Ellison and his money?" I said with a hint of cynicism.

I could tell he didn't like where the direction of the conversation was going, and he shifted uncomfortably on the sofa. I came to him and wrap myself into his arms.

"Sweetie, you are the hero in this. You swept in and saved the day. You got Heather from the bad man. You did exactly what she wanted. She knew you were clever and resourceful."

"What are you saying?" His voice held doubt.

I looked up at him and said, "Heather needed an exit strategy, and you were it."

CHAPTER 20

Sometime during the evening, Lee got his tee shirt back and forgave me for the video. Despite being back on team Lee, my uncertainty about Heather McLaughlin remained. Was this woman the innocent Lee remembered or the man-eater of Pace's recollection? The picture of Heather from the funeral gave me no answers. Working at a prestigious New York Law firm gave her access to a different world of money and power. From endearing herself to men like Maxfield Layng and Lee Mackenzie, Heather found her way to Ellison Schaeffer. When I met Maggie at the Blue Moon the next day, I said as much to her.

"Did you ask Lee where Heather got the money to pay for her mother's nursing home?" Maggie held out a tray of small fruit tarts to me. The Blue Moon's elaborate dessert case laid bare and needed filling.

An early morning command from Candace had me baking an assortment of desserts for the restaurant. Ever the helpful friend, Maggie made the job go a lot faster and gave us time to talk.

"From what I gathered from Lee, Heather told him she found a fantastic job and that money wouldn't be an issue. Then I dropped the Heather talk after he made that face again. The one that turns into a statue whenever I mention her." An ever-growing frustration with Lee over his unwillingness to truly see Heather sat in the pit of my stomach.

With the last of the desserts going inside the huge glass and steel display, I searched the restaurant for Rocket. He tagged along because his only other option meant time with his grandmother. The two mixed like water and oil. Love her as he might, Rocket tolerated his grandmother in small doses.

"Where's Rocket?" The telltale sign of red hair amongst the diners was nowhere in sight.

"In the kitchen with Bebe."

"Where's Candace?" My sense of panic made me scan the room for my sister.

An unlit stick of dynamite and Rocket equaled the same thing in Candace's view of my godson. The woman subscribed to the adage of children should be seen and not heard—ever. If left to Candace, my childhood would have been a silent one.

"Talking to one of the waitresses at the front. That's why Rocket is in the kitchen with Bebe." Though tiny in stature, my friend has an oversized understanding of the tentative nature of Candace's tolerance of her son.

"Candace won't forgive him for breaking loose in the dining room." The watchful eye I kept on my sister ensured peace and minimal bloodshed.

A flush of annoyance rose on Maggie's face. "How can you blame a two-year-old? And anyway, he wore a diaper."

"That diaper came fully loaded. Not a smell you want when you're trying to eat." The memory of half-naked Rocket as he dashed between tables as his mother and the wait staff tried to corral him made me smile. To him, the incident was one big game of tag.

"The little escape artist got away from me when I tried to change him. How many times can I tell Candace I'm sorry?"

"Rocket's safe. Bebe will insure he will not strip. There are bigger problems." With Candace and Rocket a room apart from each other, I turned to Maggie.

"Which one? Lee? Heather, or your rash?" A tiny finger pointed to my arm.

"No, something worse." My arm went behind my back.

"Worse than what? Lee caring for his friend's sick mother because he believed Heather to be a victim of Ellison's overactive sex drive."

"Last night, I regret putting the idea into his head. Now it's become this little worm eating at him. To question his relationship with Heather just makes him question everything."

"Is the idea that Heather blackmailed someone at the firm worrisome or that the blackmail might be the reason she's dead?"

When said it aloud, the words to what I believed Heather had done sat uneasy with me. Dead but not forgotten, I made a judgement on a woman I'd never met.

"Both. Let's go back to the bake shop. If Candace heard the word murder coming from my lips, she might do a little of her own."

The last of the desserts slipped into an empty spot before I closed the glass door. Through the late afternoon crowd, Maggie and I made our way to the Blue Moon's kitchen.

Inside, we found Rocket wearing oversized plastic gloves and pounding a steak with a spiked metal mallet. To complete the ensemble, he wore the apron Bebe used to butcher meats. The sight made his mother pause and give Bebe a concerned cock of her auburn brow. Bebe shrugged and instructed Rocket to pound harder.

"Watch this, Mom!" With all his effort, Rocket smashed down on the hapless piece of meat with the mallet.

If Rocket realized his efforts tenderized the meat, he didn't care. I know for a fact the chance to beat the crap out of something and not get into trouble made him almost giddy. Most mothers wouldn't walk away if their child wore a blood splattered apron and resembled a miniature Hannibal Lecter, but Maggie did. With Rocket out of Candace's way and under the supervision of Bebe, she treated the sight like another play date.

"Be careful, honey," were the only words of advice she gave her son. Rocket responded with a devious smile as he whacked the meat with several blows.

On the bake shop side, Maggie and I grabbed a cup of coffee from Mrs. Gonzales, who reassured me the bake shop was Ellison free.

Thankful for her watchfulness, I freshened up her bag of confectioner sugar she stashed behind the counter before going to my office.

"Why do you encourage her?" Maggie complained as she took a seat in my tiny office.

"If the worst that happens to Ellison is a sugar dusting, I'm okay with it."

"Hopefully, he won't show up again." The office chair squeaked as Maggie leaned back in her seat and sipped her coffee.

The likelihood I would never see Ellison again seemed thin. As long as Maxfield wanted to reconnect with Lee, Ellison would be there, lurking around like a pervert in a raincoat.

"Why is this happening?" I asked.

"The better question is what made Heather return to New York. Whatever made her come home got her murdered." A tiny finger went up for emphasis as Maggie made her point.

"Yeah, Sherlock."

First, cocking her head to the side and shaking it, Maggie glared at me.

"Why did she come back? Why call Lee? Somehow something changed to make her do both."

Maggie's words came out deliberate and slow as if I had trouble understanding the English language. This annoyed me, of course.

"If I could figure that out, I wouldn't need you." I stuck my tongue out at her. Then it came to me. "Ellison!"

"What if Ellison did stalked Heather? Not because he wanted his lover back, but he found out about the blackmail. Lee helps her disappear and he can't find her. Then his family sends him away. Then without warning, Heather returned and so does Ellison. The two might be connected. So, having Mrs. Gonzales throwing sugar at him might not be a great idea, Odessa."

Maggie's pointed expression did not reassure me. Not that I wanted to put Mrs. Gonzales in harm's way. How would Ellison respond with a face full of powder sugar? Did he draw the line at Guatemalan grandmothers?

"Do you think Ellison killed Heather?" The chair squeaked again as Maggie shifted in discomfort.

The image of Ellison's handsome face filled my head. My limited contact with him didn't give me much of an impression. All I had to go on was Lee and Pace's opinion of the man.

"To say Ellison has issues might be an understatement. If his own family wouldn't deal with him, what does that say? Does it all add up to murdering someone in a cheap hotel? Was Ellison that cold and calculating?" The uncertainty I felt grew. To accuse someone of being rude, obnoxious, and annoying was one thing. To say they killed someone was another.

"So far, if he did, he got away with murder." The words from Maggie sounded harsh, but true. Words that came with a warning as well, for me not to underestimate Ellison.

"Why that hotel?" The question swirled around my head with no place to land. An unlikely place for someone like Heather to stay, yet she did. Familiar with the hotel's location, I knew twenty dollars guaranteed privacy and an empty room for an hour. Then a piece fell into place. Why that hotel? Heather didn't go there to stay.

"Not to sleep or for the night. A place to meet someone?" My gut feeling said Heather needed to be off the radar when she returned to New York.

An auburn eyebrow rose as Maggie pushed the swivel chair back and forth as she sipped her coffee. In deep concentration, she stopped her motion after a time to stare up at me over her cup.

"Lee?" Maggie finally said.

"My Lee?" Did she think Lee would set up a meeting with Heather in a cheap hotel? That redheaded mind didn't work like that or at least I thought.

"Yes, your Lee. Remember, she tried to reach him the night she died and couldn't. Instead, she did the next best thing, she called you." A cheeky grin enveloped her entire face.

"No way. Lee didn't know Heather came back." The rash on my arm tingled, and I ached to scratch it. "Unless I'm sleeping with a super spy, Lee wouldn't lie about that."

"Did I say Lee knew?" A hand went up in appeasement. "What if Lee was the bait?"

Clear, unflinching blue eyes stared back at me.

The theory why Heather returned felt shaky at best. Though blackmail seemed like a powerful motive. Despite all of it, Heather trusted Lee. Had someone used him as bait to get her to return? Would Heather refuse Lee's request to return?

"How did Lee help her leave New York?" Maggie asked.

When Lee hadn't convinced Heather to stay and deal with Ellison, he put things in motion. First, he sold her parent's house on Staten Island. One of Lee's college friends, an investment banker, set up an offshore account with the money from the sale of the house. This allowed Heather to draw on the money any place she wanted undetected by those who might go looking for her. Before settling down, Heather traveled around a bit before contacting Lee. At first, she would call. Later they would leave text messages for each other to update her on the status of her mother.

"Well, she disappeared alright. There were no indications she worked at another firm or anyplace else. If she lived off the sale of her parent's house, how long could that last? That nursing home isn't cheap," Maggie said.

"Let's say she did blackmail Ellison. On what? The affair? As a married woman, Julia had more bang for the buck. Even Lee said so," I said.

"Stalking wouldn't garnish a byline in the press. However, didn't Heather have access to information about Schaeffer Pharmaceutical from the lawsuit? With that information, she might hurt someone."

"Enough for murder?" This made me wonder about Heather's actions. Heather went from being the focus of Ellison's affection, to a side piece, once Julia came into the picture. Did she figure out Ellison's true interest in Julia and waited patiently for the affair to run its course? Once she had him to herself again, what happened? Did he turn on her and move on to someone else? That saying about a woman being scorned never ended well.

"Let's not forget, Heather and Ellison were together when he started to harass Billy's sister. Perhaps, he gloated about Deena in front of Heather. That would have been a thorny pain in Ellison's side. Another embarrassment that might send him back overseas," Maggie said.

"If he was already on thin ice with his family, his harassment of Deena wouldn't help his case. How desperate would Ellison have to be to pay Heather off?" I shook my head, unsure of the answer. There were questions and more questions.

The possibility that Ellison could be a murderer and his sudden interest in Lee unnerved me. If he thought Lee would return to the firm, how would he respond? The last time, he used Julia against him to drive a wedge between him and Maxfield. What would he do this time if he believed Lee would usurp his place with Maxfield again? I doubt if another affair would work. First, I wasn't Ellison's type, suspicious and repulsed.

I was about to say as much to Maggie when the sounds of shouting stopped me. Something was happening in the front of the store—raised voices and one of them very distinct. From the sounds of rapid-fire Spanish, I feared it had something to do with my elderly barista, sugar, and Ellison Schaeffer.

Crap.

CHAPTER 21

What I expected to see was Ellison Schaeffer. What Maggie and I found instead were two angry men confronting Mrs. Gonzales and Esperanza. A Mutt and Jeff of angry fury covered in fine white confectioner's sugar. Mrs. Gonzales shouted in Spanish with her granddaughter by her side translating. The men seemed frozen at the sight of the angry grandmother, each fist filled with another dose of powder sugar to be thrown.

"You need to leave, leave right now." The pastry chef took a protective stance in front of the older woman. Uncertain if she did it to protect Mrs. Gonzales or the men before her. Either way, the girl was out matched.

"What the hell is going on?" I stood in the center of the bake shop with my hands-on hips in the best version of Candace I could muster.

"You!" The taller of the two pointed at me and then at Maggie. Though the men seemed familiar, I didn't think they came to try the Cherry Upside Down Cake. The short one charged. Before he got two steps, Mrs. Gonzales flung a handful of confectioner sugar that hit him square in his eyes. Several words in Spanish followed. Maybe it was a Guatemalan blessing or curse? The taller of the two sidestepped Mrs. Gonzales's second salvo and pushed passed his friend to get to Maggie and me. As if by instinct, we ran in the opposite direction, confusing our pursuer for the moment. When he regained his senses, he followed me. I stepped behind one of the small café tables for protection.

"What do you want?" The tiny bistro table gave me little comfort.

"Because of you and that goddamn video!" The man cursed with a slight eastern European accent.

"Lady, stop it," the shorter man begged as Mrs. Gonzales hit him again and again. He began coughing up clouds of the powdered sugar.

"Can we talk about this?" I tried to reason.

"You cost me money." The table went sailing as he tossed it like a toy. Before I could run, he caught me by my forearm in a grip so tight I thought it might snap my bone. The scream that emanated from me was unrecognizable.

Then the guy screamed in pain, too, and released me. The expression of sheer horror and pain blanketed his face as he turned to my defender. Rocket stood behind him with the metal mallet. Still dressed in the bloody apron, it made the man pause. How often would you see a 9-year-old red head dressed like the Bloody Barber of Fleet Street?

"Rocket!" The sound of Maggie's voice made me turn to see her by the doorway shared by the restaurant and the bakery with two court officers.

Distracted by the threat, I had forgotten their presence at the restaurant earlier. While Maggie and I were filling up the dessert case, one had asked about the coconut pie. Thank god Maggie remembered them being there. Frozen, they stood in awe. The place was a mess.

At the sound of his mother's voice, Rocket froze as well. With his pint size bravado gone, he dropped the mallet as if the offending weapon didn't belong to him. Enraged, the man grabbed the front of Rocket's apron. Like a slippery eel, Rocket wiggled free and out of the man's grasp and dashed behind me for protection. Whether from his mother or the man he'd tenderized, I couldn't tell.

The assault on Rocket caused the court officers to snap into action. One called for backup and the other had Rocket's attacker on the floor in minutes. Only when the snap of handcuff went on both men, did I release Rocket to go to his relieved mother.

"What were you thinking?" Maggie ran to her son and bent down to pull him into a tight hug.

"You said someone was hurting Auntie O." Not waiting for anyone, Rocket had come to my defense. I rubbed my bruised arm, bent down, and hugged him.

"Next time your granny wants to take you to the museum, call me," I said.

A few deep breaths helped my heart rate to slow down enough to make sense of what had just happened. The mentioning of the video made them Comaneci's men. How dumb could the landlord be after the uploaded video went online? At over 100,000 views, nasty comments, death threats, Comaneci was not a popular man.

Curiosity made me walk over to the men who squatted on the floor, handcuffed and awaiting transport to the nearby precinct. Angry, silent, and dusted with sugar, I didn't think this was the outcome they expected. The only time the men appeared worried was when Candace arrived. If looks could kill, she would have turned them to stone.

As one officer sat watching the men, the other got two espressos from Mrs. Gonzales. Esperanza boxed up some pastries for them to take. The officer didn't seem to care if I spoke to their prisoners, as long as I kept Mrs. Gonzales away from them.

"Why would Comaneci do this?" I asked. The men sat silent. It was clear they would give me no answers and the cops even less. This didn't stop me, of course. Fortunately for me, the officers had emptied out the content of their pockets on one of the tables. A roll of cash, two phones, and a switchblade lay dumped on one of the tables. A piece of paper that looked like a shopping list intrigued me. Clearly, it was Butt Guy's turn to do the food shopping. The style of writing appeared familiar. Mr. Butt Guy made the funniest letter a. The style that matched the writing on my van. I sneered at him.

This answered one of my questions. How they found me at the Bentley wedding was the other. Regrettably, I wouldn't get this from the Butt Guy, who did his best interpretation of a prisoner of war. His phone had answers though. My snatching up his phone garnished a flurry of curses in two languages as I found Comaneci's number in his contacts.

A finger from Maggie went up to quiet him. This got her a barrage of curses. The tirade stopped when Mrs. Gonzales walked over with a teapot filled with hot water and stared at his crotch. The court officers watched and enjoyed their coffee. At the zombie apocalypse, I wanted Maggie, Rocket, and Mrs. Gonzales by my side.

Everyone watched as I dialed Comaneci's number, except Butt Guy. His eyes were glued on Mrs. Gonzales and the teapot. The call was answered on the third ring.

"Why are you calling me, Pavel?" an angry, accented voice questioned.

"This isn't Pavel." Butt guy now had a name though the image of his blood-stained rear end would never go away.

Silence.

"Who is this, and where's Pavel?" a curt voice questioned.

"Hi, Mr. Comaneci. My name is Odessa Wilkes. I'm the owner of the O So Sweet Bake Shop in Queens, fiancé of Lee McKenzie, and uploader of videos. You might have heard of me."

Silence.

"Where's Pavel?" There was a hint of resignation in the tone.

"Now, he's at my bakes hop, but before long he'll be on his way to jail," I said.

Cursed language filled the phone. Luckily for me, Comaneci directed this at Pavel and his companion. I sensed that Pavel had taken it upon himself to threaten Maggie and me. Lee had been right, the landlord didn't need the drama.

Silence.

"You have to excuse me, Ms. Wilkes, Sometimes, we cannot pick our relatives. I am ashamed to say that Pavel is my wife's brother. The idiot with him is their cousin Roman." With his anger dissipated, Comaneci sounded almost charming.

"That's true, we can't pick our relatives, Mr. Comaneci, but it doesn't negate the fact they work for you," I said.

Silence. Comaneci liked his silences.

"I didn't send them, but you're right, it doesn't excuse what they did. Like a fool, I'd given the idiot that building to manage because he wasn't smart enough to do anything else. When the tenants started making complaints, I told him to deal with the problem and of course, he's made a mess of it. But family.... you know."

"You're blaming this on your brother-in-law?" I mocked.

"Let's say, my wife is the smartest one in that family. The idiot grew up watching American movies like Scarface and worships Jay-Z. It was either that building or finance his rap career." He mused.

I laughed because there was someone more condescending than Candace.

My bemusement didn't escape Comaneci notice. Especially when I told him Pavel wouldn't sit right for a week and his comrade resembled the abominable snowman. To heighten the level of embarrassment, I described Pavel's attacker.

"If you want my advice, fix that building and kept your brother-in-law away from it and me," I suggested.

"We had a conversation about this already. Unfortunately, he lost something in the translation." With a promise of restitution, Comaneci thanked me for my patience.

"Would you like to speak to Pavel?" I offered.

"No. When he doesn't show up for dinner, I will pretend ignorance and enjoy peace and quiet for at least one night."

I'd never thought I'd say it, I liked Comaneci.

The laughter was short-lived at the sight of a well-dressed woman walking through the front door. At the sight of the two men cuffed on the floor, she stopped. Behind them, the court officers chatted with Mrs. Gonzales. Still dressed like a mini butcher, Rocket sat and ate cookies with his mom.

"Hi," I squeaked out like an apology for the carnage before her.

Dressed in a smartly tailored suit, tasteful jewelry, and designer shoes, the woman looked out of place. She did a poor job at covering up her uneasiness. The disarray of the shop didn't help.

"Hello, Ms. Wilkes?" she said as she made her way toward me, carefully not to step in the spilled sugar. Still on the phone with Comaneci, the sight of the woman made me lose my train of thought for a moment.

"Mr. Comaneci, I appreciate your apology, but I have a business to run." Once again Comaneci apologized and promised the tenant situation would resolve itself soon. I thanked him and said goodbye.

"I'm sorry to interrupt..." The woman couldn't keep her eyes on Pavel, who sat on his side. Now in the dog house with Comaneci, his bluster faded. He'd been taken down by a 9-year-old with a meat mallet and kept in his place by a grandmother with a tea pot.

"I'm Ms. Derry, from Cambridge Medical."

The well-dressed woman held out a hand to shake, while keeping her distance from the mess. Before I had a chance to take it, a police van pulled up outside. It took some time before everything settled down once the two men were hauled away. Rocket went back to the kitchen to pound meat. Esperanza began to clean up the front of the shop as Mrs. Gonzales made a new pot of coffee.

A few tables away, Maggie took a seat as Ms. Derry and I sat down to talk. An associate had one of my cakes at a wedding and thought I would be a good fit for her event. Tired of the usual Manhattan bakery she utilized, Ms. Derry wanted to try someone new and that's where O So Sweet came in. I appreciated anyone who'd went out of their way to discover the shop and told her as much.

"There's an upcoming event. It's a little last minute, but I'm sure you can handle it," she reassured. I didn't need her reassurance but appreciated it anyway. They needed a cake for an anniversary party for Cambridge Medical Board of Directors. Money was no object and because it was short notice, she'd pay double the price. That got my attention. The details were hashed over for at least fifteen minutes before we settled on a design and price. By the time Ms. Derry left, she seemed pleased and insisted I delivered the cake in person. The opportunity to expand my business to a bigger market was an opportunity I wouldn't miss. Considering how the day began, I was out ahead.

If Comaneci held true to his word, the tenants would get their repairs and better management. If my work with Cambridge Medical worked out, I could have a whole new slew of high-end customers. For the longest time in a while, the rash on my arm remained silent.

CHAPTER 22

With the arrest of Pavel Zelenko, the tenants of the LaGuardia Apartments could sleep easy for a while. With that issue resolved, this left the file Billy Pace gave us. Five inches thick, it was no light reading. As to where to examine it was the other dilemma. At home, Lee would ask questions. As would Maggie's husband, Roger. That left Frank McAvoy and his office in Hicksville. The only detective agency whose owner didn't like asking questions. Frank could walk pass a corpse with a knife stuck in its chest. Unless he got paid, he didn't care.

"Hey, Frank, the Yankee's called. They got your manhood in a jar and wanted to know if you wanted it back," I said as I came through the front door of the storefront office.

Frank stood by Maggie as she sat at her small desk. Coffee cup in hand, he still wore the same buzz cut and burgundy sports jacket from the seventies. The scowl on his face told me he wasn't happy to see me.

A groan emanated from Maggie as she dropped her head to her desk. "Not today, please."

"I can go get them." I dug into my pocketbook and pulled out a small change purse. "They'll fit."

"For Christ's sake, Odessa." Maggie glared up at me.

An unusual shade of red colored Frank's face as he pointed a stubby finger at me. When he struggled to find the words to condemn me, he turned on his heels and went to his office.

"At this rate, you may never make it to your wedding," Maggie warned.

"Why do people keep saying that?" I said with genuine concern.

"Leave Frank alone, please. For the sake of my sanity." With her hands clasped together in prayer, she begged.

I gave a halfhearted promise not to torture him before taking a seat across from her. She set out Deena Pace's files before me. As was her method, Maggie organized the information to address some questions.

"What am I looking at?" Several sticky notes with Maggie's handwriting decorated much of the file.

"These are emails Pace's sister had with Schaeffer Pharmaceuticals, especially with Ellison." Maggie pointed to a stack of papers covered in sticky notes.

It took some time to go through over fifty pages of emails. Most of them started off as innocuous correspondence between coworkers. An employee speaking to supervisors about her concerns about a current project. As time passed, Deena Pace's concerns intensified. Without warning, the tone changed as did the civility of the correspondence. The company responded by removing her from the research team. This didn't stop Deena, she wouldn't let it go. One could mistake it for passion or paranoia.

One particular email got my attention. A poignant, heartfelt email described her unfailing loyalty to the company and her fifteen years of services. Then the unthinkable happened. One of Deena's emails leaked to the public.

"The company turned on her, even though they couldn't prove who leaked the email." A report detailing an internal investigation on leaks resulted in Deena losing most of her privileges.

At some point, Ellison got involved. Not only did he instigate her removal from the team, they pushed her out of the department. The move resulted in a cut in salary and duties. As an experienced and trained researcher, they reduced Deena to a job counting lab rats.

Another file slid before me.

"These are her personal records. A preexisting condition of depression appeared in her file when she first started. This protected Deena under the Heath Care Act, so they couldn't just get rid of her."

"They would make accommodations for her," I said.

When I first was diagnosed with an anxiety disorder, I wondered who would hire me after I lost my job. Like Deena, I had the choice to disclose or not disclose my pre-existing illness. If I did, I would be protected under federal law. Deena disclosed early in her career.

"What accommodation?" Maggie said sharply. "If you mean, take you away from the job you love and turn it into a hostile working environment, Ellison saw to that. After a while, it affected her work. Notes of tardiness, anti-social behavior, and poor work performance cropped up in her file. Odessa, they pushed and pushed, and it killed her."

"The Pace family had a case with these emails. The emails from Ellison were the worst because he made them personal." This made me wondered why the family settled the suit so quickly.

"Without the wherewithal to defend herself from a person like Ellison, what chance did she have?"

"Because the company belonged to his family, no one stopped him. Each vicious email attacked her loyalty, motives, and mental stability." Whatever I felt for Ellison had solidified into distain.

"Before this, all her personal evaluations were excellent. She was thorough, professional, and she knew her stuff. From what I discovered, she seemed like a nice person. She volunteered, gave to charity, cared for her troubled brother all his life, and looked out for her parents. What they did to her was criminal." Maggie flipped through the pages. Deena had collected her entire life history at Schaeffer Pharmaceutics in those files.

Across the small desk, our eyes met, both measuring our mutual contempt for all things Schaeffer. Deena Pace believed she had the best job in the world until it turned on her. Whatever happened, the fallout remained, and Billy Pace wouldn't let it go.

"The research team they kicked her off developed a series of drugs that completed its clinical trials and just received approval to sell it. The company spent millions on R&D and marketing and Deena wanted to rock the boat. They ignored her."

At some point, Deena lost faith someone would take her seriously. As a researcher and scientist, meticulous to a fault, she recorded her tumultuous relationship with Schaeffer Pharmaceuticals.

"Why collect this stuff?" The pages of information flipped through my fingers, each one damaging evidence of Schaeffer's treatment of Deena Pace. Despite all of it, there was something missing.

Maggie sat back in her chair and closed her eyes. Had she come to the same conclusion I had? Though the information in the files were hurtful, it wouldn't stop Schaeffer from selling the drugs. At best, it only would have reinforced the Pace's family's wrongful death suit against the company.

"There has to be more," I said, stirring Maggie from her contemplation.

"There is," Maggie said and flipped through several sections of the file. "Deena was a researcher and she knew her words meant nothing on their own. There's a hole in this file that points a gun at Schaeffer. She hints at it several times, so where is it?"

The thick file stared back at me with answers I couldn't see. From what I read, Deena's paranoia grew before her death. She didn't trust anyone and thought the company was out to harm her. Whether this was her illness or the truth, it was hard to tell. Putting myself in her shoes, would I leave around something that could bring down a company like Schaeffer in my apartment for anyone to find? Someone like her brother. That would only make him another victim of Schaeffer. He didn't have the background or resources to take on the likes of Schaeffer. Deena's smoking gun was something else.

"She loved that company. At any time, she could have gone public but didn't," Maggie said. "Bringing it down wasn't her goal. Saving it was."

"What's the point of having evidence if you don't use it?" My eyes fell back to the various piles of papers.

Without warning, Frank burst through his office door. His mouth thinned at the sight of me and twisted into a sneer. He stood there waiting for me to say something. I smiled instead. Frank flinched.

"Odessa," Maggie warned from beneath her breath.

Incredulous at her accusation, she assumed I'd forgotten my promise not to torture her boss. I couldn't win.

"Cross my heart and hope to die, I will never bring up the Yankees and Bronx again. In fact, I will move your seat at the reception so it's closer to the bar." This declaration didn't get me the response I wanted.

Frank frowned.

"Why?" Disbelief oozed from his gravelly voice.

In a battle of wits, he was defenseless. Frank brought safety scissors to a knife fight and wondered why he lay bleeding on the floor. I said something else instead.

"Because, I should stop acting like I'm two. You're Maggie's boss and I value our friendship." The sincerity almost made me choke.

"Friends?" Frank's confusion and doubt played on my guilt.

"We are. And I respect you as a detective," I said. The eye roll Maggie threw at me didn't help. Okay, I laid it on a little thick, but only because Frank was fragile.

"Geez, thanks." Frank's face softened and blushed.

Frank walked over to us and pulled up a seat at Maggie's second-hand desk. A Goodwill find that wasn't big enough for the two of us, let alone Frank. As he leaned his bulky frame on it, he pointed to the file in front of Maggie. The desk creaked in protest.

"As much as you gals think I can't tie my shoelaces, I looked at these here files." Frank cut a withering stare in my direction as I tried to wipe the look of surprise from my face.

"This Deena girl didn't want to leak this information. But she wanted the company to stop selling those drugs. Who was she, but some lowly researcher? She needed someone who'd make them listen and still protect the company."

"What are you saying, Frank?" Despite my teasing, Frank used to be a New York City Detective for over 25 years. He had to learn something, besides where the best donut shops where.

"I once worked at a precinct where some cops were acting out, doing things they shouldn't. A few of us wanted to stop it. Going to the press was out of the question. We couldn't burn down our own house. Instead, one of us passed it to I. A., Internal Affairs. Well, a few months go by and things changed."

"What did they do?" I asked.

Frank shrugged. "Some transferred to other precincts, others retired." Frank put an emphasis on the word retired.

"You policed yourself," Maggie added.

"How would Deena police the company? She'd gone to the higher ups, and they ignored her," I added.

Frank shook his head as if disappointed in us.

"The law firm handling the suit. Their job is to protect the company from others and themselves. What if this Pace girl sent your smoking gun to them?" Frank's hairy brows went up in affirmation.

For the first time in forever, Frank left me speechless. Would Mercier, Koenig and Layng keep Schaeffer Pharmaceutics in-check? Maxfield might and could.

"What if Deena goes to the only people who might have some influence over the company? So, she goes there and then what happens?" I questioned.

Frank and I turned to Maggie.

Maggie flipped through a few pages.

"After her dismissal from the company, within days, Deena kills herself. The drugs remained on the market but then it's abruptly pulled two weeks later."

"Why would they do it then? With Deena gone, so was the problem," I said.

"Maybe because someone else had the files and knew how to use them. Someone less loyal than Deena," Frank said.

"The firm?" I said.

Maggie shook her head slowly, as if coming to a realization.

"No, from the industry news reports, the recall was abrupt and sloppy. As if done in a hurry. Does that sound like Maxfield's law firm?"

"No, if they did their jobs right, no one would have even noticed it was gone. They would have worked the narrative to their favor." I said. Men like Maxfield were fixers more than anything else. They put out small fires before they burned your house down.

Frank tapped his index finger to his head and said. "Maybe someone put a gun to their head they couldn't ignore."

CHAPTER 23

The idea that Deena had information that might adversely affect Schaeffer Pharmaceuticals beyond her personal issues with them, made me wonder. During that time, Deena had dared to take on a company, Lee's quit, and his marriage imploded. In the middle of this, Heather McLaughlin left Mercier, Koenig and Layng. Maggie called it the perfect storm of interconnections.

"Two weeks after Deena's death, Heather leaves her job in the middle of the Schaeffer Pharmaceuticals lawsuit. Suddenly, they settled with a slap on the wrist, but then Schaeffer pulls the drug abruptly from the market when they didn't have too. Why?" Maggie asked.

"Maybe Frank is right. Someone put a gun to their heads. Someone who gave them no choice," I countered.

"Who?" Maggie posed the question, but I sensed she had an answer already, as did I.

"If Frank is right, Deena goes to Mercier, Koenig and Layng with her problem. There she met Heather, law clerk to the lawyers working on the lawsuit. A sweet friendly face willing to help."

Maggie nodded.

"Let's not forget this is during the time Ellison has an affair with Julia," she said.

This time I nodded.

"I'm Heather," I point to myself. "Someone gives me damaging information on Schaeffer and my boyfriend is doing his friend's wife. This will not make me happy."

"Would it hurt you enough to turn on him with that same information and his family's company?" Maggie asked.

I nodded vigorously. If Ellison played me for the fool the way he did Heather, I would try to make his life a living hell.

"That nursing home her mother is in is very expensive," Maggie said with a speculative tone. "Even after the sale of her family house wouldn't account for the cost. I can't find any other history of employment for Heather. Unless she's working under another name or..."

"She doesn't have to work," I said as it made me wonder more about Heather.

The chances that Deena gave whatever information she had to Heather seemed thin. Even more so that Heather used the information to her benefit. Would either woman do that? How desperate was Deena? How hurt was Heather?

"After Deena's suicide, if Heather had the information, what does she do with it? Watch Ellison flaunt his affair with Julia? On a clerk's salary and with an ailing mother what choices did she have?" Maggie asked.

I sighed in contemplation of those questions. Once again, Frank had the answer.

"If it were Maggie, she'd take it to the police five minutes after she realized what it was," Frank said, giving his prodigy a disappointed look. Then he turned in my direction. "You, on the other hand, you would make this Ellison guy walk naked during the perp walk and post billboard signs of the pharmaceutical wrong doing."

"Are you saying I'm vindictive and wouldn't want justice?" I feigned a hurt expression.

"Oh, you both would want justice, you just want yours wrapped in shame and humiliation," Frank added.

I couldn't argue with that, so I didn't. The truth was, it depended on the kind of person. Who Deena and Heather were.

I left Maggie and McAvoy Investigation late that afternoon. Though Deena's file hinted at Frank's smoking gun, we didn't know what it

150

was. Did we believe Heather had it? We did. She'd left Mercier, Koenig and Layng soon after. Then she left New York City, leaving her life and her mother behind.

My drive home had my head filled with questions. Was the thought of Heather blackmailing Schaeffer Pharmaceuticals plausible? Sweet Heather of Lee and Maxfield's memory. If Ellison dumped her for Lee's wife, how would she react? Would she be the woman scorned I'd imagined?

Those thoughts carried me through the front door to my house. Inside, I found Lee sleeping on the couch, papers on his chest and eyeglasses pushed up on his head. The cat sat on one of the armrest snoring. Since Lee needed the rest, and the cat wasn't attacking him, I left them alone.

I took the time to take a shower, do a load of laundry, and think about a late dinner. By the time I had something on the stove, Lee shuffled into the kitchen looking like he'd lost a fight with a pillow. His hair stuck up in several spots, a red mark decorated the side of his face he slept on.

"Sleep well?" I asked as I put the cover over a lid of sautéed onions and mushrooms.

Before answering, he yawned and stretched.

"One minute, I'm reading a brief and the next I smell food."

He took a seat at the small kitchen table, propped his head on his fist to stare at me as I cooked.

"You look nice domesticated," he mused.

I laughed.

"Well, since you fired the maid and the cook, you just have me." I finished the mushroom gravy with a roux of flour and water and added more seasoning before I left it to simmer. Lee watched for a few more minutes before joining me at the stove. The aroma of the baked chicken and roasted vegetables coming from the oven filled the kitchen.

"You shouldn't have let me sleep so long," he said in between another yawn.

"Trust me, you needed it," I said and tried to push down his spiking hair with no luck. "Did you work this hard for Maxfield?"

His lips tightened for a moment. As if he stopped himself from saying something he might regret he sat back in the chair. The tension gone.

"It was different. Yeah, there were long hours, but it didn't feel the same," he said finally.

He didn't have to tell me why. The faces of the LaGuardia Apartments tenants were etched in his brain. Each name cemented in his heart. He fought for all of them, instead of some nameless corporation worried about their bottom line.

A nod in understanding seemed enough for him. His time at Mercier, Koenig and Layng was a lifetime ago. Until Heather's death, he showed little regret about his decision to leave. The same way I'd walked away from a job in advertising, I'd chosen a smaller, saner life.

"Why don't you do something with this?" I gestured to his wayward hair and crumbled clothing. "And I'll put dinner on the table."

With a quick kiss on the cheek, Lee headed upstairs. It didn't take long to finish the rest of the meal and put it on the table. Lee returned, changed out of his suit and into sweats and combed hair. He took his usual seat at the table, just as I placed his plate of food down. Before long we were eating, talking about the wedding, the kilts Candace refused to let him wear to the wedding, and the cat.

"He likes you more than me," Lee said in between bites of food.

The cat sat by my foot curled up on itself and purring softly. Could I explain why an animal I didn't particularly like or want was my new bestie? No. It made itself comfortable in our house, with no plans of leaving. I could only offer Lee a shrug.

"Maybe it's the chicken livers I cook for him." My mischievous smile made him laugh. I stared down at the cat who looked like a breathing rug. His large head turned up as he opened his eyes to gaze up at me. No doubt, the words chicken livers woke him. Then a question I'd always meant to ask but hadn't popped into my head.

"What's its name?"

From the mystified expression on Lee's face, he hadn't a clue either.

"Mr. Jimenez always called him the cat." Lee shrugged.

"It should have a name," I insisted.

The cat meowed in agreement and shifted its position for a better view of me.

"What should I call you?" I asked. This was a stupid question, but it seemed impolite not to ask. "Don't worry, I'll think of something."

This seemed to appease it as it returned to its curled-up position and went back to sleep. I looked up to find Lee overcome with ripples of laughter.

"You'll see, it will be a great name." I said playfully as we returned to our meal.

After dinner, the dishes, and some television, Lee and I made our way to bed. His nap earlier in the day put him in an amorous mood. Since Heather's death, the drama of the LaGuardia Apartments, and planning the wedding, our love life had taken a hit. It was nice to get back to ourselves.

The familiar scents and sounds of him. The way he caught his breath at the last. Like a man lost, he found his way back to me when I thought he'd forgotten. We'd allowed the world to come between us and it cost us our hard-fought intimacy.

"I love you," I whispered in his ear as he lay beside me trying to gather himself. He pressed his lips to my neck, and I felt his smile.

"Will you marry me?" he asked as he rolled to his side and pulled me to spoon with him.

"I think you've asked me that already." I felt sleepy and satisfied.

"Did you say yes?"

This made me giggle, but then I stopped.

"Is that your hand?" I asked.

"No," he said with a kiss to the neck.

Sometime later, he fell into a deep sleep. Necessity pulled me out of bed and heading toward the bathroom. I found the cat just outside our bedroom door looking non-plus. It didn't so much meow at me but did that clicking sound when it seemed displeased.

"He has parts you don't, so get over it," I said as I stepped over him. From the upstairs landing, I noticed a light coming from downstairs. After a quick trip to the bathroom, I made my way to the first floor to find that Lee had left a light on in his office.

Inside, a table lamp next to Lee's chair illuminated the tiny room. Everything from his old college law books, to his current cases, the place remained cluttered with bits and pieces of Lee's life. A personal space I'd conceded to him when he first moved in with me.

"Geez, one day you'll disappear in this place and never come out," I said to no one in particular.

The cat interrupted my critique of Lee's office with his silent arrival. Without invitation, the cat stepped on piles of paper and a stack of books to take a seat in Lee's chair. The trilling sound coming deep from within him made him sound fussy.

"You haven't killed Lee in his sleep, have you?" I questioned.

The cat made a huffing sound before it purred softly. I took this as a confirmation he hadn't smothered Lee in his sleep. Pleased by its less murderous attempts at my fiancé, I rubbed its head vigorously.

It purred in pleasure. When I stopped, it went for the next best thing, an open cardboard box on the table. Its big head almost pushed it off.

"Easy there, Samson," I said, picking up the box before it fell.

Inside, I noticed it held several photographs of Lee and other familiar faces. His younger self stared back at me. A face free of regrets and possibilities. A small twinge of guilt hit me as I took out the photographs and flipped through them. Normally, I would never bother anything in the room. My discomfort from this intrusion waned when one picture caught my full attention.

"This is interesting," I said to the cat.

The cat made a series of twills, chirps, and meow sounds. Voicing his displeasure of my ignoring him.

A snap shot of an office Christmas party. Not surprising, at the center of the group stood Maxfield. Like satellites to his sun, stood Lee and Ellison. The blond woman next to Lee was a smiling Julia. Beautiful, duplicitous Julia, who would destroy her marriage for the likes of Ellison. All of them seemed happy, clueless of the pending disaster that would befall them.

What caught my attention, standing a few feet away was Heather. Her attention locked on the people before her. The tight line of her lips and the cold set of her stare didn't seem warm and fuzzy. Was that look for Ellison or Julia?

"My money's on Ellison."

The cat meowed in agreement.

"If looks could kill, his body parts would be in several states."

Again, the cat agreed.

I returned the rest of the photographs to the box, but kept the one with Heather, turned off the light, and left the room. Before going back upstairs, I put the picture inside my pocketbook, with plans to show Maggie. I hoped Lee wouldn't miss it. If he did, maybe I'd have an answer to the question that troubled me.

Who was Heather McLaughlin really?

CHAPTER 24

My Aunt Renne always had a saying about my sister, Candace. How she could recognize the woman she'd be by the child she was. Growing up with her, Candace controlled, bullied, and dictated much of my life. Nothing much has changed since then. My questions about Heather might be answered the same way. Who knew her better than the people she grew up with? The need to find out had Maggie and I visiting Staten Island.

"How did you find them?" Maggie asked as we headed toward the dress shop.

"The guest book people signed at Heather's funeral. Lee had it. I just matched it up with the most likely candidates," I replied.

With a quick computer search by Maggie, we found Becky and Martha Rafferty. The women I remembered at the service. Their presence and behavior intrigued me. Two of the few mourners who looked like they belonged there.

Becky ran the dress shop on Staten Island once owned by her mother. The shop sat on Richmond Hill Street in a commercial strip sandwiched between a nail salon and coffee shop.

Maggie and I walked through the front door, not knowing what to expect. The door chimed as we entered. We found Becky Rafferty hanging up several dresses on a rack. Rich, dark brown hair cut short in a bob, framed an oval and pleasant face. Large brown eyes stared back at me for an awkward moment.

"Morning, ladies." In an instance the weirdness disappeared as Becky morphed into a seasoned sales person when she came to greet us.

"Hi." The cheery tone Maggie conveyed counteracted some of the uneasiness.

"Have we met?" Becky's brown eyes scrutinized mine.

"At Heather McLaughlin's funeral," I admitted. There was no need to lie about it.

Her eyes widen in recognition as a croaky laugh followed.

"Why can't I find relief from that witch?"

Becky's response surprised me.

"Sorry, but since the funeral, I can't sell a dress without someone bringing up Heather."

"Why did so few people attend?" I said without thinking. "I remembered you because how upset your mother was."

"In all honesty, Heather didn't have many friends. I hate to admit it, but my mother made me go. The woman could guilt the devil out of hell." Becky chuckled.

"Why didn't you want to go?" Maggie asked.

The smirked that formed on Becky's lip told me she considered this a foolish question.

"If you have to ask, then you didn't know Heather." Becky's eyes narrowed on me. "Why were you there?"

"The man with me used to work with her a long time ago. In fact, he arranged the funeral."

"The one with the glasses, right?" Her smile turned wicked. "Tell me he didn't sleep with Heather?"

"No," I replied, waving my hands back and forth. "But it didn't stop him from playing the fool for her."

Becky's sardonic laughter filled the tiny shop. "Now that sounds like Heather."

"So, you weren't close?" Maggie asked as her attention fell on a rack of silk tops.

"Grew up next door and got along well enough. Our moms were best friends, but Heather and I didn't follow that route." Becky held up a beautiful emerald green silk blouse for Maggie.

"Nine-year-old boy." Maggie shook her head in disappointment.

"At the funeral, you didn't seem thrilled to be there." I read the shifting mood in Becky's face.

"Being at her funeral, I felt like a hypocrite considering how Heather ended our friendship," Becky said.

"What happened?" Maggie questioned as she pulled a plain gray speckled cotton blouse from the rack. The selection made Becky shake her head in disapproval.

"Heather and her mom argued a lot. The girl had dreams of being an actress, the whole Broadway and Hollywood thing. Like my mom, Heather's wanted her to be practical and get a skill she could fall back on. Mrs. McLaughlin wouldn't support her dreams unless she went to school. So, Heather ended up being a law clerk and hated every minute of it. When she found Broadway didn't need another cute girl from Staten Island that degree came in handy."

Without warning, Becky took the shirt from Maggie, grabbed a soft golden one from the same rack. The color brought out the highlights in her red hair. Pleased with the selection, Maggie went in search of a mirror.

"After that, I wouldn't see her for weeks. Then she pops up at my door wanting help with her wardrobe. Though she hated being a law clerk, she liked the atmosphere, the style, and the money. Heather didn't want to dress like one of those bridge and tunnel girls, with big hair and too much makeup." From the expression on Becky's face she didn't appreciate the reference.

"Did you help her?" I asked.

"Maybe I thought we could reconnect." Becky's hopeful expression didn't last long.

"Did you?" I wondered.

"Once I did my Pretty Woman thing on her, she didn't need me anymore. Trust me, I got the hint, fast." Becky sighed.

"Sounds like a wonderful girl," I mocked.

"The dream was to become famous. Don't misunderstand, Heather had talent, but so did thousands of other girls in this city and anyone with a bus ticket."

Becky eyes glistened, and she turned away for a moment.

"When we were younger, we'd watch those old black and white movies, where all the women were beautiful and strong. By the end of the movie, they got the guy and the happy ever after. Heather loved Joan Crawford. A woman who reinvented herself time and time again. That was Heather."

"Crawford was miserable and died alone." I remembered a vague history of the actress.

"Well, so did Heather," Becky said with bemused certainty.

There was nothing I could say to that.

"Sounds like she changed a lot," Maggie said.

"In a way, not much. Heather wanted more than her parents could give. More than what a law clerk earned. It used to frustrate me how she complained so much, like other people were keeping her down."

Becky's frustration played out with her rearranging several garments on the same rack. She quickly stopped, as if realizing what she was doing.

"When we were kids, one day I thought it would be cool to have a lemonade stand, so I asked Heather to help me. It was hot and we were doing our best but not much traffic on our block. At the end of the day Heather rips on me how stupid the idea was and how we wasted our time. So, the next day, I set up myself, but it's even worse. I found out later, Heather set up a stand by the bus station without me. Getting all the commuters coming from Manhattan before they came down our block."

"Industrious," Maggie said.

"Treacherous, more like it. But that was Heather, saw an opportunity and took it."

"Well she hid that side of her well." This made me think of the men who surrounded Heather. Fooled by her ability to play the role they wanted to see.

"The minute she started that job, things changed. The clothes, attitude, and the men. No one around here was good enough anymore. Every now and then a fancy car would drop her off like yesterday's mail. Then there were the little gifts, a ring here, a designer bag there. A weekend someplace warm and expensive." Becky shook her head.

"Ellison," I cursed beneath my breath.

"So, she was happy?" Maggie questioned.

"For a while. Then her mother got sick and Heather barely managed. My mom helped but Mrs. McLaughlin needed more. When she went into the nursing home, it broke everyone's heart. It shook Heather to the bone. The place she put her in wasn't the best, but it worked. My mom would visit as much as she could, but that didn't last."

"Why?" I asked.

"One day, my mother comes home crying. Heather moved her mother to another place without telling us. When I tried to talk to Heather about it, she brushed me off. Then she sold the house. After that, we never saw her again." Becky's tone hardened.

"Did something change?" Maggie asked.

Becky nodded.

"Mrs. McLaughlin's illness started it. Heather started talking about selling the house and moving to the city. Considering she could barely manage with her own salary, a move like that would be too expensive. Manhattan isn't cheap. Then I suspected it was that new boyfriend of hers. I was wrong about that."

This got Maggie and my full attention. Did Heather expect Ellison to be her sugar daddy? Or had she found another way?

"Suddenly, he stopped coming around. Heather's mood changed and not for the best. She didn't say much but she didn't have too. The gifts stopped and so did those weekend trips. She started to blame everyone again. Her mother, the boyfriend, and even the place she worked."

Becky leaned against a small display stand and crossed her arms. Head bowed, her hesitation made me worried she wouldn't continue. But then I realized, she had come to an uncomfortable truth about her childhood friend. That they were never friends. Heather's death guaranteed they would never be friends. When she did look up at us, she had the look of a woman resigned to this truth.

"One day she'd come home in a taxi, something she never did. I was on the front porch of my house talking on the phone when I saw her drive up. I don't know what made me ask, maybe that look on her face. I ended the call and went down to meet her on the sidewalk in front of her house. We weren't on the best of terms, but we were still talking. I asked about her mother."

I felt bad for Becky. She struggled to remain connected to a woman who wanted to cut all ties. A woman who saw her life on Staten Island as an impediment to her happiness. Friendship with Becky wouldn't make her happy, so why try?

"She gave me this kind of secretive smile, like she knew something I didn't. She tells me not to worry about her mother anymore. That everything was good, even better than good."

Maggie cocked her head to the side, like a question was stuck in her head she had to get out.

"Better how?" I asked.

"Like someone gave her the keys to the city," Becky replied with certainty. "Like fate had dropped something in her lap that solved all her problems."

Maggie and I stared at each other, knowing what this meant. Had Deena gone to Mercier, Koenig and Layng and met an unhappy Heather?

"Did she give you any idea what it was?" Maggie asked.

Becky shook her head.

"Whatever it was, it wasn't hers first. Just like the lemonade stand, she took it and made it hers."

CHAPTER 25

Before I put my life on the line with Lee, I needed to know if this was a rabbit worth chasing. Questions needed answers. First, how damaging was Deena's information? Second, did that information finds its way into Heather's greedy little hands? Last but not least, did Heather use that information to blackmail Ellison and his company? The emails in the file Pace gave us between his sister and the company were only Deena's assertions.

"There's a missing bullet to this gun. The information Billy gave us only proves that Ellison was a jerk and an embarrassment to this family and company."

"To tell you the truth, I don't think Billy would know what he had. Unlike his sister, Billy barely made it out of high school," Maggie said.

Wanting to know more, we drove to the Woodside Laundromat with questions. What we found when we got there was a forlorn Mrs. Stankowski at the front door of a closed laundromat.

"I can't get in," a frail sounding Mrs. Stankowski said as we approached. As if someone had taken away her sunshine, her wizen face stared up at us filled with hope. When I yanked on the door and peered through the darkened window, a sense of dread came over me. Where was Pace?

"When was the last time you saw Billy?" With her face pressed up against the glass, Maggie searched for the missing manager.

There was a moment of confusion on the old woman's face. A crooked finger went to her lips as she thought. Then her eyes brighten.

"Yesterday, when he helped me wash a comforter."

"Has it been closed all day?" The late afternoon sun hadn't set yet as I scanned up and down the small commercial strip of stores.

If Billy wasn't there, where was he? God help him if he went after Ellison again with a new can of paint. The thought made me pull out my phone and call him. If I could stop him from doing something stupid, I would. With a quick dial of his number the phone rang, followed by an echo of another phone ringing. This happened several times before I disconnected and tried the number again. The echoes returned.

This time Maggie pressed her ear to the window. "A phone is ringing inside."

"That's Billy's phone," I said and disconnected the call.

Before I said anything else, Maggie ran past me and disappeared around the corner. Surprised by her sudden absence, Mrs. Stankowski and I stood speechless for a moment. With an offer of a weak smile, I excused myself and went after my friend. Within a few strides I caught up with her and blocked her path.

"What the hell are you doing?" I asked.

"What if Billy's hurt?"

When she tried to slip past me, I blocked her again. Despite the possibility she might be right, why run to a disaster when you could take a breath and walk? Who knows, I might need my strength to run away if that disaster chased me.

"Okay, but let's slow down," I said and put up a hand.

"Okay, we should be professionals," she replied.

This made me laugh.

"Professional! I'm a baker and you're a secretary. Unless we want to bake Billy a cake and write a polite thank you note, professionalism has nothing to do with this."

Maggie's look of hurt made me regret my words.

"I'm not a secretary." Her lips pressed into a tight frown.

"Okay, sorry, I'm nervous," I said in earnest.

"So am I, but let's do this, please." She gestured toward the back of the building as she led the way.

Sometimes, I forget that the biggest and bravest hearts come in small packages. I followed with my heart in my throat and prayed Billy was okay.

At the back of the laundromat, we found the door ajar. With her hand at the center of the door, Maggie pushed it open. In the dim light of the backroom, I saw the body of Billy Pace. The place smelled of detergent and dampness. While I hesitated to go inside, Maggie didn't. Within seconds, she was at Pace's still body checking for a pulse

"Call an ambulance, he's alive," she shouted.

"Oh my!" A mournful voice came from behind me. At the doorway, Mrs. Stankowski stood, her eyes locked on the form on the floor. Tears followed as I went to her side and guided her away from the door. To her, Billy was more than the young man who helped her with her laundry and served her tea. They were untethered souls who tied themselves to each other at a laundromat in Queens.

As I wrapped my arm around the old weeping woman, I made the 911 call.

Just as the call ended, Maggie called out.

Mrs. Stankowski stood like an anchor I didn't want to release. Inside the darken room was a crime scene I didn't want to see. The urgency of Maggie's repeated call demanded otherwise.

"Crap and double crap," I said as I released my hold on Mrs. Stankowski and went inside.

Filled with broken laundry carts, disassembled machines, and laundry soap, the only light came from two half size windows along the outer wall. The power was off. The machines lay silent in the eerie calm. Pace lay sprawled on his back and covered with an old blanket Maggie had found. By his head was a dark pool of blood. As she tended to Pace, something in the corner of the room held her attention.

"The ambulance and the police will be here soon, we don't have much time." Maggie stepped away from Billy and went to a metal shelving unit. There, she went on her knees and peered beneath it. Out from beneath the unit came a sheet of paper, which she held out.

"What are you doing?" I asked. "And stop messing around with the crime scene."

"Look at it."

"No," I protested.

"This is evidence." A sheet of paper flapped in Maggie's hand before she shoved it in mine.

"Doesn't it make you angry that someone did this to him?" Maggie's words cemented herself as Pace's pint-sized champion as she pointed past me. "When he won't be there for her."

My gaze fell on Mrs. Stankowski, who returned to her vigil at the doorway. Something in me burned. Yes, I was angry someone had denied Mrs. Stankowski of someone who cared for her. So as much as I wanted to be in my bake shop, making cakes for hapless brides, I read the paper in my hand. Then I read it again.

"An original page from Deena's file," Maggie said and pointed to a small wooden table. "Look, another page is over there."

As instructed, I went to the table and retrieved the loose paper from beneath the table.

"Maybe he had the file in his hands during the attack," Maggie said.

"The file scatters and toss around the room, and what?" As I recalled, Deena's file contained over hundreds of pages. That amount would have covered the floor in paper.

"They took it." Blue eyes stared up at me. "The attacker never noticed some papers slipped behind the shelving unit."

Had this been a repeat of Heather? Someone came in search of information and left carnage in their wake. This time, did they get what they came for or not?

"Do you think Ellison did this?" If Ellison seemed like the obvious choice, it was because I couldn't think of anyone else connected to the file.

Maggie scanned the room, taking in every detail before she answered. Did Ellison have a motive? Billy started to harass him again. Was that enough?

"Is he that crazy?" I said.

Banished from New York, Ellison returned to find his old demons haunting him again. Pace refused to make him forget about his sister and the part he played in her death. Lee remained the favorite son of a man he worshipped.

"Put the paper back. When the police come, I want them to find it," Maggie said.

Once I replaced the paper, I checked to see if we disturbed anything else in the room. On one of the narrow work tables I found the albums Pace had shown us on our first visit. The book lay opened to a page of four pictures of Deena. With only my fingertips, I pulled back the protective plastic sheet. The eyes of Deena Pace looked back at me while I peeled the photograph off the tacky page and slipped the picture into my purse. If someone asked why I took it, I couldn't say. Maybe I needed a reminder why I was doing this.

When I turned around, the smirk Maggie wore told me I'd truly joined her on the dark side. With my cell phone out, I took pictures of the small room. The police wouldn't share crime scene photos with us, no matter how nice Maggie asked.

The moment I put my phone away, the sound of a siren blared outside the door. I went outside to meet whoever came to save Pace. Mrs. Stankowski stood next to the door, hands clutched tight and a pleading expression on her wrinkled face.

"They'll save him." A promise I didn't know if they could keep, but I needed to say something.

Two emergency service workers bounded out of the ambulance, laden down with equipment and intensity. I gestured to the open back door and tried to explain what had happen. As they disappeared through the door, I stayed with Mrs. Stankowski. A few minutes later, Maggie emerged with a withdrawn and ashen face.

The police arrived a few seconds later. They conferred with the EMS workers first before coming to us. The surreal scene found a new level when the EMS workers carried Pace's unmoving body to the ambulance as Mrs. Stankowski wept.

The unreality continued when a detective who'd arrived at the scene demanded we go to the precinct to answer questions. My protest that I had a business to run fell on deaf ears. With her concern for Billy distracting her, Maggie said nothing. Our only concession was that Mrs. Stankowski should go home. What little she knew, we could elaborate on.

"What exactly do we tell them?" I asked Maggie as we walked to the car.

"It's what we are not telling them," she declared.

I threw up my hands in confusion. "What am I not telling them?"

"That Ellison Schaeffer might have attacked Billy Pace for some damaging information. Information that would affect his family company and himself," she explained.

"Why not? Don't we want that?"

"Prove it." Her pointed gaze made me scramble for an answer. All we had was a theory and accusations. None of which proved Ellison did anything except be an annoying pain.

"I hate it when you say things like that."

Still carrying the weight of Billy's attack in her eyes, Maggie seemed disheartened. "So, do I."

Before we got into the car, I pulled out my phone.

"Who are you calling?" An annoyed expression decorated Maggie's face.

"Lee," I said with a sigh.

"Why?"

"Because, I promised him if I ended up at a precinct, I had to call him."

"Why?" Auburn brows furrowed in confusion.

"Would you want me talking to the police with an unchecked mouth?"

The smile came from understanding and adoration at Lee's forethought.

"A good thing you're marrying him," she teased.

Only Maggie could find the time for humor at a crime scene.

"Oh, shut up Sherlock and get in the car."

CHAPTER 26

Three hours at the precinct tested my patience and my sanity. Though not a suspect, the investigating detectives asked us the same questions repeatedly. Did they have ADD? Yes, we knew Billy Pace. How long? Not long. Why didn't I press charges against him when he threw the paint? What's a file have to do with anything? Lee's presence didn't help our situation. Who brings a lawyer if they had nothing to hide?

"What time did you arrive again?" Detective Pena asked me for the fifth time. A stone-faced Lee sat next to me. No doubt checking his notes for when he'd cross-examined me later. One desk over, Maggie sat, arms crossed with a scowl on her face. The detective, an officer named Pickett treated her like she might break into hysterics at any moment.

"We got several drug arrests on him," Pickett informed as if this explained everything.

"Three years ago. Now he works at the Woodside Laundromat for almost two years. The supportive housing he lives at does random drug testing. If he came up positive, they would toss him out," Maggie said with a deliberate tone she often used with her sometimes confused husband.

"You know a lot about ole Billy," Pickett said.

Maggie pulled out one of her business cards.

"Is this real?" Pickett's almost mocking tone didn't sit well with Maggie.

"You work for a P.I.?" Never once assuming she worked for herself. "What are you, like, the receptionist?"

The last of Maggie's restraint faded.

"Why don't you ask questions about the missing file? Or if there is a motive. Yet a drug history and a few misdemeanors arrests stick out for you. Why my friend didn't press charges. Did you think we'd gone there for revenge?" Maggie said.

Pickett blinked a few times as if the idea might hold merit.

"Did you...?"

Maggie reared up from her chair. Intense blue eyes narrowed on him as her tiny nostrils flared.

"My God, Billy laid in his own blood for over twelve hours."

The detective flinched in response. When Maggie acted contrary to her appearance, most people reacted like Pickett. The same way people stared when little dogs bared their teeth. In the back of your mind your thoughts are, this little dog might hurt me. Does your embarrassment stop you from running?

"How would you know that, Mrs. Swifts?" Pena asked.

Those same blue eyes turned their heated gaze on Pena.

"Odessa called his residence to tell them of what happened. Billy didn't check in that night according to their records. By the time we saw Billy at the laundromat in the afternoon, the blood on the floor, by his head, already turned a dark maroon with evidence of serum. The rest of the blood splatter crusted over. With the ambient temperature of the room, it had to be over twelve hours."

Other detectives in the room turned in our direction.

Bewilderment blanketed Pena's face.

"Do you think a secretary knows that?" I offered politely.

"The attack happened last night because Billy locked up for the night the day before. His last customer was Mrs. Stankowski at eight o'clock, because she was always the last to leave. Billy does what he always does, he walks her home, two blocks away. The other store owners on the block will tell you this. When he comes back, someone was waiting," Maggie continued.

"What do you do again?" an opened mouth Pena asked me.

"I bake cakes," I said with smugness Lee didn't appreciate.

Pena picked up his reading glasses and his notepad. He flipped through several pages, stared at me again, and flipped more. Did he want to confirm he asked me that same question two hours ago, because he did?

"Do they do this often?" Now the detective's attention turned to a stoic looking Lee.

"More than I care to admit." Lee sighed.

"Matches up with what I got from canvassing the other store owners," a reluctant Pena said.

"What about the file?" Maggie asked.

"That could be back at his apartment," Pena replied.

"Nope. I spoke to one of the resident managers at Billy's group home while the medics worked on him. He tells anyone who'd listen about his sister, Deena. The manager checked the room, and the file wasn't there," Maggie said.

"Fine, but the neighborhood had a stream of break-ins this month. Maybe our resident's thief got bolder," Pena said.

"What? How much is fabric softener going for on the black market?" I quipped. Lee gave me a withering look.

Pena chuckled beneath his breath. "It might surprise you what thieves want in this city."

"That's an old laundromat. They use cash there," Detective Pickett interjected.

The right corner of Maggie's lips lifted into a sneer of disappointment.

"Didn't you notice the sign on the wall? In large letters, it reads, the manager can't access the money from the machines. A private company comes to remove it. Which means Billy couldn't have cash on hand," Maggie chided.

"The sign is small, you might have missed it," I said to lighten the mood.

"Listen, lady, I don't appreciate—" Pickett stopped when Maggie held up a finger at him.

"Both of you have been condescending and dismissive since I arrived. It's because of how you see me, isn't it?" Maggie accused.

Pickett and Pena were silent, too silent.

"Tinkerbelle," I said in confirmation. When Maggie's responses went beyond a simple yes or no answers, they got annoyed. To them, did her complaints sound like a female on the verge of hysterics? I deferred to her when I wasn't sure. The moment Lee showed up, they deferred to him.

"My firm uses her often," Lee explained, much to the men's surprise. Yet they took his word for it. This annoyed me, too. Were our words not good enough?

"The voice, the hair, and the whole pixie things," I mocked. Lee shifted in his seat.

"What?" Pena said, somewhat confused.

"Most men want to protect her," I said to Pena. Then I turned to Pickett. "The others think she stepped out of some fantasy game and want to do things to her they wouldn't do with their sisters."

"Hey!" an indignant Pickett exclaimed.

Lee groaned.

"Can you tell me how blood coagulates? Because she can. She can tell you the make and model of your gun." I gave him a disingenuous smile. "Her boss is a former New York City Detective, and she makes him look like an idiot."

The tight line of Pickett's mouth meant he wanted to say something, something unpleasant.

"Okay, Ms. Wilkes we get it," Pena scolded.

"We tried to tell you something, but you don't want to hear us. Like, thinking while female is dangerous." This was my cue to stand up.

From the surprise on Pena's face, he hadn't expected that. From the lack of surprise on Lee's face, he had. He stood up next to me. Lee was a man who could read my change of mood from the moon. Astute enough to recognize things could go south in a heartbeat and I would drive that bus south, breaking the speed limit.

"Where are you going?" Pena warned.

This time, I pulled out my card. "Come by for coffee and cake."

Maggie followed suit, but not before giving Pickett a scornful expression.

Lee gave a slight shake of his head. There would be no more questions.

"This means nothing." Pickett held up Maggie's card between his fingers and tossed the card into the trash. He missed Pena's rolling his eyes and the trash can.

With one last disdainful side glance, Maggie turned and walked away, with her bright red hair swishing behind her. Pickett gave her a look he wouldn't give his sister.

"Detective." Lee nodded at Pena and pulled out his business card. "Call me if you need any help."

"Counsel," Pena said and took the card.

Outside of the detective room, I wondered if we had accomplished anything. Against common sense, Maggie had been right. The police wanted a simple solution to Billy's attack. We had told what we could, and they didn't care. What was next?

As we walked out, I felt we'd accomplished nothing. Without the file, there was nothing to connect Ellison and Schaeffer Pharmaceutical. Throwing them into the mix would only increase the doubt the detectives showed. To them, it was a robbery of opportunity considering the rash of robberies in the neighborhood. As for the missing file, Billy could have trashed it for all they cared. No other motives came up. For them, crime was complicated enough, why throw in a conspiracy only a baker and a office manager believed.

All the while Lee listened and said nothing. If he thought we were giving the police half-truths and omitted other motives, he kept it to himself. The most Lee said after we walked out of the precinct was that he'd take Maggie home.

"I'll take her," I said.

"No, you go home," he insisted in a tone that didn't bode well for me.

"Why?" I asked.

Lee took a deep breath as he stood between Maggie and me as if contemplating what to do with us.

"Unlike those two detectives, I have the common sense to question you two apart. Together, you share one mind."

"No, we don't," Maggie and I said in unison.

He gave me a sarcastic laugh and headed toward his parked car.

Unlike the two detectives, he was right. We wouldn't contradict or say something derogatory against the other.

"Please, if he asks you about the file don't tell him we have a copy," Maggie said.

"Why?" I asked as Maggie checked her cell phone for messages.

"Because he might come to the same conclusion, we did about it. If anyone had information about Ellison or Schaeffer Pharmaceutical, they somehow ended up dead like Heather or hurt like Billy. Lee wouldn't like it."

"I don't like it."

"Talk about Heather, that should get him going," Maggie encouraged.

Did my best friend just ask me to manipulate my fiancé?' I didn't much care if I did it, but when someone else asks, it made me wonder.

"With Roger, I bring up his baseball card collection. When he complains about money, I get him to talk about his card collection. A very expensive hobby. This gets him on the subject on how much it means to him and we're no longer talking about how much I paid for Rocket's new sneakers," Maggie said with an air of authority.

"Is that why your marriage has lasted this long?" I asked.

"Roger can't handle the truth. Lee can't handle a lie. So, give him a little truth."

"Heather." A name that seemed to lower Lee's I.Q. and throw away his common sense.

"Heather," she replied.

"You're evil." I smiled.

"All that fairy dust. I need to cut back," she said with a straight face.

This time, I laughed.

CHAPTER 27

A few days after Billy's attack, things appeared to return to normal. The attack left him unresponsive for at least forty-eight hours. When he awoke, he remembered nothing. He never saw his assailant. When Maggie told him about his missing file, Billy became distraught. One more connection of his sister taken away from him.

The late-night integration Lee gave me after the precinct stung, but I knew the pitfalls of living with a lawyer. Maggie's drive home with him must have been interesting. She called me the moment Lee dropped her off. Little good that did me. As an expert of the Maggie and Odessa tag team, he knew how to get information. Never saying a word upon his return home, he waited until bedtime. Just when I thought he wouldn't make a big deal over it, he went in for the kill.

"You both recognized the papers from the file when you saw them at the Laundromat," Lee said as he slipped into bed.

The declaration stopped me in mid-stride as I approached my side of the bed. Since I didn't know what I should confess to, I let him continue as I slipped in next to him.

"Couldn't do that unless you'd read them. More Maggie than you. You tend not to sweat the details. Second, if you told the police, they would ask you for them." Not making eye contact, Lee slipped off his glasses and placed them on the nightstand. After slipping down beneath the covers, he turned on his side to face me.

"Is that what Maggie told you?" The rash on my arm tingled as I did my best to look surprised.

With my back against the headboard, I stared down at him. Wavy, dark brown hair reached his hazel eyes. The darkening circles beneath them pulled at my guilt for giving him something more to worry about. Whatever he'd been in the middle of, he dropped it to come to the precinct to save me. This made me susceptible to him.

"Drop this, Odessa. Stay away from Billy Pace and his vendetta against the Schaeffers."

Surprised by the terseness of his tone, I took a beat to remember the last time Lee spoke that way. It was last week. Without complaint, I complied and instructed my sister to stop calling him about his tuxedo fitting. This command was different. Like raw meat, Lee waved the directive in front of me and waited for my reaction.

"Don't get involved with Maxfield Layng, since we're dictating what we should do," I complained in a huff.

"That's different," Lee said as he sat up.

"How?" Heat rushed to my face as I glared back at him. "Because they speak nice, dress well, and smile when they insult you."

"Billy Pace could be dangerous," he shot back.

My indignation found a new level. Smug elitism didn't fit into Lee's makeup and seeing it on him added fuel to my anger.

"The worst Billy ever did was throw a bucket of paint. Why don't we list the crimes that old firm of yours might have committed with Schaeffer Pharmaceuticals?"

"Alleged crimes!" Lee snapped back. Inches apart, I could see the flecks of green in his hazel eyes, bloodshot as they were. He was in full lawyer mode and didn't flinch.

"Is that what your conscience tells you, sweetheart? Because mine tells me, Billy finding out the truth about his sister and what Ellison and your Maxfield might have done to her seems more honest."

There it was, the dirty truth about why we went to the laundromat to meet Billy Pace. Why we went back a second to confirm a theory about Ellison and Lee's old firm. Why we fueled Billy's paranoia with paranoia of our own.

Lee was about to respond when a harsh hissing sound got our attention. A blur of hair and fury jumped on the bed. Beautiful oblique eyes narrowed on Lee as the massive cat came toward us. Its rage directed at Lee, the cat stepped between us. When Lee tried to push the cat away, the attack happened in a flash. The cat seemed to double in sizes as it arched its back, flattened its ears, and took a meaty wipe at Lee's outstretched hand.

"Shit!" Lee drew back his hand, but not quickly enough. Blood, cursing and escaping seemed the only thing on his mind as he hopped out of bed.

Without thinking I grabbed the cat who seemed intent on finishing the job.

"Bad cat!" The thing struggled in my arms. It was like holding a hairy sack of potatoes. As if a switch had flipped, the angry ball of fur relaxed in my arms, purred and nuzzle my neck.

"What the..." Lee glared at us both.

There I sat, stroking the cat as it licked its paw, content in its victory. To Lee, it may have seemed like I condone the behavior. My stroking stopped.

"You're bleeding," I said and pointed to the wounded hand.

"No kidding." With his hand held to his chest, he snarled back at the cat.

"Let me see."

Hazel eyes danced between me and the cat. I put the cat down and watched it saunter to the edge of the bed. Never once looking at Lee, it circled a few times before settling down to doze.

"Bad cat," I said, but my heart wasn't in it.

Convincing Lee to let me treat him required more effort. I retrieved the first-aid kit from the bathroom. With a little antiseptic and a heartfelt apology, the lines between his eyes softened.

"Let me read the file," he said as I placed a Band-Aid on his hand.

"Why?"

"Curiosity and a fresh perspective."

"Then, you're not mad?"

"I'm mad because you didn't tell me what you were up to," he said. What little details he got from Maggie, he came home intending to find out our true intent with Billy Pace. The argument was a means to get me to talk, and I fell for it.

"Would you have liked it if I told you?"

Somehow, I eased Lee back onto the bed without disturbing the cat. As if satisfied, Lee wouldn't harm me, it went about the business of sleeping. The kiss I gave Lee helped settle him.

"Sometimes, you can love someone even when you don't like what they are doing," he said as he examined my handy work on his hand.

"Isn't that what Eva Braun said about Adolf?" I teased.

"Not funny." With his eyes back on the sleeping cat, he pulled back the covers on my side of the bed, an invitation for me to join him. It took only moments for us to find our familiar positions, spooning, front to back and his arm about my waist.

"At some point, she should have asked, 'Adolf honey, why Poland?'" My German accent sounded ridiculous.

His body trembled with laughter as his lips found the back of my neck. The kiss was soft as it made its way down my neck. The relief I felt at the warmth of his touch eased me more into him.

"Careful, the cat is still on duty." The cat seemed indifferent to my warning.

Lee stopped his ministrations and gave the creature a warning, but cautious glance. A large furry head turned to glare back. For a moment, nothing happened. Then the cat stood, stretched, and hopped off the bed. It took its time to leave the bedroom. Once gone, Lee got up and shut the door before crawling back to bed. This wouldn't keep the cat out. With a broken lock Lee promised to fix ages ago, the cat learned to open the door.

♦ ♦ ♦

The following day, I asked Maggie to bring the file to Lee's office. Maggie being Maggie, she made a copy before dropping off the file. Still involved with the La Guardia tenants' case, he promised to make time for it. I took him at his word and focused on my work. The Bentley-Henderson wedding part two had a new date and venue. The last minute, Executive Board Anniversary cake had my full attention. Completed in record time, the multi layered cake was a scaled down version of the hospital.

The downtown Manhattan location of the venue was troublesome. Bebe had a rare day off and couldn't help. Eperanza needed to stay to watch the shop and her grandmother. The drive to Manhattan and the cake setup would be a solo act. For half a minute I thought of calling Maggie. She was on her way to visit Billy and I didn't want to deter her.

There were questions she had for him. If he could remember anything about the attack. Maggie wanted to reassure him, someone cared for him.

My immediate problem was a cumbersome cake. Made to serve at least a hundred and thirty people made it weighty. Esperanza could help me put the cake in the shop van but taking it out alone was the question. For about fifteen minutes, I stood in front of the open back door of the van wondering how to answer that question.

"Is there something you need to move?" a thick accented voiced from behind me said. Instinct made me dive into the back of the van to get as far away as possible. The sight of a sullen face Pavel glared back at me from the van opening. Next to him stood a well dress older man, who slapped Pavel hard on the shoulder.

"Idiot, you scared her," he scolded in the voice I recognized as Comaneci.

"Yes, you scared me," I shouted, more from my rattled nerves than anything. Despite being in front of the bake shop and the Blue Moon, near to people who would jump to my aid, I still didn't feel safe.

"Sorry, Ms. Wilkes. Pavel has the manners of a stray dog. This I tell my wife every time, but she mistakes it for a charm." Comaneci smiled, his accent not as heavy as his brother-in-law, more refine and less threatening.

"What do you want?" I search the empty van for something to defend myself with and came up with an empty icing bag.

"Please, we mean you no harm, my dear." Comaneci held up his hands to calm me and took a seat at the edge of the open van.

Pressed up against the back of the driver's seat, I realized I'd cornered myself in an enclosed space. Smart Odessa, real smart.

"As you know, I'm trying to fix the problems this fool left me. If he wasn't my brother-in-law, he'd be in jail. I still might send him back to the Ukraine to dig up potatoes on his uncle's farm."

"That sounds like a great idea. The world needs more potatoes," I said nervously.

"Well, with much regret, he's staying and paying for his stupidity. Including restitution for Ms. Ramos. She is very much happy with this."

"Happy for her." The happiness of Ms. Ramos was the last thing on my mind as I kept an eye on Pavel.

"Now it is you he must help," Comaneci said with unexpected delight. "Pavel needs to make amends, and I will leave it up to you how."

Pavel grumbled. Comaneci responded with a swift kick in his shin. Pavel grabbed his leg and cursed in a foreign language beneath his breath. When he recovered, he kept a healthy distance from Comaneci.

"Well?" Comaneci asked.

From the serious expression on his face, this was a man determined to have his way. An angry Pavel stood with his thick, muscular arms crossed, silent and obedient. Then an idea formed in my head. Anyway, who was I to stop Pavel's life lesson and emotional development?

"He has to listen?" I questioned, giving Pavel the once over.

"On pain of death. Planting potatoes by hand is demanding work. He's a delicate boy," Comaneci mused and wiggled his fingers.

Pavel huffed indignation.

"What size are you?" I asked as I eyed him up and down.

CHAPTER 28

The snug, pink O So Sweet cake shop tee fit Pavel in all the right places a discerning female gaze appreciated. When I demanded the removal of his diamond stud earring, put his wayward honey blond hair into a man bun, and check his attitude about the color of the shirt, he grumbled. A disgruntle Pavel got behind the wheel and drove to Manhattan. All the way he complained at his sudden servitude and lackluster glamor of his duties.

"Would you like for me to call your brother-in-law and tell him?" I said, as I held out my cell phone. The complaints stopped.

"This embarrassing," he complained.

I laughed and said, "No, getting taken down by a nine-year old with a meat tenderizer is embarrassing."

Pavel didn't find it amusing.

With an on-time arrival and quick set up, thanks to Pavel's beefy arms, Ms. Derry appeared pleased with the results. Per her insistence, I remained for the brief ceremony. Happy, I was willing to stay, Pavel's presence gave Derry some doubt. The last time she saw him, he was in cuffs covered in confectioner sugar.

As promised, the official ceremony took all of ten minutes. The attendees gave Ms. Derry a hearty round of applause for a well-planned event. After the speeches, the refreshment and cake took center stage. The cake included miniatures made of modeling clay that decorated the outside of the cake. Esperanza detail on the tiny ambulances drew raves. One of the board members insisted I take a picture with him and the cake. Even Pavel seemed pleased with his part. An overheard conversation of someone asking him how long he'd worked for me, he proudly answered this was his first day.

"Ms. Wilkes," a familiar voice in the mist of the chattering voice made my stomach clench as I turned to find the source. The sanctimonious smugness Ellison wore deflated my congratulatory high like a pinprick to a balloon. Ellison was the prick in question. With arms laced together like conspirators, both Ms. Derry and Ellison wore their self-satisfied satisfaction as a privilege.

"What the... Ellison!" I didn't hide my annoyance with his presence.

"The cake is a hit." A gleeful Ms. Derry beamed.

"Didn't I tell you Ms. Wilkes would be your secret weapon? And you discovered her first." Perfect white teeth grinned back at me.

"Without Ellison suggesting you, you wouldn't be here, my dear. You should thank him," Ms. Derry insisted.

She was right. The event allowed me to make new contacts. There were promises of new jobs I couldn't ignore. My forced smile had nothing to do with Derry's words, but I didn't want a scene with Ellison in front of my potential new clients.

"Thank you." I didn't put much effort in it.

"Well, you don't sound happy," a displeased Ms. Derry said. The pout she wore did her little service.

"Gives us a moment, would you, dear?" Ellison disentangled himself from the event planner. It took her moment to realize that Ellison had dismissed her. The feckless woman made a good show of being called away by some imaginary guest before she slinked away.

"A pleasure to see you again... May I call you Odessa?" Ellison took a step closer. This made me take a step back.

"No." With Ms. Derry gone, my need for pretense went with her.

"Why don't you like me? As you can see, I could be quite helpful." Ellison gestures to the room filled with hospital employees and future customers.

My mind flashed on Billy lying motionless on the store room floor and the sadness of Mrs. Stankowski. Then I thought of Deena Pace,

Heather, and Julia. This man pushed through their lives like a weed whacker.

"Why? Please don't tell me you did it for Lee or me." My hand went up to stave off any fiction he was about to conjure up.

Ellison feigned disappointment with an exaggerated sigh.

"Am I the monster Lee makes me out to be?" This man smiled at me with the guiltless innocence of a sociopath or clueless idiot.

From the few times I'd encountered Ellison, I couldn't tell if he were a monster or a spoiled overgrown child.

"If you want my appreciation for arranging this, fine. Thank you." The words came out measure and laced with caution. "The method you use I don't appreciate."

Ellison put a hand over his heart as if hurt.

"What method?"

This time, I took a step toward him.

"Manipulation. The look on my face should tell you something. There are no brownie points for this. If you think getting me jobs would endear you and by proxy Lee, you're mistaken."

"I am."

"Why?"

"I wronged him, I'll admit that. My father demands amends. I blame it on his Germanic upbringing. Poor lack of self-control to mess with other men's wives. Though he never met Julia." Ellison's lips twitched into a slight smile. I suspected he'd had a cocktail or two before he arrived. I couldn't smell it, but I knew the signs.

"When Maxfield found out about Julia, he made me end it. He thought it petty, and he expected better. Maxfield always expected better. It's what made him a great man, even when he's ripping you a new one. When he likes you, you feel less..." Ellison's words fell away.

I almost laughed at Ellison's daddy issues. He didn't like the one he had and opted for a new one—Maxfield. Despite his words, he saw Lee as a threat no matter what he said about a reconciliation.

"Less monster-like," I said, and it broke him from his reverie. His eyes darkened at my words, but his false smile returned.

"You are so unlike Julia. Lee's blond, milky skinned goddess." He emphasized each word to make a point of what I was not. "So malleable and eager to please. She loved Lee, too."

"Not enough. Not to sleep with you." My words felt sharp and angry.

"Do you know what I could do for you and to you, Ms. Wilkes?" he said in a low and feral tone. In his mind, no doubt he believed he sounded enticing.

In one sentence, he both propositioned and threatened me. I thanked my dark complexion for hiding the flush of anger beneath my skin. After all these years he still wanted to hurt Lee and use me to do it. Hell, to the no with that.

I forced a smile on my lips.

"Yeah, but in time we'd fall out and you'd get a restraining order. Or send me nasty emails that slandered my character and drive me to suicide... or blackmail," I said in a much too jovial tone for Ellison's liking. His eyes narrowed on me.

"What do you think you know?"

"What would I know? I make cakes for a living." I shrugged.

The air went out of the room as Ellison leaned in closer. To the others in the room, the gesture might not have appeared threatening. It was. They couldn't see how cold his eyes went or the stern set of his mouth.

"Why don't you answer my question?" he said.

I shrugged again. Playing dumb was the only choice I thought I had. Billy's restraining order and his sister's emails should have been the last thing out of my mouth. Maggie was right, I like poking things.

"Not talking about William Jefferson Pace, are you? That... pathetic, sick individual whose misguided delusion blames me for everything," Ellison said.

"Someone attacked him, and he is in the hospital."

The man before me acted unmoved by this or indifferent. Once again, finding Ellison's true motives eluded me. Did Billy attack him? Yes. Yet he played the victim poorly.

"And...." His tone was impatient and demanding. "Does that mean I'll have a respite from his harassment?"

"Harassment?"

"Calling, showing up everywhere. The man is psychotic and should be in jail." Ellison's anger appeared palpable.

"He misses his sister," I offered, but regretted it the moment Ellison's face twisted in anger as he lost control.

"Another misguided fool. That family had problems long before they knew my name. They saw a quick payday. Pace is just coming back for more money. Somewhere in his delusional thinking, he thinks he can get more."

Ellison believed this. Pace was nothing more than an opportunist. As for Deena, his opinion didn't change much.

"For half a minute, I thought about not pressing charges. Now, I think I need to. Maybe once and for all he'll go away and leave me the hell alone." His voice rose in anger and a few passersby took notice.

"Perhaps you should leave each other alone," I said.

Ellison laughed.

"Just when I thought you were nothing like Julia. Are all women gullible?" Ellison huffed in disgust. The mention of Julia just annoyed me.

"Julia, Deena, and Billy, your fan club keeps on growing. I think I'll join," I snapped back.

Ellison's face went bloodless. This made me wonder about my inability to keep my big mouth shut. God, I wished Maggie had come with me.

"What bullshit has Lee told you? No wonder you think I'm the devil's spawn." Ellison huffed in disgust.

I shook my head. "Lee barely talks about you."

"Then where are you getting this.... stuff." For the first time, Ellison seemed frustrated. His arms crossed tight on his chest as if to restrain himself from choking me or screaming. "Julia was a mistake. As for Pace and his sister, they both were crazy. An unstable family, especially Deena. Her brother fed into it and hasn't stopped. Every time

I try to put my life back together, he's there reminding me about his crazy sister."

"Maybe she had a reason." It took effort to sound calm as Ellison's agitation grew.

"Deena Pace was a lonely, bitter girl who failed at her job and blamed everyone but herself. Deena lost out on a promotion she thought she was qualified for and took it personal. Can you guess what her response was? To turn on the only company that supported her for years, even when she was hospitalized for her depression. Did you know that?" Ellison said in his defense.

"No, I didn't," I said, but it didn't matter. Being aware of Deena's depression didn't suddenly make them altruistic. Deena was protected by law and they had to make those accommodations.

Ellison shook his head in disbelief. His annoyance with me rising.

"Why am I not surprised you'd think the worst? Do you want to believe that we harassed her until she killed herself? Or could you wrap your mind around the idea that Deena was sick, and her illness drove her to suicide?"

A silence fell between us as I contemplated his words. Had I deemed Ellison the enemy and tossed out what might be obvious to others? Deena Pace wasn't a well woman and her campaign against Schaeffer Pharmaceuticals was all in her head. Did she feed her misguided delusion to her emotionally susceptible brother?

"As for Julia, it takes two to tango, doesn't it?" he said.

Again, he didn't seem far off there. Despite Lee's protest, Julia had to take responsibility for their marriage ending.

"What about Heather?"

Ellison took a step back as if I had slapped him in the face. The stunned expression he wore appeared earnest if not surprising. Without warning, he grabbed my forearm.

"What the hell do you think I did to Heather?"

CHAPTER 29

Whatever doubt I had about Pavel assisting me vanished the moment he removed Ellison's hand from my arm. His bad attitude, rude remarks about my taste in music on the van's radio, and comments about the color pink no longer bothered me. Make no mistake, this wannabe thug terrorized Lorenza and her son and hurt Lee. However, now he was my thug.

Only when Ellison winced in pain did I insist Pavel to let him go. Pavel, being Pavel, took a moment. Ellison's once handsome face flushed and contorted in both pain and loathing.

"Why did you bring up Heather?" Ellison said between clenched teeth as he rubbed his hand and stepped away from us. Like most people, upon meeting Pavel, you wanted to keep a healthy distance.

Pavel stood next to me, arms crossed, and eyes fixed on Ellison. The O So Sweet pink tee shirt took some edge off his fierceness, but his size and sneer made up for it. Like most people, upon meeting Ellison, you wanted to punch him.

"She worked at Mercier, Koenig and Layng, didn't she? Now she's dead," I said.

Instead of the angry denial of being connected to yet another dead woman, Ellison's face broke. The unexpected reaction surprised me. The smug demeanor he hid behind cracked just enough to see the heaviness and regret in his eyes. As if I'd punched him in the gut, he seemed to dissolve in a wave of emotion. However, in an instance the vulnerable expression vanished.

"If you're implying I did anything to Heather..." The anger returned.

Despite being in the middle of a party, we found ourselves off in a small corner of the huge space. People around us were engaged in their own conversations and self-congratulation. No one noticed Ellison grabbing me. Or if they did, they ignored it. Did the hospital benefit from Schaeffer Pharmaceutical Company? A huge, conspicuous sign hung by the door, noted the years of contributions to the hospital and this party. This made me wonder how long they would stay uninvolved if Pavel put Ellison in check. From the expression on Pavel's face, he wanted to test it.

"They wouldn't even let me go to her funeral," Ellison spat out.

I was surprised at his anger and didn't respond right away. This Ellison acted like a man denied. Did my accusation hurt him? It made me wonder who Ellison directed his anger toward. Who denied him that simple act of humanity? How much did his word say about his relationship with Heather? Once again, she had a way of affecting the men in her life that disturbed me.

"Nobody understood her like I did... Nobody." His words broke off suddenly, as if he revealed too much of himself. Ellison took a moment.

This made me think of Lee. He treated Heather as if she were some fragile thing. A sweet girl who brightened his time at Mercier, Koenig and Layng. An innocent who was taken advantage of by the likes of someone like Ellison.

"She was beautiful, and I would have given her anything."

"So, you wouldn't have hurt her?" I wanted to know more about his relationship with Heather.

Ellison's snarl returned with a vengeance. Had I implied the unthinkable?

"Why would you think I would hurt her?" he accused.

"Was your break-up amicable? Because you did dump her for Julia, didn't you? Did she forgive you your indiscretion? Or after Julia, she didn't find you worth it?"

His eyes widened in surprised. As uncertain as I was about this theory, Ellison's reaction confirmed he'd been with both women. Ellison seemed to gather himself.

"Was that Lee's theory?" A well-groomed brow arched up.

"No, mine. There's only so much a woman will take, no matter how charming the package." I offered my own disingenuous smile.

"Going after Julia was a mistake. The pleasure of seeing Lee lose everything didn't last long. It cost me more than it was worth."

"An affair with your friend's wife was your way of dealing with Maxfield getting close to Lee?" My disbelief was palpable. "Is that how you deal with things that you don't like, Ellison?"

I shook my head.

"Lee had everything already. Great job, perfect wife, he even had me as a friend. He wanted Maxfield, too." The sour tone in his voice immerged.

I laughed in response.

"That job wasn't that wonderful. A law firm whose moral compass is for sale to the highest bidder. Trust me, if Julia slept with you, I'd check her compass too. As for you, your behavior speaks for yourself."

"Do you want to check my compass, Ms. Wilkes?" His lecherous smile made me second guess my decision to have Pavel let him go. Pavel's slight shift toward me told me he thought the same thing.

"No thanks, I'd have to shower in industrial grade disinfectant and it would ruin my mani-pedi." I waggled my fingers at him

Ellison's lip twerked up in bemusement.

"Ellison, you take passive aggressive behavior to a new level, you know that? Was it worth what you did to Lee? Ruining his relationship with Maxfield? Destroying his marriage, just to get him out of Mercier, Koenig and Layng?" I questioned.

"You wouldn't understand. The affair cost him for a time, but I lost more." His face flushed again with resentment.

"Heather?" I suggested. Ellison didn't respond at first.

"Between my father and that god damn law firm, I had a plane ticket to Korea and nothing else." This statement seemed less directed at me than for his own clarity.

"The firm didn't like you messing with their employee's wives?"

Ellison gave me an indifferent shrug.

"They didn't like it, but the affair didn't put me on that plane."

"Something worse than that? Or someone worse?" I added.

Ellison's facial feature flinched. Had I hit a nerve or a weakness? How did Mercier, Koenig and Layng react to Ellison and Heather's relationship? With the reputation as a notorious playboy and part-time hedonist, Ellison's relationship with Heather shouldn't have been a blip on their radar. Or had their relationship been something more?

Ellison laughed, but it didn't feel sincere. "They're more dangerous than my father."

"How?"

Though Pavel stepped away, Ellison gave him a wary glance before he came closer. Back was his perfect face—smooth, congenial, and handsome. The smile returned along with the twinkle in his eye.

"Who do you think told me how to handle Deena Pace?" Ellison stepped away, still holding that smile.

Deena Pace had been a loyal employee to Schaeffer Pharmaceuticals. When she called into question their methods, they attacked. They degraded, undermined, and threatened her. They exploited her demons, and it drove her to suicide. I stared into the smiling face of Ellison and my stomach shifted. Deena Pace was a threat to him and his family's company. Had the firm's solution been to drive Deena out by any means necessary? Had Ellison been their weapon of choice? More than willing to play the devil, Ellison took to his job with glee.

"Are you saying Mercier, Layng and Koenig told you to harass Deena?" I asked.

Ellison's smile widened in response. With all his show of doing as he pleased, he went to Korea and begged to come back. A grown man who still agreed to the decrees of his father and the firm that executed them. So much so, he went after a helpless girl on the say so of men who needed to remove Deena at all cost.

"Ellison." Ms. Derry's voice cut through the noise at the party and the swirling fog in my head.

"Ellison, dear." Ms. Derry's pasted-on smile belied the concern in her eyes at the sight of us. I would contribute a lot of this to Pavel's demeanor and his instant dislike of Ms. Derry.

"The director wants to meet you, he knows your father," she said.

As always Ms. Derry's presence hindered me. It wouldn't be long before the event planner would whisk him away. Ellison's words about the law firm made me want to know more.

"How did they tell you to deal with Heather?" I asked before Ms. Derry came between us.

"I told them to stay away from her. What I did with her was my business, not theirs," he said in his defense. "Heather felt hurt after the affair with Julia. What she did was only natural." Again, the words were for himself.

"What did she do?" I kept my tone soft so not to break his self-reflection.

"Sometimes, she was too big for me, too much. What she wanted. What she needed for happiness. The thing with Julia was stupid, reckless, and Heather..."

"She... What?" I prompted.

"She showed me how much she loved me and how much I hurt her," Ellison confessed.

As hard as it was to admit it, I believed his remorse. Despite his reputation, what he did with Lee, Ellison showed genuine affection for Heather. Had Heather's response to Ellison's affair with Julia forced the firm and his father to put him on a plane to Korea and out of the way? Unsure of what to say as Ms. Derry slipped a possessive arm around his, I only stared at Ellison.

Ms. Derry's presence seemed to bring him back to himself. He mirrored her insincere smile and his mask was back in place.

"I'm sure you'll tell Lee about this?" Ellison cocked his head playfully to the side. Despite stating his regret about Julia and what he did with Lee, he still couldn't let it go. Ellison wanted what he wanted—Lee as far away from Maxfield as possible. That was all he had. His friendship with Lee had imploded without the hope of reconciliation. Maxfield remained. Who else would run as a point guard to his father?

"Tell him what? That I've made new contacts." I shook my head, not willing to play. Why would I feed into Ellison's end game?

"Or should I tell him about my bad behavior?" Ellison teased, back to his former self, as if I hadn't seen a more vulnerable side of him.

"Not if your mouth is wired shut from a broken jaw." Pavel cracked his knuckles and stepped toward him. Ms. Derry's eyes widened and pulled at Ellison enough to make him take a step back.

"He still would be able to write," I said as I stared at his hands. Pavel looked at them too and crooked his lips into a smile. This time Ellison's agreeable facade disappeared. Sometimes a thug came in handy.

"The director is eager to meet you Ellison," Ms. Derry insisted. Ellison allowed Ms. Derry to pull him away. I watched them disappear into a small group of people. Only once did he turned back to look at me. In that moment, I realized I knew less about Ellison than before. My dislike of him remained. Had he loved and lost Heather because of his jealousy of Lee? Had Heather's reaction to the affair made her turn on him? Did she turn on Mercier, Koenig and Layng as well? Had it cost Ellison his place in the family and the company?

"My brother-in-law will not believe this job is like my old one." Pavel's voice broke my contemplation on Ellison. The bemused expression he wore made me worry for half a minute. Then I shrugged at the absurdity of it all.

I sighed, not certain I learned anything.

"Yeah, we bakers are bad asses."

CHAPTER 30

A promised dinner date with Maxfield couldn't be avoided no matter how hard I tried. Trust me, I tried. From claiming menstrual cramps to leaving the cat alone, Lee wasn't having it. He refused to face Maxfield on his own. Knowing Maxfield's ability to get a murderer off death row, I agreed. There appeared no respite from Lee's past life.

On a balmy Friday evening, we took our time walking from the parking garage to the Manhattan restaurant Maxfield had selected. The New York evening made the walk a pleasant relief considering what was to come. Besides the weather and our wedding, the conversation fell once again on Maxfield.

"The class action suit against Schaeffer Pharmaceutical was the last thing I worked on. In court, I presented an independent third-party research to validate the company's claims that the drugs were fine. Like a good boy scout, it never occurred to me to question if my so-called independent research company had any ties to Schaeffer. I found out later it did. When I brought up the conflict to Maxfield, he brushed me off. This was how they played the game, he'd said. The company got a slap on the wrist for bad marketing and the world turned. Snake oil and bullshit." He tried to temper his anger but couldn't.

"Lee..."

His hand went up to stop me. What rationale could I give to appease his so-called sins? I entwined my arm in his and walked alongside.

"After we won, everyone gave me a pat on the back like I cured cancer. Maxfield said how proud he was. It felt wrong."

"He disappointed you," I said.

"No, I did. Because when I found out about the conflict with Schaeffer, I couldn't prove it. The harder I tried, the more annoyed Maxfield and the partners got. It made me sick, and I'd had enough. The day Ellison told me about the affair, I'd been in Maxfield's office confronting him about it. The fool burst in and brought up the affair, and I lost it. He represented Schaeffer Pharmaceutical, and Mercier, Koenig and Layng's purpose for being. He didn't care about my marriage or his family's company responsibilities. Someone had to pull me off him."

I gave him a moment as he took a breath.

"Then I found you." His smile returned, even as his eyes held the memory.

"You hit me with a pie," I teased, remembering the event.

"My charm didn't work." The delight in his voice reached his eyes. The smile on his face gave me some hope the evening wouldn't be a total waste.

When Lee and I arrived at Pouliot, a sixty-seat fine dining restaurant in Tribeca, he groaned. Less of the intimate dinner, we expected, but an open plan dining room. Maxfield wanted everyone to see Lee, the return of his prodigal son.

We found Maxfield at a center table deep in conversation with a man I remembered as Mercier. The same realization set Lee's lips into a tight line. The walk to the table felt like a walk to death row.

"It's gonna be a bumpy night," I said, quoting Bette Davis.

"This might turn into a three-car pileup." Lee's initial shock morphed into a mask of control.

"Lee," Maxfield bellowed in his commanding voice as he caught sight of us. Every eye in the crowded restaurant turned to see the indomitable Maxfield and the objects of his attention. With Maxfield's table in the center of the restaurant, Lee and I maneuvered past several watchful eyes. A few smiled up at us as if we were granted a meeting with the king. If Lee felt uncomfortable with the attention, I couldn't tell. I did. The rash on my arm flared in symbiotic understanding.

"Leland," Mercier said in such a deep, rich voice as he rose from his seat to greet us. The handsome, dark-skinned man's quick smile would be the envy of any ad exec.

"Eric." Lee held out a tentative hand to shake.

Mercier took it in both of his and held it a bit to long for my liking. It seemed a possessive act from a man who found something he'd lost and losing again wasn't an option.

"When Max told me about your dinner, I wanted to come by to apologize for the gala. Max said we ruined your evening," Mercier said to both of us. "You expected a great night out but got waylaid by a bunch of lawyers. Maxfield gave us an ear full the next day."

"We survived," Lee said with little conviction.

"Why don't you join us, Eric?" Maxfield said with a glint of mischievous glint in his eyes. "You and Lee can catch up on old times. You don't mind, Odessa, do you?"

Did I mind? Yes, I minded, and half expected the other partner, Koenig to show up and pull up a chair. The gentle kick I gave Lee told him how much I minded. In response, he turned to give me an adoring smile. The same smile he used on Candace daily.

"No, curious to hear about Lee when he was just a little boy," I joked. Everyone at the table laughed except Lee.

Within minutes, a waiter placed another table setting, and served the appetizers. The men fell into a congenial conversation about Lee's time at the firm. Mercier did much of the talking while an appreciative Maxfield watched, like a puppet master, ensuring Mercier played his part. Whether reminiscing worked on Lee, I couldn't guess. His game face remained intact. The same face he wore in when Candace got on his last nerve. I made a mental note, Lee should thank Candace for prepping him for tonight.

"The recent work you did with that slumlord, short of amazing. Has Maxfield told you we've increased our Pro Bono work?" Mercier asked as he sipped his wine.

There it was, the carrot. Not as subtle as I expected, but there. They knew Lee struggled with the civil suit against Comaneci. Without the help of Maxfield's fund, Lee would have compromised, if not settled. With the sponsorship of Mercier, Koenig and Layng, money and resources, men like Comaneci would never be an issue again. From their conversation, you would have thought Lee was a legal rock star. Praising his intelligence, fearlessness and the most billable hours of any associate, no wondered they wanted him back, despite Ellison.

"This man had a way of finding the heart of the case, a weakness in his opponents," Maxfield said with pride. "That understanding of the law doesn't come around that often in someone so young."

For a fleeting moment, I saw the appreciation in Lee's eyes. Lee once respected the men before him and wanted to be them. Yet, those same men hadn't noticed he'd changed.

"Some of our clients still ask about you," Mercier said.

Throughout the dinner, he kept throwing salvos regarding the benefits of a large firm versus a small one like Aaron Boyers. When Maxfield brought up a favorite client of Lee's, the two digressed in recalling a related case. A sour mood rose in me at the sight of Maxfield and Lee's growing closeness. My front-row seat to Maxfield Layng's charm didn't sit easy with me. The man had the ability to talk you off a cliff and convince you the fresh air would do you good.

"Odessa, you had to be there when Lee took on a U.S. prosecutor. Left the man questioning his profession." Maxfield's eyes twinkled recalling the details.

Like a well-rehearsed tag team, Maxfield focused on Lee, while Mercier turned his charm on me. I imagined more for distraction than anything else. He didn't want me competing for Lee's attention. Before he threw on the charm, I tossed in a salvo of my own.

"Did you remember Heather McLaughlin?"

Lee choked on his lamb and Maxfield stopped talking. Mercier stared at me as if I wanted to talk about Hitler's summer reading list.

"Excuse me." Mercier's eyes blinked once or twice.

"Heather? She was a law clerk at your firm." My nonchalant tone belied my disruptive intent.

"We were all shocked at her passing," a wary Maxfield interjected.

I ignored Maxfield's attempt to steer the conversation away from death and murder.

"Well, I wasn't as close to her as Max and Leland, but I remember her," Mercier offered.

This time I nodded and poked at the food on my plate. A beat passed before I let him go back to his own meal.

"Lee and I were in the middle of planning our wedding when we found out," I said with false horror.

"No doubt." Despite his comforting tone, Maxfield's eyes went to Lee. Did he hope Lee could encourage me to change the subject?

"That will stick with me for a while," I mused and ignored the unease the topic caused.

"Odessa maybe..." Lee began but stopped when I gave him another kick from beneath the table. The only one who noticed Lee's sudden discomfort appeared to be Maxfield.

"We were all at a party," Mercier recalled. "Celebrating Schaeffer's seventieth birthday. Remember, Max?"

A party? How convenient. They could be each other alibis.

"A party," I said, ignoring Maxfield's gaze.

"It was Paul's seventieth, also a business celebration. Schaeffer Pharmaceutical had just bought out Hillcrest Labs. A huge acquisition for the company," a boastful Mercier said.

"All of the firm must have been there," Lee questioned. Had he come to the same conclusion as I?

Mercier nodded as Maxfield said nothing.

"Did Ellison behave himself?" I mused, ignoring Maxfield.

"For a time," Maxfield said with some disappointment.

"That's putting it lightly." Mercier didn't hide his annoyance. Unlike Maxfield, Mercier seemed to have little patience with Ellison.

"For one evening, can we not talk about Ellison?" Maxfield said, voice cool and restrained. Even I couldn't miss the underlying irritation in his voice. He'd lost control of the narrative. I'd hijacked it.

"I wouldn't mind if we didn't talk about Ellison," Lee conceded.

"That would be a nice thought, but Ellison being Ellison, not likely. He has a way of seeping into people's lives," I said in a dispassionate tone.

This silenced the men at the table for a time. Were they remembering the havoc Ellison's presence wrought?

"He told me about the job he arranged for you," Maxfield said. "In his defense, he said he wanted to help."

The weak laugh I gave expressed my doubts in Ellison's intention.

"I had to threaten a few broken bones to get him to understand my point of view though," I teased.

Mercier's eyes widened in surprised. Lee sighed and Maxfield's lips quirked into an appreciative smile.

"He mentioned that."

Maxfield's smile vanished. A furrowed brow and annoyed expression replaced it. At first, I thought he directed his sudden harshness at me. When Lee turned to follow Maxfield's gaze, I realized his irritation wasn't at me. The focus of his ire stood at the entranced chatting up the pretty hostess.

"You've got to be serious," I said at the sight of Ellison Schaeffer.

CHAPTER 31

From a distance, Ellison Schaeffer was a handsome sight. Lean, tanned, impeccably dressed in a casual linen suit, that cost more than most average worker's salary. The way he smiled at you, made you think you were the only one he cared about. So, I didn't blame the pretty hostess for escorting him over to our table like a long-lost friend. Beneath the table, I placed a firm hand on Lee's thigh. To his credit, he kept silent and focused on the vegetables on his plate. Maxfield's tight expression took it all in, his annoyance palpable.

"Christ," a tight-lipped Mercier said beneath his breath.

"Of all the nights to give Kip the night off," I mused. Part of me wished Maxfield's constant companion would appear as he did the night of the gala and whisk Ellison away. The other part wished Pavel would appear instead and do the same. The condition Ellison would end up in might be different.

"I'll get rid of him," Mercier said and was about to stand, but Maxfield stopped him.

"Let's not make a scene. I'm sure it's nothing," a stoic Maxfield said with his eye on Lee.

Most days, I left wishful thinking to Maggie and little children under the age of ten. If he expected Ellison to act like a grown-up, then shame on him. As Lee tried to capture a wayward carrot on his plate, Ellison arrived at our table with all the innocence of a serial killer. Careful to stand next to Maxfield and a table length of Lee, he greeted us.

"Why the grim faces?" a smiling Ellison teased.

The men seethed in various degrees. For a moment, I tempted to remove Lee's cutlery. Like Maxfield, my only hope was Ellison would behave.

"Pavel says hello." The slight hint of malice in my tone made Ellison's smile falter.

He scanned the restaurant for my new employee. He recovered as his broad smile widened. I guess with the restaurant as a Pavel free zone, he felt safe. To be honest, I didn't need Pavel.

"Why are you here, Ellison?" Maxfield asked. Despite the coolness of his tone, an underlying sympathy laced his words. The dynamics of the two intrigued and annoyed me. Like watching a Greek play. You didn't understand it, but you knew it was important.

"Remember, I introduced you to this restaurant, Max. It's two blocks from my house," Ellison explained as if that were explanation enough. "Everyone here knows me. When I called for a reservation, Patty told me you were here."

Ellison nodded toward the pretty hostess.

"If you have a table, why don't you find it?" Mercier demanded. This got Ellison's attention.

Ellison gave Mercier a withering look for half a second before his smile returned. He placed a hand on Mercier's shoulder and squeezed.

"Don't think you can use that tone with my father," Ellison said with a chuckle.

Mercier said nothing.

"Ellison," Maxfield said firmly.

Ellison slipped his hand away from Mercier shoulders, but not before giving the lawyer a playful pat on the back. Mercier shifted uncomfortably in his seat. He tried to play off his discomfort when he caught me looking at him.

When Ellison turned his gaze upon Lee, I felt Lee tense. All the carrots in the world couldn't distract him. With my hand still on his leg, I gave it a gentle squeeze and worked my way up his thigh. This got his full attention. I only got so far when his hand stopped me. My efforts produced the expected smile from him.

"I see what you find attractive about her," Ellison said, his lascivious tone not missed by anyone with earshot. "All exotic and different."

The murderous look Lee gave him didn't bode well. If Ellison didn't leave, there would be a scene. Once again, he ruined a halfway decent evening. If he wanted to pick a fight with Lee, he would be disappointed. I'd punch him first.

"Ellison, please find your table," Maxfield demanded.

Like some rabid dog, Ellison only had eyes for Lee. Maxfield's words had a negligible effect.

"Why don't you stay," I said. You would have thought I'd grown a third eye, the way everyone turned in my direction.

"What!" Lee yelped.

"Maybe he can add to the conversation we were having before he interrupted us." I gave Maxfield a curious smile. With a confused look on his face, he turned to Lee.

"Odessa," Lee warned, but I was beyond any warnings. This would have been a good time to listen to Maggie's advice about poking snakes. I had three in front of me, why miss the opportunity?

"Heather," I said.

Ellison lost his smile.

"Why are you bringing her up again?" Ellison's expression showed genuine confusion.

"We didn't finish our conversation, especially about the night she died," I continued.

"Odessa, I don't think this is..." Maxfield began, but I wouldn't be stopped.

"Lee and I were in the middle of planning our wedding when we found out. From my understanding you were celebrating your father's birthday or something."

The certainty in Ellison's eyes faded for the first time.

"Two celebrations marked by tragedy." My full attention stayed with Ellison as I ignored the warning looks of the men at my table. We were in the middle of a fancy restaurant, with many eyes on us. Nobody wanted a scene, even a now uncertain Ellison seemed reluctant.

"Then we have Heather to thank for bringing us all together, don't you think?" I gave Ellison a half-hearted smile.

"You think that's a topic for conversation over dinner?" Ellison replied, his voice strained with a growing anger.

"Well, what Lee sees in me isn't either," I retorted. "Considering Heather is the only thing we all have in common."

"What makes you say that?" a surprised Mercier said.

"Well, let's see." I turned to face Lee. Ellison, no longer the focus of his ire, but me. He knew me well enough to let this play out. He'd have a better chance turning Candace into a Republican than stopping me.

"Heather worked at your law firm. Ellison dated her and dumped her. Lee befriended her even though I suspected she took advantage of that friendship. The night she died, she called me," I said.

Apart from Lee, the surprised look on the faces of the men at the table didn't surprise me. The police hadn't made Heather's phone call to me public.

Mercier recovered first. "What did she say?"

"It's an ongoing investigation, so she can't say," Lee interjected quickly. I nodded because I had no intention of telling them what Heather said. From the flushed face of Ellison, he wouldn't take no for an answer.

"Tell me what she said," Ellison's raised voiced demanded as he leaned over Mercier to face me.

"She's not telling you, so back off, Ellison," Lee barked.

"Odessa, I think it's best we drop this subject," Maxfield said politely, yet there was no politeness in his expression. A look I would imagine he mastered over the years to intimidate others.

"Why would you care what she said?" I directed this to Ellison. At first, he seemed confused by the question. "You weren't together anymore, and she didn't work for the firm. Why would any of you care?"

"What's that supposed to mean? Heather was a part of Mercier, Koenig and Layng," Mercier said.

"Then she left on good terms?" This I directed at Maxfield and Mercier.

"She did," Maxfield insisted.

"Well, if she did, why when she returned to New York City none of you got together for brunch, show vacation photos, or get tickets to a show? Ellison, I understand. Who wants to talk to someone that dumped them? We only met a few times and I wouldn't share a lifeboat with him if I didn't have too," I said with a smile.

"You don't know anything about Heather—" Ellison began, but I held up a hand to stop him.

"You told me as much, Ellison, remember? Lee thinks you stalked her and that's why she left, but we know you didn't. Heather left New York City and Mercier, Koenig and Layng skipping all the way."

"What are you talking about, Odessa?" Maxfield's congenial demeanor had gone. Lee noticed the change, too, and put a hand on my knee. Once again, Maxfield protected Ellison from himself and others.

"Why come back to a place where she didn't want to be and tell old friends she was in town?" I added.

"Her mother's here," Ellison said.

I shook my head.

"Heather returned to the city several times to visit her mother, without notifying a soul, even Lee. This time she returns and dies."

"Maybe we should call it a night," Lee said and threw his napkin over his plate. He'd had enough of my Miss Maple moment.

"I think so, too," I added cheerfully and pushed my chair back.

"Why do I think you know more than you are telling?" Mercier asked.

"There you might be right," I said, with a wag of my finger.

"Odessa, what are you playing at?" Maxfield's cold eyes locked on me.

Lee stood up, and I followed suit. Ellison took a step toward me, but Maxfield held out an arm to stop him. Did I think Ellison would do anything physical? No, not with Lee there.

"Odessa isn't playing at anything. I have questions about what happened to Heather. You should have questions, too, but it seems you don't," Lee said as displeasure laced his voice.

"I cared for Heather, you know that." Maxfield said it as if he wanted everyone at the table to believe it.

"Have you been looking into Heather's death?" an uncertain Mercier asked me.

"Yeah," I said. "Lee needed answers."

"Why would you do that?" Maxfield glared up at Lee.

"Because she was my friend, and no one should die that way," Lee replied.

"Didn't someone try to rob her?" Mercier's eyes danced between Lee and Maxfield.

"Someone must have thought she had something worth stealing," I interjected.

"Let's go, Odessa." Lee took me by the arm and guided me to his other side, away from Ellison.

"In a place like that, money," Mercier insisted, ignoring the warning eyes of Maxfield.

"Enough!" Maxfield exclaimed, silencing Mercier and the surrounding tables.

"Playing detective or something?" Ellison said snidely.

"Playing... No," Lee replied.

"Maybe I was wrong," I said as I eyed the men before me. "Maybe Heather called someone else that night besides me. Funny, except for Lee, everyone she knew was at that birthday party the night she died. I would ask if anyone of you got a call from Heather that night, but I don't think you'd tell me the truth."

"Why would we tell you anything?" Ellison said.

"True, you wouldn't tell me about a call, or if anyone of you left early that night." None of the men returned the congenial smile I gave them.

"Let's go, Odessa." Lee wrapped an arm around my waist ensuring I would leave.

"Lee, we need to talk," Maxfield insisted.

Lee sighed and gave his former mentor a pensive look. "Let me call you, how about that? Good night, gentlemen."

Before we could leave, Lee turned to face Ellison.

"Whatever you are looking for from me, forget it. You can tell your father anything you want to make him happy. But I want you to know, I never planned to go back to the firm. As for Maxfield, I know you'll always come first with him, no matter what. No matter what he tells himself or you."

"Why don't I believe you?" Ellison shook his head.

"Because you're a narcissist and a borderline sociopath," I interjected and left with Lee.

CHAPTER 32

The day after my dinner with Max and Ellison's sudden appearance, I had to contend with an overly apologetic and sober Uncle Hal at my bake shop. He stood in the doorway blocking my exit. Already late for a meeting with Maggie, I was in no mood for Uncle Hal. He insisted I tell him where the venue for the Bentley-Henderson wedding would be. When an apology didn't work, he offered me money. When that failed, he hinted at mild, indirect threats against my person.

"Don't make me call the police," I said.

"What about my rights?" he interrupted. His initial calm vanished, and bloodshot eyes glared back at me now.

"What does that have to do with me?" When I tried to sidestep him, he filled the door frame with his body.

Unfortunately, for me, I'd sent Pavel on delivery. Involving Mrs. Gonzales and her ever present bag of sugar wouldn't get me to Maggie, because the cleanup alone would take time. From the expression on Uncle Hal's anxious face, he didn't much care about my wants.

When the sound of a door opening pulled my attention, I prayed it was Pavel returning. Instead, Candace emerged through the O So Sweet and the Blue Moon's adjoining door. Knowing my sister, she'd come to steal desserts for the restaurant. When she saw me, she didn't even try to look contrite. What got her attention was Uncle Hal. She walked passed the cake display and headed in our direction.

"Hey," I said with a mock nonchalance that hinted at my annoyance. Candace ignored Hal's presence altogether and arched a well-groomed eyebrow at me.

"Aren't you supposed to be somewhere?" Dark honey brown eyes did a slow turn in Uncle Hal's direction and narrowed. "Why are you blocking her way?"

"She won't tell me where my daughter's wedding will be," a desperate Hal exclaimed. His pleading eyes searched my sister's face for sympathy. This man had a better chance at picking the next lottery numbers. At the Blue Moon, the first Bentley-Henderson wedding attempt gained legendary status at Bebe's retelling of the strange event.

"And?" Candace huffed. At the height of most men, my sister could stand toe to toe with anyone. The way she looked men in the eyes often made them check their chromosome count.

"Tell me you've lost your mind," Candace said in a tone so frosty, I felt the ambient room temperature drop. "Have you mistaken my sister and this place of business as a person or a place for an audition for The Jerry Springer Show?"

Uncle Hal took a cautious step back. "Excuse me! I have rights."

"In this world, the only guarantees are being born and dying. Since you are breathing, I can oblige you with the other." The temperature dropped with each word out of my sister's mouth.

Uncle Hal's eyes widened at the threat coming from a somewhat calm woman. His mouth opened and closed without a word spoken. With a slight cock of the head, she reached out and touched the upturned collar of Uncle Hal's crumpled shirt. He flinched. Long deft fingers straightened the collar and brushed against his neck. Hal stood frozen in fear of Candace's fingers proximity to his carotid artery.

"Instead of trying to find out where the wedding is, ask yourself why no one wants you around. Why the sight of you makes women cry and men want to punch you." Candace's words came out slow and deliberate. The grip on the collar tightened as she drew him close.

Hal nodded slowly, as his face turned another shade of red. I suspected Candace was cutting off his air supply.

"Before you cause more unhappiness and declarations about your rights, remember a sperm donation doesn't make you a father," Candace continued.

"But..." Hal tried to finish. He stopped when my sister's grip tightened.

"You'll be remembered only as the man that ruined her happiest day. You're an amateur at this. Go find a man of God and ask him the best way to earn forgiveness. It might include twelve steps and a mountain in Nepal."

In an instant, it was over with her release of his collar. Uncle Hal took it as his cue to turn and hurry down the street. I hoped in search of a priest or a travel agent.

"Take only three cakes and two pies," I instructed, knowing she would take what she wanted. Did I care? No, but I had to say something to convince myself I was in control of my shop. Candace crossed her arm, rolled her eyes, and returned inside. In her mind, she earned those desserts. She did.

With Hal a distant memory, I drove to pick up Maggie in Hicksville. When I explained about Hal and the need for Candace, she understood my tardiness. She envied my sister's ability to make grown men cry or run for their lives. The Blue Moon Chef, George, was the only man Candace wouldn't go toe to toe with.

"Why is that?" Maggie asked.

"Out of her weight class," I mused as we drove out to Stony Brook University on the eastern shore of Long Island.

Maggie had gone through all of Deena's copies of emails from the file given to us by her brother. A lengthy correspondence between Deena and a Dr. Hagemann drew a clear picture of someone who'd listen to her concerns about Schaeffer Pharmaceuticals.

"Deena belonged to the University's alumni association. Hagemann was her student advisor when she was there. They seemed to have a close relationship. I'm not surprised Deena went to him for advice," Maggie explained.

"Didn't you tell me he died of cancer? So why would we go to the school?" I asked.

"A graduate student of his worked with him as a lab assistant. Perhaps she might remember Deena. If she does, maybe she can give us a clue on what Deena corresponded with him about."

"Schaeffer Pharmaceuticals," I offered.

Maggie nodded.

"Didn't you say Ellison accused them of directing the campaign against Deena?"

The encounter with Ellison at the restaurant was still fresh in my mind. Ellison's appearance put an end to the evening of revelations. The look of 'I told you so' I gave Lee said everything. These were not nice people.

"Schaeffer Pharmaceutical would have access to her job email," Maggie said.

"If what he said was true, then reading Deena's email would be nothing. Perhaps, Ellison was too good at it and it caused Deena's suicide." I pondered this.

Deena's unnecessary death at the hands of a malicious company and an insensitive Ellison made the drive uneasy. We drove in silence for a time along the Northern State Parkway, heading deeper into Long Island.

Maggie broke the silence.

"Ellison made them question her loyalty to the company. Her co-workers abandoned her. Then her job evaluations turned negative. Then they removed her from a department she worked in for years to do underling work. From her emails, her symptoms of her depression seemed clear, but they didn't stop."

"Even after she left, Ellison didn't stop," I said.

"Why would they? Deena didn't. From the emails, she was still in contact with the company and Dr. Hagemann. Maybe she thought if she proved them wrong, she'd make them understand her motives. She wanted to save the company from itself. They would reinstate her or something." Maggie sighed with the futility of Deena's plan.

"At first, I thought Ellison went to Korea because of this affair with Julia. But I think it was something worse. Deena's death might have even been too much for Schaeffer and the firm. Afterward, they had a wrongful death on their hands. They needed Ellison out of the country," I said.

"Where does Heather come in to all of this?" Maggie's pensive expression told me she struggled with that question.

"Well, if I were Heather and my rich boyfriend dumped me to mess around with his friend's wife just to be spiteful, this would annoy the hell out of me. Then he comes crawling back. Ellison, being Ellison, I'm sure his sugarcoated apology didn't carry much weight with Heather. What would stop him from doing it again and tossing her to the side?"

The furrow between Maggie's eyes deepened.

"Didn't you say he loved her?"

This made me laugh. As sincere as I thought Ellison was in his confession of love for Heather, I didn't trust it. Ellison is a man who would confuse love with lust and loyalty with familiarity. He dumped his girlfriend just out of jealousy. Ellison thought nothing of returning with a diamond-crusted apology as if nothing had happened. The idiot thought his help would make me grateful for the hospital job. So grateful, I would tell Lee to ignore his betrayal and kiss and make up. He would have to show me a bus ticket to nowhere and promise never to come back to make me grateful.

"Ellison is in love with the idea that someone loves him," I mused.

"Let's say Deena went to the firm to expose Schaeffer and there she ran into a very helpful law clerk. There would be little doubt that Heather would have known what Deena had. Convinced Deena to hand over the drive with the promise of ensuring the right people saw it."

They did, I thought. The people Heather thought would put Ellison in his place. She wouldn't be just another ex-girlfriend of Ellison. They would give more than promises. Blackmail would offer a way out of her life and away from a cheating Ellison. Enough to put her mother in an expensive nursing home and a one-way ticket out of the city.

The crease between Maggie's brow lessened, but not by much as she fell into a silence that disturbed me. When the sign for the turnoff for the University loomed in the distance, she continued.

"If the timeline is Deena's death, the affair or Heather's blackmail happened around the same time. Anyone of them could cause Schaeffer senior to exile Ellison. One or all of them caused it."

"If Heather came back to stir the pot again, maybe her luck ran out," I said.

"Is any one of them enough for murder?" Maggie asked. "Anyway, if what you said was true, that Ellison attended his father's party, he had a room filled with alibis. So did everyone who had a reason to kill her."

"From what Mercier's said, the party didn't sound like an intimate get together for family and friends. Schaeffer also made it a business celebration. Maybe anyone of them could have slipped out to meet Heather."

"I'll look into it," Maggie promised as she turned at the exit that went to the school.

"Would any of them kill Heather for what Deena found?" Maggie questioned.

"Enough to pay Heather to get her away. Like I said, how many times can you come back to your golden goose? After a while, even the goose might complain," I replied.

Maggie pondered this for a moment. Still not convinced, I explained further.

"People always forget who the damn goose belonged to; a giant who ate people for snacks."

CHAPTER 33

Through Deena's emails and notes, Maggie found a lengthy correspondence with Dr. Hagemann. A professor of pharmacology at a state university, pharmaceutical college on Long Island. He was also Deena's former instructor. The flurry of communication between the two before her death said a lot. Much of the contact had to do with meeting up, but the underlying subtext was about Schaffer Pharmaceuticals. None of the information in the files given to us by Billy was a smoking gun on Schaffer, but they all led to Hagemann.

The news of Hagemann's death, of an aggressive form of cancer, was disconcerting. Yet Maggie found a graduate research student of Hagemann, Wilda Clark. Wilda worked with him during the time Deena reconnected with her former professor and until his death.

"She seemed happy to talk to us," Maggie replied when I asked about Wilda.

"Deena liked him enough to trust him with what was going on with Schaffer Pharmaceuticals," I said as we walked to the meeting place we were to meet Wilda. The sprawling campus took up several acres. Despite being in the middle of the summer semester, students filled the campus.

Wilda had suggested a nearby diner frequented by everyone. The Harbor Road diner appeared like most eateries that catered to the college students and academics. A funky little place that served diner food and gave you enough time and space to grab a meal and study. The placed smelled of French fries and coffee.

Maggie spotted Wilda first, from the description texted to her. Rail thin and in need of sustenance, I treated Wilda to the afternoon special. God knows how much she made working at the school. Maggie and I drank coffee as the graduate student and now a research assistant ate a huge burger. In between bites she regaled us on the brilliant Hagemann.

"A real cool dude. He made research exciting," Wilda proclaimed as a wisp of her jet-black hair dangled in her eyes. The wafer-thin girl went through two sixteen-ounce colas, half her fries, and much of the burger like a vacuum. "I took classes with him as an undergraduate and he became my advisor when I got accepted into the graduate program."

"He hired you as an assistant?" I asked.

Wilda nodded as she chewed. "The professor liked to hire his former students, like Deena. There were pictures of her in his office along with photos of his other students."

"Was that the only time you saw Deena Pace?" Maggie questioned.

Wilda shook her head, took a long sip from her drink, and sighed in satisfaction.

"At my job at the school's research lab, I met her there when she came to see the professor. Hagemann kept it below the radar and after hours."

"What did Hagemann do for her?" Maggie asked.

"At first they talked about her work at Schaeffer. Then one day a package arrived from her. When I unpacked it with the professor, there were reports and drug samples. The professor went through them while I ran tests on the samples as he instructed." Wilda shoved fries in her mouth. We waited as she chewed.

"We found two research files, an initial one and another. The files included all the research and clinical trials done on the drugs. They differed greatly in their results. Of course, they used the favorable one for approval. What Hagemann found was the drugs had initial benefits, but not worth the risk of putting it out there on the market. With millions spent on research, the company refused to abandon the drug."

"Is the first report still important?" Maggie asked.

"Yes, it's damaging and proved the company manipulated the results to get approval," Wilda said.

"How did they change the results?" Manipulating the market in advertising happened all the time. I knew, because I used to do it. How did you do it with pharmaceuticals?

"They skewed the study in favor of a positive outcome for the drug by being selective of their test subjects and the size of the sample or how they downplayed the false positives. Any number of ways to make the drug sound better than it is." For someone so young, Wilda had a cynical view of her profession.

"Hagemann thought most pharmaceutical companies were self-serving. They're in it to make money with the next miracle pill on the horizon. They pour millions of dollars in research and needed a marketable outcome. Sometimes, it's just smoke and mirrors, he'd say."

"Why are these two reports important?" Maggie asked.

"Because the first one no longer exists. Deena said all information on the first drug trials vanished from the company records. Since she was involved in the original research she had access to both trials. She kept a copy of the original report and never told Schaeffer she had it," Wilda explained.

"So, Schaeffer lied?" Maggie asked.

Wilda shrugged.

"What was Hagemann's expertise?" My understanding of pharmaceuticals went as far as the medicine cabinet in my bathroom.

"He had a variety of research projects he'd been working on. But his passion was for nephrotoxic."

Maggie's expression mirrored my confusion.

"Substances that damages or destroys cells in the body, especially the kidneys. Some medications can do that if you take them too long. Even over-the-counter ones can cause kidney damage and even death if left unchecked." Wilda gave a knowing nod.

"How could they approve a drug if it did that?" Maggie's frown deepened.

Wilda gave a slight smile.

"Happens all the time. The FDA can approve a drug and later recall it if they found that severe side effects popped up after the approval. They'd take the drug off the market for safety issues, if the risks aren't worth the benefits."

"Really?" I said.

"You know those drug commercials that tell you the wonderful things it does. They grow your hair, fix your penile dysfunction, and teenage acne. But at the end they give you those warnings. You might experience side effects that sound worse than the original disease. Stroke, impotence, or facial scarring." Wilda's smile turned wicked.

"Yeah," I nodded, recalling one. When I once had to deal with anxiety, my doctor gave me little blue pills. At that moment, I didn't care if side effects included growing horns and blue skin. I'd do anything to get that one-ton gorilla off my chest.

"Warning labels don't just come on packages of cigarettes. Every drug has a risk, even a common aspirin. If the benefits outweigh those risks, you take the drug. The percentage should be low. When it's not, that's when good drugs go bad."

"If they found the Schaeffer's drug were harmful, what would the company do?" I asked.

Wilda frown. "They would have to remove the drug off the market, before the FDA did. Trust me, you don't want them to pull a drug. The publicity could cost the company billions."

"What if they didn't take the drug off the market?" I asked.

"The FDA would crucify them. Along with the public if they found out they didn't recall a dangerous drug. A god damn lynch mob would form and then the lawsuits would come." Wilda grinned and stuffed her mouth with fries.

"Did Professor Hagemann get sick soon after he sent Deena his research outcome?" Maggie asked.

"He got diagnosed with cancer and left the school three months later. Everything happened so fast. He was a great guy," Wilda said.

"How did he give his results to Deena, verbal or written?" I questioned. We waited as Wilda chewed the last bit of her hamburger.

"When he finished, he got all serious and made us erase his files, both hard copies and electronic. Pace stressed secrecy. The professor hated her loyalty to the company, but he complied. Only three graduate students worked with him on the testing. I don't think even the school knew what he was up too." Wilda leaned in close, suggesting Maggie and I do the same, which we did. Wilda seemed to enjoy the intrigue.

"Dr. Hagemann was on the eccentric side. He loved all those spy novels and kinda play at this research for Pace like it was corporate espionage. Which I guess when you thought about it, it was. I think he wanted to be Q from James Bond or something. Not my thing, I'm more into Warcraft. Maybe he did it as a joke, but he put the file on a USB flash drive in a heart-shaped locket," Wilda whispered.

"What?" Maggie and I said in unison.

"All the girls at school wear them or something like them. Kinda pretty if you like bling. They limit storage, but enough for what Professor Hagemann needed."

To prove her point, after she finished her burger, Wilda took us to the store that catered to the students and faculty. True to her word, at the register hung an assortment of USB flash drives in various styles and capacities. In a small locked glass case were the more expensive variety. Hanging from an eighteen-inch chains were gold and silver heart shaped memory USB flash pen drives.

"It could be jewelry, and no one would know," Maggie said in amazement.

We stared at the various drives, each one designed to look like something else—key chains, pens, and even jewelry. This made me wonder had Deena given one to Heather? Did Heather have it with her the night someone killed her?

"Maybe finding this thing might not be as safe as I thought," I said to Maggie.

While we talked Wilda wandered off to a magazine rack. Had Hagemann told her the ramification of what his investigation meant? Should we have told her that someone might have died for it?

"Maggie, how did you find Wilda?" I watched from across the store as Wilda scanned the rack filled with magazines.

Maggie followed my gaze to the young girl as she flipped through a magazine before replacing it and selecting another.

"I researched Hagemann through Deena's emails and established a timeline. From there, I checked with the school as to who might have worked with him in his lab at the same time and was still on campus. Didn't have time to find the other assistants."

As if reading my thoughts, Maggie frowned. Had we put Wilda in harm's way? Would someone come looking for her as we did?

When Wilda selected a magazine from the rack and joined us at the register, I had to say something.

"Wilda, it might be a good idea if you don't mention the USB locket to anyone," Maggie stated.

"Why?" Wilda's large brown eyes widened in alarm.

I didn't want to scare the girl, nor did I want Billy's attacker out looking for a locket. Wilda's helpfulness wouldn't benefit either one of us.

"Let's just say if someone found out about the USB drive, they might destroy the information on it," I said with caution.

Wilda nodded in understanding. "So not a word?"

"Yeah, like top secret," I added.

Wilda's lips quirked up into a smile. "Dr. Hagemann was Q."

Outside of the store, Maggie asked Wilda to contact her if anyone came around asking about Hagemann. We left Wilda with the idea Hagemann was way cooler than she remembered. After leaving, we also came away with the idea that the killer hadn't found the locket when he killed Heather. Maggie believed if Billy had it he would have used it against Schaeffer Pharmaceutical and Ellison right after Deena's death. He hadn't. So whatever Billy's attacker was looking for, he wouldn't find it with Billy. It was still out there, filled with information, enough to kill for.

CHAPTER 34

Finding Deena's heart shape locket wouldn't be easy. The police were our best bet and may have found it amongst her belongings found at the hotel. Unfortunately, the police wouldn't talk to a baker and unlicensed investigator. If Lee asked, they might tell him. How Maggie and I knew about the locket came with problems. This made my rash itch. Instead of worrying about our upcoming wedding, I was running around with Maggie doing God knew what!

"Don't you think he should know about the USB drive?" Maggie put on the mother knows best tone. "If we find it, it won't matter how we knew."

As usual, Maggie had a point.

"Does it bother you that you're always right?" I gave her a questioning look. Her response was typical Maggie, practiced innocence.

"That's not true," she said with a straight face. "Most of the time."

As much as I didn't want to call Lee, I did. I got Amber instead. Quick to apologized, she explained Lee had given her his phone to update his contact list. This didn't surprise me. The slick new phone came with a thousand options Lee refused to wrap his brain around. Amber became his personal tech slave.

"You should charge him by the minute," I teased in earnest.

A multitude of polite apologies followed as Amber explained Lee was in a meeting with Comaneci. Thankful I got a reprieve from confessing to him directly, I took the life line. I explained everything to Amber. She promised to relay the message as soon as possible.

While I dreaded Lee's reaction, he would have time to calm down when I saw him next. At least I hoped so. As Maggie drove us back to Queens and ultimately, Lee's office, I leaned back in my seat and enjoyed the view outside my window. It took a moment to notice Maggie hadn't taken us back the way we came. I sat up as we entered the borough of Queens and stayed on the Belt Parkway. When the Terminal Hotel came into view, everything itched.

"What the…" I said as Maggie turned off on an exit.

The Terminal Hotel stood like a middle finger just off the Belt Parkway. On a small triangle plot of unkempt land, it sat between an airport car park and a no name car rental. The red-painted concrete facade now faded to a nauseating dull pink. Its ornate trim hinted at an attempt to give the place a Parisian style. A sick Twilight Zone version of Paris.

"You've got to be kidding," I complained.

Rusting security gates covered the first-floor windows. A variety of handwritten signs regarding the dos and don'ts of being a guest adorned the front door. The place felt more like a jail than a hotel. Outside of the hotel, a motley group of men stood by the front entrance. From their wretched appearance, none had taken advantage of the hospitality suites or the showers.

"It's not the most welcoming places but I have my reasons," Maggie said as she parked the car into the hotel's small lot.

"Should I even ask why we need to go inside?" My disbelief bolstered my indignation.

Maggie's angelic face offered an apologetic smile. I'd been to this rodeo one too many times where Maggie's unchecked curiosity got the better of both of our common senses.

"I want to talk to the housekeeper who found Heather." She made this explanation sound simple. Like, let's go pick up milk and eggs at the corner grocery.

I cared less about the housekeeper when one man in the small group in front of the hotel pointed at us. He smoothed out his rumbled clothing before heading in our direction. Like the hotel, the man hadn't aged well. A thick, unruly beard covered much of his face and layers of soiled clothes covered him.

"Why here? Couldn't you ask to meet someplace else where someone hasn't died?" My eyes still locked on the man as he approached the driver's side of the car. Was I surprised he went straight to Maggie? No, because she radiated vulnerability and an easy mark. I on the other hand, had a strong desire to leave. Before I could express that, Maggie was already out the car and chatting it up with her new friend. For half a minute I sat there in mild disbelief. It would serve her right if she got kidnapped by a mass murderer who lived at the Terminal Hotel. This feeling passed, of course.

"Maggie." I hopped out the car.

By the time I caught up with them at the hotel entrance, Maggie had already exchanged names, a preference for Dunkin Donuts coffee over Starbucks, and the name of the front desk manager. Bartow, who Maggie explained only went by one name, ensured her the housekeeper who found Heather was on duty. Bartow also guaranteed if we gave the manager a twenty, he wouldn't care if we spoke to her.

"Twenty bucks gets you a room for an hour?" Maggie explained.

"Along with bed bugs and a social disease," I snapped back.

Undeterred by my resistance, Maggie allowed Bartow to lead the way into the cramped lobby that smelled of heavy-duty disinfectant and now Bartow. Bartow spoke in hush tones to the manager. A suspicious-looking reject from a Quentin Tarantino movie glared back at us.

"Twenty-five," he croaked out.

Before I could complain, Maggie pulled two twenty-dollar bills and waved it at the manager.

"Give me the room where that woman died," Maggie demanded.

I joined the manager and Barlow in a look of surprise. Not so much on Bartow's part as his eyes focused on the money in Maggie's hand.

Catching Bartow's interest, the manager snapped his fingers in front of him. Bartow blinked and licked his lips. I was in a Tarantino movie.

"Whatever. I'll tell Elsa to meet you." The manager picked up the phone, but before he dialed, he held out his hand. Maggie walked over and handed him the bills.

"Room 425 at the end of the corridor," he said gruffly.

"Come on, Bartow," Maggie instructed.

"Hey why is he going up there?" the manager complained. Thank god he asked. Because, despite Maggie's sudden kinship with the homeless, I didn't need a tour guide.

"Do you ask any of your guests who can come to their room? Do you even care?" Maggie stood with her hand on her hip and glared at him.

As if taken aback by Maggie's brusqueness, the man remained silent. In not so many words, Tinkerbelle told him to mind his business.

"Whatever." The manager gave us a dismissive wave of his hand and disappeared into a small room in the back. What looked like a small cot and a portable television sat against the wall. We were no longer his problem.

"I'll show you where it is," Bartow said with a grin that was missing a few teeth.

The ride in the elevator was awkward but informative. Bartow explained why he preferred St. Catherine's Food kitchen over the one down the block. How the night manager slept all the time and doesn't care who came and went. There had been many a night when several of his friends found an open room. A quick shower, and a night's rest on a bed were the highlights of their day. Once a wife found her husband with his girlfriend and got into a serious fight. The night manager didn't notice until the police woke him up.

"Maybe he's only pretending to be asleep. You ever think of that?" I said.

Bartow's face held a look of displeasure and disappointment.

"That's very cynical," he said.

I shrugged.

"He's a night manager, at a hotel where people don't want to be seen. He's perfect," I replied.

Bartow's face morphed into a surprise contemplation as if he were reassessing me.

"You're not a cynic, you're a realist, with a dash of irony," Barlow mused.

"It's my super power," I said as the elevator doors opened.

The hallway was narrow and dark. Many of the overhead lights were missing. The enclosed space had a muted yellows hue to it from the outdated fixtures. The well-worn carpet smelled of mildew and age. The peeling wallpaper had a slight sheen that reflected the dull lighting. At the end of the hall, the shape of a woman stood next to a cleaning cart and hotel room door. The rash on my arm tingled, and I held my breath at the sight of the door. Heather died there.

"You're not the police?" A hint of a Caribbean accent permeated her voice.

"God no." I laughed at the obscurity of the question. If Brody and Starzynski knew we were at the crime scene talking to a witness, they would put us under the jail.

"Okay," she said and gestured us to come.

Elsa stood small in stature, with tiny neat rows of braids that hung down her back. Deep, nervous brown eyes danced between Bartow, Maggie, and me. Despite not being the police, Elsa seemed uncertain of our presence there. As uncertain as she was, she pulled out a set of keys from her uniform pocket. The jangling noise echoed down the dark, empty corridor. With one hand, she pushed the heavy door open. We peered inside an outdated and empty hotel room. Maggie stepped into the room first, leaving Elsa, Bartow, and I standing by the door. Regardless of being empty, the room still had the left-over detritus from a crime scene. Which made me think the room hadn't been used since Heather.

"Is that a good idea?" I said.

A Candy Coated Lie

Maggie ignored me but stepped with caution on the worn rust colored rug. Elsa followed, her hands braced close to her chest. I entered with reluctance. Bartow stayed outside keeping the door open and stood guard. I didn't want to ask what he was guarding us from.

"What are you looking for?" I asked.

Covered in the same rust-colored hue were the rug, bedspread, and curtain, the room looked unchanged since the early seventies. A single bed anchored the room. A dust covered old-style tube television sat in the middle of a faux wood dresser. On the wall hung a faded replica of a French impressionist that reminded me of every boring art history class I took in college. A sour scent hung in the air--heavy and stuffy. It made Bartow seem refreshing. The need for fresh air drew me to the room's only window. When I tried the window latch, it wouldn't budge.

"The owner, he sealed them, so the guests won't smoke in the rooms," Elsa said apologetically.

"What if there's a fire?" Maggie's furrowed brow expressed her concern. Elsa didn't seem to have an answer. Considering the condition of the building, sealed windows weren't the only code violation the Terminal Hotel had.

At the window, I stared down at the pavement below. If a fire didn't kill you, the four story drop to the ground would. The view wasn't much better. The corner room gave a partial view over a high brick wall. On the other side, a small garbage dump sat next to several parked garbage trucks of a private trash company. That explained the smell.

The moment I step inside, I thought of Heather. With its dingy rug, outdated furniture, and ever-present smell of garbage, she had died in this room. Whether it was the way the police believed or something else, it didn't matter. The face I remembered from the photograph at her funeral was of a beautiful, young woman whose desires might have gotten her killed in a place like this.

CHAPTER 35

An hour and half later, we left the Terminal Hotel with Elsa's version of the night's event. Maggie jotted down every word while I listened. Much of it matched what she told the police, some of it didn't. Less flustered by us, she had time to think about what she saw.

"A lot of men come to the Terminal that way, just another day. Not wanting to be seen," she'd said with a shrug.

The sound of raised voices and a heavy thud hitting the wall caught her attention. Cleaning in a room next door, she'd been wearing ear buds and listening to music, so she didn't hear much. The thud against the wall got her attention, and she pulled out her buds. No other sound followed. When she went to the hallway to check, she saw a man walking toward the elevator. Medium build, blond, maybe light brown hair and drunk. At one point he braced himself against the wall to steady himself. A hint of alcohol lingered in the air.

"He came back later," Maggie added. "She'd forgotten something in one of the rooms and came back to the floor. A man burst out of Heather's room and ran down the fire exit. There was something in his hand, long and dark."

"He didn't seem drunk then," I said as we pulled up to the familiar brick building.

As Maggie found a place to park the car, we debated over what we should tell Lee. During the elevator ride up, she opted for the truth and I struggled to come up with a lie he'd believe. By the time we walked through the door and found Amber, Lee, and Comaneci in the conference room, the truth won out. Not that I believe the truth would serve me better, but every lie I came up with sounded more ridiculous than the last. Maggie demanded I give up when I added a fairy, fortune telling, and acts of God.

The moment Lee saw us heading towards him, his expression told me I should have given acts of God a shot. He stepped out of the conference room to face us.

"Should I ask about the locket?" Lee said in a calm and pleasant tone. This was a trap.

Though Maggie and I stood side by side, Lee only had eyes for me. For half a breath, lying to him was winning the debate in my head, when Maggie saved me.

"Why don't I explain." She stepped in front of me as to counter any thought Lee might have on murdering me. Once again, I'd held back something from him. This was not a good way to start a marriage. However, I took this as a cue to go in the opposite direction.

"I'm going to say hello to Mr. Comaneci," I said and stepped to pass them as fast as I could.

"Odessa." Lee's nostrils flared as I stepped passed him. Maggie already had him by the arm and guiding him away from me to his office. If anyone could soothe him, a little redhead truth charmer could. He might not forgive me fully, but it wouldn't hurt as much. Happy for the reprieve, I went to see Comaneci and Amber.

"Mr. Comaneci," I said when I entered the small conference room. Who would have thought Comaneci's presence would cheer me up? At the sight of me, the older man jumped from his chair, arms out stretched to embrace.

"Ms. Wilkes." Wearing her trademark congenial smile and stylish pump, Amber did a little bow in greeting and stood off to the side.

"Call me Cezar. We are family now." He pulled me into a hug that threatened to cut off my air supply.

"We are?" Who would have thought I had Ukrainian relatives?

"So happy to see you. Lee said you might be by, so I waited." Again, he pulled me into another hug. I didn't know many Ukrainians, but were they all this friendly?

"Nice to see you, too." The words came out a little breathless as I pulled away from his embrace.

"How did you get Pavel to dress like a grownup?" His surprise seemed earnest.

How would I explain to him that working with Pavel came with issues? His size and demeanor made him a poor choice for the front of the shop, so I put him to help around the workshop. At first, Esperanza appeared wary. When she saw he could lift large bags of flour and sugar without breaking a sweat, her trepidation vanished.

"He gets up early in the morning, dresses like a man with a job." Comaneci beamed with pride.

Although pleased with Pavel's transformation, I wanted to get off the subject of his servitude. Instead, I asked about the LaGuardia Apartments and tenants. He both sighed and smiled.

"Your fiancé is bleeding me dry and yet I'm good." His accent made the words sound playful. If Lee were taking advantage of him, he didn't seem to bother with it.

"Mr. Comaneci put a management company to run the building. Repairs are underway. Also, they've started a tenants' board to address any issues," Amber chimed in. I'd almost forgotten she was there.

"The repairs will put the building in line with the rest of the neighborhood development. This will increase its market value. That's good for me. The tenants even praised my intervention and now I'm a hero. It said so in the newspapers." A mischievous smile decorated Comaneci's face.

"A hero?" I almost laughed. "You sent them Pavel."

Comaneci feigned a pained expression.

"Yet, because of you and your little redheaded friend, you've brought Pavel's misdoings to my attention. He is being punished as we speak." Comaneci pointed at me.

"Working at a bakery is punishment?" a curious Amber asked.

"For someone whose idea of working is posing, yes." Comaneci huffed in disgust.

I laughed at the contentious relationship between the two men. This gave Comaneci an excuse to pull me into another hug. As he did, he brought me close enough to whisper into my ear. "I must speak to you... Alone."

When I stepped out of the hug, Comaneci had that same generous smile. Yet his eyes said something else, something urgent. Whatever he wanted to tell me, he didn't want an audience.

"Cezar, can I talk to you about Pavel before you go? It is a little delicate." I put as much sincerity as I could without sounding suspicious. Picking up on my cue, Comaneci blustered about being busy, but thought he could spare a few more minutes.

"I'm sure Pavel has done something embarrassing. If there is an embarrassing way of opening a jar of peanut butter, Pavel will find it." Comaneci's tone was apologetic to Amber, who blushed.

"Why don't I work on the copies for you, Mr. Comaneci," Amber said with her usual efficiency.

You would have thought she'd offered the crown jewels or something, the way he thanked her. It was a little overboard for my taste, but it got an embarrassed Amber out of the room.

"What is that American saying about a lying like a carpet," Comaneci said as we watched Amber leave and head to the copy machine.

It took a second to translate what he meant. "A rug, you mean."

Comaneci bobbed his head from side to side as if to say that semantics weren't important.

"Despite what your fiancé is doing, you got me out of a mess with Pavel. For once, one of my wife's relatives has a real job. Now, I can sit at my dinner table and not want to kill my brother-in-law."

Pleased as I was Pavel wouldn't die a horrible death, he didn't need to kick Amber out of the room to say it.

"So, when I tell you this, it's because I care." Comaneci nodded at the open door. Through it I saw Maggie and Lee leave his office. He no longer appeared like he wanted to murder me. Instead, Maggie and he walked over to Amber by the copy machine. Lee handed Amber his phone. The three huddled close together, eyes on the tiny screen.

"That girl is a liar," Comaneci proclaimed.

My perplexed look must have told him I was clueless.

"Maggie?" I asked, still confused.

Comaneci shook his head.

"No.... Silly girl, the other... Amber." Comaneci pointed at the threesome. Still sensing my confusion, he pointed again.

"The times I've spent with your fiancé, I know he is an honest, determined man. Even after Pavel pushed him down the stairs, he took the high ground. For a lawyer that says a lot. Your little redheaded friend can't keep her eyes off me, like she's taking notes for the police. Much to like there. I even like the fat boss guy, he has fine taste in scotch and he loves your Key Lime Pie."

"Are you talking about Amber?"

"Yes, the pretty girl. All the time I talk the small talk with her, she lies. Lies, lies, and more lies. Small talks help me judge people, you see. Politicians, lawyers, and even my butcher, who always lies about his meats. People are less careful when you talk unimportant things with them. It helps me to recognize... Excuse my language, the bullshit." Comaneci's stance dared me to contradict him.

How was I supposed to respond to that?

"I talked the small talk to McKenzie, nothing too much, little things. Like your sister won't let him wear his Scottish skirt thing for the wedding." Comaneci gave a disagreeable shake of his head.

"It's a kilt," I informed, and I liked Lee's family tartan.

Comaneci didn't much care and shrugged.

"The small things from Amber, she put on the false face, smile, and lies. Your man is clueless to this. There, he's not so smart."

"What lies?"

"I asked about the pretty watch she wears. A gift for my wife I need so I ask. To tell me it's a fake is foolish, that she bought it off the street. Who lies about a real gold watch? Or the diamond studs in her ears, she calls cubic Zirconia. Lies."

I stared at Amber, in her designer knock offs, that were too good to be knock offs. Showing Lee how to work his phone and so happy to help.

"How many receptionists know the exchange rate of the euro, or the time zone to Beijing?" Comaneci gave me a knowing nod. "I have an administrative assistant I stole from a hedge fund guy and they are cut from the same cloth. I know the type."

I once admired Amber's efforts to fit into the tiny neighborhood office. Attentive to people's needs, especially Lee's. Aaron said she was too good to be true and even thought about keeping her. If you got passed the pretty face, her polite mannerism and impeccable grooming, I saw what Comaneci saw. An over qualified, highly skilled woman working as a receptionist? I played every conversation I had with her. What surprised me more than anything was what little I knew about her. What angered me more, she knew almost everything about me.

"I can check her out for you," Comaneci said conspiratorially. "I have a guy."

My gaze went to Maggie as I shook my head. "That's okay. I got a girl."

CHAPTER 36

The Comaneci's speculations about Amber had my head doing a few back flips. Unsure of what to do with this information, I said nothing. There wasn't much time to contemplate it because Lee took the time to chastised Maggie and me. Though she had given him a compelling explanation for searching for the USB drive, the news didn't go down well with him. He thought the connections were circumstantial. He had no qualms about bringing down Schaeffer; however, he had doubts about Max and Heather's involvement. For it to be true, this meant Max hadn't changed, and Heather wasn't a saint. Despite that, he promised to talk to the police to see if the locket was with her belongings found at the scene.

"Asking you to stop would be stupid, right?" he asked halfheartedly.

"It would be stupid if we stopped searching for the truth," Maggie said.

From the determine set of Maggie's tiny chin, he'd have a better chance at stopping a hurricane. As for me, I had no interest in stopping and told him as much. Like Maggie, I believed Schaeffer Pharmaceuticals had done something wrong. Though he accepted my decision, we went home that night saying little to each other. Once again, Heather had come between us. My doubts about Amber would have to wait. Talking to him about her would be like trying to shove another clown in a fully packed clown car. It was just too much.

The next day my questions about Amber remained on hold. My focus lay with the Henderson-Bentley wedding. Once again, Naomi's father went all out for his baby girl. Set at a secret location, Mr. Bentley didn't skimp on anything, especially the security. It was a Hal free day. Family drama forgotten.

"I want to bake," Pavel announced unceremoniously as he stood next to me and watched as the hundred-plus guests enjoy the festivities. When I turned to him, I could have sworn a little light bulb hung above his head.

"What about residential management?" I queried.

The scornful snort Pavel gave me made me smile. I suspected something was going on when I saw him reading some of Esperanza's baking magazines.

"I can teach you." I mused at the idea that my shop now included a Guatemalan grandmother and an ex-Ukrainian thug. The ringing of my cell phone interrupted my enjoying the obscurity.

"Hey," I said to the picture of Maggie on the screen as I engaged the call.

"How's the wedding?" she asked.

"No Uncle Hal. Naomi is dancing with her new husband and her father is smiling."

"Good. Can you come by the office when you finish?" Maggie asked.

"What's up?"

"Amber."

With the promise I'd come right away, I disengaged the phone.

My thoughts toward the receptionist turned dangerous.

"Something wrong?" Pavel asked, reading my shift in mood.

I shook my head and took in the sight of Naomi and her father hugging. Uncle Hal a distance memory. The sight made me think of the lies we tell. How we coat them with candy and eat them whole. Naomi's genetic connection with Uncle Hal, my sister's passive aggressive resistance to me marrying out of my political party, Lee's unwavering belief that Heather was a sweet and giving girl. You could sprinkle sugar on horse dung and someone would eat it.

"Lesson one, know your customer. They won't tell you everything."

Forty minutes later, Pavel and I walked back into a shop filled with customers. Mrs. Gonzales sat at her station giving free advice and her excellent coffee. In the back, Esperanza worked on a groom's cake in the shape of the Stanley Cup. In my office, I found one of my baking books and sat Pavel down to read it.

"This is the first book I bought when I wanted to take my baking seriously."

Pavel flipped through the well-worn book and then look up at me. The light above his head shone a little brighter.

I left my ever-growing employees in the shop as I drove out to Hicksville. Comaneci's assumptions about Amber had me in a spin. First came denial and then anger. By the time I pulled up to the Hicksville strip mall that housed McAvoy Investigation, my desire to water board Amber won out.

Inside the small office, I found Maggie at her desk and her son, Rocket, on the floor piecing together shredded papers. Next to him sat several pages neatly taped back together.

"Hey, Auntie O," he said at the sight of me.

At nine years old, Rocket's resemblance to his mother went beyond the red hair, blue eyes, and slight build. He had a penchant for the mysteries of life, at least for a small boy. His often-adventurous nature got him into trouble. But wasn't the lot of small boys?

"What are you doing?" I hovered above him.

"Frank is giving him fifty cents for every page he puts back together," Maggie explained. "It's part of a divorce case for Aaron. The husband likes to shred stuff."

I was surprised Frank McAvoy enlisted Rocket in one of his cases, considering he didn't like Rocket in the office. With Rocket around, Frank had to curb in his profanity and answer Rockets ten thousand questions.

"How much so far?" I asked my godson.

"Ten dollars and fifty cents," the 9-year-old said proudly.

"Good for you." I gave him an enthusiastic thumbs-up before I joined his mother at her desk. "Later, I'll renegotiate your rate."

"Stay out of it, Odessa," Maggie warned.

"That's okay. Momma says I shouldn't take advantage of Frank."

I threw some shade at Maggie. Rocket's ability to take advantage of Frank was the highlight of my day.

"Frank wanted to do five cents a page, but Rocket got him up to fifty cents. By the time they finished, Frank begged me to intercede," Maggie said.

I gave Rocket another thumbs up.

"You want the good news first?" she offered as I took a seat across from her.

From my sour expression, Maggie understood I didn't much care how she gave the news.

"Twenty-six years old, single, and lives at Riverside Park in Manhattan."

"Nice neighborhood. Kinda expensive, don't you think?" I said.

"Paid for her condo in full two weeks ago."

"On a temp's salary?"

"No criminal record. Graduated from Tufts University in business management. Worked for a big west coast marketing firm right out of college."

"As what?"

"An assistant market analyst." Maggie gave me time to digest this bit of information. Why would a business graduate work for a small neighborhood law firm?

"All this sounds pretty innocent. So what's the real bad news?"

Maggie leaned forward.

"The temp agency Aaron normally uses didn't send her. When I called, they said someone rescinded the request. Then Amber showed up."

"No one questioned it?"

"She was so good no one complained," Maggie said.

"Have you told Aaron or Lee?" I asked.

JILL BROCK

"No, of course not. Aaron would pounce on her like one of your pies."

A tough sounding Maggie had a point. For whatever reason, Amber had placed herself in the firm. Eventually, Lee and Aaron would need to know why.

"Comaneci thinks Amber wants to seduce Lee or something crazy like that?" I said.

Maggie's auburn brow cocked up. "Your Lee?"

We both laughed at the absurdity of the accusation.

If Lee picked up any romantic vibes around Amber, his discomfort level would rise like a red flag. Once a new secretary flirted constantly with him. Reluctantly, he asked me for advice when he didn't know how to get her to stop.

"Simple, introduce us," I explained confidently. Despite being able to confront judges, criminals, and other lawyers with the confidence of a man possessed, he was a chicken with women with boundary issues. So, he introduced us, and she stopped. Nothing got your attention more than the object of your affection's girlfriend, giving you the look of death. She didn't last long.

"You know the thing about the internet. Facebook, Twitter, Instagram, and Snapchat, most people think their information is private. It isn't. Even if you take precautions, you're still as naked as a newborn."

"How naked?"

"Amber Kim is social, pretty, single, and wasn't in this country before coming to Aaron."

"Where was she?"

"Working in South Korea."

My eyes widened in surprise. "Our Amber?"

"Though she's American, she has close family ties in South Korea. From her online post, she visited a lot and even worked there off and on. She only just returned home."

"There's more, isn't there?" I said.

"Amber worked for a marketing firm that dealt with a lot of American companies. One of those companies happens to be Schaeffer Pharmaceuticals."

The rash on my arm flared. Once again, Ellison Schaeffer had found a way into Lee's life. His banishment from New York City included time in Asia. I doubt that he spent the time sightseeing.

"That bastard!" I exclaimed.

"Auntie O said a bad word," Rocket admonished with a giggle.

"Sorry, sweetie," I said in the best sugary tone I could. "But Auntie O wants to kill someone, and I couldn't find a better word to use for him."

Rocket nodded in understanding and went back to his task.

"It's too much of a coincidence," Maggie said.

"It's not enough he shows up everywhere. He spied on Lee. Jesus, that's borderline crazy." I crossed my arms because I thought I might hit something.

"What do you want to do?" Maggie leaned forward in her chair. "Do we tell Aaron?"

The first thing I should have done was call Aaron and tell him of our suspicions about Amber. But I didn't. The memory of Ellison showing up at the restaurant stopped me. He knew Lee and I would be there with Maxfield. He knew because Amber told him. Helpful Amber, who did everything without complaint as she worked below her pay grade.

"She bought Lee's new phone," I remembered

This got me a pensive stare from Maggie.

"While you were in talking with Comaneci, Amber helped set up his phone's email app."

"When I called after leaving Wilda, she picked up. Damn it, she's on it more than him."

Ever since Lee lost his phone, Amber stood by his side helping him with his new one. I thought nothing of it and Lee thought even less.

"Do you think she's done something to it? Because she could."

Despite looking like a pixie and a soccer mom, Maggie prided herself on being up to date on the latest investigative tools and methods. She scoured the internet, read books, and asked questions. So, when she suggested that Amber might have done something to Lee's phone, I believed her.

"Like what?"

"From tracking Lee's whereabouts, to listening in on his phone calls, reading his emails."

If Amber did something to Lee's phone and spied on him, water boarding might be too good for her. However, getting her to confess about this wouldn't be easy. Why would it? She had no problem lying to lawyers who deal with liars every day.

"I need to know," I said as I watched Rocket sitting on the floor next to me piecing together the shredded files. Someone wanted to hide the truth. The task seemed mind numbing dull, yet the little guy went at it like a miner digging for gold. Like his mother, he had the tenacity of a bulldog. Everything about Heather felt like shredded paper. So much of it meant nothing. Yet Deena and Billy Pace added to the coherency of the clutter. Even Heather's motives for returning put the pieces together.

"There is a way of finding something out," Maggie offered with caution.

I turned back to her and saw the glint in her curious eyes.

"Am I going to like it?"

Maggie shook her head.

"Will it involve water boarding?"

Again, her head shook.

I took a deep breath and braced myself to ask.

"We need Lee's phone."

CHAPTER 37

After leaving Maggie and Rocket, the conclusion we'd come to about Amber left my head throbbing. Why she situated herself at the law firm could be anyone's guess. Like Lee, all of this could have been circumstantial. Unless, we found the locket or the truth about Amber, I wouldn't rest easy.

When Lee found me on the sofa later that evening, I had a cool towel on my head and the cat nestled warmly at my feet. Inside my jean pocket were instructions from Maggie. Her detailed tutorial on how to deal with Lee's phone and see if Amber tampered with it.

"Bad day?" he said as he hovered over me.

"If you only knew the half of it." I moaned.

"If I sit next to you, will that cat attack me?" He waved his scratched hand at me and glared at the hairy mass acting as my leg warmer.

"Hasn't moved in about ten minutes, so it's either dead or doesn't care." The thing had grown a weird attachment to me, neither of us couldn't explain.

While he kept a sharp eye on the cat, he took a seat next to me and touched my cheek. The heat from my skin got some relief from the coolness of his touch. Concerned as he was for my wellbeing, I could tell he had something to say.

"Talked to the detectives." His eyes found mine. "No locket."

The news seemed to tighten the vice in my head. Without Deena's file we had nothing on Schaeffer Pharmaceuticals or Ellison. Where to look next eluded me.

"Are you hungry?" he asked as he danced away from the touchy subject. "How about Chinese takeout?"

Considering my current state, food was the last thing on my mind. Yet, I appreciated the time I spent alone with Lee. If I had to fake an appetite, I would.

"How about dinner and a movie?" he asked with a hopeful smile. An ardent movie buff, Lee could name the actors, the subplot, and the box office receipt at the time of release. He found amusement in my running contemporary commentary when we watched movies dated before the 1950s. For example, his appreciation of "Gone with the Wind" waned after my observation of the nostalgic classic. I saw it as over romanticized, wishful thinking, if not a delusional version of the old south. Even as a romance, it rankled my feminist sensibilities.

"Why don't you take a shower and I'll call it in." Eager to show interest in the evening's plans, I pushed myself off the couch. Then I thought of something. "Take a long one, then pick a movie."

"Something scandalous." The corners of his eyes creased in delight. I struck.

"Forgot to recharge my phone. Let me borrow yours."

Oblivious of my deception, he dutifully handed me his phone from his suit pocket. My brief hesitation at first to take it, I blamed on my guilt for my dishonesty. I took the phone anyway.

Lee stood for a moment, watching me and his phone.

"Something wrong?" The smile I wore didn't feel right.

He said nothing at first.

"Don't get the Chicken Lo Mein, didn't much like it last time."

I nodded in agreement as he turned and bounded up the stairs to the bathroom. If Amber put spyware on his phone, it wouldn't have taken much effort, I thought. Not much at all.

First, I called in the dinner order. I didn't know how long it would take me to follow the instructions Maggie gave me. The shower, getting dressed, and a search for a movie I had about thirty minutes. Before I started, I waited for the sound of the shower. The minute I heard running water, I pulled out the paper Maggie had given me. After reading the instructions twice, I engaged Lee's slick, new phone. As expected, there was no password to open it. This made me cringe at his naivety.

It took time to stroll through several useless apps before I found the App Store. Once in, I downloaded the software in the instruction. This took forever. At one point the shower stopped. With the download half complete, my heart raced. The download bar seemed to stand still. Each sound coming from upstairs unnerved me. Finally, when it finished, I opened the app and let it run. Five minutes later, a flashing warning sign came on the screen that it found spyware.

"Did you order extra spring rolls," Lee shouted from the bedroom.

I almost dropped the phone.

"I put in a double order," I lied.

While the phone's screen continued to flash the warning, I called in a double order of spring rolls. When the program asked permission to remove the spyware. I pressed 'Okay'. This took time—too much time. As the program worked its way through, Lee came ambling down the stairs. Hair still wet from the shower and dressed in sweats, he waved a DVD case at me.

"Little Foxes," he grinned triumphantly with his choice

I nodded as I gripped his phone.

"Something wrong?" Lee peered over his glasses at me.

I shook my head.

When his eyes danced between me and his phone I held it tighter. The program hadn't completed yet and kept flashing.

"Are you spying on me?" he said with a straight face.

My heart went directly into my throat and choked off my works. The incredulous face I tried to make felt unsuccessful.

"Why would you think that?" I feigned hurt.

"Because you're clutching my phone like you found a dirty secret." His arms crossed as he stared at me.

The software was ninety-five percent completed.

"How can you be so smart and so careless," I chided and held up the phone to wave at him. If I kept it close enough to the truth, the pit in my stomach would stop rolling.

Lee took the phone from me and stared at the screen. "What is this?"

"What do you think it is?" My indignation felt hollow.

Lee blinked at my accusing tone.

"It says I've been infected."

"You don't have a log on password, or any kind of antivirus to protect your phone or information. That's really careless." Without asking, I snatched the phone back. "Maggie explained this once about malware or something. I'm putting on some protection and a log on password," I insisted.

With his index finger, Lee pushed his glasses back up his nose and gave me a thoughtful frown. Just as he was about to say something, the doorbell rang. He stood there for a moment, sighed, and heading for the door.

"Don't make the password too hard that I can't remember," he called out as he answered the door.

I didn't know whether to be grateful or annoyed at his gullibility. At ease for the first time, I let the program finished. By the time Lee set up the food and readied the movie, his phone had a new password and the spyware removed. Whoever placed the malicious software could no longer track him. If that person was Ellison, that was fine by me. For the next ninety minutes we ate and watch Bette Davis' visceral performance in "The Little Foxes" in amicable silence.

"You like her, don't you?" I said, referring to Davis when the movie ended.

Lee wiggled his brows and gave me a playful grin.

"A woman with a little bite."

"That explains a lot." I said, as I slapped away his approaching hand. "Wasn't she involved in a famous feud?"

The name of the actress slipped my lips. Yet an image came to mind of an intense looking woman with boxy shoulders and major eyebrow action.

"You mean Lucille Fay LeSueur." Lee stood to clear up the takeout.

"Who the hell is Lucille Fay LeSueur?"

"Joan Crawford." He laughed and headed for the kitchen.

Seriously, who'd name their kid Lucille Fay LeSueur? An odd sense of déjà vu hit me. The name repeated in my head several times because something about it tingled at the edge of my senses. Something that had nothing to do with old movie actresses or a feud. The first connection hit me when I remember what Heather's old neighborhood friend said.

"Did you know Joan Crawford was Heather's favorite actress?" I called out to Lee.

Lee paused in the kitchen doorway with two bowls of green tea ice cream.

"How did you know?" He frowned, possibly wondering how I would know that. He continued to the sofa and sat down. "We used to joke who could take who in a fight."

"Crawford, easy," I said with certainty as Lee handed me my ice cream. "Because she had nothing to lose."

"Bette could take her," he said.

I could tell he wanted to start on Bette's defense. My hand went up to stop him. The fighting skills of two dead actresses didn't need debating. Something more important wrestled around in my head. Something only Lee could answer.

"How often did Heather visit her mother?"

Lee's brow furrowed deeply. His hesitation to respond told me this wasn't the direction he wanted the evening to go.

"Not often. She said she found it hard seeing her mother like that."

"You believe Heather stayed away from her mother because of her illness?" Whatever I thought of Heather, it never occurred to me she was a neglectful daughter.

"In the last two years, Heather didn't visit," Lee replied.

I shook my head slowly, knowing what I was about to tell him might hurt. Hurting him was the furthest thing from my mind.

"When Heather first died, I had Maggie look into her for me." Before he responded, I pushed on. "You were acting weird about a woman I'd never met. She found out about Heather's mother and the nursing home. That's how I knew you were taking care of her mother."

"Heather was my friend," he insisted.

"A friend who asked you to help her disappear because of Ellison; a friend who made you responsible for her ailing mother. You say she wanted to start a new life away from Ellison. I don't believe Heather feared him. Played him yes, but not fear."

He said nothing, and I continued.

"If Heather got a hold of that locket and used it as leverage for blackmail, she wouldn't want to be found, especially by you. How helpful would you be, knowing what she's done?"

"That's not how..." Lee put down his ice cream and began to pace.

"Did you know where she was? Did she care to see how you were doing? Why did she move her mother from a perfectly good nursing home on Staten Island to the one in Brooklyn?"

"The care was better?"

Again, I shook my head.

"Maggie said the biggest difference is the one in Brooklyn is a more secure facility. The only visitors allowed to see her mother were you and someone else. They're better than Fort Knox about divulging information."

Lee stopped pacing.

"If anyone odd came sniffing around her mother, she'd know. More importantly, anyone interested if she came back to New York City."

Lee sighed in annoyance, not willing to play along. "Ellison."

"Maybe, but someone dangerous to her financial health."

"Odessa, what the hell are you getting at?"

"You were right, Heather didn't seem to visit her mother much. But I believed Heather cared about her. That was her mother. Despite worrying about who might want to know if she was back in the city, she did visit, regularly. She just didn't visit as Heather. Maggie found out someone did visit Mrs. McLaughlin often. A woman called Lucy LeSueur. Secretive, paranoid Heather, who comes to New York telling no one. Careful Heather, who stays at a low-rent hotel, not for the view, but because it's only minutes away from her mother and the airport. A place that doesn't much care about checking in or out or how long you stayed."

Lee's jaw clenched.

"When Maggie threatened the night manager with calling the fire department on why he locked all the room windows, his memory improved. He remembered her. If you know the hotel's type of clientele, she stands out. Lucy LeSueur visited Mrs. McLaughlin more than Heather did. What's the likelihood she might have kept something with her mother for safekeeping? Something pretty and shiny and close at hand?"

CHAPTER 38

Maybe to prove me wrong, early the next day, both Lee and I arranged a visit to Mrs. McLaughlin at the Magnolia Adult Care and Housing in Brooklyn. Once again, I left Esperanza in charge of the shop. I felt guilty for about half a minute. My sense of guilt died when the young baker told me not to worry and take as much time as I wanted.

"The shops in good hands, another day at O So Sweet Bakery," she said with a cheeriness that seemed out of place. Did I say she was a horrible liar? Her voice resembled a twelve-year-old the further away from the truth she got. Also, she always does it out of earshot of her grandmother.

"Pavel wants me to teach him how to bake," she blurted out.

I felt disappointed and a little hurt by her revelation. I kind of enjoyed the idea of teaching him. Why did he opt for Esperanza?

"He's afraid of you," Esperanza admitted.

Pavel and his cohorts intimated an entire building of people. He threatened me, my staff and attacked Lee. The only reason he worked for me was because of his brother-in-law. Along with a threat to return to the potato fields of the Ukraine, his collection of hip-hop CDs would be buried in the same field. Why would he be fearful of me?

"He has about a hundred and fifty pounds on me," I reminded Esperanza.

She didn't answer at first. This was her way of being polite. I loved the girl to death, but I didn't have time to wait her out.

"Esperanza," I prompted.

"Well, Ms. O, you and your sister have a way of looking at people, especially, Ms. Candace. The other day, the liquor distributor stopped by the shop because he needed time to brace himself. He had to meet her, and he needed my grandmother's double espresso to do it. The man looked terrified."

I sighed. I knew the liquor salesman. A timid man who collected stamps and taught Taekwondo on the side. Once I had to intervene between Candace and the salesman when she threatened to send his man parts to meet his maker. There had been a question about replacing some high-end stock with one of a poorer quality.

"You equate me with my sister?" I said with some indignation.

"Have you ever noticed that when a bride comes looking for over the top cakes either they can't afford or impossible to make, then stop asking after about fifteen minutes?"

I had to think about it. With the abundance of cook and bake shows on television, some brides thought a six-tier cake was a commercial away. The need to correct them was my civic duty if not my sanity.

"And Pavel?" I said in the hope to come to a point.

"When he took a cookie out of the cookie display the other day, you grabbed him by his ear. Then you dragged him into the shop, explained how long it took to make that cookie and how much it cost. You made him pay for the cookie and apologize for wasting my time to make the cookie."

"And?"

"Ms. O, you did it in front of the sergeants Lopez and Steiner from the 113th precinct." She sounded embarrassed.

The image of the congenial Lopez flashed in my head. Then the sight of Pavel munching down on one of Esperanza's cinnamon oversized cookies flashed as well. An hour earlier, I sent him to the Blue Moon for lunch. A lunch that included a double helping of George's meatloaf, loaded potatoes, and two slices of a berry pie. Pavel ate as if we'd never feed him again. I had to stop him with the cookie.

Just because he worked in my shop and I shared ownership in the Blue Moon with Candace, didn't make it an all you can eat buffet.

"Fine, teach him," I conceded but couldn't help but say something. "Tell him I'll test everything he makes."

Esperanza fell into another silence before speaking. "Can I tell him later... Much later."

"Whatever," I said. There were more problems beside Pavel's appetite. Lee and I were on our way to the Magnolia Adult Care and Housing to see if Mrs. McLaughlin had Heather's locket. Lee had called Amber to let the office know he needed the morning.

When we arrived, the sight of Magnolia Adult Care and Housing was impressive. It looked more like an apartment complex or a hotel. Dance classes, computer training, and the gray hair set getting dating advice filled the activity rooms.

We found Mrs. McLaughlin in a Magnolia Adult Care and Housing's large arts and crafts room trying to work out a complicated puzzled of a photograph of an English garden. Aiding her in this task was another woman, whose method of doing the puzzle was to force the pieces into place. Each time she tried to force a piece, Mrs. McLaughlin waited until her companion's attention focused on another piece and removed it. At this rate, they would never finish.

"Mrs. McLaughlin," Lee whispered.

Dull blue eyes looked upward. They focused for a moment before returning to the puzzle. I could tell where Heather got her looks. Time had taken its toll, yet the fine bone structure remained. The edge of her bowed lips lifted in a smile as she turned her gaze on me.

"Josephine, you've lost weight," Mrs. McLaughlin said, her voice low and uncertain. "What will Harold think?"

I turned to look behind to see who had gotten Mrs. McLaughlin's attention. There was no one except two elderly men chatting up one of the pretty attendants.

"Excuse me," I said. Certain she had mistaken me for someone else.

"She thinks you're a nurse who works here." Lee leaned in close to whisper to me

Not willing to correct her, I nodded in response of the compliment.

"Do you remember me, Mrs. McLaughlin?" Lee asked. He bent down to face her. Her eyes brightened.

"You're Heather's boyfriend? Is Heather with you?" she scanned the room to look for a daughter that would never come.

"Heather's boyfriend!" My indignation was palpable. Lee gave me a slight shake of the head. Mrs. McLaughlin's puzzle mate cocked a brow at me. Her scrutiny became uncomfortable when her gaze stopped at my engagement ring. It was then I noticed she wore several pieces of costume jewelry. Somewhere in the woman's head was Mardi Gras.

"That's pretty," she said in a way that didn't hide her intent. I stood a little closer to Lee, who was trying to have an unsuccessful conversation with Mrs. McLaughlin, who asked questions about Heather.

"Did she come see you?" he asked, tone gentle and warm.

"Can I try it on?" Ms. Puzzle asked with a smile as she batted her lashes at me.

I shook my head.

"Please," she whined. She got up from her seat and came over. The elderly woman stood like a small child, with her hands behind her back and swaying side to side. About shoulder height, with a bluish white shortcut hair and wide set of tiny black eyes, she reminded me of a garden gnome. I shook my head again. She held out a hand. This ploy must work, as evident by the excessive amount of jewelry she wore.

"Beatrice, stop bothering Josephine. Harold won't like it," Mrs. McLaughlin said.

Beatrice huffed in disgust and leaned closer.

"You're not Josephine, and Heather is as dead as my third husband," Beatrice whispered. Her coy demeanor gone as she eyed my ring. When she turned her gaze on Mrs. McLaughlin, her intent seemed clear. Reminding Mrs. McLaughlin her daughter was dead had clear consequences only Beatrice comprehended. I didn't want to find out. It would also stop Lee from getting any answers from Heather's mother.

Beatrice's knowledge about Heather had me curious. More importantly, something around her neck caught my eye. A prize pink crystal necklace took center stage. Beatrice preferred wearing her jewelry box. With many rings on her fingers, a stack of bracelets, she wore several necklaces draped around her neck beneath her house dress.

I nodded toward the activity room door, in the guise of giving Lee and Mrs. McLaughlin privacy. Beatrice's smile broadened as she followed, in the clear belief I would pay for her silence with my ring. In the world of extortion and bribery, I was an expert.

Candace once threatened to tell our parent's I'd snuck out of the house on a school night to meet my boyfriend. Candace's compromised was to have me clean her room for a week. I took this opportunity to steal her diary and in return blackmailed her. There's nothing like telling the boy your sister liked that she really, really liked him to keep a girl in check.

"Beatrice," I said with a grin and a twenty-dollar bill I pulled from my pocketbook.

Beatrice's eyes widened.

"You share a room with Mrs. McLaughlin, don't you?" I said.

"Yeah, they put me in with her a week ago. How'd you know?"

Maggie wasn't the only one with deductive abilities. Sometimes even Doctor Watson had a clue or two. From the guilty expression on Beatrice's face, I hit the mark. Considering how inactive most of the residence were, a roommate like Beatrice could be problematic. Especially, if she took a liking to your things. Most residents would complain. Mrs. McLaughlin wouldn't complain, let alone remember.

"It's not important how I know. What's more important, is that you stole a gift a dead woman gave her sick mother. How will that play in the Magnolia Adult Care and Housing newsletter?" I said.

"We don't have a newsletter," a confused Beatrice said.

"Well, how about Daily News or Post? It might interest them in the theft going on at Magnolia," I said with a little too much smugness.

A Candy Coated Lie

The fact I was harassing a woman old enough to be my grandmother bothered me.

"You wouldn't," Beatrice threatened.

I snapped my fingers and pointed at her neck where her collection of jewelry lay. "Lady does this face look like it can't get loud and obnoxious if it wanted to?"

My raised voice made several staff turn in our direction. For the first time, doubt rippled on Beatrice's face. The doubt slipped away as her gaze fell back onto my ring.

"The ring for the necklace," Beatrice said between clenched teeth grin.

I laughed. The Red Sea would part, and Republicans and Democrats would agree on a Tax Code first before I handed over Lee's ring to an ageing kleptomaniac. I shoved the twenty in my purse, placed my hands on my hip, added a smirk, and glared at Beatrice. If needed, I would be as loud and obnoxious as a 1970s stereotype.

"How can you take advantage of an old lady?" Beatrice cursed as she dug around her neck for the locket. A wrinkled, aged spotted hand held out the heart-shaped locket.

"How could you, Beatrice?" I replied and held out my hand. Out came the locket and what looked like someone named Robert Glickman's medical medallion. Beatrice pouted as she handed me the necklace.

"What about the twenty?" she said with hopeful eyes.

I hoped my warning expression told her what I thought about the twenty-dollar bill. Still hopeful, she smiled at me.

"Don't get too happy. I plan to visit Mrs. McLaughlin every chance I get. If I find out you've been stealing from her again, your next roommate will be from Rikers," I warned.

Beatrice made a disgusting sound before scurrying away down a corridor. No doubt to pick the pockets of some comatose patient. I would have to tell Lee about Beatrice, but for the time being, I was contented to have Deena's locket. Its heart shaped case held the fate of a multi-million-dollar company. If I were lucky, it might change Ellison's current residence to Rikers.

When I returned to the arts and crafts room, I found Lee chatting with Mrs. McLaughlin. They were talking about her storm drains or something like that. I didn't have the heart to break up the conversation, so I waited. Five minutes later, a dejected Lee ended his talks with Mrs. McLaughlin with a kiss on the cheek. She beamed in delight. When he turned to see me, I held up the locket.

To anyone looking, the truth looked shiny.

CHAPTER 39

My excitement on finding the necklace didn't last long. With resolving the LaGuardia Apartment's case, Lee's caseload doubled. Taking the morning off had been a luxury he could no longer afford. A call from the office had him racing to the court house to replace one of the firm's lawyers named Tillman. Tillman complained of a slight fever and an abdominal tenderness before doubling over in court. He was in the middle of his opening remarks. Diagnosed with acute appendicitis, they rushed him to the hospital. Lee had to step in and left me with the locket. Before he left to save the Tillman's case, he instructed me to put it some place safe.

"How about the cookie jar," I teased.

"Funny." Lee groaned. "Maybe I should take it."

"Trust me, I'll find someplace safe." I said. "Anyway, we'll need someone to explain what's on the drive to us.

"Let me see who I can find."

"Why not Wilda Clark?"

"A graduate student won't do." Lee shook his head.

I scoffed at his dismissive tone. Considering Wilda was one of the few people who knew the reason for the research. With little time to argue the point, I agreed.

"Don't wait up for me. With the Tillman's case, it will take me awhile to catch up." He sounded tired already. The hope he might clear his cases before the wedding dimmed with each new disaster. Thank you, Tillman.

With work of my own to deal with, I headed for the shop. Along the way, I called Maggie to tell her about the locket. Earlier that morning, she sent me a text about her plans to visit Billy at the hospital.

"He had no recollection of the attack or the days that led up to it. His main concern was the laundromat. He never discussed Ellison and I didn't push it," she said.

"Maybe that's a good thing." With the death of his sister, Billy's life had been a struggle.

"We talked about Deena a lot. When I asked about the time she might have given the drive to Heather, he said something interested. Her mood changed and seemed more hopeful. It was short-lived though, because she killed herself soon after." The hint of sadness in Maggie's voice told me the conversation was difficult to have.

"Heather gave her false hope. Instead, she took the information and money and ran. Leaving Schaeffer free to do what they wanted and Deena with nothing."

"Speaking of Schaeffer, Frank and I went to the place where they held that big party. A place called the North Shore Country Club. Ellison's father is a member."

"Frank! Did he volunteer?" My surprise made me giggle.

"Not exactly," Maggie replied, making me curious how she got her boss to help.

"Exactly how?" I had to know.

"Rocket promised to give him a thirty percent discount if he helped me," she confessed.

An image of Rocket negotiating with Frank made me smile. Once again, he was out negotiated by a 9-year-old.

"Find anything?"

"Frank pulled his retired cop routine and got a copy of the surveillance tapes for that night. Told them we were on an insurance case and a guest sideswiped a car the night of Schaeffer's party. I'm going through it now."

Now and then Frank came in handy.

"Sounds like a plan," I said before saying goodbye.

The news about Billy hadn't been great, but at least he would recover.

At the shop, the day flew by. As promised, I let Esperanza teach Pavel. What surprised me the most was the intensity in which he went about it. Like with LaGuardia Apartments, Pavel had a take no prisoner's attitude. How good his baking was, was another conversation.

Around seven o'clock I returned home. I heated the leftover Chinese food and found another one of Lee's old movies. This time I picked a Joan Crawford movie, "Mildred Pierce". By the movie's end, I understood why Crawford was Heather's favorite. Alone or abandon by some man, Crawford's characters fought her way to the top, bloody knees and all.

After the trials and tribulation on Mildred Pierce, I readied for bed. The cat followed me upstairs like a lap dog. Most nights, the cat slept on the couch, but with Lee pulling another late night, the company would be nice. Anyway, trying to keep him out of the bedroom was hopeless. Once, when Lee closed the door on him, we watched in silent horror as he managed to turn the knob and push the door open. Short of barricading the door, we threw up our hands.

"You better behave yourself," I warned. The large round face stared up at me with an indignant gaze and proceeded to hop on the bed. After a quick shower, I slipped between the sheets and fell asleep, with a warm hairy body at my feet.

The sound of hissing and shrieking of the cat woke me. Disoriented and still half asleep, I read the bedside clock at 1:17 a. m. Something thudded hard against a wall, followed by the sound of scrabbling feet.

Someone was in the house.

Instinct propelled me out of the bed. At the open bedroom door, I listen for sounds. Tentative steps to the second landing brought me to the edge of the stairs. I peered down into the darkness and saw nothing. Then the cat snarled again, loud and aggressive.

I needed to call the police. My phone sat on the nightstand and I dashed for it, like a bad television action star. When my toe banged into the edge of the large dresser, I cursed loud enough that anyone in New Jersey could hear. My foot throbbed as I hobbled to the nightstand to grab my phone. Any pretense I was asleep vanished.

"I called the police and I have a weapon." My voice broke from fear.

A stranger was in my house and my only defense was a cat. All the scenarios running in my head ended with me dead. The idea I would never see Lee, Candace, and the people I loved forced me to stop shaking long enough to dial 911. It took forever for the call to connect.

"What is the nature of your emergency?" a much too calm voice said.

"Someone's in my house," I said in a hushed voice. The operator asked for my address. This information eluded me for a minute, my head felt jumbled.

"Are you in a safe place?" she asked after I gave her my address.

"I'm in a house with a murderer or rapist or burglar. How safe can I be?" I almost shouted. I'd position myself on the far side of the bed with a clear view of the closed bedroom door.

"We have dispatched police to your location, please stay on the line," the woman said. Her voice steady.

A wave of fear rolled over me as my stomach twisted in a knot. My eyes stung as tears rolled down my cheeks.

"In a few weeks, I'm getting married."

"I need you to stay calm," the operator said.

"Calm! The only thing between me and a maniac is a bedroom door and my cat," I yelled

"What?" The woman sounded surprised. "Did you say your cat?"

I heard the cat growl and give a long threatening hiss.

"Yes, my God damn cat," I scream. I was losing it.

Then there was silence. Crouched down by the bed, I peered over it. My eyes locked on the closed door. If I couldn't keep a cat out of my bedroom, how would I stop a mass murderer?

When something knocked against the door, I yelped. I clutched the phone to my chest, dropped to my knees and prayed. When the door pushed open, I shut my eyes.

Then I heard a soft meow. The cat meowed again. When I opened my eyes, bright glowing eyes stared back. In the darken bedroom, all I saw were those eyes.

"Lady, are you all right?" The operator's calm voice had vanished. In that same instance, I saw flashing lights decorate my bedroom wall.

"The police?" I yelled in triumph.

"Great!" Her calm facade had gone. "Are you okay?"

At first, I couldn't answer. Someone had broken into my house and I wanted to fold up into a ball. Instead, I watched the cat lick his private parts, hop up on the bed, and lay on Lee's pillow.

"I think I'm okay." I said.

Twenty minutes later, I sat in my kitchen drinking Chamomile tea and frying up chicken livers. My house was a mess. Whoever came ransacked Lee's office and the living room. All the valuable electronic remain untouched, including my laptop, which I left on the sofa.

"What time did you go to bed again?" a uniformed police officer asked. When he and his partner had arrived at the scene, they made me wait outside as they searched the house. Certain the intruder had gone, they allowed me back inside. What surprised me was they found no forced entry.

"Maybe you left a window open?" one of them suggested.

I shook my head and remembered I hadn't set the alarm. An exhausted Lee would crawl home and I thought nothing of not turning it on. It was a careless and a stupid mistake.

"Change the locks for good measure," the police instructed.

"That's the biggest cat I've ever seen." An officer stared down at the cat as he sipped coffee I'd made. A panicked Lee was on his way home and they didn't mind waiting. The coffee and homemade chocolate chip cookies helped.

The cat stood by my side licking its paws and waited for the chicken livers. If I could have served the thing kitty champagne I would, but chicken livers would do. Pleased with itself, it stretched out its long furry legs. We all took notice as it displayed a long set of curled claws. I bent down for a closer look.

"Is that wise?" one of the officers warned.

"There is blood on it," I explained, taking the big paw in my hand. "Are you hurt baby?"

The men leaned in for a closer look but kept a healthy distance. You would have thought I was petting a Bengal tiger. One of them nodded.

"He got a piece of someone," he said in admiration.

The cat rubbed up against me and I stroked it about the ear. It made that weird chirping sound when it was pleased. When it had dumped enough of its hair on my leg, it sat back on its haunches and licked at its paw. It only stopped grooming itself when I put the plate of chicken liver before it.

I stared down as it ate. Unconsciously, I pulled the necklace from beneath the robe. The reassuring feeling as it slipped through my fingers calmed me. A panicked Lee came bursting through the front, setting off my nerves again. Only when the police promising to patrol the area for the next couple of days, did Lee relax a little. No matter how hard we tried, the only one who got a good night's sleep that night was the cat.

CHAPTER 40

After the break-in, the next day Lee called the shop several times before I told him to stop. That morning, he'd been reluctant to leave me, but he had the Tillman case. I didn't want him to. What I wanted was to deal with Amber. Besides Lee, everyone at his office knew he'd be working late, especially Amber. Home alone made me vulnerable.

"She seemed like such a nice girl," Maggie said.

"I'm a nice girl and trust me, I can do some not so nice things," I reassured her as we sat in her car just outside Lee's office.

"Don't you think you should have told Lee what you were up to?"

I laughed. "This is the not so nice part."

"When he finds out..." Maggie began, but stopped when she saw my face.

"He'll be grateful I didn't waterboard her," I snapped back, my nerves still a little frayed from the night before.

"Did it ever occur to you we might meet up with someone who might have killed Heather?" Despite my anger with Amber, the truth was we might connect her to that person. Despite Deena's file, Billy's attack and my break-in, the heart of that shredded mess was Heather. If she'd gotten Deena's drive and used it to get as far away from Staten Island, it might have cost her a life.

"The thought has crossed my mind."

In all honesty, I ran right passed that thought just to get to Amber. My sense of payback overrode my common sense. I knew it, Maggie knew it, and I didn't care. Memory of that fear as I huddled in the dark still lingered at the edges of my mind. The crazed part of me couldn't run away from it. Maggie might have called it poking the snake. I preferred to call it getting the asshole that made me feel that way.

"Using Lee to set her up will not make a happy groom." Maggie's warning tone had no effect on me. If Amber arranged the break in, Maggie should worry more about the unhappy bride-to-be. Reading my mood, she stopped asking about Amber's future state of health.

"Did you get the same one?" I asked.

"Yeah." From her large satchel pocketbook, Maggie pulled out a small university shopping bag. From it she pulled out a heart shaped USB drive. The same drive that held Deena's information.

"If we timed this right," I checked my watch, "Lee will be back in the office around three for a client meeting. That gives Amber about two hours to do whatever duplicitous people do."

"Time enough, I think." A wary Maggie placed the new drive in my hand.

"Showtime." I gave Maggie a disingenuous smile before I got out the car.

"Try not to strangle her, please," Maggie begged.

I huffed at the idea about wasting that much energy.

When I reached the reception area of the law firm, Amber greeted me first, along with a few others. Certain Lee had informed them of what happened, the most sympathetic was Amber, and it took all my efforts not to strangle her. I thanked them all for their good wishes but pulled Amber to the side to ask a favor. Happy to comply, she all but groveled at my feet.

"Lee won't be home for a while and I'm still a little shaky after what happened last night." Having to put a sense of unease in my voice didn't take much. "So, I thought maybe you could help me."

"Ms. Wilkes. Anything. Please, I want to help." Her eager face and heartfelt sincerity surprised me. "When I found out what happened, I couldn't sleep or eat or anything."

I took a beat to see past the empathic expression on her face. At one point, she placed a hand on mine and gave it a gentle squeeze.

Somewhere passed my anger, I thought she might care. Before I lost my nerve, I pulled out the duplicate USB drive and dangled it in front of her. To the unsuspected, it was just a piece of costume jewelry. From the reaction in Amber's eyes, it was much more.

"What's this?" She took the locket in her hand to get a closer look. "Pretty."

"If you like this kind of stuff." I shrugged off the compliment. "Could you give it to Lee for safe keeping for me? Tell him I don't want it in the house." I dropped the locket in her out-stretched hand. Before she had a chance to refuse, I turned and walked away.

"Ms. Wilkes," she called out. I didn't turn around but gave her a wave as I left. My plan to give Amber the locket had been more elaborate. Her show of concern played a little with my head. Did she care or was she the best actress in the world?

"Gotta go," I said as the elevator door closed. Inside, I took a deep breath and prayed I hadn't made a fool of myself.

When I reached the car, my uncertainty grew. By the time I got in the car, I second-guessed myself.

"Amber must think I'm crazy," I blurted out as I fell into the passenger seat. "She seemed really upset about what happen at the house. God, what if I'm wrong?"

Azure eyes stared back at me. Judging how crazy I was, considering moments before I wanted to strangle the receptionist, Maggie sighed. She reached out and gave me a gentle, yet condescending pat on the shoulder.

"I'm serious, Maggie. What if I'm wrong and this is all just coincidence? You're right, pissing Lee off before the wedding is the dumbest idea in the history of the world. Why am I doing this? I should be concentrating on my guest list, checking my wedding dress and cake." All the air from the car seemed to vanish and I couldn't breathe.

"Odessa!" Maggie shouted. "I would slap you, but you might hit me back."

"I should have listened to you."

Instead of slapping, Maggie gave me a hard pinch on the arm.

I yelped in pain.

"Why did you do that?" I rubbed the spot.

"Because you need to relax," Maggie scolded.

How does causing someone pains help you relax? That's like curing a headache with a hammer.

"Let's wait and see what happens. If nothing does, then nothing will. Lee or Amber won't be any the wiser, so breathe," she reassured.

I took a deep breath and then another. The rash on my arm tingled and when I went to scratch it, Maggie slapped my hand away. While I tried to breath and not scratch, Maggie pulled out the hand-written notes she'd gotten from the housekeeper from the Terminal Hotel. This was Maggie's way of distracting me from my crazed behavior.

"The police were right. Her description of the man she saw on Heather's floor made no sense. Medium height, blond or light brown hair, dark suit and drunk." She flipped through the pages in search of something.

"That's odd," I said.

"She'd been cleaning rooms on the floor. A noise came from the room next door and thought nothing about it until the sound of a door closing and someone walking down the hall. She peeked out and saw someone walking down the hall away from Heather's room. In that darken hallway, she couldn't make out the details. Except she noticed his unsteady gait and smelled alcohol." Maggie closed the notebook.

The assumption that he was drunk seemed reasonable. It wasn't the first time at the hotel, she'd encountered a drunken guest. With rooms to clean, she forgot about him until she saw him later. When she returned to the floor, she saw a man burst out of Heather's room with a weapon and ran. Had he sobered up?

"Look." Maggie pointed just beyond me.

Outside of the law office building Amber Kim stood. Her face now filled with anxious desperation. In fact, if I had to put money on it, I'd say, she seemed anxious and scared. A few minutes later a black car pulled up. Before it even stopped, Amber ran to the driver's side and handed what looked like the locket to someone. From our position, we couldn't tell who was in the driver's seat. A fretful Amber talked excitedly. An adamant shake of her head followed each word.

"She's not happy," Maggie said and pulled out her phone and took several pictures of the transaction.

Without warning the car sped away, leaving an overwrought Amber in its wake. As far away as she was, I could tell she was crying. The unexpected sight surprised me. Standing alone, in front of the building and acting for no one, Amber Kim looked lost. For half a minute I felt sorry for her. Then I realized the car that had taken the bait had driven off without us.

"Why aren't you following them?" I scanned the street, I saw it turn a corner.

"Don't have too."

"Yes, we do," I insisted.

"Nope, I know that car." Maggie reached into the backseat and retrieved her laptop. She turned the laptop screen so I could see. In a media program a video of a parking lot appeared. Even though the scene was at night, you could see clearly.

"The North Shore Country Club video Frank got." Maggie tapped the screen.

At one corner of the lot, a group of men I recognized stood by a black sedan. Maxfield, Waller, Ellison, and another older man I didn't recognize. Without the sound I couldn't tell what they were saying, I didn't have too. Maxfield tried to take a drink from Ellison's hand only to have it tossed at him. The older man shouted something to an unresponsive Ellison. The only thing holding Ellison up was Waller, who struggled to put him in the backseat. Frustration showed on Waller's face, even in the dim lighting.

"I guess that was the incident at the party." I peered in closer for a better look. Moments later, the rest of the law firm joined the men out in the lot. "God, they all look alike."

All the men were dressed in the typical tailored black suit. Christ, did they shop at the same stores? Maxfield's white hair distinguished him, as did Mercier's dark skin and Koenig's girth. A brief discussion occurred before the older man returned inside of the country club entrance. The rest of Mercier, Koenig and Layng each went to their cars and left.

"They all left at the same time." Maggie froze the frame on a license plate. From her note pad, a neat list of license plates took up much of the paper.

"Who is it?" I peered in closer for a better look.

"Koenig, from Lee's old firm."

The smug look on Maggie's face said a lot. Once she got the video file from the country club she took down every license plate of any car that left the party around the time of Heather's death. Then used Frank's connection at the DMV to put names to the plates.

"Are you telling me Mercier, Koenig and Layng broke into my house?" I couldn't hide my anger.

"Don't know. All we can say is that they knew about Amber and the locket." Maggie closed the laptop.

I suspected Ellison for this. A reckless loose cannon even his father couldn't contain. With Lee's old law firm added into the mix, I didn't know what to think. Schaeffer Pharmaceuticals remained their biggest client. If nothing else, there were fixers. With Heather's death and with what they believed was Deena's file, they'd done their job. My question would be, how far did they go to get it?

CHAPTER 41

The news of Amber's sudden resignation didn't surprise me. Just over two hours after I gave her the fake locket, news of her resignation reached me at my shop. The news made its way to my shop with a call from Lee. He'd called to check up on me and lament about the receptionist's leaving. His tone of regret was palpable. Part of me wanted to tell him about what Maggie had found. I didn't. An image of that clown car popped into my head. It was all just too much.

"I'm sure you will find someone just as good or better," I reassured. Lee's response seemed doubtful

To cheer him up, I promise to swipe a nice bottle of wine from the Blue Moon's bar for dinner. Picking up on my mood, he threatened to make the only dish he knew how to make.

"Spaghetti and meatballs... Mmmm." I feigned enthusiasm. Since the sauce came out of a jar and included frozen meatballs, there wasn't much home to it. "I'll steal two bottles."

This made him laugh. Though we talked about dinner, the wedding, and the weather, I still sensed Lee's displeasure. Amber was easy to like, and he'd miss her. Who else would help him with his phone? After falling in a silence, he told me he loved me, as if that put a salve on an uneasy day.

Discovering Amber's true reason for ingratiating herself into the Aaron's office still angered me. She'd fooled everyone. Fool me once, shame on me. Fool me twice, you better find a zip code in an alternate universe.

The moment I hung up with Lee, my phone rang again. It interrupted my murderous contemplation toward Amber. Maggie's face appeared on the screen. Ever since our trip to the Terminal Hotel, Maggie and I debated over what Elsa told us. Like the police, Maggie found Elsa's recall confusing. Nor could she explain why a man who seemed drunk, could return and sprint down several flights of stairs cold stone sober.

"I was about to call you," I said and explained about Amber.

"That was quick. I would have loved to talk to her," Maggie said.

"What I have to say to her, you wouldn't like," I said.

"Don't you want to know who sent her to Aaron's?"

"Ellison, who else?"

"That's a no brainer, but why would someone for Mercier, Koenig and Layng come pick up the locket?" Maggie asked.

With Amber's betrayal, I didn't think pass what was next. I should. Why would someone from the firm contact the receptionist? If Ellison set Amber up at Aaron's office, I could write it off as his jealous feelings toward Lee. If Max's firm sent Amber, everything felt more calculating.

"What if it's both? Ellison starts the ball rolling by placing Amber in the office to spy on Lee. Max or someone in the firm finds out and sees this as an opportunity. The firm takes control of Amber and the job turns from keeping an eye on Lee to finding Deena's file." Certain threads I felt were loose seemed to tie together.

"You mean, once Heather was dead the file remained out there in some form or another? With Heather gone, her mother and Lee were the only links to the drive. Heather's mother would be of no help, and they didn't have access to her," Maggie said and tied up a few strings of her own.

"After Heather's death, they had Lee. At least Maxfield did." The words stuck in my throat. Max's appearance at the funeral took on another meaning.

"The file stolen from Billy would lead a trail straight to Dr. Hagemann. Wilda wasn't the only graduate student working with him.

If they found out Hagemann and Deena put the information on that USB drive, they would try to find it, by anyway means possible."

"Like the idiot I am, the moment we found out about the locket, I ask Lee to contact the police. Amber heard all of that and told someone. When we found the locket at the nursing home, someone tries to break into my house." I wanted to kick myself for leading them straight to it.

"Don't beat yourself up about it. When they try to access that duplicate we gave them, all they'll find is Rocket's science homework and some nonsense files I downloaded," Maggie reassured.

"That make me smile," I mused.

"Did Lee find his expert?" Maggie asked.

With reluctance, I'd given Lee the locket. Though Amber no longer worked at Aaron's, I wanted to keep Deena's file close.

"Aaron found one. A professor friend of his from NYU. Lee's going to meet with him tomorrow. Once the drive is authenticated, Lee will give it to the police."

Before we said goodbye, Maggie wanted to go back to the Terminal Hotel one more time. She explained that Bartow told her several of his friends situated themselves around the hotel all the time. They might have seen something.

"Most sleep in the back of the hotel where it's quiet and no one bothers them. Maybe they saw something that night."

Maggie going back to the hotel by herself bothered me and I told her so. The workload in the bake shop stopped me from accompanying her. Tempted as I was to send Pavel, I didn't. He'd scare everyone away.

"I'm good," she said with confidence.

This didn't reassure me. However, I didn't want to treat her like Frank, or even her husband, Roger. Despite her natural ability, persistence, and eagerness to learn the trade, they only saw her as a wife and secretary.

"Just call me when you're done," I insisted. She promised.

The rest of the day whizzed by in a hectic cloud. By closing time, a rush order for ten dozen cupcakes sapped the last of my strength. Pavel didn't help. With Esperanza teaching him how to bake, every cupcake, banana loaf, and cookies made its way to me. For a man who threatened countless tenants, a lawyer, a 9-year old boy, and his future boss, Pavel was terrified of bad critiques. He cringed, flinched with every word. Then he placed a perfectly baked sponge cake in front of me. When I had nothing bad to say, he thought I lied to save his feelings. He refused to believe me.

"If you don't believe me, take it to Candace to taste. Trust me, she won't lie," I said.

An expression of betrayal, hurt, and disappointment played across his face in an instant. You would have thought I was offering him up as a virgin sacrifice. I couldn't win.

"Why would you do that to me, Ms. O?" a dejected Pavel replied.

By day's end, I settled Pavel's nerves, finished the last dozen cupcakes, and called my last bride. When I reached home, the sun had set. The muggy summer evening had my neighbors inside taking advantage of cool central air. I hoped for the same as I entered our house.

Tired and hot, it took me a moment to realize how dark the house was. The darkness inside looked like a gaping mouth ready to eat me whole. At the entrance, I unburden myself from the wine I'd taken from the Blue Moon, my keys and my pocket book on the small foyer table.

"Lee!" I called out as a sense of unease hit me.

Nothing.

The silence pressed me in place as the feeling grew. It rooted me to the spot. Even the cat was absent. It had become its habit to greet me at the door, hoping for a treat or an early meal.

"Well, don't just stand there," a familiar voice from inside the darkness made me jump.

Ellison was in my house.

As my eyes adjusted to the darkness, I made out the shape of outstretched legs jutted out of the kitchen doorway. Instinct made me run to Lee's side as he lay unconscious on the kitchen floor.

"Lee!" I screamed as I fell to my knees beside him. My voice made him stir and exhale a moan. My hand scanned his body for injuries. When I got to the back of his head, something wet covered my finger.

"What did you do to him?" I yelled.

Alone in the dark, Ellison sat in one of the living room's accent chairs that faced the kitchen, legs outstretched, with his arm dangling from the side. He held a bottle of scotch in his hand that Lee always kept in his home office. Much of the content now in Ellison's stomach.

"Have you lost your damn mind?" The words came in a rage. My entire body tingled with heat.

"Where is it?" His words came slow and slurred.

"Get the hell out of my house!" My only thoughts were of Lee as I stood up to turn on the kitchen lights.

"Don't do that," Ellison patted an object resting on his right leg. Hidden in shadow, I hadn't noticed the gun resting on his leg. "Father has a wonderful collection, you know."

The sight made me freeze. Lee moaned again, and it stirred me from my stupor. Without caring, I entered the dark kitchen and grabbed a roll of paper towel. Wadding enough to make a makeshift compress, I returned to Lee. When I press the paper towel to the site of the wound, Lee winced in pain at the contact. His eyes fluttered open. At the sight of me, his eyes widened in panic.

"Dessa." My name came out like a croak.

"It's okay," I whispered to him. The rash on my arm screamed as I tried to force myself to calm down.

"I asked Lee for it, but being the stubborn son-of-bitch he is, he said no." Ellison's snarky tone irritated me.

"Deena's drive?" What else would Ellison want, I thought.

"That little trick you played on Amber wasn't nice," Ellison said.

I ignored the confused look on Lee's face when I helped him to sit up. The effort made him lose what little color he had as he swayed. Lee was not a small man, and I had to brace him against me.

"You don't want to do this." Thoughts of arguing with an armed and drunken Ellison, was the last thing on my mind. Getting Lee to the hospital was my priority.

"I can't blame Amber. She did her best, but let's say I wasn't happy." Ellison's impertinent voice filled the silence.

Though I had no fondness for the receptionist, the thought of Ellison doing something to her concerned me. This disaster was of my making. I'd given Amber the fake locket. Amber's job was to help him play the hero to the men he'd looked up to. The same men who looked down on him. The night of his father's party, did he go to the source of his problems at the Terminal Hotel? Would he try to deal with me the same way he dealt with Heather?

"So, will you give me what I want?"

Even in the darkness, Ellison's desperation hit me like the odor from the Terminal Hotel. My stomach protested as my mind struggled for a solution as Lee's weight pressed into me. He seemed unable to steady himself, even with me holding him. The sound of his labored breathing and his efforts to mask his pain pulled at my concentration

"I'll make this right," I said like someone who wasn't in control of the only gun in the room. "I will fix this."

CHAPTER 42

When I started my day, I thought my worst problem would test Pavel's attempts at baking. Ellison topped that. Somehow, he'd gotten into the house and surprised Lee. From the mess on the kitchen floor, Ellison interrupted him in the middle of cooking his spaghetti and meatballs. Powered up on a pint of scotch, Ellison had a captive audience.

"I used to admire his taste in women," a smug sounding Ellison said to Lee.

Lee didn't respond. Even in the dim light, I could tell something was wrong with him. The blow had knocked his glasses off and left a nasty bruise on the back of his head. Staying alert appeared to be a struggle. Talking was out of the question. My worst fear was that Ellison had turned his brain to jelly.

"You can get what you want and walk away." I said it in a way that didn't sound as calm as it should, praying that Ellison's hubris wouldn't impede something he wanted more than taunting Lee.

"Leland wasn't forthcoming, which explains his current condition. Why would you?" Ellison pointed at me.

As I held tight to Lee, I forced a hapless smile. "I can fix this."

"No," Lee mumbled. Even in this state, he worried about my moral compass.

Ellison and I ignored him.

"How?"

That was the million-dollar question. When I worked in advertising, often a client would ask me about my idea that would sell his brand of toothpaste, car, or hemorrhage cream. I'd fortified myself with the confidence I didn't have, stare them straight in the eyes, and told them what they wanted to hear.

"I know where the drive is, and Lee is in no condition to stop me," I said.

My betraying Lee brought a smile to Ellison's face. His affair with Julia had done the same. Thank God, it had nothing to do with exchanging bodily fluids. His pleasure was short-lived when my cell phone rang.

From the foyer table the familiar ethereal music I'd designated for Maggie's calls fill the room. The intrusion deflated Ellison's mood. After several rings, it stopped. Not in a space of a breath, the ringing started again. One thing I knew about Maggie, she was persistent.

"That's my friend Maggie. If I don't answer, she'll call until she reaches me." At worst, she might come looking.

"That redhead." Ellison got up from his seat slow, as if any quick moves would send him to the floor. "Amber told me about her. She asked a lot of questions."

The phone rang again. He walked over to the foyer, dug in my bag, and pulled out my phone. He studied it for a second before he bought it over where I sat huddled with Lee. When he held the phone, the sight of the gun made me hesitate to take it. Indifferent to my reluctance, he dropped it into my lap.

"Put it on speaker." Ellison wagged the gun at me.

I put it on speaker.

"Are you all right?" Maggie's concerned voice steadied me, allowing me a moment to think.

"Hey, girl," My voice cracked as I tried to sound upbeat. "Sorry, Lee and I were going over the wedding plans, you know how much he loves to be involved."

Maggie said nothing at first, possibly trying to digest my lie. Lee's involvement in the wedding consisted of him showing up.

"Yeah, that sounds like him. I stopped by the Blue Moon and Candace said you went home already." With her hesitation gone, she fell into our natural rhythm of conversation. "I thought of stopping by, if that's okay."

Before answering, my eyes went to Ellison. Intoxicated as he was, he was no fool.

"No... Lee's a little under the weather and you might catch it, too."

It only took a beat for Maggie to respond.

"A cold or something worse?" She laid on the concern thick, but Ellison missed it.

"A serious stomach flu," I said. "I might have caught it from Mr. Poulsen."

"Poulsen, really? That's too bad." Maggie trailed off.

The Poulsens were the last job Maggie did for Aaron. A contentious divorce that needed the police to put an end to it. The Poulsen's marriage had devolved into heated and often violent confrontations. I prayed Maggie would remember.

"Will you be okay by the fifth?" she chimed back.

To show his annoyance with me, he took a step closer. A face I once thought of as handsome, now filled with loathing and suspicion. Whether to intimidate, or to hurry me off the phone, he heightened my discomfort. When he sank to one knee beside me, I drew away. This caused Lee to slip from my hold. He sank back and only stopped from banging his head against the floor by me grabbing him. This caused the phone to drop.

"Odessa... O, are you all right?" This time Maggie made no attempt at hiding the panic in her voice.

Desperate not to shatter the pretense, I picked the phone up before suspicion clouded Ellison's face.

"Sorry the phone slipped." Trying to hold up a full-grown man made me breathless. "Listen, Maggie, I have to go. As for the fifth that's fine. I hope that doesn't put you into a bind?"

With a malicious grin, Ellison dipped his head by my neck, sniffed, and made a face.

"No, sweetie. Since Lee isn't feeling well, I'll try to get someone to help you. Don't worry, take care of him and we'll talk tomorrow." For Maggie, her tone felt cool and detached. An image of a woodland fairy strapping on army boots popped into my head.

"Good..."

Ellison grabbed the phone before I finished and tossed it to the side.

"Now, give what me I want, and I'll go away," he said between clenched teeth, but then his face brightened. "Technically, Deena stole that information from us, so the drive belongs to Schaeffer Pharmaceuticals."

The look of incredulity on my face could have been seen from International Space Station. Holding two people at gunpoint didn't win his argument, but I kept that opinion to myself. What I wanted was some distance between us.

"Did you use that argument with Heather?" I asked snidely.

Ellison glared down at me. A surprise hint of hurt appeared before the façade of control returned.

"Don't want to talk about Heather, so don't say a god damn thing about her," he spat out. With each word, he stepped away.

"Isn't this all about Heather?" I said and took a moment to check on Lee. His steady breathing reassured me, but his lack of alertness didn't. "For Lee, Maxfield, and you."

"What do you know about Heather?" Without taking his eyes off me, he paced.

"She tricked Deena out of that drive and used it to blackmail you." What I needed more than Ellison's righteous indignation was time. Time enough for Maggie to get help. So, if I must bring up Heather, I would.

An angry Ellison shook his head.

"Mercier, Koenig and Layng, not me. Schaeffer Pharmaceuticals, not me." He tapped the gun to his chest to emphasize this point.

For one brief shining moment, I had the heady thought he might shoot himself. Unfortunately, he didn't, and I had to keep him talking.

"Then, did they send you here?" Considering Ellison's drunken condition, I doubt it. The firm was subtler, the way snakes were before they killed you. By the time you realize they're there, it's too late. Using Ellison was like using a tank at a knife fight.

"They didn't know Deena went back to her old professor for help, but I did. Her brother kept her papers around like they were the Holy Grail, claiming they'd bring me down. Where is he now, the fool?"

In the hospital recovering from an attack, I thought. From the way he took out Lee, the coincidence was hard to ignore. My question was why the sudden interest in Billy after all this time?

"Wasn't Billy just a nuisance to you?"

"The fool called me up and told me he'd hired a detective." Ellison laughed.

This made me pause. Did Billy tell him about a little redhead gung-ho to find the truth? Did our talking to Billy make Ellison see him as a threat? Serious enough threat to go to the laundromat and find out what he had, but instead found his sister's file?

"In his way, he kind of did," I said.

"That redhead?" He gritted his teeth in annoyance. "Amber said she dressed like she shopped at Kmart, but they liked using her for cases."

"Amber." I sucked back a breath at the memory of Amber's smiling face. "If she dressed like she shopped at Kmart, no one would have caught on to her. When I gave Amber the fake drive, you knew I'd found it," I said in self-condemnation.

"When I found out it was you, I thought you might set your own terms." His lips curled up in a sneer.

I didn't like what he implied, but I went with it.

"You mean like Heather, blackmailing everyone except you?"

Ellison's lips went bloodless.

"You'd never understand what I had with her."

"Did anyone?" I questioned.

"Max understood how I felt. He didn't laugh or mock me. He even talked to her after my affair with Julia to make her understand why I did what I did."

Ever the helpful, enabling Max. He might not have encouraged Ellison's narcissistic tendencies, but he didn't discourage them either.

"When she died, he went to the service because he knew I couldn't. He knew my father wouldn't want me to go. Told me she was in a better place and God was watching over her." Ellison's voice broke.

This was a man I'd accused of confusing love with lust and friendship with familiarity. Did I think Ellison was a narcissistic sociopath? I did. Would he kill the woman he loved? I didn't know.

A knock on the front door made me jump and sent my heart racing again. Ellison turned like a drunken iceberg, slow and dangerous.

"Odessa, it's me," Maggie familiar voice said from behind the door. "I brought chicken soup from the Blue Moon."

What the...

Had this been Maggie's plan? Walk up to the front door and say hello? What I expected was a call to a SWAT team. Light's flashing and a cute hostage negotiator, talking Ellison off the edge. I didn't expect goddamn chicken soup.

"Get up!" Ellison said in a harsh but hushed tone.

When I didn't do this quick enough, he stomped toward me. When he grabbed my arm, he yanked me up. Lee slumped to the floor, like a rag doll.

Whatever Maggie's plan was, I didn't want to open my front door. As much as I admired her deductive skills, I didn't expect her to play superman. She was someone's mother and wife. Ellison didn't care as he pushed me hard toward the front door. He stood on my right, just behind the door as I opened it.

A smiling Maggie stared back at me holding a large Blue Moon takeout bag in both hands. I looked past her, in the hope I'd see several police cars. Nope, it was just her.

"Hey, I thought I'd bring sustenance," she said, snapping me back into reality.

"Hey!" Another familiar voice said from behind me. It seemed surreal as both Ellison and I turned at the same time to see Pavel. In one swift move, he grabbed and twisted Ellison's gun hand. Ellison screamed in pain as I heard something pop. When the gun dropped, Pavel gave me a quick, yet satisfying smile before he punched Ellison hard in the face.

The only thought in my mind was, bakers were bad asses.

CHAPTER 43

The moment the police arrested Ellison, my level of anxiety magnified with each passing moment. In a dingy Queens precinct, I sat with Maggie on hard chairs wanting to be somewhere else. The rash on my arm threatened to push me over the edge every time Detective Brody told me I had to stay. I needed to leave. Lee lay in some hospital bed miles away without me. His only company was Candace. A woman whose constant joy was to question his choices in life.

When I called with the news of the attack, my sister didn't hesitate to be by Lee's side. This only confirmed how serious the situation was when Candace just said yes. A memory of them bickering over appetizers almost brought me to tears.

"Odessa." Maggie put a gently hand on my knee to stop me from pumping it up and down like a piston. My body parts were revolting and if I didn't do something, they'd leave without me.

"I can't stay here," I said as I checked my phone for the umpteenth time. Candace hadn't called. No news was a good thing, right?

"Relax," Maggie replied in a hushed yet calming voice.

Moments like this helped me appreciate Maggie's mothering tendencies. They didn't make things better, but helped you cope with it. At the end of the world, Maggie would pour everyone cocoa and recite Hallmark cards. A deep inhalation readjusted my nerves and prevented my leg from pounding a hole in the floor, but nothing else.

"Ms. O, I wanted to try this bread tomorrow. Why do I put water in the oven?" Pavel said as he showed me a picture of rustic French breads. He'd gotten into the habit of carrying several baking magazines with him. When the police removed his personal items, they didn't have the heart to take it. The fact he read unperturbed while cuffed to a bench said a lot about Pavel's past life experiences. Why he was cuffed was another source of my anxiety.

"It helps form a crust. You promised to be quiet," I said, taking a quick look at the photo he showed me. The answered seemed to appease him and he returned to his reading. God, it was like babysitting. Still dressed in his O So Sweet pink tee shirt, he hadn't had time to change when Maggie asked for his help.

"Do they know we can hear them?" Maggie questioned. The closed door of the detective squad lieutenant's office did little to muffle the raised voices coming from behind it.

"It's like the Cone of Silence, they think it works." I shook my head in frustration.

The joke registered on Maggie's face with a smile. A fan of the 1960's comedy, she understood the absurdity of the moment. Inside the small office, Detectives Brody and Starzynski dealt with Ellison's enraged father and a conciliatory Maxfield as he struggled to keep the peace. Kip Waller stood just outside the door, arms folded, head bowed and keeping his distance from me. Ellison sat in a holding cell with his hand in a cast and a broken nose trying to sober up.

"Rocket and I watched a rerun and he loved it," Maggie said fondly and turned a watchful gaze to Waller.

Every time the lawyer looked up, she made a point of catching his eyes. Regulated once again to wade hip deep into Ellison's disaster of the day, he looked miserable. Was defending Ellison against assault and unlawful restraint on his career goal list? I doubt it.

"There you are?" The familiar voice of Cesar Comaneci boomed in the opened detective squad. He looked out of place, dressed in a yachting outfit.

"You have a boat?" Maggie asked as she abandoned her gaze on Waller and took in Comaneci's outfit.

Comaneci stared down at what he was wearing—a red, white, and blue polo style shirt with khaki shorts and tan boat shoes. The captain's hat clinched the ensemble.

"Oh, no. Boats are dangerous. But the New York Yacht Club makes a fantastic Tom Collins." Comaneci smiled, then lost it at the sight of Pavel. "I was on my second when I got a call from the police. Once again, Pavel you are my biggest regret."

"Cesar!" Pavel pleaded, but stopped when Comaneci sneered at him. Pavel pouted and gripped the magazine like he wanted to strangle it.

"Pavel is a hero," Maggie said, quick to come to Pavel's defense.

Comaneci looked doubtful.

"If it wasn't for him, Lee might have died. You should be very proud of him. Scolding someone all the time hurts his self-confidence," Maggie admonished.

Comaneci laughed at Pavel's lack of confidence. "He wears bravado like an eyeliner. I think his ego is okay."

Maggie disagreed with her usual passion.

"Although Pavel manhandled my son, threatened a building full of people, and pushed Lee down a flight of stairs, he's trying to change. Your constant doubt is undermining his change."

Comaneci laughed and raise his hands in resignation. The scowl on Comaneci's face softened enough to give his brother-in-law an appreciative smile.

"I told you, bakers are bad assess," Pavel said proudly.

"Then why are you in handcuffs?" Comaneci pointed to Pavel's cuffed hand.

Like some trained seal act, Maggie, Pavel, and I pointed to the lieutenant's office. The raised voice emanating from the office told me I was no closer to leaving.

"Give me... the gist... of it." Comaneci snapped his fingers.

At first, unsure of what he wanted, I realized he needed exposition. How did a little redhead, a baker, and a baker's apprentice end up in a

Queens precinct? Maggie did the honors because she was good with details. If I spoke, it would only ignite my anger.

In a hushed voice, Maggie explained about Heather, Lee's old firm, Ellison and Schaeffer Pharmaceuticals. How a death at a run-down hotel had put Lee in the hospital and me on the verge of losing my sanity. My leg pumped, my rash screamed, and Comaneci listened patiently.

"I got this!" Comaneci held up a hand to stop any complaints. He offered a gentle smile before it vanished. Replaced with set determination that bordered on scary.

We watched him in strange fascination as he walked passed a protesting Waller into the office. Suddenly, the shouting stopped. For a long time, nothing happened. Had Comaneci made the matter worse? His only horse in the race was Pavel. He owed me nothing and Maggie even less. All I could think of was Lee, lying in a hospital and my anger rose. Just when I thought I couldn't take anymore, the men emerged and headed for us. None of them looked happy.

There was a flashback of being sent to the principal's office as the men stood before us. Maggie and I huddled close as Schaeffer senior gave me a nasty look. Maxfield stood next to him, his face indecipherable. As always, Kip Waller stood off to the side, trying hard to be invisible. Maggie glared at him.

"You want to explain yourself," Detective Brody demanded. His gruff and inpatient demeanor irritated my already jangled nerves. As if reading my unease, Detective Starzynski stepped up.

"Ms. Wilkes, we know you've had a rough night, but you can't say what you told Mr. Comaneci here and expect us to believe it," he said.

Did they believe I would make up a story, just so I could leave and go to the hospital? They were partially right. Getting out of the precinct was my main goal. But, I would tell the truth and give a reason Heather McLoughlin died at the Terminal Hotel.

"This is ridiculous," Schaeffer voiced in a tone so filled with disdain, it made Comaneci blanch.

"Let the ladies speak and we'll see how ridiculous this is," Comaneci barked back. "I'm good friends will several newspapermen."

I couldn't help but smile, considering those same newspapermen wanted to lynch him right after I released the video. Now he was there hero, at least in Comaneci's mind.

"I wonder what they would say about my family member being held because he protected Odessa and her fiancé from your psycho son."

This silenced Schaeffer. Pavel smiled as Comaneci came to his defense.

Undeterred, Maxfield spoke up.

"Cooler heads need to prevail here, gentlemen. Accusations made in the heat of the moment aren't helpful, so everyone please calm down."

I didn't want to be calm. I wanted to tear everything down. Anything that got me closer to Lee.

"I'm calm," I said in a way that belied the anger I felt.

"Ladies," Starzynski prompted. I could tell he wanted the crazy to stop.

Maggie pointed toward Starzynski's desk. On it lay several evidence bags. One had Deena's heart-shaped USB drive. Another held the gun Ellison used to hold Lee and me hostage. Another held a long nine-inch leather encased heavy gauge weight, Detective Brody called a Slap Jack.

The gun was problematic. From Schaeffer senior's gun collection, the starter gun from the Helsinki 52 Olympics shot only blanks. If I had known, Ellison's broken nose and finger would have had company. It was the Slap Jack, Ellison used on Lee that got him arrested. Schaeffer tried to argue that Ellison came to the house to talk to Lee and resolve their issues. Since Lee had attacked him before, he'd brought the weapons as self-protection. Schaeffer could only sell this story to someone with a questionable IQ and sense of humor.

"Byron, please. Lee is in the hospital. All Odessa wants is to go to him." Maxfield made everything sound reasonable. "Tomorrow, when we are all clear-headed, we'll sort all this out."

Clear-headed, I thought. A part of me found his words amusing. So, when I smiled, he returned it.

"I won't have my son in jail," Schaeffer insisted.

My smile widened because that was exactly what I wanted. I wanted Ellison Schaeffer dressed in prison orange and worried if his bunk mate wanted to braid his hair. I wanted the men of Mercier, Koenig and Layng to disappear from my life. If it were my only way to be by Lee's side, I would burn this house of lies down around them.

"That heart-shaped locket is the reason Heather came to New York, time and time again. Each time, Schaeffer Pharmaceuticals paid her not to release information on one of their drugs," Maggie began.

"That's a lie!" Schaeffer exclaimed. Maxfield held up a hand to silence him.

"Odessa, don't do this. You're upset. I understand. What Ellison did was reckless. Let us deal with him and I promise you he'll never bother you again," Maxfield pleaded. He hovered over me, his eyes urgent with concern and maybe a little fear.

I couldn't trust that concern because I believed it wasn't for me or even Lee.

"You told Mr. Comaneci that you know who killed Heather. That's a serious accusation," Starzynski said. From his expression he worried about my sanity. I'll admit they had to drag me kicking and screaming to the precinct. My priority hadn't been the arrest of Ellison, but an unresponsive Lee.

"Please, Odessa, let me make this right." Maxfield's words cut through the fog in my head. A fog caused by the sight of Lee's motionless body as an ambulance drove him away. That kind, fatherly face stared down at me, hoping I'd do what was best. Like Schaeffer, did he believe an apology and a nice wedding gift might appease me? A small misunderstanding between old friends and colleagues had an easy answer.

"I trusted you not to get Lee hurt," I replied. "He warned me, but I didn't listen."

I looked passed Maxfield and stared at Kip Waller. All eyes turned to him. He seemed to shrink at the attention. Helpful Kip, always at Maxfield's side, ready to fix the unfixable. He foolishly thought standing alongside Schaeffer and Maxfield, he could join their club. Or at least he hoped he could. In his desperate need to be at the right hand of Maxfield a woman died, Lee lay in the hospital, and my wedding anxiety had morphed into a killer rash.

CHAPTER 44

To describe Ellison as a monkey with a can of gasoline and matches in his hand would be an understatement, but I said as much. The disruption of Schaeffer's fragile peace with Heather lay at Ellison's feet. He'd come back to New York City, sober, focused, and determined to please his father once and for all. When I first met him at the gala, he appeared to be all those things. Over time, he devolved back into the person his father banished to South Korea. Why the rapid change?

Kip Waller

"I wondered why Ellison kept showing up. At the dinner, the restaurant, and that job for the hospital." My eyes danced between the men before me. "Each time, he was increasingly obnoxious, drunk, and unstable. Anyone with half a brain could tell I dislike him, and he felt the same. Yet there he was tripping over every twelve steps to mess in my life."

"What's that have to do with Heather?" Brody asked.

No one disputed Ellison's sudden downward spiral, not even his father. His cold, detached demeanor was the opposite of Maxfield's fatherly concern. No wonder Ellison turned to him repeatedly.

"One thing I've learned about Ellison, he's no mastermind. What you see is what you get. His greatest feat was recruiting Amber Kim in Aaron Boyer's law office, so she could spy on Lee."

"That's a lie," a defensive Schaeffer cursed.

"Not really," Maggie said and dug into her pocketbook and pulled out a slip of paper. "This is Amber Kim's contact information. She worked as a receptionist at Lee's firm, but abruptly resigned. She met Ellison in South Korea. On a promise of a job at Schaeffer and a hefty monetary incentive, she came to America. All she had to do was keep an eye on Lee. She didn't bargain for the rest."

"Why?" Starzynski prompted.

"Where are you going with this, Odessa?" Maxfield's word felt less like a question than a warning. Starzynski gave him a warning look of his own.

"Heather had a USB computer drive filled with damaging information on Schaeffer Pharmaceuticals. Deena Pace complied information on a series of drugs she helped research. She even went to an old college professor, Dr. Hagemann, to verify her findings." Maggie gave Schaeffer a scathing glance.

"The drugs had problems, initial results had the drug failing miserably, then suddenly the results changed magically. When the FDA approved the drug for the market based on the second research and testing report, Schaeffer sent it to market making millions. Dr. Hagemann confirmed Deena's worse fears on the original results. Schaeffer wouldn't listen to her, so she went to their lawyers. There she met Heather. Heather used the drive to blackmail Schaeffer and the firm for years. With her death, the drive went missing. The only person who had contact with her was Lee. They thought he might have it."

The room exploded in denials and accusation. Schaeffer threatened me with a libel suit as Maxfield warned me to stop. A shouting match began between Brody and the senior Schaeffer about the question of my character. Maxfield pleaded for me to see reason. It was all a crap.

"The drive isn't important!" I yelled above the noise.

Everyone stopped and focused on me.

"What?" Schaeffer said. For years, it was all about Deena's information and managing Heather. With Heather gone, there was only Deena's file.

"Heather has been blackmailing you for years. Even when she demanded more money, you didn't blink an eye. God, you probably wrote her in your yearly financials between research and marketing. You and the firm had Heather handled." I directed my words at Schaeffer and Maxfield.

They said nothing to confirm that fact. It would take more than my words to prove Schaeffer's payment to Heathers. That would come.

"But then Ellison came home," Maggie added.

"Recently recovered from a stint in an overseas rehab and a few years working in South Korea, Ellison arrived. Like the prodigal son, only with fewer morals and even fewer brain cells."

Schaeffer blanched at the insult. Certain he saved such abuses for himself. It was okay for Ellison to feel worthless in his father's eyes, but no one else.

"Little Ellie hatches a plan. This would get him back into his father's good graces and make up for his behavior towards Deena," I said.

"Ellison did nothing to that woman!" So quick to come to his son's defense, Schaeffer didn't notice a tiny redhead flushed with anger.

"I've read those emails your son wrote, and those calls Deena's recorded," Maggie said tightly. "If my son had said those things I would question how I raised an insensitive, morally vacant human being."

That made everyone take a moment.

"Who are you again?" a defensive Schaeffer asked.

I shook my head. "You don't want to piss her off, trust me."

"Can we stay focused, people?" Brody barked.

I sighed and cleared my throat. I hadn't finished my story.

"Anyway, Little Ellie hatches a plan to get the drive back from Heather. First, he needs her back in New York City. The only way he can do this is through Lee. With Amber in place in Lee's office, she steals his phone to get Heather's contact information.

"Lee and Heather were friends and he managed her mother's care. He was the only one from the firm still in contact with her. Even

Mercier, Koenig and Layng didn't know where she was. Heather would come to New York, get her money, and leave." I gestured toward Schaeffer and Maxfield with a playful grin.

"Do you think this is amusing, Odessa?" Maxfield sounded like a man at the end of his patience. I hadn't seen that side of Maxfield, the one that made U.S. prosecutor quake in their pants.

"It's either that or screaming." I stopped smiling.

"Lee admitted he communicated with Heather through texts only. She seemed to prefer it that way." Maggie shrugged. "Anyway, pretending to be Lee, Amber sent a text to Heather with the stolen phone. Something about her mother's care and papers needing signatures. Heather took the bait. To insure she wouldn't have any contact with Lee to contradict the text, Amber did something brilliant. Playing off Heather's paranoia, she told her that Lee's phone was hacked, hinting it might be the firm and provided a new number for her to call. That cut her ties with Lee all together."

"You expect us to believe you?" Schaeffer said.

Maggie pointed to the slip of paper she handed Starzynski.

"Ask her. When Amber realized what Ellison had her do, she felt afraid and trapped," Maggie explained.

"So, Heather comes to New York to sign a few papers, visit her mother, and go about her business. But that didn't happen. There were no papers to sign and she couldn't get in contact with Lee. Amber made sure of that at the office. By then, Lee had a new phone and new number. Heather's number was blocked just in case. Not knowing what to do, Heather calls the next best thing—me. She didn't have my cell number, but she found the number to my shop and left a message," I clarified.

Brody, who only seemed half interested in this tale straighten in his stance, his attention now fully focused.

"Someone lured her here," Maggie said.

"Ellison?" Starzynski questioned.

"That's a lie," Schaeffer bellowed.

"Bryon, please," Maxfield said in a calm but placating tone. "This is all speculation, Odessa. Guessing is not evidence. As for Ms. Kim—"

I held up my hand to him.

"Story isn't over. Let me finish and you judge if it's interesting," I said.

"No, I'm not," Maxfield said more sternly.

"I am," Starzynski said in a manner that advised no argument.

"Did you ever wondered why Heather ended up at the Terminal Hotel? Of all places, why there?" Maggie asked.

When no one answered, she continued. "After leaving the assisted living facility, a confused Heather tried to contact Lee at the office. When that failed, she sent him a text. Amber answered as Lee. She sent an urgent message he needed to see her. Heather agreed. She trusted him, so why not?" I said.

"This is preposterous!" Maxfield said. "Even you admit Ellison couldn't do this."

"Handled Amber, trick Heather into coming to New York, spy on Lee, yeah you're right. It takes a cool, calculated head to do that. Someone with motives of his own." I made a show of staring passed Maxfield. Behind him, Kip Waller stood, silent and trying to disappear. The often self-assure expression he always wore, now gone, and replaced with something else. The realization his dream of becoming the next legal star was fading. All eyes turned to him.

"Kip, what is she talking about?" Maxfield's frosty tone sent even a chill down my spine.

"It might have worked. Ellison could have talked Heather into handing over the drive, with the promise of reconnecting. But that wasn't the plan, was it Kip?" Maggie asked him.

"I don't know what you're talking about?" He seemed to shrink away with each word.

"Your plan was for Maxfield to make your career. A few more years with him, and you would have been a shining star, not some third-rate associate playing gofer. A dream you put all your hopes on until Ellison returned. You pushed and pushed him, didn't you? You whispered in his ear and fed his demons and pretended to help him."

"I talked to the wait staff at the country club where Schaeffer had its party. One of them told me that you paid him fifty dollars to keep Ellison's drink filled," Maggie said.

"That's absurd," Waller said.

"Kip?" Maxfield asked, as his eyes danced between Waller and a tiny redheaded dynamo.

"You and Ellison are just alike. You wanted Maxfield to yourselves. Ellison thought Lee was the serious threat, but you were." I glared at Waller. "Ellison came home. That cushy job of being Max's gofer turned into babysitting Ellison and digging him out of whatever hole he'd fallen into. But what if you had a way of getting rid of Ellison? Maybe his father would ship him back to Korea or at least another stint in a rehab," I said.

"You convinced Ellison in trying to get the drive from Heather. Then you concocted this elaborate plan to entice Heather back to New York. Ellison knew Amber and what she could do. He placed her at Aaron's firm. From there, you handled the rest. Coached Amber on what to say."

"But something went wrong. Heather dies. You don't have the drive and you're still stuck with Ellison. How long would it be before he told Maxfield or his father about what you two were up too? So, you push him toward the edge," Maggie said.

"Like a loaded gun, you aimed him at Billy Pace first, then at me, and ultimately, Lee." My voice went hard with controlled anger. "To think you would have gotten away with it if it weren't for Heather dying."

"No... no... no," Waller mumbled.

"Are you saying Ellison killed Heather?" inpatient Brody asked.

Maggie and I shook our heads.

The detectives glared at Waller, who eyes widened in realization.

"No, I didn't kill her!" he yelled.

I signed, knowing the next part would be hard.

"The plan was for Ellison to go to the Terminal Hotel and confront Heather. Heather being Heather, she wouldn't take kindly to being manipulated. Her reaction would be predictable and messy," Maggie explained.

"What you didn't expect was Ellison got so drunk at the party and couldn't confront anybody. Someone else went instead."

"Who?" Starzynski looked at the surrounding men.

Maxfield leaned on his cane, unsteady as he took a seat in a chair. The color drained from his face before I even said his name.

"Max."

CHAPTER 45

Though I teased Maggie often about her resemblance to Sherlock, I played her Watson happily. I followed when I asked her to chase the rabbit, and she did. When she took it upon herself to confront Amber, she excluded me. I trusted her to get answers, and she did. Also, she thought I might rearrange Amber's chromosomes for spying on Lee. Her decision to revisit the Terminal Hotel on her own, said a lot. Along with a threat from the fire department, a box of donuts and coffee, she got more answers. She was my superhero.

"What's this?" Brody asked. Maggie's laptop sat on her lap in full view of everyone. Everyone could see the small screen, except Maxfield. Maxfield sat turned away.

"The surveillance recording of the country club parking lot, where Schaeffer Pharmaceutical held its party the night of Heather's death. Notice the time stamp in the corner." Maggie pointed to the corner of the small screen. The detectives leaned in while Waller and Schaeffer stood behind them. Brody's squinted as he got closer.

"This is about fifteen minutes after Ellison had a fight with his father about Heather. Ellison told him of his plans to confront her. The wait staff said they were loud enough that one of the assistant managers had to intervene."

Schaeffer's indignant scowl lessened as he averted his eyes when I looked up at him. Once again, his son had humiliated himself. As for Waller, if he could vanish into a wall, he would. The weight of what he'd done pushed him into a corner he couldn't escape with charm and manipulation. He'd set in motion a tragedy that resulted in Heather's death.

"You notice a drunken Ellison?" Maggie said.

Even in the dusky surveillance video, the sight of an inebriated Ellison shouting at his father was disturbing. At one point, Maxfield struggled to take a drink away from him. The drink splashed over Maxfield and anyone near. Finally, Kip intervened and put Ellison in the backseat of the car. A few feet away the older Schaeffer stood, angry and frustrated. If I felt anything for Schaeffer, it was pity.

"This means nothing." Schaeffer's once pompous air faded. His defense of his son felt like a man drowning in open water with no relief in sight. A disengaged Maxfield sat heavy and unresponsive. Waller was no help. He needed a lifeline of his own.

"The intent was to take Ellison home. Maybe in the car he told Maxfield everything. Whatever happened, Maxfield knew if he didn't put an end to it, Ellison would find his way to Heather. He needed her to leave New York, keep to their arrangement, and never return. They went to the Terminal Hotel. The place Ellison had set up Heather to meet him. Using Lee as bait, they knew exactly where she was," Maggie said.

I couldn't help but look at Maxfield. All the energy drained from his broad shoulders as they slumped. Yet, a hint of the man Lee once admired remained. His dignity shone through despite the night's events.

"The night of the Carmen Smythe Gala, I saw it. It took time to realize what I'd seen that night and connect it to the Terminal Hotel. How light affects how you see things. In the hallway of the hotel, most of the lights are out because the owner is too cheap to replace them and they're incandescent. Making what you see as a trick of light. A weird yellow tone to anything white, like hair."

"I'm confused." Brody threw up his hands.

"She's talking about Mr. Layng. His white hair under the Terminal Hotel's hallway light makes it look blond or light brown," Maggie explained.

"Then I remembered, he said something in passing about Heather's last view of the world was a garbage dump. He also mentioned the smell. How did he know the room had the only view of a private garbage hauler? Only the corner room could see over the wall," I said.

"What about the housekeeper? Ellison was drunk. It could have been him," Starzynski asked.

"You saw how drunk he was. He could barely stand." I shook my head. "Again, at the gala, I saw Maxfield walk without his cane. If you didn't know better, you would have thought he was drunk. And if you wondered about what housekeeper said the second time she saw someone, it was Waller. Carrying what she thought was a weapon. It was Maxfield's cane. He left it in the room," I said.

"Maxfield panicked and left it there. Kip retrieved it. What she saw was two different men, first Maxfield and then Kip," Maggie explained.

"You can't prove anything," Waller said.

"Shut up, Waller," Schaeffer barked.

"You'd gone back upstairs to get the cane," Maggie glared at him. "The million-dollar question is, how you got into the room?"

Like a bear waking from a long winter, Maxfield turned his icy gaze to Waller. His grip on his ornate cane tightened as he took in the cowering sight of the younger man. His brow furrowed in a questioning looked he already had the answers to.

"Maxfield, did you look for the USB drive in Heather's room?" I asked.

His glacial stare turned to face me and soften in an instant as he shook his head. As if the answer came to him in waves of realization. His eyes clouded by memory. When his eyes returned to Waller, they were replaced with rage.

"What caused Heather's death?" Maggie asked.

"Head trauma, several blows to the head," Brody said flatly. Yet, something in his eyes said something else.

"There was bruising about the head. The initial trauma to the side of her head." Starzynski pressed his hand to the left side of his head. "An odd bruising, we couldn't figure out."

All eyes went to Maxfield's cane, with its heavy silver wolf's head.

"The final blow hit here." Starzynski's hand moved to the back of his head.

"There was no blood in the room, was there?" This question got Maggie a scrutinizing scowl from Brody.

"If you knew the room had the only line of sight of the garbage dump across the street, then you know there was no blood," Brody replied with a sneer.

"The medical examiner believed the first blow dazed her but didn't kill. The blows after did. Caused a bleed in her brain," Brody said with an emphasis on the last word. Never once did he take his eyes off Waller.

"What are you saying?" Maxfield asked as his eyes danced between both detectives.

"What they're trying not to say Maxfield, is that you didn't kill her," I said confirming the same. How had Waller gotten into the room? "When the housekeeper saw you in the hallway on Heather's floor, her door was closed. The door is weighted in a way that it closes on its own if you don't stop it. With a slam lock you can't get back in without a key or someone let you inside."

"I... I..." The word spluttered out of Maxfield's mouth.

"Say nothing, Maxfield," Schaeffer begged.

"This is the crazy speculation of two..." Waller faltered when I gave him a searing look.

"Hypothetically, you went to talk to Heather, not to hurt her," Maggie said, her voice soft and low. "You argued, and Heather got physical. In your defense, you stuck out at her with your cane and hit her harder than you meant to. You thought you'd killed her. In your panic, you dropped your cane and returned to your car downstairs. Kips in the car with Ellison, passed out in the back seat. You tell him what happen about Heather, the attack, everything."

"Waller to the rescue. He runs upstairs to retrieve the cane. On the floor he finds Heather, not dead, but dazed from Maxfield's blow. Maybe she tries to leave when you found her. When you realized she was alive, she posed another problem. She wouldn't take Maxfield's attack on her likely. What was already a mess would just get worse, especially with Ellison in the mix. So, you hit her again until she couldn't say anything," Maggie said.

"Now your plan to get rid of Ellison is shot to hell. Being the opportunist you are, you look for the USB drive, hoping for some leverage. You couldn't find it though. You returned to the car and confirmed Maxfield's belief he'd killed Heather, maybe to control him and the situation. You convinced him not to worry, you were his man, and his secret was safe. An intoxicated Ellison wouldn't talk or even remember the night," I added.

"That's a lie," Waller cursed.

The deep sigh coming from Maxfield pulled everyone's attention. "I didn't kill her!"

The words sounded like a well-earned revelation. A burden lifted on a man who thought he had to fix the world.

"Maxfield!" Waller begged.

"I'd forgotten her temper, that rage she always had beneath the surface. With such a beautiful face, you don't expect such anger," Maxfield mused wistfully. "She hated us, you know."

Maxfield's eyes went to Schaeffer.

"We were obstacles and demigods who blocked her a happiness. When she took up with Ellison, you railed against her. I helped him end it. Maybe she did love him. Blackmail was too good for us," Maxfield said in a bemused tone.

"She was an ungrateful, greedy bitch." Schaeffer's venomous tone didn't surprise me. Years of payoffs and Ellison's obsession didn't garnish warmth from the elder Schaeffer.

"I guess Deena Pace was ungrateful, too," Maggie replied with a little fairy venom of her own. Schaeffer found a spot on the floor to examine.

"Do you have something to say to us, Mr. Layng?" Schaeffer prompted.

"Don't do this," Kip demanded as he pushed passed Schaeffer to stand before Maxfield.

"If you tell me you killed her for me, I won't help you," a somber sounding Maxfield said. Whatever Waller was about to say, he stopped. Possibly, recognizing something in each other. The choice of dealing with this on his own, or with Maxfield by his side, was clear to everyone in the room, especially Schaeffer.

"After what he did to Ellison!" An angry Schaeffer shook his head and pushed Waller to the side to face Maxfield. "He ruined his sobriety and manipulated him. If he killed that woman, it's his own fault."

The hands around Maxfield's tightened around the cane's wolf's head. The knuckles on his hands turned white. When he finally glared up at Schaeffer, a man that shaped the course of his life, you would have thought he saw a stranger.

"Why don't I take responsibility for Kip and you Ellison?" Maxfield said. "These are monsters of our own making, aren't they?"

A dumbfounded Schaeffer reared back as if struck by the truth Maxfield told. When he turned my way, gone was the reproachful looks.

"Was getting Deena's USB drive worth all this?" I questioned.

It didn't take him long to respond. "Not really. We were foolish in our thinking. First, to get Lee back under our influence. Second, in the misconception we ever controlled Heather or Ellison."

I shook my head and replied, "It had more to do with a selective memory. You'd forgotten why you banished Ellison. That's the healthiest thing for him was to be as far away from you and his father. As for Lee, you forgot why he left. Because he didn't want to turn into any one of you."

Maxfield laughed and nodded. With bowed head, he said nothing. His hands caressing the wolf's head cane. When he stopped, he gave it one last look before handing it over to Starzynski.

"I think you'll need this."

CHAPTER 46

Precincts are not my favorite place. The promise I made if I never saw another one might cost me my favorite pair of Jimmy Choo shoes. When Maggie and I finally left the detectives with the mess Heather's death caused, I never looked back. Only when I reached the hospital and sat by Lee's side did I take a breath. Pale, sleeping, and gloriously alive, I reveled at each breath he took. The doctors assured me his recovery was a matter of time and patience. Work was out of the question, and if he didn't overdo it, our upcoming wedding would be fine.

"What planet do you think we live on where Lee sits and does nothing?" I explained to the pleasant-looking doctor who didn't have a clue.

"Really?" He appeared surprised and glanced at my sister.

Candace stood in the corner with her arms crossed and a smug expression. This made me wonder how she managed while I was at the precinct. I'd called her in the middle of the restaurant's dinner service. Still wearing a beautiful, floral printed dress and low heels she favored, I'd disrupted her evening. Since Lee was the cause of that disruption, her almost guardianship surprised me.

"He'll behave," Candace said firmly.

"Really?" I echoed the doctor's surprise and glared at my sister.

The doctor cleared his throat nervously.

"Mr. McKenzie became upset when he awoke and you weren't here. To be honest, your sister calmed everything down quickly."

A Candy Coated Lie

Candace had a way of calming things down. The most effective way was to threaten bodily harm. Since Lee was already in pain, she probably had to use coercion of another kind. I shuddered to think what but didn't ask. Happy that Lee was alive and well.

"Thank you, Candace." I was thankful she took charge of Lee and that put me at ease.

The night had evolved from a nightmare to a reassuring quiet. The gentle beep of Lee's monitors and his steady breathing lulled me into a peaceful sleep as I rested my head on his bed. The dream I fell into was a kaleidoscope of color and warmth. The anxiety that plagued me melted away and for the first time in forever, nothing itched.

In the days that followed, news of how Schaeffer Pharmaceuticals and Mercier, Koenig and Layng handled the scandal caused by Heather's death and Deena's USB drive was hard to ignore. I tried. Except for the occasional calls by Starzynski and Brody, I did my best. This was harder for Lee. Part of him wanted to talk to Maxfield while another part knew he shouldn't. Banished from work, he was at a loss with what to do with himself. The cat tolerated his presence to a point.

"Does that cat remember I saved him from a fate worse than death?" Lee complained.

"It's a cat, honey. He doesn't much care what you think," I reminded him.

"I think it's why he likes you so much." His lips curled up in a smirk.

I suspected Lee might be right considering the cat's return to his previous owner seemed unlikely. One of Mr. Jimenez's daughters took him in after his discharge but refused to take the cat. Since the cat was like feeding a small child, we understood.

Between territorial bouts with the cat and vegetating in front the television, I needed to get him out the house. Dinner at the Blue Moon usually worked to brighten both our moods, despite Candace's constant interruptions. Though discussing seating arrangements, music selections, and whatever signature drink we wanted didn't bother us anymore.

"What's wrong?" Candace's eyes danced between our smiling faces.

"Did I thank you for doing this for us?" Lee said sweetly.

Candace frown.

"We're grateful," I added with enthusiasm.

Candace reared back as if we'd slapped her. Then her steely eyes focused on me.

"He had a concussion, so what's your excuse?" she said. "I'm not buying this act."

I feigned hurt and put on my biggest smile.

"You planning the wedding is a Godsend," I said.

Without saying another word, Candace stood up with a scrutinizing sneer that could melt the polar ice caps.

"If you even think about eloping, I will hunt you down and drag you kicking and screaming to the church. I know people." Candace pointed to several people having dinner in the Blue Moon dining area. Many of them were in uniform and she knew all of them. From the smile that replaced the sneer, she might enjoy dragging us to the church in handcuff.

"Wouldn't think of it," Lee said with a ridiculous grin.

This made Candace huff in indignation before she turned and left. It was a pleasure to watch her go. Thankfully, we'd finished our meal before she interrupted us with wedding planning issues.

"At the hospital, she was a menace to the staff," Lee mused as he gazed upon my sister. At the front of the restaurant, she berated a waitress for something. The waitress looked like she wanted to sink into the floor. "I didn't want for anything. However, the minute they discharged me, she reverted to the enforcer we love and fear."

"Yeah, I know. She acted that way because you were vulnerable and helpless. She likes a fair fight."

This made Lee laughed.

The waitress Candace had berated came over with a coffee pot to top off our cups. I gave her an understanding nod when she finished.

"I would tell you her bark is worse than her bite, but that would be a lie," I said.

"I don't know how you do it, Ms. O," the young girl said with a sigh.

"First, listen to every third word as if it matters. Second, pick your fights, don't expect to win any of them, but have conviction. Candace's likes conviction. Last, but not least, show no fear," I said with certainty.

Lee nodded in agreement. "It helps if you have a concussion," he added before forking in a mouthful of dessert.

The waitress's eyes widen but relaxed into contemplation on what we said. Then she shrugged and headed for another table. For a time, we said little and enjoyed each other's company. Candace kept her distance most of the night. Lee seemed content. That ball of worry that sat in the pit of my stomach the moment I'd first heard Heather's name vanished. Though the aftermath of that death remained, it was no longer our priority.

"Max called me today," Lee said as he took a sip of the steaming coffee.

The mention of Maxfield Layng felt like an unexploded bomb placed in my hands. I didn't know what to do with it. The police brought charges on Maxfield, Waller, and Ellison. Maxfield got off the easiest. Mostly, due to his age and health. It didn't hurt that his reputation still carried weight. Out on bail, Maxfield kept his word to Waller. He stood by the associate's side when the district attorney charged him with murder. The fact Maxfield got the D.A. to reduce the charges to manslaughter said a lot about his ability.

"Yeah, what does he have to say?" I didn't much care, but Lee did. So, it felt important that I listened.

"When we first talked after they charged him, all he could say was how sorry he was. How leaving the firm was the best thing I could have done."

"Will he defend Schaeffer against the legal crap storm that Deena's drive put them in?" I asked.

Lee shook his head.

"He hasn't returned to the firm. Something about his heart not being strong enough anymore, or something like that. He feels responsible for Waller and Heather." Lee played with the remains of his dessert. Caught up in some memory, I would rather have him bury.

"He used to always tell me to learn from my mistakes because to repeat them is a fool's art." Lee's eyes held uncertainty. "I asked him why he always forgave Ellison."

Again, I couldn't care less about any profound revelation Maxfield Layng claimed.

"Because no one would." He pushed the plate away and sat back in his chair. The noisy room of the dinner crowd seemed to fall away. "Ellison was exhausting but needed him. When I came to Mercier, Koenig and Layng, he saw a calm in me. Maybe he thought I'd rub off on him."

This made me laugh and break the somberness of the moment.

"A chisel, therapy, and a 12-step program couldn't rub off on Ellison. Don't get weepy about Maxfield. He used you to get Deena's drive. He wasn't man enough to come out and ask you for it because unlike him, you have a soul," I complained.

I could tell Lee didn't want to hear it, but I continued.

"Maxfield wraps up his lies in convenient nostalgia and Daddy issues. Since the moment Heather died, his only focus was to get Deena's drive and save Schaeffer Pharmaceuticals and Ellison. Not only did she have Hagemann's report on Schaeffer's drugs, but the original drug trial reports from Schaeffer Pharmaceuticals. That was what they wanted to hide the most. They realized the drugs had problems and ignored it."

"Aaron's expert explained how they manipulated the second clinical trials for a better outcome. The worst part was the Deena had all the original drug trial documentation. Solid proof of what Schaeffer did. All because they didn't want to lose what they had invested in the drugs," Lee said.

From the news report I read, it would take years for the company to survive the onslaught of legal issues Deena's information revealed. Bad publicity from Ellison's arrest hurt even more. The realization the coming trouble on the older Schaeffer's face was reward enough for Maggie and me. A little payback for Deena and Billy.

"Not to bring up Eva Braun again, but if she had told Hilter the truth, that he wasn't all that and a bag of chips, the world would have been better off. If Maxfield, had called Schaeffer Pharmaceutics on the shady practices and made them pull the drugs, people wouldn't have suffered. Deena might be alive."

"Odessa, please," he begged.

"I'm about to marry you. You have bigger troubles to worry about than Maxfield and what's about to happen to him," I warned.

Lee cocked a brow at me. His face held uncertainty.

"Candace will be your sister-in-law. This will make you family," I explained.

From his confused look, I realized I had to explain further.

"Candace tolerates your presence because of me. Those days of questioning your choice in wives, political affiliation, and religion are over. Since you will be part of the family, it's within her right to dictate those choices now. Welcome to my world, honey."

Lee scanned the restaurant. His eyes set on Candace. With a smiling face, she stood by a table chatting up the guests. As realization dawned on him, he pouted.

I leaned over and gave him an encouraging kiss on the cheek and said, "Show no fear."

CHAPTER 47

I expected locust, hellfire, and my body covered head to toe in a horrible rash. The morning clouds had threatened more rain. Lee and my cousin Earl got into a heated argument about the Yankees at the rehearsal dinner. Maggie cried when she told me the dry cleaner lost Rocket's suit for the wedding. She would have to find something else for him to wear as my ring bearer. The day before, I got a phone call from Aaron's wife. She threatened to report me to the American Heart Association if I didn't stop feeding him pie.

"Get out of bed, Odessa Marie Wilkes," Candace demanded at 7:30 in the morning. Dressed in a house robe, curlers, and a cleansing mask, she was a frightening sight.

"No, God will strike me dead if I do," I said with a pillow over my head.

"That's blasphemous and I'll tell Auntie Rennie." She yanked the covers off me. I felt exposed and vulnerable.

My attempt to get the covers back failed. Candace had hands like a vice.

"You were right, I shouldn't marry him," I said. Her momentary shock allowed me to pull the blanket from her grasp. For insurance, I cocooned myself in it.

"Great time to decide on the day of your wedding," Candace shouted.

She tried to pull the covers again, but I was a human burrito wrapped up tight. Failing to retrieve the blanket, she hit me hard with something. I threw the blanket off my head to see her with her house slipper.

"I always knew you were violent," I hissed.

"And you are crazy," Candace yelled.

"What is going on here?" The familiar voice of Maggie pulled me away from my sister's attack.

"She tried to kill me," I protested. The idea of Maggie taking on an armed Candace would be wishful thinking, but a girl can hope.

"She won't move. She says she won't get married. Well, you tell her for all the money I spent on this wedding, she's going to marry someone. If not McKenzie, then I'll find one of the busboys," Candace threatened.

"Let me talk to her," Maggie said in a conciliatory tone.

"Somebody better talk to her," Candace demanded. "This is ruining my facial treatment."

Candace gave me one more whack before stomping off in a huff.

"You told me it would be a bad idea to stay over at Candace," I complained and sat up in bed to face Maggie. Dressed in her usual garb of jeans and a tee shirt, it made me happy that something remained normal.

"Don't you think you're acting a little silly here?" She sat on the edge of the bed.

"I only wanted an extra ten minutes before Ms. Godzilla came in like some psychotic drill sergeant." I fell back onto my bed exhausted. Fighting with Candace took a lot out of me.

"So, you do want to get married?" a patient Maggie asked.

"Not to a busboy," I quipped.

"I guess Lee's it?" she replied nonchalantly.

The mention of his name made me smile.

"He'll do," I sat up again.

"Rain stopped." Maggie craned her neck toward the window. A hint of sunshine peeked through the window.

"I found Rocket something to wear for the wedding. In fact, he picked it out himself."

She had the prideful look of a mother, whose child has been potty trained.

"This should be interesting. I'm glad someone's happy." I cocked brow at her. I wrapped the blanket around again.

Maggie came to sit closer and put an arm around me.

"You're going to marry Lee. That will make you happy. You'll join the wife club," she mused.

"Does it come with a golden key or card? Do we have a secret oath?"

Maggie made a silly face.

"This is your day, so enjoy it. You're the most anti-bride I've ever met. The day will be perfect," she reassured.

I wanted to believe. Things had gone wrong in my life. Five years ago, when I thought my world was perfect, it exploded right before my eyes. Starting over was hard. Now that I was about to have what I wanted, would a five-hundred-pound cartoon anvil fall on my head?

"Here." Maggie pulled out her cell phone and dialed. She waited until someone picked up and handed it to me. I took the phone and listened.

"Maggie?" Lee said. He sounded sleepy.

"No, it's me!"

"Hey, is something wrong?"

"No, I'm good," My unease decreased. "Except Candace wants me to marry one of the Blue Moon busboys."

Lee's laugh filled the room.

"Which one?"

I huffed. "The cute one."

Maggie took that as a signal to leave.

"You okay?" I'd been concerned about him since Maxfield's arrest.

He took a moment to answer. "I'm good. Shared the bed with the cat last night."

"Don't worry, the cat doesn't swing that way, so you're safe," I teased. "You want to hear something great?"

"Candace was kidnapped by gypsies."

"Funny. I gave the cat a name," I announced.

"I was getting used to calling him the cat."

"Samson, the mighty Samson." Memory of the cat taking a swipe out Ellison made me smile.

"Perfect."

Oddly, we fell into an awkward silence.

"I visited Max yesterday. He's home," he said.

The shift of conversation jarred me. I'd put Heather and Mercier, Koenig and Layng in my rearview mirror. Lee hadn't. Between things we had to do for the wedding, the shop, and his cases, we hadn't had much time to talk about Maxfield.

"He's doing well, you said."

Maxfield suffered another mild heart attack at the precinct. Despite Maxfield's part in everything, Lee was the first to his side. If he never saw the older man again, there would still be a connection between them. Both Lee and I would have to live with that truth.

"He wants us to be happy."

"Did he say anything about Ellison?"

"We don't talk about him or Kip."

"Will he receive any backlash about Heather's blackmail and Deena's file?"

"The court will sort that out. Schaeffer Pharmaceutical will get hit hard. There's talk of lawsuits and a Federal Investigation. Maxfield Layng is the least of everyone's concerns."

"That's good. Is it true someone saw Kip from the hotel?"

"Yeah, that surprised everyone. A few of Maggie's homeless guys from the Terminal Hotel. They were too afraid to come forward. The detectives threw Kip in a lineup and got several positive IDs. One saw him coming out with Max's cane."

"That's Maggie for you."

"Now Kips claiming it was an accident." Lee couldn't hide the disgust in his voice.

"Did he hate Ellison that much?" I asked.

Lee huffed. "Ellison's easy to hate."

I had to agree. Cleared as a murder suspect, Ellison went on the attack to defend himself. He still had blackmail and theft charges to contend with. He claimed Lee had set him up for revenge because of his affair with Julia. Ellison's legal issues were the least of his problems. With Schaeffer Pharmaceutical under fire, his father has little patience for him. Maxfield no longer willing to buffer his father's contempt. Ellison was on his own.

"Keep thinking about what Maxfield said about the beasts he'd made with Kip and Ellison."

I sensed Lee's darken mood creeping into his words. We let the past derailed us one before. First with Heather and then with Ellison, I wouldn't let it happen again.

"Max didn't make Kip and Ellison demons. He might have fed them, but they were monsters already."

The silence fell between us worried me.

"I should have told you about Mercier, Koenig and Layng and why I left. Heather's death was the wrong way to find out."

"You didn't lie about it, you just didn't tell me," I mused in the hope of lightening the mood.

"It was a lie of omission," he said.

"You didn't want to hurt me." If nothing else, I believed that.

"I wrapped it in candy to make it easier to take, that's all. I fooled myself into thinking I was trying to protect you. The truth was I didn't want you to know that person who could go along with Mercier, Koenig and Layng."

I had a few of those moments when I worked in advertising. Once my firm wanted to push a questionable product toward a certain demographic. I cringed now when I remembered how I sat in those meetings and said nothing, did nothing. I understood.

"My mom used to do that when I was sick. Give me something sweet when she had to give me medicine. It still left a horrible taste in my mouth," I said.

"No more lies," he said solemnly.

"Not even the candy coated one," I said playfully.

"Not even those," he replied firmly.

"Okay, I'm good with that." I'd shed myself of the blanket.

"Can I marry you now?"

I couldn't help but smile and stretched out my hand. My engagement ring shone bright in the morning light. For the first time in weeks, my rash had gone. No more red spots and a desire to scratch my skin off.

"Odessa, this the part where you say yes," Lee said.

"I'm thinking about that busboy."

"Funny, real funny." Lee laughed. I missed that laugh.

"See you soon," I said before we both said goodbye.

I hopped out of bed and headed downstairs to the kitchen. I found Maggie at the table drinking coffee.

"You look better," she said.

"Where's Candace?"

"Removing her mask or something. She's pissed at you, you know."

"Different day, same Candace." I took a cup from the drain for coffee and filled it to the rim. I sipped the black liquid and felt an instant calm come over me.

"Ready?" Maggie asked.

"Never been so ready," I said to my best friend.

That afternoon, I married Leland McKenzie in front of family and friends. Rocket carried our wedding rings dressed in his new dark blue Cub Scout uniform. With pride, he displayed his entire collection of badges. He was the best ring bearer ever.

At the reception, Candace put a folded printed tee shirt on each seat.

WILKES FAMILY REUNION

P.S. ODDESA AND LEE'S WEDDING

Who would have guessed my sister had a sense of humor?

Lee's sister, who flew in from California with her husband, gave me a framed photograph of Lee with he was nine. After I stopped laughing, I looked at that awkward boy. He stared back at me with oversized glasses, unkempt, dark hair, and bright hazel eyes. He had the unmistakable expression of youthful enthusiasm. I looked up to watch Lee dancing with Candace. I had hope for mankind.

"That's a sight I never thought I'd see." Maggie watched them dance.

"Yeah, I kinda expected locust and hellfire," I mused.

"How do you feel, Mrs. McKenzie?" She returned the picture to me.

"Like I'll do my best never to lie to that man," I said.

"Yes, you will." Maggie grinned. "You'll tell him he's taller than he thinks he is. That his hair line isn't receding. Or that he fixed the toilet when you hired a plumber after he broke it. It's the kind of lies you tell. The one that pulls you together and not the one that pulls you apart."

"What's the difference?" I said with all seriousness.

"For Roger, it's... Oh, I don't know where the weed whacker power cord is. For Lee, it might be different."

"Maybe."

The music stopped. Candace and Lee broke apart as the music revved up again. One dance was all they could tolerate and parted. He walked over to Maggie and me.

I put on my best smile.

"You and Candace dance well together."

Lee gave me a doubtful look.

"No, I wouldn't lie about that," I said with a straight face.

Maggie began to step away. She wore a pleased grin before she walked away. Lee put an arm around me as we looked out at the large reception hall at our family and friends as they dance, ate, and laughed. I still held the photograph of the young Lee and thought how funny fate can be. I couldn't have imagined the things that brought us together. In reality, it had been the disasters in each of our lives. The way each of us survived and became something else.

"What to dance, Mrs. McKenzie?" Lee held out his hand to me.

A Candy Coated Lie

How could I say no to that?

Made in the USA
Columbia, SC
09 April 2022

58754361R00190